Praise for *Shaded Light*

"Ontario police detectives Paul Manziuk and his new partner, Jacqueline Ryan, make an odd team—he's white, an abrupt, patronizing veteran, while she's a recently promoted, vivacious black woman—but in Lindquist's debut mystery the two rub elbows and tempers to captivating effect....

Like Agatha Christie, Lindquist spends a lot of time developing a believable web of personal relationships before introducing the murders. However, she updates the Golden Age template with modern police techniques (Ryan has degrees in both psychology and criminology). The result is a cozy that will delight fans who appreciate solid, modern detection."

Publishers Weekly

"Highly recommended.... Paul and [Jacquie] make a fabulous team as their divergent personalities harmoniously clash to the benefit of the reader. The who-done-it is well designed with a wonderful investigation to add to the pleasure…"

Harriet Klausner, *Under the Covers*

"Detailed characterization, surprising relationships, and nefarious plot-twists provide ample diversion…."

Library Journal

"*Shaded Light* has all the elements of a classic mystery—a body in the garden, a mansion full of suspects, and two mismatched police officers. Combine them and you have a page-turning, keep-you-up-all-night mystery where the murderer isn't revealed until the very end.

"This well-written first mystery by author N. J. Lindquist is reminiscent of Agatha Christie; the houseguests gather, tensions run murderously high, a body is discovered. Enter Paul Manziuk, a "cop's cop" who's been a police officer forever, and his partner, Jacquie Ryan, a young, black female who has had to work hard to get where she is. Together they interview the houseguests. And some very curious clues and red herrings emerge.

"If you are a mystery fan, *Shaded Light*, the first in the Manziuk and Ryan series, will keep you reading until the end."

Linda Hall, author of *Steal Away, Chat Room, Sadie's Song*

"*Shaded Light* is a recipe for murder and mystery that simmers slowly and emits an enticing aroma reminiscent of earlier delights. It's not a taut, edge of the seat thriller but then it wasn't intended to be…. *Shaded Light* is just that—a convergence of shadows. Purposely patterned after Agatha's best, readers are led down the garden path where nothing is quite as it seems, and suspects appear at every turn…."

P. J. Nunn, *The Charlotte Austin Review Ltd.*

"A cozy reminiscent of the best Agatha Christie had to offer…You have humor, complications, and characters so real that you can just about touch them and smell their sweat. Good stuff!"

Midwest Book Review

"N.J. Lindquist works every twist imaginable in her modern cozy-meets-police-procedural…. This excellently plotted novel … kept me reading and guessing until the very end."

I Love a Mystery

"An admirable first outing for a pair of detectives readers will look forward to hearing from again."

The Mystery Reader

"Lindquist writes a very compelling mystery that keeps you guessing until the last minute. Through her ace detective combination of Paul Manziuk and Jacquie Ryan, she leaves no stone unturned and entertains many possibilities…. Lindquist's story succeeds in keeping the reader's interest and the tale never wanes in its action. A very good novel by an accomplished writer."

Rapport Magazine

"Ellen Brodie hopes to outshine Martha Stewart as she plans the perfect house party for the partners at her husband's law firm. However our hostess is confronted with a major faux pas when a corpse is discovered in the garden. The party becomes mayhem even before it's discovered that the guest list includes a blackmailer and perhaps a murderer. Throw in two mismatched Ontario police detectives; stir and you have brouhaha worthy of Agatha Christie."

Greensboro Library

"If you like to curl up with a good mystery, one that has humor, a thread of romance, its share of twists and turns, pick up *Shaded Light*...."

Joan Hall Hovey, author of *Nowhere To Hide, Chill Waters,Listen to the Shadows*

"Riveting. Lawyer Peter Martin and his devastatingly beautiful, trophy wife, Jillian, captured my interest right from the beginning of this page-turning mystery.... I didn't guess 'who done it' until Lindquist was good and ready to tell me."

Elma Schemenauer, author/editor of 100+ books

"*Shaded Light* is what I would call a cozy police procedural. It's the kind I especially like: traditional closed community, lots of suspects, clues, detection, and interesting characters.... Lots of skilled interrogation provides leads, and of course the crime is finally solved. In the process we are treated to varied and carefully delineated characters that hold our attention, to good, unclichéd, lucid writing, and to a well-sustained pace as we try to match wits with the detectives."

***The Bookdragon Review*, Gene Stratton,** author of *Cornish Conundrum, Killing Cousins, Fit for Fate*

Jo Monica

you go girl!

Shaded Light

A Manziuk and Ryan mystery

N. J. Lindquist

N. J. Lindquist

Markham, Ontario, Canada

Shaded Light

Published in 2000 by St. Kitts Press (hardcover)

This novel is a work of fiction. Names, characters, and events are
the product of the author's imagination, and any resemblance to actual
persons, living or dead, is purely coincidental.
The city of Toronto, the Toronto police, and any other entities
that seem familiar are not intended to be accurate,
but come totally out of my fantasy world.

MurderWillOut Mysteries is an imprint of
That's Life! Communications
Box 487 Markham ON L3P 3R1
Call toll free 1-877-THATSLIFE
(in Toronto area 905-471-1447)
E-mail: info@murderwillout.com
http://www.murderwillout.com

Library and Archives Canada Cataloguing in Publication

Lindquist, N. J. (Nancy J.), 1948-
    Shaded light / N.J. Lindquist. -- 2nd ed.

"A Manziuk and Ryan mystery."
ISBN 0-9685495-6-X

    I. Title.

PS8573.I53175S53 2004   C813'.54   C2004-904757-4

Dedicated to my husband, Les, who has encouraged me in every way he possibly could.

Acknowledgements

I would like to acknowledge the role books have played in my life. From *Anderson's Fairy Tales* and *Alice In Wonderland* through *Trixie Beldon* and *Little Women* to *The Grapes of Wrath* and *Crime and Punishment*, and countless other titles, I have been entertained, challenged, and delighted through words on pages.

When I am feeling blue, I reread Agatha Christie, Dorothy Sayers, Georgette Heyer, Jane Austen, Desmond Bagley, Dick Francis, Louis L'Amour, and now Peter Robinson. Books are more than words on a page; they are my friends.

I also have to acknowledge my debt to a different kind of writer. Hank Williams, Johnny Cash, Marty Robbins, and others taught me at an early age the magic of how a few words could carry volumes in emotion and depth of meaning. As I write, the poetic music of Ian Tyson, Prairie Oyster, Clay Walker, Paul Brandt, or Brad Paisley drowns out the rest of the world.

And there are a few people I need to thank for their practical help and encouragement. My great-uncle Frank for introducing me to the fascinating world of books when I was seven years old and knew little beyond Dick and Jane. Bob Wilton for opening my eyes to creativity. Barney Thordarson for keeping me awake in those 8:30 AM first-year English classes and teaching me how to organize my thoughts. Professor Grant for challenging my mind with 16th-and 17th-century literature. Margaret Epp and Maxine Hancock for letting me see that writers are "ordinary people," too. Norman Rohrer, Leslie Keylock, Ken Peterson, and Larry Matthews for their advice and encouragement. Audrey Dorsch for maintaining a writing conference so I could meet writers and editors, learn, and later try my wings. Former police-woman Gail Hayes for her advice on Jacquie's character. The people at *Writer's Digest* for producing all the wonderful books I have used as resources. Crime Writers of Canada, Sisters in Crime, and Murder Must Advertise for helping me learn the ropes and find community. The many writers I now count as friends, especially those who are members of The Word Guild.

Thanks to Laurel Schunk of St Kitts Press who first pub-lished *Shaded Light* in hard cover.

Finally, I would like to thank Carole Anne Nelson, who I met at Bouchercon in Denver in 2000. I was lost in a sea of strangers, wondering what on earth I was doing there. I was sitting alone at a table near the registration area when Carole Anne arrived. She set her belongings down on a chair near me, and we ended up talking for nearly an hour. Later, she invited me to be on a panel she was moderating at Malice Domestic and treated me as if I belonged there. Carole Anne has left us before her time, but I will always remember her as a larger than life person who welcomed me into the mystery community and made me feel I belonged.

And, of course, I have to thank my family. My four sons for letting me spend hours cooped up in my room plotting and writ-ing and rewriting. My husband for doing many of the household chores to give me time. And also for encouraging (challenging?) me to write this book in the first place. One Christmas years ago—either 1982 or 1983—I threw down a library book in dis-gust and made the typical, "I could do better than that!" com-ment.

My husband, while giving me "the look," said, "Then why don't you?"

So I did.

Shaded Light

Major Players in Order of Appearance

Peter Martin — boyish 40-something lawyer who enjoys the good life

Jillian Martin — Peter's beautiful, yet grasping, fourth wife

Shauna Jensen — Jillian's shy, older sister who finds books easier to understand than people

Kendall Brodie — son of the senior partner, who is about to join the law firm

Nick Donovan — Kendall's annoying roommate who prefers ski moguls to law books

Ellen Brodie — the hostess whose nice little family party has plainly gone out of her control

Bart Brodie — the black sheep nephew who always turns up when you least want him

George Brodie — senior partner in Brodie, Fischer, and Martin, whose ulcer is acting up

Douglass Fischer — partner in the law firm, whose mind is occupied with domestic matters

Anne Fischer — a menopausal wife and mother with recurring headaches

Lorry Preston — a terrific catch for Kendall if only Nick will stay out of the way

Hildy Reimer — a neighbor who chose the July long weekend to have her apartment redecorated

Mrs. Winston — housekeeper par excellence, who's too busy to know what's going on

Crystal Winston — Mrs. Winston's daughter and an observant future journalist

Paul Manziuk — one very tired cop (pronounced *Man's hook*)

Jacqueline Ryan — a newly promoted policewoman with an attitude

Part I

Half light, half shade,
She stood, a sight to make
an old man young.
                    Alfred, Lord Tennyson

Chapter One

"You self-righteous liar! But then you never think of anyone but yourself!"

As Peter Martin stepped into the front hallway of his penthouse in an exclusive residential area of downtown Toronto, he was surprised to hear his wife's angry voice. The voice he'd been hearing a lot lately. The one he hadn't realized she possessed until several months ago. But this time she wasn't speaking to him.

He had come home early from the office to pack for their weekend trip, expecting to find his young wife in the midst of deciding what clothes she should take to dazzle their friends. Instead, she appeared to be telling someone off. Unless by some miracle she was annoyed with herself. "Yeah, right," Peter said softly.

"But, Jillian, I wrote you weeks ago, and I asked you to let me know if this weekend wasn't convenient." The answering voice was soft and apologetic. Peter recognized it as belonging to his wife's older sister, Shauna.

Peter crossed the tiny front hallway into the living room.

Jillian Martin, Peter's wife, was seated on the sofa. Tone-on-tone embroidered ivory cushions served as a perfect backdrop for her flowing golden hair and tangerine lounging pajamas. As was inevitable when Peter saw her, he found his eyes caught and held by the smoothness of her tanned skin and the perfection of her delicate features.

But today he had to shift his glance to Shauna, Jillian's opposite—tall, gangly, mousy-haired, and pale—standing awkwardly before Jillian like a child on the carpet, her hands clasped, shoulders hunched. The small suitcase at her feet only served to make her position even more embarrassing.

Jillian's voice dropped to a purr. "Peter, darling, I'm so glad you're home. Shauna has just arrived on the doorstep. She says I knew she was coming, but I didn't, Peter. I'm sure I didn't!"

"Hello, Shauna." Peter held out his hand as he walked toward her. "It's good to see you even if there is a mix-up."

In spite of the thick lenses of her black-rimmed glasses, he could see relief in her eyes as she put her hand into his. The hand was limp and cold, and he held it for only an instant before moving to the sofa beside Jillian and inviting Shauna to sit down and make herself at home. Simultaneously, a part of his mind wrestled with the question of what to do with her.

"I've told Shauna I'm sorry, but we just won't be here, will we, Petey?" Jillian's clear blue eyes, big as saucers, gazed at him with a studied helplessness he was getting to know well.

"She's right, Shauna. We're going to one of my partner's homes for the weekend. A house party. But perhaps we can work something out."

Shauna had tentatively seated herself on the edge of a plush ivory chair. Now she leaned forward and twisted her hands. "Oh, please, don't worry about me. I must have made a mistake. If you're going away I can just get a bus back home. Or I could stay here while you're gone and look after things. There are a couple of books I wanted to buy. I could read them."

"What an utterly boring weekend!" Peter said with the involuntary shudder of a man who regarded books of all forms as work. "I think we can do better than that."

Jillian placed a beautifully manicured hand on her husband's arm. "But there's nothing wrong with that, Peter. She can stay here and read or watch TV. She'll be fine."

"Yes, really I will, Peter." Shauna sat forward eagerly, and he was almost convinced.

"So it's settled," Jillian said as she rose gracefully from the sofa. "Well, I have to get back to packing. You can put your things in the guest room, Shauna. I had a late brunch, so if you're hungry you'll have to fix yourself something. I don't know what there is." As she left the room, she turned to her husband and said, "Don't give it another thought, Peter. Shauna's always preferred books to people."

He had been ready to agree that Shauna should stay in the apartment. Now, perversely, he changed his mind. "No, she isn't staying here. She's coming with us."

Jillian stopped in the doorway. "She's what?" Her voice rose perilously close to a shrill note.

"I said she can come with us. George has a big house. One more person won't make any difference."

"You can't be serious!"

Shauna rose halfway out of her chair. "Oh, no, Peter! I don't want to go. I couldn't possibly just go there uninvited. I don't even know them!"

"They were at our wedding last year. You met them then. And you've seen George once or twice since. Ellen's easygoing. She won't mind."

An edge to her voice, Jillian said, "Peter, Shauna doesn't want to go, and she needn't go."

Peter stood up and took a few steps toward his wife. Clearly and softly, he said, "My dear, if Shauna says she told you she was coming this weekend, I believe her. She wouldn't make a mistake like that. So it's not her fault we weren't prepared, and we are going to do the best we can to give her a good weekend. That means taking her with us."

Jillian opened her mouth but shut it without making a comment. Instead, she fluttered her eyelashes. "But, Petey." She came toward him, her eyes mutely distressed, lips in a beautiful pout, hands reaching up to grasp his lapels and pull him toward her. "It wouldn't be fair to either the Brodies or Shauna. She would never fit in."

"Oh, no, I wouldn't, Peter." Shauna's voice was distressed. "Jillian's right. It's very nice of you to suggest taking me, but I wouldn't fit in at all. I'll be just fine here when I get my books. Or—or I'll go back home."

"Either you go or we all stay here," Peter said. Again, the words seemed to slip out of their own free will.

"That's nonsense!" Jillian snapped.

"You can't mean that!" Shauna's eyes darted from her sister to the man in front of her. Peter saw fear in those eyes. Of whom, he wondered. Himself or Jillian?

"Peter, why are you being so silly? Shauna doesn't want to go, and besides, she won't have proper clothes."

"She can borrow some of yours, can't she? You're the same size. I thought you'd given her quite a few of your things."

The look Jillian flashed him was not one of unbounded love and affection. But Peter continued without regard for that look. "I came home to pack. I have to get back to the office for a meeting with a client. I'll be here to pick you up about four. You should both be able to get ready by then." He moved toward the bedroom. "By the way, Jillian, I tried to call you this morning around eleven. There was no answer. I didn't know you were going out."

She followed him into the hallway. "I had shopping to do. Should I have checked with you first?" Her voice made him think of tempered steel.

"No, of course not. I only wondered if there was a problem."

"No problem, Petey." She walked up to him, her slim hips swaying in the silky pajamas, and he waited for her to come close.

"You look tired," she said. "You know you shouldn't work so hard. Do you really have to go back?"

"Yes," he said bluntly. She was right, though. He was tired. Of his job? He didn't think so.

Her slender hand came up to caress his cheek. But his mind ignored her touch and focused cynically on the very large, glittering diamond. The one he'd bought her. Stupid middle-aged fool, he thought ruefully. Then he remembered the wife before Jillian. No, he wasn't a middle-aged fool. Just a fool.

She kissed him and he responded. Might as well get something for what he'd paid.

As she felt his response, she pressed against him.

His arms tightened.

She whispered in his ear, "You didn't really mean that about Shauna's going, did you? You were just teasing me."

He kissed her again before replying, his voice as soft as hers. "I meant every word I said, and you'd better be nice to her or I'll cut your clothing allowance in half."

She pulled away, her blue eyes blazing with anger.

He touched his index finger to her lips. "Not a word or I'll do it now." He went into the bedroom and began packing the clothes he thought he'd need for the next three days.

A few minutes later, Jillian came in and stood watching him speculatively.

"Are you finished packing?" he asked after a moment.

"Haven't started. But don't worry, *darling*, I promise I'll be ready on time."

She had emphasized the word darling a little too much. So she was angry. Well, maybe he was, too. Angry and something else. Maybe wondering when he'd grow up. A lot of people would say a forty-three-year-old man who took a twenty-two-year-old bride needed to grow up.

"Have you talked to Douglass?" his bride asked.

"Briefly."

She picked up a necklace and wrapped it around her fingers. "Are he and Anne going?"

"I believe so. Does it matter?"

"Of course not. They're a couple of old stuffed shirts, anyway. Who else will be there? Besides George and Ellen, I mean."

"Their son, Kendall, and his college roommate. You've met Kendall, I think."

"I'm not sure. Does he look like George?"

"I guess. His hair is brown, as I believe George's was before it turned gray. He has a lot more than George, of course. Reasonably good-looking. Not too fat, not too thin. Medium height."

"Doesn't ring any bells. You said his roommate was coming. Male or female?"

"Male. I doubt if you've seen him. But we've offered to let both Kendall and him come into the firm. At George's request, of course."

"Does George always get what he wants?"

"He's the senior partner."

"Who else will be there?"

"That's about it. Oh, no. Some female cousin of Ellen's is coming. From out west."

"That should be fun."

She did sarcasm well, he thought. "Maybe Shauna will take care of her."

"You were rather nasty about Shauna."

"Was I? Sorry." He finished packing and shut the suitcase with a quick snap.

"It's not as if Shauna wants to go."

"Maybe it bothers me that no one in your family ever cares

what Shauna wants. And that reminds me. Fix her up with some decent clothes and some makeup. And try to do something with her hair!"

"Peter, she's an old-maid librarian, and that's exactly what she looks like. She doesn't want to change."

"She's what, twenty-seven? Hardly an old maid. Especially these days. Anyway, I don't have time to worry about Shauna. I have to get back to the office. See you at four."

As he shut the door of the apartment, he took a deep breath. Funny how the air in there always stifled him. Maybe it was that perfume Jillian insisted on wearing. The stuff that cost a hundred dollars an ounce. Ridiculous! But he had to humor her. Her. Them. All of them were the same, weren't they?

He got into the elevator and traveled from the penthouse to the ground floor. While he descended, a subtle change took place as his mind turned from domestic matters to legal ones. He was back on solid ground.

And he was feeling good. He had a very rich, very important client coming to meet him in half an hour. And just that morning, he'd found the loophole his client needed to solve his tax problems, thus saving said client a good deal of hard cash, even after he'd paid his legal fees.

Twenty minutes later, Peter nodded to his secretary as he walked past her desk. His glance was casual, but thorough. What he saw pleased him. As always, her mahogany hair was perfectly sculpted, her makeup flawless. She was thirty-three, well-groomed, businesslike rather than seductive, yet feminine enough to rate a second glance from any client. Like the plush carpet, expensive leather, and mahogany wood, she gave his office the right tone, that of a successful person who knew how to deal with success.

Peter himself gave the same impression. His features were regular and misleadingly boyish. His light brown hair was longish and curling in the back, carefully styled by an expert; his clothes were the latest in business wear, discreet yet individual; his diamond-studded watch and gold ring were distinctive without being flashy. He had gained a little weight lately, it was true, but he visited his club enough to keep fit, and the filling out of his face and slight paunch only added to his sleek look. The picture of a contented man.

Peter poured himself a drink and relaxed against the smooth leather of his executive chair, waiting for the lucky client to appear.

His thoughts returned to Jillian and Shauna. Women! They had you no matter what you did. It was the same old story of "can't live with 'em, can't live without 'em."

And that reminded him. He needed to give his secretary a raise. No way he was paying her enough for her to afford the designer clothes she'd been wearing lately. She sure looked good, though. That figure was worth some expense. Better still, she had class. All in all, she was the ideal secretary. Easy on the eyes, unobtrusively in the background yet alert to his every need, intelligent yet deferential. She'd even thought to fib about where he was to Jillian a few times when she sensed he hadn't wanted to be bothered with his wife's petty requests.

Jillian's shrill voice popped into his thoughts. No tact there. Why hadn't he seen that before? She had deceived him. Okay, maybe he had allowed himself to be deceived. But he saw her now for what she was. Selfish. Grasping. Out for all she could get. If he tried to divorce her, she would fight him every step of the way.

He smiled. As if she could defeat him. He would have to be careful, that's all. Find a way to rid himself of her without losing everything he had worked so hard to get.

His intercom rang and he pressed the button. "Yes?"

"Mr. Jennings is here to see you, Mr. Martin." She had a nice voice, too.

"Send him in."

"Yes, Mr. Martin. Is there anything you need, Mr. Martin?"

"No, Miss Parker. Not right now." But you never know, he thought as he stood to welcome Mr. Jennings. An engaging smile lit his face. You just never know.

2

Eight blocks from the offices of Brodie, Fischer, and Martin, Attorneys-at-Law, the newest member of the firm, Kendall Brodie, only son of the senior partner, set down the cellular phone he had been using and sank into an ultramodern chair designed in one of the Nordic countries and sold in a large carton to those who didn't mind putting their own furniture together. It was impossible to sink far, and Kendall quickly straightened up. Stupid chair. He had wanted black leather, overstuffed and relaxing. But Nick had to have this beige plastic stuff that was supposed to be good for your posture. It also showed every speck of dirt. But Nick didn't care. His idea of decorating was to buy something cheap and throw it out when you tired of it. False economy!

The chair, however, was merely an annoyance. What was really bothering Kendall was the fact that Nick had been gone since seven-thirty the night before. He'd come in from who knows where, changed from jeans and a T-shirt into black linen pants, red sports shirt, and gray tweed blazer, yelled something about a sudden date, and rushed out. Likely a pick-up, Kendall had thought in disgust.

And where was he now? Maybe lying in an alley someplace with no ID.

But no. Someone was at the door, fumbling with the knob. It was locked, of course. And, as happened not infrequently, Nick had forgotten his key. Kendall waited until the bell rang before he pulled himself out of the chair.

"You're just a little bit late," he commented as Nick walked through the doorway. "In fact, I was wondering if you were going to show at all."

If Nick noticed the tone of reproach in his roommate's voice, he hid it well. "What a babe!" was all he said as he collapsed his lithe six-foot frame into the twin of Kendall's chair. "I wouldn't have missed last night for anything!"

"Where'd you pick her up?"

"Well, actually, she picked me up." The soft baritone that women and law professors adored changed to a Hollywood falsetto. "She's an actress, dahling. At least she hopes to be. And she didn't know anyone in the big city and I looked so tall, dark, and handsome I must be an actor, mustn't I? And it didn't matter anyway, because I was just so good-looking, all she could think of was running her fingers through my hair and would I mind terribly if she did?"

"You fell for that?"

"Kendall, the lady was gorgeous!"

"So what?"

"So—it was a mutual admiration party. We even had champagne. And when things got a little fuzzy, we finished the party up in her hotel room."

"You've been there till now?"

"You have a problem with that?"

"I just think you should use a little intelligence, that's all. You can get diseases from casual encounters like that."

"I'm not stupid, Kendall. Anyway, it isn't as if you've never had a little fun. What's the real problem? Jealous?"

Kendall faked a swing, which Nick parried with his arm. "Just annoyed. You left me behind to answer the phone when Candace called last night looking for you. What was I supposed to say when she wanted to know where you were?"

"What did you say?"

"I told her you were out with some of your skiing friends. The male ones."

"She buy it?"

"What do you think?"

"Oh, well, I'm becoming a little tired of Candace, anyway. She's starting to get possessive."

"Good old love-'em-and-leave-'em Donovan, huh?"

Nick grinned. "Did Marilyn stand you up last night? Is that why you're in a bad mood?"

"Marilyn and I played squash and ate a late lunch together yesterday, as a matter of fact. I told her I was busy last night. I thought we could talk. You and I. Seriously, for a change."

Nick rose and strolled to the kitchen where he rummaged in the fridge for a couple of cans of Coke. When he returned, he threw one to Kendall and sat across from him. "We've been over this already."

"You haven't given it serious thought yet."

Nick smiled and threw Kendall a quick glance. "I've given it a little."

"And?"

"And I don't think I'm ready for it."

"You may never get another chance like this. A job with the law firm of Brodie, Fischer, and Martin is a dream come true."

"For you, maybe. Not necessarily for me."

"Do you know how much money you would be making?"

"I'm making fairly decent money now."

Kendall shook his head. "Oh, sure. Risking your neck all the time. One of these days you'll break a leg or maybe your back and then what? You'll have to start right at the bottom in some no-name office. Maybe even from a wheelchair."

"I like skiing."

Kendall stood up and walked in a circle in front of Nick. His voice was earnest, as though he were pleading with the jury to understand a client's alibi. "So do I. But as a hobby. Besides, freestyle isn't skiing." He walked a few steps further and turned back, hands outstretched. "Okay, I like to watch. But you would never catch me doing it for a million bucks."

"You can't do it. I can."

"All right. You're good. And you've been fortunate. So far. But one bad fall and it's game over."

"So then I'll give law a shot."

Exasperation replaced Kendall's earnestness, and his face took on a boyish look of chagrin. "You're nuts! Why did you bother going to law school in the first place? Why waste the time and money?"

Nick remained relaxed. "You know I paid my way through by skiing. The servant became the master, that's all."

"But won't you even think about it? Talk to Dad? Ask him to tell you about the opportunities?"

"I don't know what he could say that you haven't."

"Not good enough. Nick, this weekend is a perfect opportunity! They're all going to be there, Dad, Douglass, and Peter. Once you've met them, you'll see what I mean. You'll want to be one of them instead of…"

"Instead of what?" Nick prodded.

"Instead of whatever you call yourself."

"Whatever I call myself?" Nick's voice was mocking, his eyes filled with laughter. "I call myself a free-style skier, and a good one at that!"

"You can do a lot more good as a lawyer, Nick." Kendall was pleading again. "And Brodie, Fischer, and Martin is one of the top legal agencies in the city. Think of what you could accomplish with their backing!"

"Speaking of backs." Nick finished his Coke and stood up. "I think I'm going to hit the shower and wash mine. Then I'm going to pack—assuming I'm still invited, of course. After that I'm going to allow myself to be driven by you to your parents' home where I hope I won't have reason to regret the impulse that made me accept the invitation."

"I don't want you to make a mistake you'll regret for the rest of your life."

"Kendall, I've roomed with you for three years. Why, I don't know. But not so you could tell me how to run my life."

"I'm only thinking about your own good!"

"You're not my mother. And that line is a cop-out."

Kendall's normally pleasant face was set in a hard line. "Somebody has to do your thinking for you. Right now you act like life is one big party, but there'll come a day when you'll wake up and realize you've blown it. I don't want that to happen."

"How old are you again? I could have sworn you turned twenty-five last month, but you sound more like fifty-five."

"Nick, come on!"

"Kendall, there's lots of time for settling down. Right now, I just want to be free to do what I want to do." Nick grinned ruefully. "Can you seriously see me in a three-piece pin stripe with a briefcase and Gucci loafers?"

But Kendall didn't smile. "You're really going to turn down my dad's offer?"

"Your dad's offer? But it was your idea, Kendall. You talked him into it. And you didn't even ask me if I was interested."

"I was going to surprise you! I thought you'd be thrilled. And I wasn't sure he'd do it. As a matter of fact, I had the devil of a time talking him into taking you. And now…"

"And now?"

"Now, thanks to you, I'm going to look like a complete idiot! Nick, you've got to take this job!"

3

Surrounded by windows dressed with yard upon yard of fabric flowers in rose, blue, yellow, and white, seated on a matching soft floral chair, Ellen Brodie was able to take a few moments to sip a ginger ale and get herself ready. She smoothed the skirt of the chic turquoise dress from the small boutique on Yonge Street and patted her hair, which was dark brown freely intermixed with gray, and had been put up in as modern a style as her despairing hairdresser could get her to approve. Cutting it was out of the question. Her hair had been waist length all her life and she couldn't fathom it any other way. Besides, George liked it long.

Her figure was good—comfortable, she called it. She'd put on a few pounds over the years, but not enough to worry about. In fact, she rarely worried. And she wasn't worried now. Only she did hope this weekend went well.

As she looked through the glass doors at the patio with its brightly colored umbrella tables and fabulous gardens, she wanted to pinch herself. She still found it hard to believe this spectacular house, mansion, really, was hers. She had spent her entire life in Cabbagetown, one of the oldest areas in downtown Toronto: her childhood in a small, battered third-story apartment, her first four years with George in a dingy basement, the next ten years in a narrow row house, and finally, the last twenty-four in a very comfortable three-story house on a large, well-treed lot. Cabbagetown had been home.

But this spring, George had decided Cabbagetown was no longer good enough for them; they should move far from the heart of the city to a suburb where other affluent people lived. It took some getting used to. She suspected her feelings were much like Cinderella's might have been after the honeymoon when Prince Charming carried her over the threshold of the castle and said, "Okay, honey, this is home now."

But this one room she loved. She smiled as her eyes moved from the view through the patio doors to the interior of the room. She called it the "day room" because the real estate agent had deemed that to be the proper name, but she thought of it as her own personal refuge—a soft, gentle space, perhaps a little large with its numerous groupings of chairs and coffee tables, but bright and cheery and comfortable. The feminine equivalent of her husband's heavy book-lined study. Only in this room did she really feel at home. But it was to be expected that it would take some time to get used to living in a mansion.

A bright whistle from outside broke into Ellen's thoughts and she started, turning her head toward the now-open patio doors.

"Hello, Aunt Ellen."

Ellen's glass of ginger ale tumbled from suddenly numbed fingers. Amber liquid seeped into the thick rose carpeting.

A tall man in his mid-thirties stepped through the patio doors. Backlit by the bright sunshine, his silhouetted frame looked thin to Ellen, and somewhat stooped. His face, indistinct at first because it was cast into shadow by the intensity of the sunlight behind him, was an ordinary face, unremarkable except for the complete baldness of his shaven head.

He set down a worn dufflebag, walked over to pick up one of the foil-wrapped toffees threatening to overflow an elegant crystal swan candy dish, and sank into a floral recliner chair. "You've certainly done well for yourselves," he said.

Ellen leaned toward him, her back stiff, every muscle taut. "What on earth are you doing here?"

"Just dropped in to see my favorite aunt."

His favorite aunt looked anything but pleased to see him. "What on earth have you done to your hair?" Her voice changed suddenly. "You aren't sick, are you?"

"It was turning gray at an alarming rate. Made me look old. It was either dye it or shave it. This seemed easier. Besides, baldness is in these days. Very sexy."

"Does George know you're here?"

"Not yet."

"Bart, you know how upset he'll be. We have guests coming! There's no room."

"You mean you'd turn me out in the cold? Your own flesh and blood?"

"You aren't either my flesh and blood! You're George's nephew. And it's not cold out. It's July, and so hot you could live outdoors easily. You probably have been.

"And what happened to the money George gave you? Surely you haven't gone through it already? You know he said it had to last the rest of the year."

"Slow down, Aunt Ellen. You're getting all worked up. The truth is I've had a bit of bad luck. But I can get the money back with a little ingenuity. I was in the neighborhood, so I dropped in. I'll leave if you don't want me."

Bart stood up and reached for his dufflebag. As he picked it up, he said, "Sure is hot out there. I had to walk for miles."

Ellen said nothing.

At the open patio door, he turned. "Are you really going to send me penniless into the cruel world?"

She stared at him. There was something of her husband George there, and something of their son Kendall, too. But it was muted by the lines of dissipation on his face and the cynicism in his eyes. She hoped with all her heart that life would never do to Kendall what it had done to Bart.

"Well?" He set the bag down and held out his hands. "What's the verdict?"

There was nothing about him that looked beggar-like. He wore an expensive black tweed sports coat, gray slacks, and a white silk shirt, and his loafers were thin, well-cut leather. But the clothes were dusty. And the way he shuffled his feet made her think they were sore. Neither the clothes nor the man were made for walking along a highway thumbing rides.

It must have been a year since she'd seen Bart last, though George had given him money a couple of times. He looked older and—and lost somehow. The baldness seemed to draw attention to every bone in his face. Made him look harsh, even tough. Made his eyes stand out. Hard eyes. Perhaps even wary? He must be thirty-five, the only son of George's favorite sister, long dead. A hustler, sometimes living it up, sometimes owning only the shirt on his back. But the shirt was inevitably silk.

However, despite his faults, which were many, he was family, and despite the hard-nosed appearance George presented to both client and associate, he had a strong sense of family. Even though he'd never liked Bart's father, and had been very angry with his sister for marrying him, for his sister's sake he'd given Bart an allowance, which Bart had used for gambling. He'd pulled some strings to get Bart a job in a bank and then paid off the bank so that Bart wouldn't be arrested for embezzlement. He'd offered all kinds of incentives for Bart to make something of himself, and, at last, offered to give him money so long as he stayed away—a modern version of the old remittance man.

But he hadn't stayed away, and George would not be pleased to see him, especially not this weekend with the partners and their wives here. But then, she thought, Bart was always a good actor.

He was still standing, waiting for her, probably knowing how much she hated to make anyone unhappy.

"You might be useful," she said at last. "You've always had a way with women."

Bart raised his eyebrows quizzically.

When she didn't continue, he asked, "What exactly do you have in mind?"

"Oh, come back and sit down! I shouldn't even be thinking of this. What George will say—!"

The door was shut, the dufflebag dropped in a corner. Bart reached for another toffee before settling himself back in the recliner. "I'm all ears, my dear—no, my favorite, aunt."

"Do you think you can exercise your charm for a weekend without straining yourself?"

"Are you implying that my charm is wearing thin?"

"Not at all. If you had half as much ambition as you do charm, you could probably get elected to the government."

"How sweet of you to say so, and how intolerably revolting a thought."

"Never mind. I've got your uncle's law partners and their wives coming for the weekend. Can you concentrate on keeping the wives busy? You know, amuse them for me. They'll be far more interested in talking to you than to me. If you can keep them happy, I'll put in a good word for you with George."

"When you phrase it that way, how can I possibly refuse?"

"You'll have to see if Mrs. Winston has time to make up a bed for you. There's an apartment for a chauffeur over the garage, but so far George hasn't saddled us with one. I dare say there are a few mice, but they shouldn't bother you."

He chose to ignore her assumption that he was familiar with rodents. "And where do I find Mrs. Winston?"

"Go straight past the hallway when you go out of here and turn left at the first door. You'll be in the kitchen. She should be there."

"Oh, and Bart," Ellen cautioned as he picked up his dufflebag, "don't waste your charm on Crystal Winston. It wouldn't be appreciated."

"Crystal?"

"Mrs. Winston's daughter. She's eighteen and idealistic. Just the type who takes to you. So see you mind your own business where she's concerned. George wouldn't like it one bit if you made Mrs. Winston unhappy."

He saluted. "I shall amuse wives, not maids."

"See you do."

He started to turn toward the kitchen.

"There's one other girl who's going to be here," Ellen said thoughtfully. "Her name is Lorry."

"Yes?"

"Stay away from her, too."

Bart raised an eyebrow. "That sounds intriguing."

"Not at all. She's the daughter of my favorite cousin, and she's not in the least your type."

"Your cousin's daughter, eh? Now why do I suspect something? Could she perhaps be Kendall's type?"

"Perhaps. But it's none of your business. Just stay away from her."

"Your wish is my command." He bowed to kiss her hand. "What time will they start arriving?"

"Dinner is at eight, but I told them they should try to come in the afternoon. To avoid traffic, you know. And they might like a dip in the pool first."

"Then I'd better waste no time in getting settled and learning my way around so I'll be ready to go into action when your guests arrive."

He wandered toward the kitchen and Ellen leaned back in her chair. "Stupid," she said aloud. "I should have sent him packing."

That's what George would say, and he would be right. George said she had a soft spot for Bart. Her only excuse was that most women did.

She stood up, and wetness seeped through the flimsy straps of her sandal.

The drink she'd spilled! She'd forgotten all about it. She hurried out to find a cloth and stain remover.

Chapter Two

George Brodie glanced at the grandfather clock in one corner of his spacious office. Time he was packing it in for the day if he was going to be at the airport on time. Ellen was afraid Lorry would be upset if she arrived in that huge terminal and he wasn't there to meet her and help with her luggage. And he supposed she might be right. Lorry had never been to Toronto before, and the large, bustling airport would no doubt be an intimidating place for a young girl from the country. Besides, he was having trouble concentrating on work.

He signed a few more papers and then buzzed his secretary. She was through the door in less time than one would have thought possible. Sometimes he wondered if she sat on the edge of her seat, poised to spring at the sound of the buzzer.

"Yes, sir?" said the woman as she advanced into the room. Nadia Estmanoth was in her fifties, with graying hair worn in a tight bun and a flowered sari covering her from chin to toes.

George smiled at his secretary. "I have to go and pick up my wife's cousin's girl. Which terminal was it?"

"Terminal two, Mr. Brodie. I was just coming to let you know it was time for you to leave. Won't do to have her wandering around the airport looking for someone she's never seen. How will you know her?"

"My wife says I can't miss her, so I'm sure she's correct. That is, if I'm there on time. Otherwise, I'll just have her paged."

"Of course."

He gave her several folders. "These letters need to go out today. By courier."

"Yes, sir. The courier is coming," she said, glancing at her watch, "in half an hour. That will give me plenty of time to make copies and get them ready."

She was gone as quickly as she had come. George cleared his desk and packed up his laptop computer. He glanced around, wondering if he'd need anything else. He pulled one file from his in-basket and added it to the papers in his briefcase. Then he checked his pocket for his wallet and keys.

"Have a good weekend, Mr. Brodie," his secretary said as he strode through her office.

"I hope so," he replied. Then, in afterthought, "You, too. See you Tuesday."

He was soon driving his black Lincoln in the downtown traffic. But his mind was on the weekend. Ellen had wanted a simple house party with themselves, Kendall, and Lorry. Inviting his partners and their wives had been his idea. He and Douglass and Peter had a few things to discuss and it had seemed to him they could do some work on the side. Now he was starting to realize it had been a stupid idea. You couldn't talk business with the wives hovering in the background. The naked truth was he'd forgotten that the other two women weren't like Ellen. She never got in the way. But Anne and young Jillian? Another kettle of fish entirely.

Then there was this thing with Kendall. Stupid to get talked into offering Nick a job. Even though he showed a strong streak of brilliance, the last thing they needed was a woman-chasing, part-time lawyer. And now Kendall seemed to expect him to sweet-talk Nick into accepting the offer! That was a rum job! Why he'd ever let Kendall talk him into doing it!

But he wasn't sure either of these things was what was bothering him. There was something else. An intangible. Nothing he could put a finger on. Just a sixth sense that something was going on behind his back. Something he couldn't control.

His sixth sense had never failed him in the past. People thought he had achieved what he had because of his brains. Maybe a little. But it hadn't been his brains that had told him to face up to the owner of the local newspaper forty-odd years ago when he was a wet-behind-the-ears-kid of seventeen. Cocky. That's what he'd been. But that particular owner, Mr. Anscotti, had liked the cocky kid from Cabbagetown enough to promote him several times and eventually put up the cash to send him to college. Later, he'd made his money back, in spades, as silent partner of the law firm of Spencer, Jones, and Brodie, with Brodie the only one who actually existed.

Later, when George's intuition had told him to risk everything and branch out from Cabbagetown into the business center of Toronto, he had done it. And it had paid off. His clients now were primarily millionaires. The elite business class.

Luring Douglass Fischer from a rival firm had been a solid coup—once again due to his intuition. Convincing Peter Martin to join had completed his quest for rock-solid respectability.

And his private life was solid, too. For thirty-eight years, Ellen had been there, seeing that his home was kept the way he liked it, doing everything a man could expect of his wife. She had never interfered. Always agreed that he should do whatever he wanted. Encouraged him to stretch.

And she'd never worried about finances. Early on, when they'd lived in one room in a basement, not knowing if there'd be food on the table the next day, Ellen had not once complained. The truth was, she took no notice of the things money could buy. She'd still be choosing her dresses from the nearest Walmart if he hadn't put his foot down and told her it didn't look right for his wife not to wear things from the designer shops. And the new house he'd bought her! He chuckled. He'd almost had to force her to agree to the move. But she deserved a house like this. A setting worthy of the wonderful person she was. And he could certainly afford it.

No, Ellen was not the cause of his concern. Neither was Kendall. Their only child was doing well. Joining the firm. What a terrific thought! His own son carrying on. Not like George's life. His old man had been a failure from start to finish. An Irish immigrant, cast off by his family because he lived in a fog, incapable of manual work. A dreamer, writing poetry and earning dimes and nickels for his readings and his ability to dazzle children with coin tricks. Nothing there for a son like George to emulate. What had impressed the young boy was not his father's golden words but his mother's rough, reddened hands, made that way from washing floors so she could put bread on the table.

Well, Kendall would have something more to remember of his father. And, unlike George's own mother, Ellen had never worked a day in her life. It would have killed him if she had. No. He shook his head. Whatever was bothering him had nothing to do with Ellen or Kendall.

He relaxed. Perhaps this weekend was going to turn out to be a good idea after all. Give him opportunity to talk to his partners in a casual way. Find out how they were feeling. Likely his feeling of anxiety had something to do with them. Maybe it was his intuition noticing something that didn't quite jibe. He'd have opportunity this weekend to discover what it was. Likely nothing important.

2

Like his partners, Douglass Fischer had been busy in his office for most of the day. Consequently, he arrived at his Rosemont home later than he would have chosen. The traffic flowing north out of the city was always heavy by four o'clock. Douglass had hoped to be soaking in the pool on the Brodies' new estate by that time. But it hadn't worked out. It never did.

He drove past the triple garage to stop his car in the circular drive which swept in front of his three-story brick home. A red Ford Mustang was already parked there. Douglass recognized the car with a grimace of annoyance. Did Luc have to spend every waking hour here?

He strode heavily up the steps and through the front door. If Anne had the packing done, they could still be at the front of the rush hour traffic.

He found his daughter Trina and her boyfriend Luc in the family room. Music was blaring from the CD player and he had to turn it off to make himself heard. They broke guiltily away from each other.

Aside from a cold stare at Luc, he ignored them. "Where's your mother?"

Trina shrugged. "I think she's upstairs." She paused, then added, "She's in one of her moods."

With a grimace, Douglass turned away and headed for the stairs. After the day—no, the week—he'd had, that was all he needed!

The heavy drapes were closed, making the room dark. Anne lay under an afghan on the king-size bed, her back to him.

"I suppose it would be too much to expect you to be ready to go to George and Ellen's," he commented from the doorway.

She rolled over, and he saw she was clutching an ice pack to her forehead. "Is that you, Douglass?" Her voice was thin and tired. "What did you say?"

"I asked if you had packed before—before this."

"This?" Her voice was sarcastic. "It's called a migraine, Douglass, as you well know." She spoke softly, as if afraid someone might overhear. But there was a querulous tone, too.

He was too preoccupied to care. "I know what the name is," he said roughly. "Are you packed?"

"No, I'm not."

He sighed. "I had hoped we'd be there by now."

"Well, we aren't." She turned away again.

"You'd better get up and pack now. We'll leave after the traffic has gone. That gives you a couple of hours. Surely you can be ready by then." Without waiting for an answer, he walked out.

Ignoring Trina and Luc, who were back in their own world in the family room, he strode into his den and used a key to open a locked cupboard. After a moment's thought, he chose a bottle of rye and poured himself a drink. He swallowed it quickly, without any enjoyment. Setting the glass down, he loosened his tie, then undid the top button of his shirt. He took a deep breath, and his chest expanded, stretching the rest of the buttons on the Italian silk. He needed to buy some new shirts. All of his seemed to be shrinking. Nobody made quality anymore.

After a moment, he walked to his desk and, picking up his phone, pressed familiar buttons and waited. When a woman's voice answered, he spoke quietly, holding his hand cupped around the receiver. "It's me." He listened for a moment, then said, "I'm not sure. She has a migraine."

A pause while the voice on the other end of the line murmured.

"I'll do my best," he said roughly.

The other voice spoke again.

"You have no right to say that! I'll manage!" His voice was louder now, and angry. "I already told you I'd do it as soon as possible! You'll get what you want!"

He hung up, then turned to pour another drink. Again, he took it straight and swallowed quickly. His eyes stared at the glass for a moment. Then he poured a third drink. Raising it to his lips, he held it there, suspended in space, his eyes focused on a spot in the air five feet in front. With a sudden oath, he sent the glass cascading toward the corner of the den, spraying its contents in an impromptu shower over the imported rug.

Hand still raised, he stood motionless, as if awestruck. When he finally broke from his trance, he half-ran to the door, calling, "Trina! Trina, I need you! I've spilled something on the carpet."

But when Trina discovered her father wanted her to clean up, she only laughed. "Sorry, I don't do housework. We pay somebody for that, you know."

Luc whistled. "Boy, if my father spilled his drink on our carpet, my mother would have a fit. Boy, would she be mad! If we so much as spill water, she goes crazy. She'd have a field day with a full glass of beer, or whatever. Does your dad drink a lot?" he asked Trina as the two went back to their interrupted tête-à-tête in the family room.

As they passed the foot of the stairs, Trina called, "Hey, Mom, you better come look after this mess!"

Douglass was trying to wipe up the spill with a towel from the powder room when Anne walked in. She was wrapped in a pale blue housecoat with matching slippers. Her medium-length brown hair was unbrushed and limp. Her voice was flat and cold. "What happened?"

"It's nothing. I just spilled something. It was an accident."

"I'll clean it."

"No. I can do it."

"You don't know how. I'll do it."

He stood and watched while she went for cloths and cleaning solution from the laundry room.

"Where's Mrs. Young? She should be doing this," he said as she came back. "Isn't she here yet?

"I told her we'd changed our minds."

"You what!" His face took on a deep red shade and, as he towered over Anne, he felt the urge to take a swing; to show her once and for all that she couldn't do things like this to him. Instead, he made himself walk away. "What's her number?"

Half an hour later, they were still in the den, no closer to being ready for the house party. Douglass was insisting that she get packed and Anne was moaning vehemently that she was not well enough to go.

Trina walked in without knocking. "Are you two still at it? Now what's the problem?"

"Your father tells me I should just forget my migraine and hurry up to get ready for the wonderful weekend party. Of course," Anne added bitterly, "he's never had a migraine, so naturally he knows more about them than I do."

"Anne, I only—"

Trina tilted her head to one side. "Luc and I are going out. I'll be back around midnight. I've got my keys. See you on Monday." Douglass watched her leave. Her torn jeans and oversize shirt looked like something a beggar might wear; her make-up and hair made him think of a horror movie. Was this how teens dressed nowadays?

"And besides," Anne said, watching him, "I don't think we should leave the kids alone that long."

"You can't leave them alone for two lousy days? Trina's nineteen and Jordan's sixteen. What are you worried about? And they won't be alone! Mrs. Young is supposed to be staying with them. She'd be here now if you hadn't told her not to come."

"I don't want to go!" Anne screamed. "Don't you know that? I hate them! All of them!"

"George and Peter are my partners," he said evenly. "They've never done anything to you. And you've always gotten along okay with Ellen."

"Aren't you forgetting someone? Or do I mean omitting? You wouldn't forget her."

He sighed. "I don't see why you can't get along with Jillian. She's never done anything to you, has she? Well, has she?"

She looked at him for a long silent moment, her eyes raking his. "Fine," she said at last. "I'll be the good little wife. Look after the house and the kids and be your loving spouse and ignore when you flirt with other women. That's all you want from me, isn't it? I'll go and pack and I'll spend a weekend being miserable just so you can have an excuse to be near Jillian!" She walked out of the room, then came back. "By the way, Jordan isn't home from school yet. Or hadn't you asked?"

She went upstairs. Douglass's shoulders sagged, and he stared for a long moment at the doorway. Something told him he should go after her, try to reason with her, but what was the use? Instead, he thumbed through his address book until he found the phone number for Mrs. Young, the lady who came in twice a week to clean the house and occasionally stayed with the kids for a weekend. When he found it, he told her they'd changed their minds again and he'd be over in half an hour to pick her up. Then he trudged wearily up the stairs to make sure Anne actually was packing their clothes.

As for Jordan, surely at sixteen he was old enough to take care of himself!

3

As Peter Martin unlocked the door of his penthouse apartment for the second time that day, he was relieved to be greeted with silence. Immediately, he began to worry that the silence might be of the icy variety.

But no. As he entered the living room, he saw his sister-in-law reading a paperback bestseller he'd picked up the week before when he and Jillian had spent five days in Tampa. A number of friends had told him he should read it, but he hadn't managed to get past the first few pages even though those pages had tried very hard to do their job of grabbing his interest. They appeared to have succeeded in grabbing Shauna's interest. She was so engrossed in the novel that she didn't even look up as he entered the room.

"Good book?" he asked as he came within a few feet of her.

She jerked as if someone had hit her. The book fell. "Oh! I— I didn't hear you come in. I have your book. It's one I wanted to read. I saw it and Jillian said you wouldn't mind. But I'll get my own copy. I meant to, only…"

"Hey," he said, "you're welcome to the book. Keep it if you want. I never find time to read anyway."

"Oh, no, I wouldn't dream of keeping it. I just thought— Jillian said I could take it so I have something to read if…"

"If you find yourself bored to tears by the rest of us. Bring it along by all means." Tired of keeping up the conversation with Shauna, who always seemed to be apologizing for something, he changed the subject. "Are you ready? Did Jillian find you some suitable clothes?"

"Oh, yes. They're very nice. Too good for me. Expensive. Not for a small-town librarian."

"Well, for this weekend, pretend you aren't a librarian. Pretend you're a—" His eyes took in the cover of the book she was reading. "Pretend you're the heroine in one of these books. Off for a weekend at a castle someplace or jetsetting around the world. Having a romantic weekend. There'll be a couple of young men there, you know. Anything might happen."

Her cheeks turned pink, and he was afraid she was going to lecture him about the difference between fiction and reality. "Is Jillian here?" he asked quickly.

"In the bedroom. She was having trouble deciding what to take. She sent me out because—well, because I was in the way."

Peter grinned, then sauntered along the passage to the enormous bedroom he shared with his young wife.

As Shauna's words had led him to expect, Jillian was standing at the door of her walk-in closet holding up two expensive dinner dresses. "Petey, which one should I wear tomorrow? I have something for tonight, but I don't know what to take for tomorrow."

"I think I can help with that decision." He took a small box from his jacket pocket. The box was covered in gold foil, with a red ribbon tied jauntily around it.

"For me?" she breathed, tossing both dresses over the nearest chair and coming toward him.

"See which dress goes best with this." He held the box out and received the kiss which she dutifully paid before she grabbed the box and tore it open.

"Oh, Petey, it's gorgeous!"

"Just a little something I picked up on the way home. To make sure you're in a good mood for the weekend." His smile took any intended sting out of the words.

"Silly," she said. "I was selfish not to want to take Shauna. You were right." She came to him. "Put it on. I want to see what it looks like."

He placed the large diamond pendant around her neck and fastened the clasp. His hands moved down, along her shoulders.

She gazed at her image in the mirror. "It's gorgeous, Petey. And I know just what to wear with it. What a wonderful way to solve my dress problem!"

She turned in his arms and lifted her face to be kissed. As he responded, she wrapped her arms around his neck.

He had shut the door on the way in, and he knew Shauna wouldn't bother them. She was likely deep in the book again, imagining herself as—as what? The heroine? Or perhaps the villain. Who knew? Or cared. Anyway, she wouldn't notice how long it took them to get out of the bedroom.

He had been wrong to become angry over Shauna. He didn't want Jillian wondering if he was becoming unhappy with her. The pendant would assure her that everything was okay. For a while at least. Give him time to figure out his next move.

4

Across town in an underground garage, Kendall Brodie unlocked the trunk of his graduation present, a black Porsche, and tossed in a leather suitcase. "Come on, Nick, hurry up!" he called to his friend, who had stopped to talk to another resident of their apartment building.

Kendall was annoyed because Nick was wasting time, but more annoyed that Nick seemed to be on a first name basis with every attractive woman they saw.

The truth was Nick had even introduced him to Marilyn several months before. When he'd brought them together, he'd said, "You ought to suit each other to a T. And if you run out of other things to do, you can always discuss my bad habits."

They had hit it off right from the start. Marilyn had everything Kendall liked in a woman: fair hair that hadn't come out of a bottle, baby blue eyes, small bones and delicate features, a soft voice, and a gentle style. She liked having doors opened, chairs pulled out, and all those things so many modern women seemed to take as condescension. She was, for lack of a better word, a lady. He was certain his parents would approve of her.

Nick had met her at the home of another skier. She was the sister of a friend of a friend, and Nick had thought she was perfect for Kendall. Nick went for the modern, no-holds-barred variety. The kind that phoned at all hours, didn't seem to care how much skin they displayed, and were game to try anything at least once. Kendall found the sum total more like a torpedo than an attraction.

"No class" summed it up nicely.

Nick was through talking now and he strolled leisurely toward the car and tossed his suitcase in beside Kevin's. "Waiting long?" he asked with a grin. Kendall knew that as usual Nick had read his thoughts.

They took their seats in the powerful car. But the number of horses under the hood was of little use once they hit the Don Valley Parkway. Traffic was stop and go, with more stop than go, and after a while they ran out of mundane conversation. Kendall coughed. "About the job—"

"Not that again!"

"I just want to say—"

"I'll jump!" Nick unsnapped his seat belt and reached for the handle.

"That's scary. We're going maybe five miles an hour."

"But you promised!"

"I promised I wouldn't keep bugging you about it. All I wanted to say was please keep an open mind. Talk to my dad and the others. That's all."

"And if I promise to do that, you won't mention it again?"

"Cross my heart."

"Okay. I'll keep an open mind. Now, any new CDs?"

They listened to music for a while, but the slow traffic was annoying. Kendall began drumming his fingers against the steering wheel.

"Traffic's going to be bad all the way," Nick commented.

"Everybody's heading out of the city. Cottage time."

"Yeah. Too bad, but you can't blame 'em."

"Wouldn't have been busy if we'd left a couple of hours ago."

Nick covered his face with both hands. "I know. All my fault. What's the penalty?"

"You can entertain my cousin or whatever she is for the weekend."

Nick lowered his hands and stared at Kendall. "The one from out west?"

"Country cousin. I'm not sure what our relationship is. Her mother is my mother's cousin. So we're—second, isn't it?"

Nick adopted a British accent he sometimes used. "Not close enough to bother about, what?"

"I told you I think my mother is matchmaking. So it's up to you to run interference. Enthrall her."

Nick switched to a Clouseauish French. "Aha, ze plot thickens. I deduce you have not yet told maman about ze so-beautiful Marilyn?"

"I was going to before she sprang this cousin on me. I thought it better to wait. She'll be disappointed when Lorry what's-her-name and I don't hit it off, and she'll be in despair that she'll never have grandchildren, which is the main reason she wants me to fall for Lorry, and then I'll pop up with Marilyn and Mom'll fall all over her with joy. Sound good?"

"Sounds like you've been reading trashy romance novels instead of law books."

"Very funny. Don't you think it'll work?"

"Well, I guess when you consider the material at hand, it might work."

"There's nothing Mom won't like about Marilyn. Is there?"

"Nothing I know at any rate. And don't look at me like that. I thought when I met her she was perfect for you, so I reserved her for you."

"Thanks."

"I expect to be Uncle Nick to all your little Brodie brats."

"How about being Papa to a few Donovans?"

Nick's cheerful face clouded over. He stared out the window at the cars in the other lanes. "Not a chance," he said quietly. "Not one in a million."

A wall had come up, but Kendall pushed against it. "Who knows? Maybe my country cousin will turn out to be a smoldering dark-eyed gypsy who'll sweep you off your feet in the good old-fashioned way, huh?"

Nick grinned. "Sure she will," he drawled, relaxing once more into the cushions. "More than likely she's coming to Toronto because she figures with the higher population of males here she'll be able to find someone who's both deaf and blind."

5

At that moment, in Pearson International Airport, George Brodie, as promised, was watching for Lorry Preston among the passengers disembarking from Flight 203 from Edmonton.

Ellen proved correct; Lorry was very easy to spot. With that flaming red hair—no, not really red, more what they called auburn—neither too short nor too long, shining like a brand new copper penny, breathing elegance and good-manners against the background of a very smart moss-green suit, she would have caught George's eye no matter who he'd been waiting for.

He stepped forward to greet her, and was surprised to see that her complexion was not the combination of freckles and easily burned skin that was the bane of many redheads. Rather, it was clear and creamy. Her eyes, like the suit, were green. Green and intelligent and clear. Not a cover girl, perhaps. Her mouth was a trifle large, and her chin a little too square. But she would never lack for admirers. He began to understand Ellen's desire for Kendall to meet this young woman.

As their eyes met, a smile lit her face, and he was caught off guard. In his business he was used to meeting people who were trying to hide something. Rarely had he seen a smile so genuine.

They shook hands. George took command of her luggage, and within a few minutes the canvas suitcases were stowed in the back of his Lincoln and Lorry was comfortably seated on the passenger seat in the front.

They spoke briefly about the flight and the weather, and George mentioned that his partners and son would be at the house. Then they relaxed into silence.

Lorry didn't mind. She needed time to assimilate what was happening. She was in Toronto! Seated in what she thought was rightly called a limousine, in traffic that seemed to go wall to wall, being driven by a wealthy city lawyer. Her eyes sparkled with excitement. She glanced over at George, but he was staring straight ahead at the road and he seemed completely preoccupied. With all this traffic, one would have to concentrate.

Her eyes narrowed. George was dressed in clothes that looked wellcut and expensive. But he didn't quite live up to the clothes or the car. In fact, her first impression was that he reminded her of a neighbor who worked as a plumber. The smallish stature (Lorry was 5' 5" and, when she was standing beside him in her heels, George had been only slightly taller), thinning gray hair, matching mustache—somehow it didn't add up to what she would have expected the senior partner of a very prestigious law firm to look like. But he was certainly at ease behind the wheel of the expensive car.

She allowed herself to relax into the cushions. Her mind drifted. She had come to Toronto for the summer to join a group of people who worked with street kids. She didn't expect to have a lot of fun. Rather, she knew there would be long hours of hard work and lots of frustration. Still, she couldn't wait to get started! After four years of studying youth and psychology, she was ready to put what she'd learned into practice.

Spending the summer in Toronto also would give her a chance to look objectively at her life. While there were several young men whose company she enjoyed, she was not ready to settle down with any one of them. "Haven't met Mr. Right!" was how she put it. But in actuality there was someone who had been trying for several months to persuade her she was mistaken.

So far, she wasn't convinced. But lately she had been wondering if she knew her own mind. After all, Dean was intelligent, trustworthy, capable, and, as he repeatedly said, crazy about her. And she liked him very much. But was that liking the kind of love that would last for fifty years? It was hard to decide. So it was good to get away, to have the opportunity to think about him from a distance.

Her mind returned to the weekend before her. In a way, it was an unwelcome distraction. So different from what the rest of the summer would be like. When the letter came inviting her, she had wanted to write back and refuse. Frankly, she didn't feel some people should have large houses and everything money could buy when there were starving people in the world.

But not to go or to cause a scene would be rude.

So here she was, committed to spend a weekend with relatives she barely knew and didn't expect to like.

Butterflies took up a fast polka in her stomach. She shut her eyes and began to pray that she wouldn't do or say anything really stupid.

Beside her, feeling guilty because of his lack of conversation, George Brodie glanced over and noticed her eyes were shut. He was pleased. He intensely disliked small talk and had no idea what to say to this girl. Good that she was taking a nap. With all the traffic, he hoped it was a long one.

Watching the other cars with one part of his mind, he allowed the other, larger part to return to where it had been before he went in to meet Lorry. He knew his doctor would just say this uneasy feeling was caused by the ulcer he was treating. But George honestly didn't think so. The only thing he'd inherited from his Irish father was a sort of second sight that often gave him a premonition of good or bad to come. Right now, he felt that something bad was about to happen. But what?

6

If George had envisioned what was happening in a very modern, beautifully decorated and furnished apartment in North Toronto, just a few miles from his new home, more warning bells might have pealed in that receptacle of his intuition which he privately acknowledged as his gut.

In that apartment, which was a dream of soft taupes and warm grays highlighted with splashes of vivid red, a woman stood in front of a stone fireplace and stared intently at the single picture on the mantel. A blond, blue-eyed child stared back at her, his face captured permanently in a sweet boyish grin.

But the woman's face bore no sign of an answering smile. Her red mouth was set in a hard line, and her gray eyes were cold and grim.

She turned away and paced the room for a bit, her feet in their sensible low heels sinking into the taupe carpet, her hands restlessly clenched at the sides of her expensive charcoal suit, man-tailored, relieved only by white ruffles at the neck of the silk blouse and rubies on the lapel and in her ears.

She stopped pacing and stepped close to a mirror framed in oak. For a long moment she stared intently at her face. Not bad, she thought. In another year she'd be forty, but she looked five years younger. A bit hard, maybe, but what could you expect? She'd had to make it up every rung by her own sweat.

So she hadn't had it soft. So what? She was a fighter, wasn't she? She'd scratched and shoved to get where she was, and she wasn't going to lose what she had gained. Not one tiny bit! No, she would never give in. Not if it took all the strength she had.

She turned again, forcefully, and strode over to the low table where she kept her phone. Earlier, when she had made her plans, she had memorized the number. Now, jaw clenched, she flipped back the short, coal-black hair expertly cut forward on one side, back on the other, and picked up the receiver to dial. She knew exactly what to say.

"Hello, Ellen, darling? It's Hildy Reimer, from the horticulture club. Listen, Ellen, I've a big favor to ask you. I don't want to be any trouble, but the truth is I've got painters coming and I can't stay in my apartment this weekend. Stephen is going to a friend's house and I had made plans to be away, but my plans have fallen through. I could go to a hotel of course, but that's sort of depressing. I wondered, well, I remembered your telling me about all the room you had in your home, and it would be so nice to see those gardens I've heard about... Oh, thank you, Ellen. That's so sweet of you. Now, you're sure you don't mind?... All right. I'll be over this evening... No, I wouldn't dream of intruding on your dinner. I'll come later. Thanks so much. You're really a lifesaver."

Hildy hung up the receiver, then rubbed white knuckles. There had always been a chance it wouldn't work. But it had. Poor Ellen, always trying to please. Hildy smiled wryly as she glanced at her recently wallpapered living room walls before shrugging and going to her bedroom to pack.

But before she could start, the phone rang. A child's voice was on the line.

"Stephen, I told you not to call.... No, of course not. Nothing's wrong. I just thought I'd be away by now. I'm going someplace this weekend.... Yes, you're to stay with Aunt Susan. I'm going to a place kids aren't allowed. It wouldn't be any fun for you. You'll have a good time playing with Diana.... No, I can't give you a number. I'll call to see how you're doing. Just stay with Aunt Susan. And Stephen, don't go out of the yard unless Aunt Susan or Uncle Art takes you. And for heaven's sake don't go anyplace with anyone else! Do you hear me? Nobody, not even if a policeman comes to tell you I'm hurt. Just run inside and tell your aunt. Do you understand?... Good. I'll see you Monday night. Is Aunt Susan there?... Let me talk to her now. Bye, Stephen. Stephen? I love you.

"Susan?... Yes, I'm just going.... I'll call you Sunday if I can. Keep a close eye on him. Don't let him outside alone. I'll try to settle things.... Don't worry."

She hung up the phone and stared into space for a moment. Then she pulled open the top drawer of her nightstand and took out a small revolver. After carefully burying it in her purse, she pulled a suitcase out of the back of her closet and grimly began to choose what she would wear.

Chapter Three

Ellen Brodie set down the receiver and wondered whether she should kick herself. Why had she invited Hildy to come for the weekend? She barely knew the woman. Had only talked to her twice at the horticulture club meetings she'd impulsively decided to attend after moving from downtown Toronto to this mausoleum George had insisted they buy.

What did she know about gardening? Nothing! But the house she now called her home had some of the most admired gardens in the entire city. So she'd thought, naturally enough, that she ought to learn something about them.

But Hildy Reimer? Ellen was only vaguely aware of the younger woman. Knew what she looked like and that she seemed smart as a whip. And she knew a lot about flowers and such. Or maybe that was someone else she was confusing with Hildy.

She sighed. It was all so difficult. She just wasn't cut out for this lifestyle. Of course, it was a credit to George. A smile touched her lips. Yes, it was wonderful for George. When you considered where he'd started, he had to be a genius to get where he was now. And he was so happy about it all.

So why was she so—so what? Unsettled? Out of her element? Like a small flower taken out of its hothouse and planted in a strange environment. She was afraid she would fail, would prove somehow unworthy of George, though she knew he would be the first to call her thoughts ridiculous.

Her guests should be arriving soon. She'd expected some of them earlier, before George arrived. But now he might beat them all. Traffic would be heavy from the airport, of course, but it was impossible everywhere on a summer weekend. So nice to be out here where one never heard all the noisy city traffic. Here, there was quiet.

It was all very different.

Not that the house would be quiet once their company arrived. She shuddered slightly. Although she'd had to do quite a bit of entertaining over the years, she'd never done anything like this before. All these people in the house. Supper and the evening was one thing. But the whole weekend! She could handle the arrangements and the food and all that, but what would they talk about?

Then she relaxed. It wasn't as if she had to be responsible for everything. Throughout their married life, George had always been there when she needed him. She would take care of the arrangements and let George worry about keeping everyone entertained. He had a knack for that and for a lot of things. Since she'd first met him at the age of fourteen, she'd leaned on George, who was only one year older, but a lot older in every other way. She could always depend on George. And their life together had been good.

Her only regret was that there hadn't been more children. She would gladly have adopted, but for some reason George couldn't bring himself to raise someone else's child. Such a miracle Kendall had been born when she was thirty-six and had all but given up hope!

She hoped Kendall and Nick would arrive first, so she could have her son to herself for a few moments before the other guests arrived.

That reminded her. Where was Bart? He had eaten as though starved at lunch, then lazed around the pool for hours. At four, she had sent him to dress so he'd be ready to help with suitcases. This was one of those rare times when she regretted the lack of a butler or chauffeur, but most of the time there was simply no need for any other servants. Mrs. Winston looked after the cooking and running the house, and there was a woman who came in twice a week for cleaning. And of course the gardeners. What else did they need?

Was that a car? Oh, dear. She still had to warn Mrs. Winston about Hildy's coming. Fortunately, Kendall's room had twin double beds; he and Nick would have to share it. Then Hildy could have the room Mrs. Winston had readied for Nick. She hurried to open the front door.

2

George had pulled up in front of the house and was opening the passenger door for Lorry.

Ellen rushed down the front steps. "George, I'm so glad you got here first. The others haven't arrived yet. Lorry, my dear, you look wonderful! We're so glad you were able to come!"

Lorry emerged from the car into a hug from Ellen. After the hug, Ellen held her at arm's length. "You're gorgeous. And that hair! I know women who would kill for that hair."

It was real, too. Ellen remembered the pictures of a chubby red-haired cherub with a mischievous grin and sparkling green eyes. The eyes still sparkled. But the chubbiness had been replaced by curves in all the right places and the grin had turned into a lovely smile. She was intelligent, too. She would make a delightful daughter-in-law.

Perhaps a little old-fashioned. With the father she had, she couldn't help that. But Kendall would bring her up to date.

Lorry was looking all around. "This house is breathtaking."

"Isn't it?" Ellen agreed. "I have no idea why George thought we needed a place this grand. But it will certainly come in useful this weekend."

Leaving George to handle the luggage, she escorted Lorry indoors and, after giving her a quick tour and pausing to speak with Mrs. Winston, led her upstairs to a room with pink ruffles and twin beds and, after another hug, left her there to unpack and freshen up.

Ellen hurried downstairs. She had suddenly remembered that George didn't know about Bart.

She was wrong.

After George carried Lorry's luggage into the front hall, he drove his car around to the garage. Puzzled by the open door leading to the unused apartment above, he went upstairs and found Bart in the process of sweeping a pile of dust onto a dustpan. "Of all the—! What are you doing here?"

"Glad to see you, too," Bart said easily. "Apparently, no one's been up here for a while. No end of spider webs, and dust an inch thick."

"What are you doing here?"

"Cleaning up."

"Ellen knows you're here?"

"Afraid so, old man."

"You're not getting another cent from me this year! I already told you that."

"You did. It makes life very difficult for me. I'm down to throwing myself on the mercy of my nearest and dearest. Of course, Aunt Ellen did give me a job."

"She what?"

"Entertaining the ladies for the weekend. She thought I might be able to take them off her hands."

George grunted. "And I suppose you're eager to get started."

"Well, Uncle George, if you want me to leave, I will. But, you know, I can't think that the headlines would look very nice."

"And what headlines might we be talking about?"

"The ones saying 'Prominent Lawyer's Nephew Arrested for Vagrancy on the Doorstep of Million-Dollar Estate.' Some of those trash mags really go for that stuff, you know. Might even pay for an in-depth account of the nephew's story. They'd love to dig up all the old stuff about how I was almost arrested for embezzlement that time, or how you paid off that girl's father— the one who wanted to charge me with statutory rape. Of course, I don't think he'd have won. And weren't there some other incidents? Not sure I can remember. A couple of forgeries, maybe? Impersonation? I think someone wanted to charge me with theft. A lot of people would enjoy reading about my past. Vicarious thrills, you know."

"Has anybody ever mentioned that you're nothing but scum?"

"I think you may have alluded to something like that once or twice."

"You do what your aunt tells you this weekend. And you stay on the line. One step over and I might change my mind and throw you to the dogs, no matter what the headlines say. Got it?"

"Got it. Now, may I finish cleaning up? I have to get ready to assist with the guests."

"There are some suitcases in the front hall. You can start earning your keep by carrying them up." So saying, George turned on his heel and walked out. As he went down the stairs, he slammed his fist against the wall. If he'd needed any proof that something was wrong, here it was. Whenever Bart turned up, there was bound to be trouble of one sort or another.

Ellen was standing in the front hall when George walked in.

"I saw Bart," he announced immediately. "You should've sent him packing."

"Did you?"

He grunted.

"I didn't know what to do with him." She slowly shook her head. "Such a waste."

"I wish somebody would waste him." Her puzzled look caught him up. "Waste is slang for killing. I wish we could get rid of him."

"Killing him would be a little harsh, perhaps?" she offered.

"Not too harsh for that weasel. Oh, I know, it's my own fault. I never should have helped him out in the first place. Stupidity. No, pride. He's got my name. Didn't want it dragged through the mud. I was a fool."

"You did what you felt was best, George. It might have turned out differently."

"He's never had a single grateful bone in his body."

"Well, no. Even as a young boy, he was never very trustworthy. Always looking out for himself."

"I guess he's the cross I have to bear. But if I can think of some way to get him off my back, I'll do it in a minute."

"Yes, George."

"Never mind him. He'll do what you want this weekend. He needs money. But after that—! Where are the others?"

"Douglass phoned to say they'd be here in time for supper. He had to work later than expected. And Peter called from his car to say they're on the way and he's bringing a surprise. He said he hoped we don't mind. I don't know what he meant. If it's a surprise, why should I mind?"

"Who knows? Well, I'll have a quick shower and change. Talking to Bart always puts me in a sweat."

3

Twenty minutes later, Kendall's Porsche pulled into the driveway. He grinned at his passenger. "How do you like it so far?"

"This is a house? I thought you'd changed your mind and stopped at a resort."

"Snappy, huh? Some guy from the mob built it. He wanted to be very private. Later, he decided he didn't like being so far from downtown, so he sold it. To the senior partner of Brodie, Fischer, and Martin. Think about it."

The front door opened, and Ellen Brodie appeared. "Nick, it's so good to see you again. You're looking even handsomer than at your graduation. I'll bet you've got all the girls waiting in line, eh?" Her voice dropped and she clasped her hands. "I have to warn you, though, that we have a small problem. I had planned for you to have your own room, but I hope you don't mind sharing Kendall's. It seems our house is going to be fuller than I thought. Of course, he has two beds in his room, double beds at that. It's like a motel room, really. Well, don't just stand there, you two."

She gave Kendall a hug. "Come on in the house, and Nick can tell us how he likes it."

She waited while they got their suitcases out of the trunk and then led them inside, where she gave Nick a quick tour of the house before leading him and Kendall upstairs and making sure they had everything they needed.

Five minutes later, Ellen was standing in the hallway looking out the window in the front door when Kendall's voice startled her. "What are you doing? Planning a coup?"

"What? Oh, it's you, Kendall. Gracious, you frightened me. I didn't hear a sound."

"Deep in thought?"

"I was just wondering when they'll get here. Soon, I hope. There's so much traffic that of course one always worries about accidents. There are so many of them. Not always tragic, of course. But still worrying. And the delays they cause—" Another thought flashed across her mind. "But never mind that. Lorry's here. Your dad met her at the airport. I think you'll like her. She's really quite lovely. And she's so sweet."

She would have continued, but the sound of a motor reached her ears. She opened the door and peered out along the circular drive. The nose of a silver Mercedes came around the corner. Ellen hurried out, followed by her son.

Peter cheerfully blamed their delay on Jillian. "She's never ready on time," he said. "It's simply a fact of life I've learned to accept. And I hope you don't mind, but Jillian's sister is visiting and we couldn't possibly leave her alone, so we brought her with us. She and Jillian could share a room if it would help," he said with his endearing smile. "I'll sleep anywhere, in the car if necessary."

Flustered, Ellen said that of course he wouldn't have to sleep in the car and there would be no trouble arranging a place for—what had he said her name was again?

"Shauna Jensen." Peter laughed again. "Jillian, Shauna, Charmaine, Brandy, and Angelina. Their mother reads Harlequin romances by the dozen."

A tall, thin woman dressed in beige emerged from the back seat of Peter's Mercedes. Square black glasses stood out on the pale, though not unpleasant face. Shauna stepped forward. "I hope I haven't put you out. I didn't want to intrude, but Peter insisted."

"Of course he did. 'The more the merrier,' as my dad always used to say." Inwardly, Ellen groaned. What on earth was she to do with this unwanted guest? A couch somewhere? That would never do.

A Cadillac pulled into the drive and came to a stop behind Peter's Mercedes. Douglass Fischer hurried around to open his wife's door and help her out of the car. Anne got out slowly, as though she had arthritis. She was wearing an A-line mint green linen skirt with matching short-sleeved jacket. The jacket had white cuffs and a white Peter Pan collar. Her shoes and purse were also white. She had pulled her hair back and twisted it into a knot. Large pearl earrings dangled from both ears. She wore dark sunglasses and carried an emerald green tote bag.

Douglass tried to take the tote bag from her, but she ignored him and walked toward Ellen. Douglass shut the car door and followed. He kissed Ellen's cheek before turning to talk with Peter.

Anne's words rushed out to fill the empty space. "Ellen, how sweet of you to have us. It's so nice to get away for a change."

"Anne," Ellen responded with equal enthusiasm, "it's so nice you were able to come. I was thinking afterwards that you should have brought your children. They must be almost grown now." As they hugged, Ellen wondered why Anne's makeup looked streaky. And why her voice sounded so brittle.

Peter was opening the trunk to get suitcases. Douglass was stooped over to assist Jillian. Apparently Peter's wife had dropped her purse in the car and was having difficulty finding the contents. Ellen and Anne moved toward the house. Then Ellen stopped and turned. "By the way, everyone, dinner is at eight. I know that doesn't give you a great deal of time, but I hope you can manage. Just come as you are, of course."

Nick was descending the wide sweeping staircase as Ellen and Anne entered the entrance hall. "Oh, Nick, if you're looking for Kendall, he's out front with some of our guests."

Nick paused with a smile.

Ellen introduced Anne to Nick and then led her up the stairway. As the two women walked through the upper hall, Lorry's door opened and she stepped out. Ellen watched in amusement as Anne's eyes narrowed in a clear appraisal of the younger woman.

Having made quick introductions and shown Anne to her room, Ellen went back to talk to Lorry, who she had asked to wait for her.

"I have a real problem," Ellen confided. "I hate asking you this, but Peter and Jillian Martin have turned up with Jillian's sister and I have no more rooms. Would you mind terribly if I asked you to share your room? There are two beds."

"I don't mind one bit," replied Lorry. "The room is so huge I was afraid I'd get lost in it by myself."

"Thank you so much, dear. I'll make it up to you. Now, let's go down and find you something to do until supper is ready."

As they reached the bottom of the stairs, Ellen was surprised to see Nick standing in the open front doorway. He appeared to be watching the people outside. At the same moment she noticed him, he turned. She was immediately aware of a difference. In the few minutes since she'd last seen him, he seemed to have paled, although with his tan it was hard to imagine how.

To cover her confusion, Ellen began to talk. "Nick, you haven't met Lorry yet." She made the introductions.

Lorry smiled.

Ellen watched Nick to see his reaction, but there was none. Perhaps because he had been looking into the bright sunlight, he had trouble focusing in the darker hallway?

Ellen went to the open front door to call out, "Kendall, come and meet Lorry."

Douglass was still at Jillian's side of the car, leaning over. Kendall was talking to Shauna and Peter, but he waved to acknowledge his mother's words and came inside.

When Kendall was in, Ellen introduced him to Lorry. Then she waved her hand in the direction of the games room. "Perhaps you'd like to have a game of billiards while you wait for supper."

She didn't wait for an answer, but started toward the front door to look after her other guests. As she walked out the front door, she was wondering what was wrong with Nick. His easy habit of conversation seemed to be absent. Maybe she was imagining things, but he looked like someone who had just seen a ghost.

4

Still seated in the silver Mercedes Peter had given her as a wedding present, Jillian Martin shut her voluminous purse. "That's everything!" she announced. "Thanks for helping, Douglass. You're such a sweetheart." She raised her voice. "If we've missed any little thing, you'll find it later, won't you, Petey?"

"Sure, I will. But I suggest you come along now. You heard what Ellen said about supper." Peter glanced at his watch. "We have less than an hour. You'll have to hurry if you're to be ready. You, too, Douglass."

"I'd better see that our suitcases are all out," Douglass mumbled as he headed for his own car.

"Oh, well." Jillian shrugged. "I suppose if I'm a little late it won't really matter. She'll understand."

"She might, but I'm not so sure about me. I missed lunch today." Peter laughed and patted his growing middle.

Jillian ignored him as she got out of the car. "Let's go in. I want to see what our room looks like. What a huge house! Come on, Shauna. Our hostess is waiting for us."

Ellen led the way upstairs. "I've put Shauna in with my young cousin," Ellen said as she opened a bedroom door.

"I hate to cause all this trouble." Shauna twisted the handle of her purse.

"Shauna could have managed perfectly well on a couch somewhere," Jillian said. "I hope your cousin isn't inconvenienced."

"Oh, yes. This is really far too nice for me. Just a small cot somewhere would have done."

Ellen chose to ignore the comment. "Jillian, I remembered that you look lovely in all those bright oranges and yellows, and so I thought the room with those colors would be perfect for you. And, of course, I put Anne and Douglass in the green room because she wears a lot of greens and grays. Clever of me, don't you think?"

"Very clever of you, Ellen," Peter said. "And now, we'd better get to that room, Jillian, or we'll never be on time for supper."

She acquiesced and, leaving Shauna, they followed Ellen.

Shauna was staring at a picture Lorry had placed on the nightstand next to her bed when there was a knock on the door. She jumped. Guiltily, she moved away from Lorry's side of the room.

"Come in," she said in a frightened voice.

The knock was repeated.

She forced her voice to become louder. "Come in."

The door opened and the new suitcase Jillian had lent her appeared in the doorway. Behind it stood a strange man.

"Oh!"

"Delivering luggage. This is yours, I hope?"

"Yes. Thank you. I—thank you."

"You're welcome. Where would you like it?"

"Oh," she said vaguely, "anywhere."

"It's heavy."

"Oh. Maybe—?" She glanced around the room wildly and then gestured to the bed beside her. "Here. On this bed."

He lifted the suitcase onto the bed and made sure the right side was up.

He was going out the door when she called, "Wait! Shouldn't I pay you or something?"

"Do I look like the butler?" he replied. "I'm not."

Her face flamed. "Oh. I guess I'm not very—very—"

"George Brodie is my uncle."

"Oh."

"Well, see you at supper."

"Yes. Yes, I guess so."

"I'll be eating it, not serving it."

He shut the door and she moved over to stare at Jillian's suitcase. After a moment, she opened it. It was full of the clothes Jillian had thrown at her. A couple of dinner dresses. A nightgown and matching robe. Some jewelry. Underwear. Bathing suit. Two sundresses. A skirt and blouse. Even shoes.

She pulled the garments out and hung them in her closet. She couldn't keep from opening the other side of the closet. Clothes were hung neatly. One navy suit, two skirts, a few blouses, and three dresses, one green and two floral patterns. Nice, but ordinary. Not glamorous or sexy, like the things Jillian wore. Not expensive-looking, either.

Shauna went back to the bed. At the bottom of the suitcase were her own things. Jillian had said to leave them at the apartment, but for some reason she had brought them. She took out what she thought she might need. Toothbrush. Other toiletries. A few odds and ends. Her book. Then she put the suitcase, her own clothes still in it, at the back of the closet.

She sat down on a rose-colored chair and stared at the clothes in her closet. Maybe wearing them would get her through the weekend. Maybe she would be able to fool people into thinking she belonged here. Except that man. The one she'd thought was a servant. He knew she didn't belong.

From now on, she would copy Jillian. Her sister always knew how to act.

But then, her roommate was Mrs. Brodie's cousin. So maybe she should copy her. Do what she did.

It was all so difficult. She picked up the book Peter had let her bring. She'd worry about clothes in a little while.

5

Instead of playing billiards, as Ellen had suggested, Kendall had recommended a tour of the rose garden, to which Lorry readily agreed. Nick wandered along behind them.

The rose garden consisted of walls of wild rose bushes dotted with arches and trellises covered with climbing roses, several fountains with small cherubs gamboling, white wrought-iron love-seats for sitting, and a myriad of different roses, from flori-bundi to hybrid tea and miniatures to grandifloras, all of them beautifully cared for and many of them spectacular.

"However do your parents look after all this, Kendall?" Lorry asked in amazement.

Kendall laughed. "If you think either of them has a green thumb, forget it. As far as Dad's concerned, if looking after the place was up to him, this would be a slab of concrete, possibly painted green. I guess Mom likes it, because she raved about it when they bought the house. But my personal opinion is that she likes it because it's a status symbol. You know, 'Won't you come to tea in my rose garden, dear?'

"Anyway, there are two full-time gardeners looking after the grounds. Plus a part-timer to do the heavy work. And if you like this garden, wait until you see the Japanese one."

Lorry shook her head, then moved on, exclaiming about first one and then another rose.

Kendall waited for Nick. "Cat got your tongue?" he asked quietly. "Or are you coming to your senses?"

It was a moment before Nick replied. "No," he said slowly. "I remembered something and started thinking about it. Sorry."

"No problem. It's only that when you're around attractive women you aren't usually quiet. Unless of course you got to thinking she might prefer the strong, silent type."

Nick half-grinned, looking rueful. "Am I as obvious as that?"

"Usually. But then I know you better than most."

"Well, I'll try to be better company." He looked over at Lorry. She was standing in the shade of one of the enormous trel-lises. As she leaned forward to smell one of the roses, a shaft of bright sunlight hit her, making her face glow and her hair shine like new copper. As if seeing her for the first time, Nick said, "She is attractive, isn't she?"

Kendall smiled. "Not exactly what you expected." He snapped off a dead flower and threw it under the bush. "Not what I expected, either, to be honest."

"So, do I have a clear field?" Nick grinned. "You still prefer blue-eyed blondes?"

"Well," Kendall teased, "I may regret this, but don't worry about me."

"Sounds like you've met your Waterloo. I'll make sure I let Marilyn know how faithful you are."

Kendall traced the curve of a large rose petal with one finger. "You in any danger of meeting yours?"

"You wish." Nick smiled, but his eyes remained grim. He walked over to Lorry, who was staring at a spectacular Chicago Peace rose. "Nice, huh?"

"Breathtaking."

"Yeah, I agree."

She looked up, saw he was looking at her rather than the rose, and blushed.

Nick then began a guided tour of the garden, making up names for the roses, and before long all three were laughing as though they were old friends.

They were interrupted by the chime of a clear bell.

"Mom's idea," Kendall announced. "This place is too big to yell. The bell means, 'Dinnah is served, m'lud and lady.' Shall we?" He held out his arm, and Lorry, after a small hesitation, took it.

Nick bowed and dutifully took Lorry's other arm. "Amazing things one learns at law school. How to escort a lady to a formal dinner."

"Really?"

"One of our classes had a very large book on etiquette as required reading. As a lawyer, one has to be polite at all times. Even if you call someone an idiot, there are ways to do it politely. Don't laugh; it's true. One of the many reasons I'm not a lawyer."

"I know you're joking about the book. But I thought Ellen said you had both graduated from law school."

"We did. But unless I actually practice law I defy anyone to call me a lawyer. I am a skier."

"So am I, but—"

"You ski?"

"Whenever I get the chance."

"Any good?"

"Average."

"Downhill?"

"Uh huh. You?"

"Anything. Mostly moguls and aerials."

"Really?"

Nick laughed. "No, I made it up. Just kidding. I'm a freestyle skier. Competitive,"

"Oh, that's great. I love watching freestyle skiing. But isn't it difficult?"

"No more difficult than a lot of things."

"And not nearly as remunerative as law," put in Kendall, who had been silent since Nick began to talk.

6

The party gathered in the enormous living room. Like the rest of the house, it was a show piece. One entire wall was a fireplace made from white marble. Indirect lighting brought out its gleaming charm while contrasting it with the large pictures on the other three white walls—abstract pictures of giant royal blue and emerald green flowers. Four white satin brocade sofas held court on the off-white carpet, amid a scattering of bright green and blue Queen Anne chairs and white marble end tables. Gold-tone lamps with white shades speckled with tiny blue and green flowers rested on many of the tables. Here and there were green or blue vases of various sizes holding a profusion of fresh roses and other flowers from the gardens.

Lorry, Nick, and Kendall entered the room just ahead of Douglass and Anne. The room became the topic of conversation. Kendall assured them that a decorator his father hired had full responsibility for every room in the house except the den. "Dad said to spare no expense, and she didn't."

They all turned as Anne gave a brittle laugh. "Jillian seems to be missing. She obviously knows the effect of an entrance."

Douglass's face reddened slightly in the short silence, then Ellen said something innocuous about how nice it was to have such a nice large gathering. Conversation was beginning to flow again when Peter and Jillian walked in, with Shauna trailing behind them. Jillian had changed into brilliant orange cocktail pants with a matching scoop-necked overblouse. Her golden hair shone, reflecting the orange glow. The gold-embossed chain of crystals she wore sent shimmers of light radiating in all directions. The smooth, expertly made-up face glowed with vitality. One could not really fault Peter for the look of pride on his face.

"Hope we didn't keep you waiting," he said with a smile.

Polite answers were given, and Ellen and Kendall led the way into the dining room. Jillian glided to her chair and waited while Peter pulled it out. She smiled serenely at everyone. "Sorry I'm a wee bit late. I really don't know how I managed to get here this quickly." Her voice was soft, like a shy child's begging to be forgiven. Several male voices rushed to say there was no problem.

Nick turned to Lorry, who was seated between him and Kendall.

"Where do you usually ski?"

Since Lorry had been one of those mesmerized by Jillian, Nick had to repeat the question. When she did hear him, she simply said, "Banff and Jasper," and continued watching Jillian. After a moment, it dawned on her that she had been rude. She turned to smile at Nick.

In the rose garden, her attention had been on the flowers, so she had not really looked at him closely. Her impression was one of a nice-looking, confident man. Now, however, as she took in the darkness of his wavy hair and black sports jacket, contrasted against the white of his smooth shirt and finely chiseled face, and in the midst of this starkness, brilliant blue eyes gleaming like sapphires, she was shocked into thinking he was quite possibly the most attractive man she'd ever seen.

Not that his looking somewhat like a movie star meant anything, of course. It was what was inside that mattered.

She didn't allow herself to look at him again. But she did glance once more at Jillian. She was so—even the word beautiful seemed inadequate. Dazzling? Like you would expect a famous actress to look.

Lorry saw Jillian's head tilt slightly as she listened to something Peter was saying. Saw her eyes widen as she stared down the table at Nick. Saw a smile touch those perfect lips. Then Jillian turned back to say something to George on her other side.

For a second, Lorry felt just a tinge of—what? Annoyance? Stupid. It was natural that Jillian would find Nick attractive. Who wouldn't? She scolded herself for thinking like a schoolgirl. He wasn't her type at all. He'd probably be right at home with someone like Jillian. And what a couple they would make! The thought did not entirely please her.

"Lorry, do you think you could pass the butter?" Nick's voice startled her. "Not for me. I wouldn't dream of interrupting your thoughts. But Anne wants it."

"Oh, I'm sorry." She quickly found the butter and gave it to him. "I guess I was deep in thought."

"A penny for those thoughts," Nick said. "Or are they worth more?"

"More than you could afford, sir."

"You know, ma'am, I'd rather if you called me Nick. Of course, you could call me Nicky, or even Nicholas, or perhaps Hey, You, but I rather prefer Nick from my friends. You are going to be my friend, aren't you?"

Lorry felt her cheeks turning pink. Just like a schoolgirl! "Eat your supper, Nick."

Nick laughed and Lorry looked down at the beautifully prepared plate that had just been placed before her, but her eyes were drawn irresistibly back to Jillian, and to her surprise she saw Jillian look away.

Why on earth would Jillian be watching her? Likely she was just looking around the table, perhaps wondering who everyone was.

There were several people Lorry hadn't met yet. Douglass Fischer. Peter and Jillian. The mousy-looking girl Kendall had said was Jillian's uninvited sister. And Bart Brodie. He was a type she had never met. Not that she had met many people like the others, either in the small town where she'd grown up or in the city of Edmonton where she'd gone to college the last four years.

The truth was, she felt she had been plunged into a completely different world, where money flowed freely and standards were very different from those with which she had grown up, and which she had adopted for her own.

Lorry bowed her head and said a silent grace. *God, thank you for this food and for bringing me here, and please keep me from making too many social blunders this weekend. And help me to remember what's really important. Let me see through your eyes.*

7

After supper, George strolled off to his den with Peter and Douglass, ostensibly on business.

The rest of the house party followed Ellen back to the formal living room with its marble fireplace, vaulted ceiling, and groupings of sofas and chairs. Coffee and tea were set out on the central coffee table, and as Ellen poured, she protested, "Those men. If you ask me, all they're going to do is find a bottle of something that George has stashed away and that will be the sum total of their so-called 'business talk.' They think they can pull the wool over our eyes."

"And can't they?" Bart asked. He was leaning back in an overstuffed rocker, lazily studying the rest of the group. "Can't they?" he demanded.

"Well, not most of the time," his aunt replied. Then she laughed. "All right. You're an exception. No one ever knows what you are liable to do."

"Sounds intriguing," Jillian said as she selected a cigarette from a gold case. "What do you do, Mr. Brodie?"

"If you find out, let us know. That is, if he does anything at all," Kendall commented.

Jillian laughed. "You wouldn't by any chance be the black sheep of the family, would you, Mr. Brodie?"

Bart smiled. "How astute of you, Mrs. Martin."

"Jillian."

Ellen relaxed. It looked as though Bart would be able to keep Jillian amused. Now if she only knew what to do with the sister.

Nick lounged in a small bay window. His hands idly fingered a small object he had absent-mindedly pulled from his pocket.

"You look bored," Kendall said as he sat down in a near-by chair.

Nick started. "What?"

"What are you thinking about? How you'd like to own a place like this? If you joined the firm, someday you could."

"No, actually, that's not it at all. I was thinking about fate."

Kendall's eyebrows rose. "Fate?"

"Yeah. Like—oh, I guess whether things happen by chance or not."

Kendall's voice registered the astonishment that showed in his face. "What on earth has got you talking like that?"

Nick laughed and put the trinket back into his pocket. "I don't know. You, I guess, with all your talk about making decisions and having to live with them. It's not nearly as easy as you make it sound. And if you choose wrong, what do you do? Can you ever go back and start over, or do you have to go on from where you are?"

"'Two roads diverged in a yellow wood...'" Kendall quoted.

"Yeah. Do we really have a choice, or is it all fate?"

"You've got me. But I don't think you need to spend too much time thinking about joining the firm. It's obvious which is the right choice here."

"'And I—'" Nick finished the quotation, "'I took the road less traveled by...'"

Since they were to be roommates, Lorry thought it fell on her to do what she could to make Shauna comfortable. But she quickly found that drawing the older girl out was not going to be easy. If Shauna had had a shell, she would probably have been huddled inside. As it was, she was doing her best to disappear into the large chair in which she was sitting.

"I guess we're going to be roommates for the weekend," Lorry said with a smile.

"Yes."

"You're Jillian's older sister?"

"Yes."

"Do you live in Toronto, too?"

"No."

"Outside of the city?"

"Yes."

"Do you have an apartment?"

"I live at home."

"Oh, that must be, er, interesting. With your parents?"

"Yes."

"Do you have other sisters or brothers?"

"Three sisters. Besides Jillian."

"Are they at home, too?"

"Yes. They're in school."

"Oh. Do you work?"

"At the library."

Even though she appeared to be engrossed by Bart, Jillian must have been listening to at least part of her sister's conversation, because she suddenly swiveled in her chair and said, "Oh, for goodness sake, Shauna, the girl is only trying to be polite. If you could hear yourself! A moron could talk better!"

Shauna looked down at her hands, folded in her lap, but she said nothing. There was a moment of uncomfortable silence.

It was broken by the sound of a chime echoing through the house.

Kendall jumped up. "I'll get it."

Ellen started slightly. Who could it be at this hour? She sought for something that had slipped her mind. Something she had forgotten. Oh, no. She had completely forgotten about Hildy!

"I don't believe I mentioned it, but there's to be one more guest for the weekend. A friend of mine. Well, not a friend exactly. Someone I know reasonably well. We're in a club together— oh, here she is now. Everyone, this is Hildy Reimer."

But no one was looking at Hildy. Instead, they were staring at Jillian, who had suddenly burst into laughter. "I don't believe it!" she said at last. "Who invited the wicked witch of the East? Or did you invite yourself? I always thought you had a lot of nerve, Hildy darling."

Chapter Four

As if by premonition, Peter chose that moment to come in from the den. He said, "Shut up, Jill." Then he turned to the other woman. "Hildy, what the devil are you doing here?"

The attractive woman with short, black, blunt-cut hair and a deceptively simple gray silk suit with an ice pink blouse stepped forward. "Hello, Peter," she said evenly. "I didn't expect to meet you here."

He took the hand she offered and held it briefly.

Jillian stood and walked insolently toward the older woman. "Come to spy on us? And did you think you'd be welcome?"

"Jillian, cool it!" her husband ordered.

Jillian laughed, turned her back on Hildy, and sat down on the arm of Bart's chair.

Peter radiated embarrassment. "I guess we'd better get this over with. Hildy is my former wife. My second wife. I had no idea…" His voice trailed off and he glanced at Ellen.

"I had no idea she was your ex-wife," Ellen glanced apologetically at Hildy. "If I had, I certainly wouldn't—I mean, I would—I mean—Oh, dear."

"It's perfectly all right, Ellen," Hildy said. "I'll just go to a hotel. I should have done so, anyway."

"Don't go on my account," Peter said. "We're still friends, aren't we?"

"Don't go on my account, either," Jillian drawled as she leaned close to Bart so he could light another cigarette for her. "This is all terribly amusing. Did you know Peter still has your picture in his desk? Perhaps we could compare notes?"

Neither Hildy nor Peter spoke.

Ellen filled the gap. "Kendall, would you take Hildy's luggage to her room, please? The blue one next to yours. Hildy, may I get you something? A drink, perhaps?" The two women moved away from the others.

Jillian continued to lean close to Bart. "The nerve of her," she said softly.

"Maybe Peter likes women with nerve."

"Meaning?" she dared.

"Don't worry. I like women with nerve, too."

"You do, huh?" The fingers holding her cigarette touched the back of his hand lightly. "And how many ex-wives do you have in your closet?"

"None. When I get tired of them, I drown them in a lake. Tidier that way. No loose ends to walk in and surprise me."

She laughed, a throaty chuckle that carried across the room to where Ellen and Hildy were talking as Hildy finished her drink.

After a moment, Hildy set down the drink and said she'd like to go to her room and unpack.

"Oh, certainly," Ellen said. "I'll take you up." They left the room and Jillian's laughter followed them into the hallway. "I can't begin to tell you how sorry I am," Ellen apologized. "I had no idea you even knew Peter. Or any of them. You could have knocked me over with a feather when Jillian said those dreadful things."

"Jillian is a dreadful young woman. What Peter sees in her is completely beyond me."

"Well, yes, I do sometimes wonder, but, then, it's none of my business."

"Nor mine, I suppose. Although I hate to see anyone made a fool of, even Peter."

"Oh, I suppose he can look after himself," Ellen replied uncomfortably.

"Sure, he can. In a courtroom. But in the bedroom? Not a chance."

The subject of the women's conversation was seated on a stool at the bar, which occupied the east wall of the games room, wondering aloud at the luck of attending a house party with a wife and ex-wife. "Oh, well," he said finally, "I suppose they'll manage. Hildy's the most level-headed woman I know, and Jillian... well, she may be young, but boy, she won't let anybody get the best of her. Not my Jillian!" He finished with a note which George took as amused pride.

Douglass coughed.

George poured three double Scotches. "I understand it's going to be sunny tomorrow," he said. "Should be a good chance for some tennis in the morning before it's too hot. I hope some of you play tennis?"

In the living room, Nick had moved over to sit with Lorry and Shauna, and they were talking about Shauna's job and what it was like living at home when you were twenty-seven and had three teenage sisters around. Lorry was amazed at how voluble Shauna had become. Nick's moving over and taking an interest in the conversation seemed to have worked like magic.

But at the same time, Lorry decided Nick was bored. For the last ten minutes, his hands had been fidgeting with a chess piece he had picked up somewhere.

When Kendall came back from carrying Hildy's suitcase and suggested drinks, Nick half-rose from his chair. Jillian and Bart also rose, but Anne said, "Nothing for me. I think I'll just go to my room and freshen up."

Nick sat back down and looked at Lorry. "Do you two want drinks?"

"I *don't*," Shauna said.

"Don't what?" Nick asked.

"Don't drink."

Nick eyebrows rose. "What? Not anything?"

"Not anything, oh, you know, with alcohol." Her words began to rush. "I know it sounds silly and people think I'm weird. Jillian says it's stupid of me. But, well, I'll tell you. You see, our father drinks. Too much, I mean. And when he's been drinking, he acts like such a fool. I don't ever want to be like that. So I thought if I never drank at all, then I'd never get to liking it and I'd never act like he does." She looked down at her feet. "I guess you think I'm an idiot, too."

"Well, I can't very well think that," Lorry said, "because I don't drink alcohol either."

Shauna looked up. "You don't?"

"Nope. I just decided I didn't want to. But I wouldn't mind a Coke or something. Do you think they'd have that, Nick?"

Nick had been watching Lorry as she spoke. He had stopped smiling and his voice was serious as he said, "Yes, I expect they do. Should I go and see, or do you want to come?"

Finding unexpected support, Shauna became brave. "Let's all go. I'd love to see the rest of the house. Isn't it just like something in a book?"

Ellen watched Nick come into the games room with the two young women. Somehow, her matchmaking had gone astray. Why was Lorry with Nick? And where was Kendall? She looked around and saw him getting drinks for Bart and Jillian. Being a good host. But she was annoyed. He didn't need to look after them. It was Lorry he should be taking care of.

As she watched, Kendall left the room. Now where was he going? Everyone else was here, except—she looked around the room, mentally clicking off names—Anne was missing. Not surprising. She hadn't looked particularly well at supper. And she seemed nervous. Or even afraid. Ellen mentally shook her head. Of all the silly ideas. She had to stop watching those soap operas in the afternoon. She was starting to imagine everyone was living in intrigue.

Nick had found a soft drink bottle and was pouring its contents into a couple of glasses, and he and Lorry were laughing about something.

Ellen walked over to Shauna. "Did you want something to drink?" she asked. "Oh, you've been taken care of," she said as Nick handed Shauna a glass. "Not that I drink much myself, you know. One will do me all night. Just to be sociable. The truth is I've never really learned to like the taste. Now, Bart," she said, noticing him standing alone by a window, "he can drink gallons of the stuff. Can't you, Bart? And no one would ever know. So George says, anyway."

Thus addressed, Bart came over.

Ellen continued, "Whenever you've been here, George has either complained about the expense of having you around or else admired the way you can drink so much without even walking unsteadily. However do you do it?"

Shauna stared at the floor. Bart gave Ellen a bored look and then, having read Shauna's mind perfectly, said, "I know you really don't want to listen to my aunt's rather fabulous tales of my consumptive powers. Would you like to get a breath of fresh air instead?"

Startled, Shauna stammered, "I—oh, no—that is—I—"

"Why don't we go out this way?" Bart took her elbow and smoothly guided her through the patio doors onto the terrace, and then past the pool into the rose garden, which was lit by a multitude of small indirect lights.

As she saw the garden for the first time, her shyness dropped away. "Oh, how lovely!" she exclaimed. Ignoring Bart, she ran ahead. "It's like a fairyland!"

A tolerant smile touched Bart's lips. What a strange young woman! Jillian's sister, too. Remarkable how two such totally opposite people could be so closely related. Amused, he let her lead him about, answering a few questions but mostly observing her child-like enthusiasm. Ellen had better get her checkbook out. He was definitely going beyond the call of duty on this one.

If she'd thought about it, Ellen would have been very thankful Bart was looking after Shauna for her, but just now she was relieved to see Kendall coming back into the room. She moved toward him. "Is anything wrong, dear?"

"No. Why would you think that? I just had a couple of phone calls I needed to make, and I thought no one would notice if I was absent for a few minutes."

"Oh, that's fine. I just thought—!"

"Yes?"

She shook her head. "Nothing important."

He went over to Nick and Lorry. "So, how's it going? You two made plans for a midnight dip, yet? Or do you prefer dawn?"

Lorry replied, "Actually, I was wondering about trying out your tennis court. That's more my speed."

George overheard Lorry's mention of the tennis court and, always the perfect host, gallantly offered to partner her. He looked at Nick and Kendall impishly. "Anyone mind?"

"Not one bit," Nick said. "I'm going to spend the whole morning on a raft in the pool—that is, if I can talk Mrs. Winston into giving me a glass of lemonade to take with me."

Peter disclaimed any tennis ability. "Hildy's good, though. You get her out there. She'll say she's not good enough, but she loves the game. Jillian and I will relax at the pool. Swimming's my thing, and I don't get nearly enough time for it."

"You play tennis, Kendall," Ellen said.

"Usually," her son agreed. "But I'm afraid I twisted my ankle yesterday playing squash and it's still a little sore." He saw the worried look on his mother's face and added, "It's okay for walking; I just don't want to try running and turning on it for a few days."

So George obtained Douglass and a rather reluctant Hildy as opponents. Then he went to refill his glass.

"George is good, you know," Nick warned Lorry. "So's Douglass. Either one could leave me cold. Think you're up to it?"

"I'll do my best." She smiled.

"As I remember, Lorry's mother was provincial champion a long time ago," Ellen said. "I rather expect Lorry got her first racquet when she was still in her crib."

Nick smiled at Lorry. "I take back my words, then. It should be a good game. I hope Hilda—no, it's Hildy, isn't it?—is up to you."

2

Hildy was sitting alone against a wall close to the bar. If she was feeling any embarrassment at barging in on her ex-husband and his wife, she wasn't going to show it. She knew she looked cool and calm, and while she was no competition for Jillian, she was certainly adequate competition for any woman her age, or even ten years younger.

She stirred her piña colada and spoke when, from time to time, someone addressed her. But she was not looking for conversation. She had a purpose in coming here. And befriending these people was not necessary. However, although that purpose was uppermost in her mind, she was content to wait for the appropriate moment.

Douglass Fischer, too, was waiting, drumming his fingers absently on the bar. Frankly, he would have preferred to go to bed. But here he sat listening to inane conversations and planning tennis matches for tomorrow with Peter's ex-wife as his partner—what on earth would he talk to her about? And where was his own wife? If she held true to form, she'd taken three or four pills and gone to bed.

She was always so tired lately. And always complaining about headaches. But the doctors could find nothing wrong. Menopause, he expected. She was only a couple of years past forty, so she was young for it yet, but it was quite possible. And she never got a light dose of anything, although he suspected half of her problems were simply in her head.

Of course, she hated Jillian with a passion. Just because Jillian was young and full of life. He shook his head. And so beautiful.

Douglass finished his drink and sighed. What time was it, anyway? Eleven-forty-five. Still fifteen minutes to wait. He heard Lorry say that despite the fact it was two hours earlier in Alberta time, she was still tired after her flight. Kendall and Nick walked out into the hallway with her. Hildy left a few minutes later.

He'd have one more drink. Then he'd make his excuses, say anything and get outside where the air wasn't so stifling.

A little while after Douglass had gone out, Jillian asked George to make her another drink, then looked meaningfully at Peter. "I'll be up in a minute, Petey. But first, I think I'll go see what Shauna and Bart are doing. They've been out in the garden far too long.

"You don't need to worry about Shauna," Peter said, laughing. "She's a big girl."

"I know that, silly. But I don't think she's anywhere near Bart's league." Jillian picked up her drink and went out onto the terrace.

"How is the Guiardini case going?" George asked.

"We'll win. The records are in such a mess, they'll never be able to prove different from what Jake says."

"Good. Did you find the bank teller Jake said could back him up?"

"Not yet, but we've got a line on him, and we expect to have him by Tuesday at the latest."

"Good. Well, it's too late to be talking shop. Good night."

Thus dismissed, Peter headed toward the stairs. He looked to see if anyone was watching him, but there was no one around. Instead of turning to go up, he went quietly to the front door and, easing it open, slipped outside.

Ten minutes later, Kendall found his parents in the living room.

"There you are. Guess I'll go to bed. Don't lock the doors. Nick went outside when Lorry went up. Said he needed air."

"I never lock them," Ellen said. "There's really no need when we have that huge fence all around."

"Is the gate shut?" George finished off his drink and set the glass on the table beside his chair.

"I asked Mrs. Winston to shut it after Hildy arrived."

"What's that woman up to?" George asked. "She must have known Peter was going to be here."

"I don't know," his wife answered vaguely. "She said her apartment was being painted."

"Well, I think you should keep an eye on her."

Ellen looked at him in exasperation but didn't bother to ask how she could be expected to keep an eye on a grown woman. Oh, well, maybe she could get Bart to spend some time with her. But there were more important things on her mind just then. "Kendall, are you feeling all right? You disappeared a couple of times tonight. Is everything okay?"

"Sure. I'm fine. I just wanted to be by myself for a while. I don't have much opportunity, you know."

"You mean Nick follows you around all the time?" George's voice was sardonic.

Kendall flushed. "Of course not. I just had some things to catch up on. A phone call or two. Thought I'd get them out of the way so I wouldn't have to worry about them. I do have some work to do now I'm joining the firm, you know."

"George, I don't think he should have to work on the long weekend," Ellen said. Before George could protest his innocence, she turned to Kendall. "I would like you to spend some time with your cousin. Get to know her. She's going to be in the city all summer. Be so nice if you could get to know each other."

"Okay, Mom. I'll do my best."

"You're not upset about Nick's not wanting the job, are you?" George asked.

"I still think he'll change his mind. But if he doesn't, it's his problem, not mine."

"That's okay then." George stood up and headed toward the stairs. Ellen shut off the lights in the room and then she and Kendall followed.

Moments later, Bart and Shauna came through the patio doors into the games room. Shyly, she said, "You shouldn't have bothered with me. But thank you, anyway." Then she fled to the stairs.

Bart shook his head and went to the bar to pour a drink. What a way to spend a weekend!

He emptied his glass and poured another drink. After putting the bottle away, he turned off the lights and sank into a comfortable chair.

Five minutes passed. A shadowy figure slipped into the games room through the patio door and went noiselessly across the tiled floor. Jillian. Where was she? Bart asked himself. Then he stiffened as a man came in from the patio and went toward the bar. The man grabbed the nearest bottle and downed a quick drink. He swore. Then he continued toward the hall and upstairs.

"Douglass, eh," Bart mused thoughtfully. "I wonder." He continued to nurse his drink. Minutes passed. A noise outside was followed by yet another entrance to the room. In the dark, Bart raised his eyebrows. Only one of the men had worn a white short-sleeved shirt. Nick. Now what had he been up to outside? And which one had Jillian been with? Or had she found time for both? Bart smiled.

Nick shut the patio door with much more force than was required. A pillow was lying on a sofa near his path. Picking it up, he threw it into a far corner. With a heavy sigh and a muffled oath, he left the room.

Bart finished his drink, then stared at the empty glass. Perhaps he'd had enough for tonight. Then again, with so much going on, perhaps one more wouldn't hurt.

3

Saturday morning dawned sunny and hot. Those who chose to appear for breakfast were served in the dining room from silver serving dishes. Anne settled for a cup of coffee in bed. But Jillian appeared in an ivory sundress that accentuated her golden tan and vibrant face. Beside her, Shauna had all the glow of a church mouse, and Jillian complained in a stage whisper heard throughout the room, "Shauna, you look sick! If I were you, I wouldn't let anyone see me."

Shauna did not reply.

Peter laughed. "Maybe she's like me and needs her morning coffee."

On Shauna's other side, Bart, who had entered the room in time to hear Jillian, leaned over and inquired softly, "Do you always let her talk to you like that?"

Shauna ignored him and buttered a piece of toast.

He persisted. "You can't possibly like the way she puts you down."

"Oh, please hush."

Bart ignored her. "You ought to give her back some of her own."

"She's my sister."

"So what?"

"My *younger* sister!"

Baffled by this statement, Bart thoughtfully took some bacon and eggs from a silver platter and began to eat. What kind of maggot did the ridiculous woman have in her head? He would have to talk to her later. It was always interesting to observe human nature. Even more fun to manipulate it.

Now, Lorry was a different story, he thought as he glanced around the table. Younger than Jillian. Much less sophisticated. Straightforward. A man would know exactly where he was with her. No mystery there.

Pity the man who had Jillian. Not that any man would have her long. It was the other way around. She would do the having. Bart's mouth curved in a slight smile. Be interesting to see if the tables could be turned. To see if he could attract Jillian and break her heart the way she had likely broken the hearts of a score of men. Always assuming, of course, that she had a heart to break.

Shauna shifted in her chair, and Bart glanced at her again. Jillian had no heart where her sister was concerned. But why? Surely not because of competition. When it came to attracting men, Shauna would be left on the bench. She wasn't even in the game. And yet... His eyes narrowed. The material wasn't that bad. She had horrendous taste, of course. Those glasses were totally wrong. So was the hair. And the tiny bit of makeup she wore was as wrong for her as the clothes. With a start, he realized the main problem. She was wearing ivories and beiges that, on Jillian, would have come to life. On Shauna, they had all the impact of a shroud. Bart's mind drifted off. What if...?

Breakfast over, the house guests scattered. Nick, true to his promise, got in the pool and found a floating chair to lie on with the large glass of lemonade Ellen had asked Mrs. Winston to make for him.

"You know I was joking," he protested with his disarming grin.

"Of course I do," Ellen said with a smile. "But I thought it was a great idea if you really want to relax. Though I must say you don't seem like the relaxing type. You're usually rushing somewhere—down a hill or across a football field or on a date somewhere."

"That's why this is such a welcome change. Thank you very much." He kissed her lightly on the cheek and launched his chair.

Shauna wandered off to see the rose garden by daylight.

After studying the locations of each of the others and stopping to speak for a moment with Jillian, who was lying on a chaise lounge watching Peter dive, Bart followed her.

He cornered her against a trellis of climbing roses. "So, tell me, why do you let Jillian criticize you in front of everyone, or even in private for that matter?"

Shauna watched her foot make a circle on the thick grass. "It's no concern of yours."

"Do you enjoy it?"

"No, but, you would never understand!"

"I might."

"She's beautiful and mature and elegant!"

"You think she's perfect?"

"Yes." Shauna looked up at him for the first time. "She is, isn't she? Perfect! She always has been. Even when she was a little girl, people always noticed her. She had long golden hair and you just always noticed her!"

"And I suppose you got left behind all the time?"

"Oh, I didn't mind. You see, she loved all the attention. I'd have hated it. I'd much rather curl up with a good book or go for a walk. She loves to be with people and have them admire her."

"Sounds boring."

"Oh, but see how well she's done! Married to a wealthy lawyer who gives her everything she wants. All those beautiful clothes!"

"You're not jealous?"

Her eyes widened and again she looked at him. "Jealous? Of Jillian? Of course not! I'm delighted for her. Her life is just what it should be, but it would never suit me."

Her sincerity took Bart by surprise. For a moment he said nothing. Then he remembered his original question. "But that doesn't explain why she talks to you the way she does. Or why you let her."

Her eyes returned to a careful scrutiny of the grass at her feet. "Oh, that."

"Yes, that."

She shrugged her shoulders. "It's just her way. And I do exasperate her so. I guess I wish she wouldn't say things in front of other people, but I don't really blame her."

"You don't?"

"She's tried to help me, even given me clothes, but, well, it doesn't help much."

Bart chose his words carefully. "Have you ever tried to do anything about your—your—"

"My ugliness?"

"You aren't ugly. Just a little dowdy, maybe."

She quickly averted her face and walked away.

He let her go. He knew he had hurt her. But it was most definitely true.

She had gone only a few feet when she suddenly spun around. He was prepared for tears and anger, but he saw neither.

"You think I'm dowdy? Dowdy? What do you mean?"

Bart was for once at a loss for words. "I—er—"

"I want to know. Dowdy means drab or outdated. But this dress is quite new. And it's one of Jillian's favorite colors for daytime. What's wrong with it?"

Bart blinked. All right. She had asked him. "Then let Jillian wear it."

Her forehead wrinkled. "I don't understand. Do you mean it would look good on her but not me?"

"That's right."

"Then you do think I'm ugly."

"No, I just think Jillian should wear that dress. Not you."

"But…"

"Do you have any money with you? Or a credit card?"

"Upstairs in my purse. Why?"

"Well, if I had the ready cash, I'd buy you a new dress and some different makeup and get your hair cut and styled. And I'd get new frames for those glasses, or, better yet, contact lenses. And I guarantee at the end of the day you wouldn't know yourself."

Shauna stared at him. "But Jillian—"

"You aren't Jillian! And you don't have to be a poor imitation of her, either. Be yourself!"

"Do you really mean it? You could show me how to look good?"

"Let's go."

"Oh, no. I couldn't. There must be a dozen things you'd rather do."

"Nonsense. I'll get a car and meet you in the front drive in fifteen minutes."

"Oh, no, it wouldn't be right." She was slipping into her shell again.

"You're a big girl, Shauna. You can do anything you want."

"I mustn't. Maybe I'll see what Jillian thinks."

"Then I won't take you."

"What?"

"If you tell anyone, you would spoil the surprise. No one must know. Not even Jillian."

"The surprise?"

"Sure. Let's surprise the lot of them."

Shauna's eyes widened again. "Could I, do you think? Oh, I don't know what to do."

"Go up and get your purse. Meet me out front in fifteen minutes. And don't tell anyone. Surely you can handle that."

"Well…"

"On your way. And don't chicken out on me."

"I—I'll see."

4

Peter and Kendall were practicing dives at the deep end of the pool. Nick was prone on his lounge chair in the middle. Jillian found herself a floating chair and paddled it toward Nick.

When she was only a few feet away, Nick rolled off his raft and swam to the edge of the pool. He pulled himself out of the water and shouted, "You game to try some tennis, Mr. Martin? For amateurs only?"

Peter paused at the foot of the ladder before waving and calling back, "Sure. Why not? One more dive and I'll get ready." He did a perfect somersault before following Nick to the change room.

Kendall refused an invitation to accompany them. "Too hot. I'm going to do a few laps and then go inside and read for a while,"

Alone on her red raft in the middle of the pool, Jillian lay back in the warm sunshine. Only her left hand moved, tapping against the side of the raft in short, hard jerks. She watched Peter and Nick leave, and her blue eyes were as hard as diamonds.

On the way to the tennis court, Peter said, "Hadn't occurred to me before, but a good game of tennis is just what I need to work up an appetite before lunch. This lazing around isn't really my style." He touched his stomach. "Course, Jillian says I should go on a diet, but I don't see it. I've worked hard all my life, worked for everything I've got, and while I can afford good food, I'll be darned if I'll go on a diet. I'm going to enjoy myself. That's my philosophy, Nick. Work hard, and when you get the money, spend it on what you want. Some men work all their lives and put every cent in the bank and then leave the whole thing for their kids. Not me. No, sir. Good wine, good women, good everything. What about you?"

"Pretty much the same, I guess. Use what you have while you've still got it."

"George says there's some doubt about your joining us. Are you sure you know what you'd be turning down?"

"I guess I'm just not ready to settle in yet. Maybe I never will be."

"Haven't met a woman to give you roots, eh?"

"I've got no plans involving women."

"Do I detect a hint of bitterness there? Had some bad luck?"

"My parents are divorced."

"Oh? Mine might as well have been. My father was never around. It's hard, but the strong survive." Peter paused. "I guess you know I've been divorced a few times myself. Jillian's the fourth. And not likely the last."

Nick gave him a grim look.

"You don't like that, eh, Nick? You've got a lot to learn. When I was your age, I had a wife and three kids. A few years later, we called it quits. Truth was, the only thing we had in common was sex. Too much, too soon, if you know what I mean. After Patty, there was Hildy, and Genevieve, and now Jillian. Life goes on."

"I don't think I could do that."

"Neither did I when I was twenty-five. But things happened. Now it's part of my program for having the best. You get what you pay for. That shocks you, doesn't it? It would shock Jillian, too, if I told her I know she married me for my money. She's convinced herself I'm head-over-heels in love. What a sweetheart!"

They had reached the tennis court, so Nick was spared having to reply. For a few moments, they watched the foursome play. The teams had been well-matched. Douglass, although normally a better player than George, was not quite at his best today. Lorry and Hildy were very even, Hildy's experience and desire to win making up for Lorry's youthful speed. It made for a good spectator game, and Ellen, comfortably reclining in a lawn chair, had enjoyed herself thoroughly.

As the game ended, George called to Nick, "Come take my place! Lorry's young enough to manage another set, but I'm going to go and just drop into the pool."

So Nick took George's place and Peter coaxed a reluctant Hildy into staying when Douglass left with George.

"You realize the caliber of play is about to plummet?" Nick called to Hildy. She smiled.

5

Kendall had gone into the house shortly after Peter and Nick left. He paced back and forth in his large bedroom, wondering what to do. He didn't like telling lies. In fact, he hated it. Yet he had been lying to Nick for the past month about his relationship with Marilyn. It was true they were friends. In fact, he liked her a lot. But only as a friend.

Oh, there was someone all right. But he didn't want anyone, especially Nick, to know who it was. Not yet. Once he joined the firm and everything was under control, then he would introduce her to the world as his chosen bride. For now, she was a secret that gave him goosebumps. He wasn't used to lying. Not that he was lying, exactly. Just not telling the truth. Perhaps it would be best if he did make a bit of a fuss over Lorry, though. Make his mother happy. Keep her from asking questions.

Left to herself, Jillian paddled her raft to the edge of the pool and gracefully rolled onto the cement without getting wet. She stood up, lithe and tanned in the revealing cream floral bikini.

Anne was lying on a lounge chair near the pool. She was wearing an expensive plain green one-piece bathing suit with a matching green and yellow floral sarong. She had been lying there for some time watching the others, pretending to read a magazine from a stack on the table. As Jillian stood up, Anne looked over the top of the magazine.

Unfortunately, Jillian turned at that exact moment, and their eyes met. Anne quickly looked down at the magazine.

"Don't you wish!" Jillian said in what Anne considered a most insolent voice.

"I'm sorry?" Anne replied haughtily. "Did you speak?"

"What a drag it must be to know you're middle-aged, over-weight, and over the hill! But then, I don't expect you ever looked this good."

Anne clenched her jaw. With dignity, she replied, "I don't know what gutter Peter found you in, but he would have done himself and everyone he knows a favor by leaving you in it."

"Oh, the lady has teeth, does she?" Jillian smiled. "Nice try, but if you think an insult from you is going to affect me, you're not very smart."

"I expect you'd only understand four-letter words."

"Yeah, four-letter words like cold, hard cash."

"Well, you're certainly cold and hard, and it's obvious you like cash."

"Mmm." Jillian's brows arched gently above her twinkling eyes. "It's so nice we understand each other."

"I told you yesterday morning I don't have my own money. Everything is joint. He'd know."

"Are you telling me you can't make up a good lie? Now why do I find that hard to believe?"

"I could tell Peter."

"Go ahead. See which of us he believes. And then, of course, you never know what Dougie might do if Peter did become annoyed with me. Dougie is such a gentleman. Just the kind to act as Sir Galahad to a lady in distress. And I would be in such distress."

"You—you—!"

"Anne, dear, why can't you just accept that I always win? Make it easy on yourself and give me what I want."

Anne's voice was brittle. "And exactly what do you want?"

Jillian tilted her head to one side in a puzzled way.

Anne said the words slowly, clearly, as if speaking to a child. "How much money am I going to have to give you before you take your claws out of my husband?"

Jillian shrugged. "Oh, I should think twenty-five thousand would be adequate."

Anne gasped. "I can't possibly get you that much! Certainly not without Douglass's finding out. I can't!"

Jillian was examining her nails. "Don't you think he's worth that much?" she asked carelessly.

While Anne sought for words, Jillian stood up and walked away. A slender gold bracelet above the tanned ankle seemed to wink and laugh in the sunlight, warning Anne how foolish she was to think she could stand up to the younger woman.

Anne set her magazine down and walked, head held high, up to her room where she closed the drapes, gulped down several tranquilizers, and threw herself, sobbing, onto the bed.

Chapter Five

Lunch was served on the patio and consisted of plates of fresh vegetables, fruit, dainty sandwiches, and several salads.

Ellen watched as Nick gravitated once more to Lorry. Kendall was there, too, but it seemed to Ellen that Nick was giving Kendall no chance to be alone with the girl. Annoying to see her plans go awry. She should have insisted Kendall bring Nick another time.

But perhaps there was still hope. Lorry would be in the city all summer. And although she was attractive, she really wasn't Nick's type at all. Perhaps later on.

George sat down beside his wife. "Lost in your thoughts, or are you too hot to eat?"

Ellen smiled. "I'm never too hot to eat Mrs. Winston's food. I think we ought to give her a raise."

"Just don't let her get it into her head that she's too good to be working for ordinary people like us."

"As if she would," Ellen replied cheerfully. Then the two of them sat back to enjoy their lunch, comfortable together even in silence.

Across the patio, Jillian's pretty mouth set into a hard line. Unaware, she thrust her jaw forward. Her eyes were on Nick, who was smiling at something Lorry had said.

Out of the corner of her eye, Jillian saw Peter coming toward her. She cried out, "Petey, darling, what's taken you so long? Do sit here beside me, love. I've hardly seen you all morning."

Peter laughed and set his plate on the table. Then he leaned over and kissed her. "My dear, I didn't know you cared." His eyes were laughing. But she responded by reaching up and kissing him passionately. This time there was a glimmer of surprise on his face.

"You have to realize there are as many areas of law as there are medicine," Nick was telling Lorry. "Contracts, wills, civil suits, copyrights, any number of business areas from mergers to lawsuits, not to mention defending criminals of all sorts and a ton of other things that most people don't realize."
"Which area interests you the most?"
"There's good money in what Brodie does. Business law."
"And is money the priority?"
He shrugged. "I'd just as soon have it as not," he replied after a moment. "What about you? You've been going to college, haven't you? What are you going to do?"
"I majored in psychology, and I love teenagers, so I'm hoping to find a job working with young people. If I don't get one by the fall, I'm thinking of going to another country for a year. There are lots of opportunities for people who can teach English as a second language. And I could learn a lot that way. Or I may go back to get my master's degree. But right now, I'm volunteering with an organization that works with homeless youth in downtown Toronto. So I'll be here for the summer."
Nick's expression was one of pure bewilderment. "Volunteering?"
"Yes."
"So you aren't getting paid?"
"Right."
"Would you get paid if you go to another country to teach English?"
"Probably not. Or, if I did, it wouldn't be much."
"So money isn't your priority?"
She smiled as she shook her head.
"What does your dad do? He bankrolling you?"
"Not really. He's pastor of a small church in a town near Edmonton, Alberta."
"And your mother?"
"She looks after her home and family, directs the choir, plays the organ, teaches children, and leads a Bible study."

"None of which pays, right?"

"Right."

"Sounds like one big happy traditional family—right out of the fifties."

Her eyes twinkled merrily into his. "It does, doesn't it?"

"But you talk like a twenty-first century woman. So why would you choose a job that barely pays and gets you nowhere?"

"Why not if I think it's what I should do?"

"Should?"

"I think it's what God wants me to do."

"What has God got to do with it?"

"God is a very important part of my life."

"You believe there really is a God?"

"Yes, I do."

"But even if there is, you still have to live. You know. Rent. Food. Clothes. Little things like that."

"Is money a priority with you?"

"I like having it."

"Is that why you ski? For the money?"

"You know it isn't. Though it did start out that way. I was working my way through law school. Freestyle skiing sure beat construction work."

"I guess the best thing is a job where you enjoy what you're doing and make money, too, huh?"

"Of course. But I don't see you ever making much working with youth. Unless you became a psychiatrist or something."

"Hmm. Maybe someday. Right now, I just want to use what I've already learned. Help someone. I guess helping people is more rewarding to me than making money."

"And being a woman, you probably expect the guy to make the money."

"The guy?"

"Boyfriend, husband, you know. You do what you enjoy and let him sweat to pay the bills."

"You sound bitter."

"Going to start analyzing me?"

"No, of course not." She finished her lemonade.

Nick stared off into space for a minute. Finally, he turned to Lorry and smiled. "You know, this isn't the normal kind of discussion I have with a pretty girl."

Lorry returned the smile. "Why don't you tell me some more about freestyle skiing then? What kind of things do you do?"

He proceeded to describe his last competition, but although his conversation was as easy as ever, there was a grim look in his eyes. Anyone who knew him well would have noticed he was not quite himself.

Kendall, talking to him an hour later, did notice. They were upstairs in the room they were sharing. Kendall was looking at a car magazine and Nick was stretched out on his bed. "How are you enjoying the weekend?" Kendall asked.

"Okay."

"You don't sound very positive."

"It's fine."

"You've been with Lorry a fair bit."

"I thought you wanted me to keep her busy so your mother wouldn't get ideas."

"Yeah, I do. She's good-looking, huh?"

"Not bad."

"Well, not in Jillian's class, maybe, but she's definitely right up there."

"I guess."

Kendall studied him silently. "Something on your mind?" he asked at last.

"Nothing important. Say, about the job, the answer is no. Final."

Kendall threw his magazine on the floor. "You know you're out of your mind?"

"Forget it. It's a dead subject."

"You won't even give it a try?"

"No."

"Something wrong with the people?" Kendall's voice was distant, even defiant.

"No, of course not. I like your dad, and the other two are okay, I guess. Let's just say that there's something wrong with me and leave it at that."

"There is. You're crazy."

"Okay." Nick forced a smile. "But can we still be friends?"

Kendall hesitated before answering. "Yes, of course. But— well, I thought I was giving you a terrific opportunity."

"And I've shoved it back in your face? I'm sorry."

"Don't worry. There are dozens of guys out there who would jump to get the chance."

Nick sat up. "Hey, come on, Kendall. Don't get upset."

"Why shouldn't I be upset? I'm watching my best friend destroy his future. It's as if only half your brain is working."

There was silence for a minute. "I guess I've got something on my mind."

"It's not Jillian, is it? I've seen her looking at you."

"No, it's not Jillian."

"Lorry?"

"Well, sort of."

"She isn't your type."

"She's okay."

"That's what I said."

Nick laughed. "Thanks a lot!"

"You know what I mean. She's my second cousin or something, remember. I know a little about her. Her dad's a minister for some church in a small town near Edmonton. She may look pretty good, but I'll bet she's about as exciting as a door knob."

"Not that bad, surely."

But Kendall was unable to laugh. "Oh, forget her. I just—"

"What do you think of Jillian's sister?"

"I don't know, and I don't care. You're just trying to change the subject." Kendall got up and walked out of the room, closing the door a fraction more heavily than necessary.

Nick lay back on the bed, eyes open, staring at the ceiling.

2

Jillian sat at her vanity brushing her golden hair. From long practice, she worked rhythmically, automatically counting the strokes while humming to herself. At one hundred, she stopped brushing and sat gazing in the mirror for a moment.

Satisfied, she stood and tied an amber-colored scarf around her hair. Again, she looked in the mirror, craning her neck to see the back of the checked sundress she wore. The one she had picked up at that strange little boutique in Paris.

She was at the door, her hand on the knob, when a sharp rap made her step back. She bit her lower lip, then opened the door.

Hildy was standing in the hallway.

"Well, won't you come in?" Jillian said, a confident smile curving her lips. "Peter's somewhere downstairs, so we can have a nice, cozy chat."

Hildy stepped inside and waited until the door was shut. Then, hands on hips, face rigid, she said in a low, even voice, "All right. Just what is this all about?"

"Excuse me?"

"I want to know just what you think you're up to. Stephen is mine. I have custody and you aren't going to get even one of your dirty little fingers on him."

"Won't you sit down?" Jillian motioned to a chair beside the fireplace. "I think it might be better to discuss this without all the hostility you so obviously feel."

"You want hostility? I'll give you hostility!" Hildy reached into the pocket of her full skirt and pulled out a small revolver. Pointing it at Jillian, she said, "Now you listen to me, you little snake. You touch one hair of my child's head and I'll kill you. Understood?"

Jillian opened her mouth to speak, but Hildy was already going out the door. A wave of intense rage swept over Jillian. Turning blindly, she fell on the bed and began hammering the mattress. Not satisfied with that, she struggled to her feet and picked up the first thing she saw, a large yellow vase filled with flowers. Holding it above her head, she threw it against the door, where it shattered into a hundred fragments of pottery, petals, and water droplets.

3

Lorry was sitting beside the pool when Nick came out of the house. "Want to go for a walk?" he asked diffidently. "I'm told there's a great place behind the house."

Nick led the way through the rose garden and a large treed area toward a gate in the wall at the back. He tried to open the gate, but it was locked. Reaching into his pocket, he said, "Not to worry. Mrs. Winston gave me the key." The gate swung open to reveal a path winding through leafy trees and to a ravine on the left. "Looks okay, huh?" he asked.

"It's great."

Nick led the way, and for some time they walked along the path in silence, Lorry several steps behind. Finally, Lorry asked, "Is this a race? Should I have worn a number on my back?"

Nick came to an abrupt halt and laughed self-consciously. "I'm sorry. I was thinking."

"That's okay." Lorry caught up to him. "Isn't this a wonderful location for a house?"

"Most girls would have asked if I was thinking about them."

Lorry laughed. "Do you make a habit of going for walks with girls so you can walk ahead thinking about them?"

"It does sound a little odd, doesn't it?"

They walked on, with Lorry occasionally stopping to examine a tree or exclaim over a wildflower and Nick watching her.

After about twenty minutes, they came to a grassy spot and Nick sank down against a tree stump. After a moment's hesitation, Lorry sat nearby.

Neither spoke at first. Then Nick said, "I was talking to Kendall a while ago. He said you're not my type."

"Did he?"

"Yeah. He said you're dull."

"Oh."

"Are you?"

"Well, I guess some people would say I am."

"Different. You're definitely different." There was a moment of silence before Nick asked, "How about me? What type am I?"

"I don't know you well enough to say."

"Come on. From last night and today, what do you think I'm like?"

"Well, just from what I've seen this weekend, I think you're kind of a moody person. I don't mean that in a negative way. You just often seem to be deep in thought."

Nick looked at her in surprise. "You think I'm moody?"

"Well, maybe it's just this weekend. It's kind of a strange setting. For me, it sure is. I don't know about you."

"You're used to a small town where everybody acts normal, is that it?"

"Well, I wouldn't say that. All people are individuals. But the—I guess I'd have to say, the wealth and the—I don't know what a good word for it is, maybe social status, is something I'm not used to. I don't know if you are or not. I only know you're

Kendall's roommate at law school and you ski."

"If you mean did I grow up with the ability to buy everything I wanted, the answer is a definite no. My mother raised me by herself after I was eleven. My father didn't even pay child support, and my mother's health was never very good, so we had to rely on her family and on welfare. I put myself through college and law school. But nobody has ever called me moody. If anything, I'm the exact opposite."

"The life of the party?"

"Something like that."

"If so, what's making you act differently this weekend?"

"Mostly you are."

"Me? You don't even know me."

"No, I don't. And according to Kendall you aren't my type, either. Which I assume crosses over to mean I'm not your type."

She shook her head. "No, I wouldn't think so."

"Do you have somebody special back in Alberta?"

"Sort of."

"Sort of?"

"I haven't decided yet."

"Well, that's good to know."

Something in Nick's voice made Lorry say, "Boy, I'm thirsty. It's so hot. We were crazy to come without getting a thermos. I can taste Mrs. Winston's lemonade." She got to her feet. "Coming?"

Nick had a half-smile on his face. "All right," he said as he got up to follow her. "But I will bring up the subject again."

4

Supper had been planned for seven so there would be plenty of time afterwards for those who wished to go to a nearby nightclub. By six-thirty, Jillian was already well into her preparations. About the same time, Lorry and Nick finished a close game of tennis and returned to the house, laughing. Nick was complaining that the only reason the match was close was because Lorry had been taking it easy on him. Peter, who was having a martini at the bar, told them they'd better get a move on or they'd be late. Then he called Nick back. "What'll you have?"

"You just told me to hurry."

"You've got time for one drink. I expect you can shower and change in fifteen minutes. Not like the ladies, who have to arrange every eyelash just right."

Nick laughed and took a stool. "Scotch then. On the rocks. Not much."

"Kendall says you've definitely decided not to join us."

"That's right."

"Not a very wise decision. From my viewpoint, at least."

Nick sipped his drink. "Well, that's the way it is. Let's just say I'm not in a mood for making a long-term commitment."

"It's your life," Peter said. "Perhaps I'm being a little smug, but our firm strikes me as not having anything to apologize for, so if you turn it down, I can only assume you have a few rocks in your head as well as in your glass. Nothing personal. Just the observation of a successful lawyer to one who seems to be turning down the chance of his life. Another drink?"

"No. I should be getting ready for dinner." Nick stood, but didn't move. "Look, Mr. Martin, you shouldn't think I don't appreciate being offered a place in your firm. I do. But maybe I do have a few rocks in my head as you suggest. I just don't feel right about it. Maybe I can't see myself in a pinstripe suit sitting behind a desk. Sometimes I even wonder why on earth I ever got into law in the first place. I'm a lot more at home skiing down a mountain, I'll tell you."

"You could afford quite a few ski holidays on the money you'd make."

Nick laughed. "Yeah, I guess so." He paused for a moment. Then, "To be perfectly honest, I'm surprised you even offered me the job. Kendall I understand. But I'm not a relative and I was nowhere near the top of the class."

"As you say, Kendall's a relative. And he did very well. There's no question of his going elsewhere. And he's steady. He'll do okay. As for you, when Kendall asked us to offer you the job, I have to admit I wasn't too pleased. But George likes you, and he's a pretty good judge of people, so Douglass and I went along. But now I've had a chance to get to know you, I have to admit there's something I like about you. Maybe even your turning us down. It shows you're either stupid or unique, and I don't think you're stupid. In fact, I expect you could have been at the top of your class if you'd wanted to."

"Thanks for the compliment. But since you're dressed and I'm not, I'd better get a move on. I doubt if Ellen will think I'm unique if I keep dinner waiting. I'll see you later."

Nick turned and hurried up the stairs, taking them effortlessly, two at a time.

By 7:02, all but four of the members of the house party were seated in the living room, waiting the formal call to the dinner table. Nick had been the last to come in, moments behind Douglass and Anne, who bore the appearance of a couple who had recently finished an argument. Or perhaps not finished.

Nick sat on a chair next to Lorry's, but since she was talking to Kendall, on her other side, he contented himself with watching her profile.

Ellen spoke in a whisper to her husband. "Bart said not to wait for him and Shauna. He wasn't sure when they would be back. I can't understand what he's up to. He asked for my car, and, of course, Shauna was with him so I couldn't very well say no. But I would sure like to know where they were going. She looked scared stiff, but not of Bart, I don't think. She reminds me of a frightened rabbit."

George wasn't very interested. Bart needed money from him. It was highly unlikely that he would do anything stupid, especially with someone like Shauna. "I'm sure she's okay." He went over to talk to Douglass and Anne, and Ellen, remembering her role as hostess, went to see if Hildy wanted a fresh drink.

Conversation was flowing when Douglass glanced at the doorway and speech froze on his lips. Anne and George followed his gaze. Soon the entire room was still, watching a vision in a Paris original enter the room. Jillian's golden hair and tawny skin were framed in fluttering soft peach, cut very low and accented by a spectacular diamond pendant hanging from a glittering gold chain. Her movement was graceful and poised as she floated into the room, her laughter delightful as she said over her shoulder to Peter, "Now do you think this dress was worth the price?"

George and Kendall both jumped up to escort her to dinner.

Douglass also made an involuntary movement, then paused as his wife's hand grasped his wrist and her icy eyes met his.

Jillian looked around the room. "Where's Shauna?" she asked.

"She went out with Bart." Ellen's voice was apologetic. "I'm sure they'll be back soon, but they did say not to wait supper for them. So I guess we can go in."

"That little—!" Jillian began, her eyes flashing.

Peter laughed. Jillian glared at him before taking George's arm and leading the others to the dining room.

Kendall turned to escort Hildy.

Lorry looked up to find Nick waiting for her. At first glance, he appeared to be the only man in the room not drawn by Jillian's magnetism. Yet Lorry couldn't escape the feeling that something wasn't quite right. For one thing, she was quite certain that it had been Nick at whom Jillian looked when she made her entrance into the room. And that he had noticeably stiffened.

They were finishing the first course when they heard a door shut and voices move toward the dining room. Bart's and Shauna's voices. Mrs. Winston's daughter, Crystal, who had been doing the serving, hurried to the kitchen to get the appetizers that had been set aside.

Eleven pair of eyes stared as Bart entered the room followed by a striking woman with a glowing face, a short pixyish hairdo, and a dramatic black-and-white dress, off the shoulder on the white side, long sleeved on the black, slit from the knee in front.

The silence became more pronounced as, one by one, the members of the house party realized that this stranger could only be Shauna.

Peter was the first to find a voice. "Well, this is a surprise. Shauna, you look absolutely—dazzling. I had no idea…"

"It doesn't look a bit like me, does it?" the woman said softly. Her dark eyes shone with pleasure.

"You look wonderful," Ellen commented smoothly. "There are two places here if you haven't eaten yet."

The two moved around the table and Bart made a point of holding Shauna's chair and making sure she had everything she needed before he sat beside her. Then his eyes traveled around the table, stopping as they reached Jillian, whose icy glare momentarily disconcerted even him. After a moment, his eyes defiantly meeting hers, he laughed.

Until Crystal began to clear plates and bring in salads, there was an uneasy silence, broken only as Bart began to ask how everyone's day had gone. He was clearly enjoying himself, and, slowly, the dinner party loosened up and people chattered once more, though later few could remember what the talk was about.

When the delicious food had been eaten, and the wine drunk, Jillian announced that she wanted to go dancing. Her voice soft and teasing, she leaned toward Kendall and asked him if he would like to take her since she had chosen his father over him to escort her in to supper.

Kendall blushed and stammered something about Peter's minding.

"Oh, Petey doesn't mind, do you, Petey? He hates dancing just after he eats. Who else will come? Douglass? You'll come, won't you? George? Get your wives to come. Nick? I know you love dancing, don't you, darling? I'll just get a wrap. Shauna, why don't you help me?" She glided out of the room, and, after a moment's hesitation, Shauna followed.

The others began to organize into those who wanted to go dancing and those who didn't. By the time Jillian returned, Kendall and George had their car keys out and Douglass had persuaded Anne to go with him and George and Ellen.

"Bart and Hildy are coming with us in my car," Kendall announced to Jillian.

"Fine. Let's go, then, shall we?"

"Isn't Shauna coming?" George asked.

"No, she was exhausted. Today was such a big day. Bart, you ought to have known all the excitement wouldn't be good for her. She's utterly done in. I gave her a couple of extra-strength Tylenol and an ice pack and sent her to bed."

"Well, let's go, then," Kendall said.

"Aren't Nick and Lorry coming?" Jillian asked.

"Lorry didn't want to come, so Nick offered to stay with her."

"Oh, he did, did he?"

"Yeah. I expect he'll find the evening pretty dull. She'll likely want to talk about religion. That'll serve him right."

"Yes," Jillian agreed, "it's exactly what he deserves."

5

A few minutes after the two cars had driven off, Peter, now wearing swim trunks, entered the games room to find Lorry and Nick in the middle of a game of eight-ball. After watching for a few minutes, and commenting in surprise when Lorry won, he said, "Lorry, I wonder if you would mind going upstairs and asking Shauna to join us. She's in her room."

Lorry moved to hang up her cue. "I thought she went with the others."

She left and the two men wandered out to the pool, where Peter slipped into the water. Nick, hands in pockets, sat on a deck chair and stared into space.

Upstairs, Lorry knocked before entering the bedroom, and heard a muffled, "Leave me alone!" in reply.

Unsure what to do, Lorry decided to enter. After all, it was her room, too.

Shauna, wearing only her undergarments, was lying on the bed, face down. The new dress was in a heap on the floor.

Lorry picked it up to hang it in the closet and involuntarily dropped it in horror. The front of the dress had been ripped from the neck down to the top of the slit. No one would wear that dress again. "Shauna, what happened?"

"Go away."

"But, Shauna, your dress—?"

"I hate it! Go away. Leave me alone!"

"I—we wondered if you'd like to join us downstairs. Peter and Nick and I."

"No!" came the muffled reply.

"Are you all right?"

"Leave me alone!"

"Are you sure, Shauna? If there's anything I can do to help…"

There were more muffled sobs. In between them, Shauna said, "No. Just go away. Leave me alone. Why can't everyone just leave me alone! I never wanted to come in the first place! I knew something would go wrong. It always does."

Instead of leaving, Lorry sat on the edge of Shauna's bed and put her arm around the girl's back.

"I'm not leaving you alone, Shauna. Just a few moments ago, you came in looking on top of the world. What's happened?"

"Go away!"

"No. Shauna, look at me."

There was another outbreak of tears. "No!"

"I'll have to go and get Peter."

"No, don't!"

"Then sit up and tell me what's wrong."

Slowly, the older girl raised herself onto her left elbow and swung up so she was sitting. But she kept her right arm across her face.

"Shauna, look at me. What's happened?"

"I'm fine. Just leave me alone."

"I don't think you are fine." Lorry gently took Shauna's arm and pulled it away from her face. Shauna fought, but Lorry had already caught a glimpse of the bruising on her left cheek and around her eye. She had seen, also, the scratches on her shoulder. "Shauna, who did this? Was it Bart?"

Chapter Six

Horrified, Shauna cried out, "No!"

"Not—surely not Jillian?"

Shauna's lips trembled as she stared down at her clenched hands.

"Why, Shauna?"

"She didn't like the way I looked. She said I shouldn't have done it. She said I looked like a call girl. She was very angry."

"Are you all right? I mean, are you hurt anywhere else?"

"No, I'm okay. I'm just so—so embarrassed. I feel like a complete fool."

"Well, I don't know much about call girls, but I don't think you looked like one. I thought you looked terrific. And your sister has no right to hit you, Shauna. You mustn't let her get away with it."

"She's always had a temper. Ever since she was little. She doesn't realize what she's doing. She didn't really mean to hurt me. And I'm okay. Besides, it was my fault for listening to Bart and going behind her back."

"Why don't we see if we can find something to put on those scratches. And maybe we can put some makeup on the bruises. Peter and Nick are downstairs. You should come down with us."

"Is everyone else gone?"

"Yes."

"All the others? Bart, too?"

"Everyone went except the three of us. We were just going to sit by the pool. It's hot, though. I thought I'd put shorts on before going back down."

"That's a good idea." Shauna got up. "I have prescription sunglasses I can wear. But you mustn't say anything. Jillian never meant to hurt me. Promise you won't tell anyone?"

Twenty minutes later, Lorry and Shauna, both now in shorts, joined Nick. Shauna's face, partially hidden by dark glasses, looked puffy and red despite the makeup. But Nick didn't comment on it.

"Working in a library, you must read a lot of books," Lorry said. "What kind do you prefer?"

On safe ground, Shauna became quite voluble.

From books, they drifted to television, movies, the upcoming election, and recycling, with Nick throwing in a comment every so often.

After a while Peter joined them. "I don't think I've ever known anybody who's gone to a Bible college, except perhaps a few ministers I met at my weddings. Why would a bright, attractive young woman want to waste her time learning about something as out of date and stuffy as the Bible?"

"I guess," Lorry began, "because I don't find it out of date or stuffy. Even though it was written long ago, it's ageless. And because God himself speaks through it, it's always relevant. I learn something new every time I read it. "

"You mean the ten commandments and that sort of thing?" Peter leaned forward. "Do good to others and all?"

"Yes," Lorry said, "but not only those. There are lots of stories about people who faced challenges just like I do. And there are other principles to live by. And of course, the whole story about Jesus is there."

"So do you try to obey all the commandments and rules?"

Lorry smiled. "I try, but I don't always succeed. I don't think anyone can obey them all."

Peter laughed and settled back in his chair. "You see? What's the use of wasting time on something you've just admitted is impossible to follow?"

"But that's why there are two parts to the Bible," Lorry replied. "The first part is about how God created people so he could have relationships with them, but how people often mess up. But the second part is the story of God's Son, Jesus, who was sinless, and who died for us. Jesus taught us that we can't earn

God's love by obeying rules because he already loves us more than we can ever understand."

"That sounds awfully grim coming from a pretty young girl. You should be thinking about boyfriends and having fun! Not stuff like that. How old are you? Twenty-two at the most?" Lorry nodded and Peter shook his head.

But Lorry countered, "Ever known someone who died when he was twenty-two? Or fifteen? Or talked to an older person who's wasted his life on things that really didn't matter? I don't have to worry about the future, or try to grab happiness from pleasures that only last a short time. Because of my relationship with God, I am content with who I am and what I have. How many people do you know who are content?"

Peter chuckled, "Little lady, if I were content as I am, I'd be a pretty poor lawyer. You have to keep striving to get better, or you might just as well give up."

Lorry smiled but didn't argue with him.

Peter took that as permission to go into a detailed explanation of his success and plans. Lorry continued to listen and answer his questions. A little apart, Shauna sat listening intently.

Nick quietly got up and walked away. When he reached the tennis court, he stopped. Spotting a racquet someone had left out, he picked it up, clenched his jaw, and tried to snap the racquet in two. When the aluminum failed to yield, he flung it as far as he could and strode off toward the gate at the back of the yard.

2

At the same time, in the powder room of the Wily Fox, a night club with middle-of-the-road music and a passable bar, Anne had been giving Ellen a sample of her dislike for Jillian. "I don't know why he can't see through her, but I'll save him from her. I'll stop her somehow, no matter what I have to do!"

"Anne, you've been drinking too much tonight. Just think," Ellen said in exasperation. "Even if she is tired of Peter, she'd hardly try to get his business partner. Especially a married man with two kids. No one would be that crazy."

Hildy came out of a cubicle and the two women stopped talking. They had believed they were alone. Hildy began to wash her hands. "For your information," she said slowly and thoughtfully,

"Jillian is neither crazy nor stupid." Hildy dried her hands on a paper towel before she went on. "She is cruel and malicious. She enjoys hurting people." Hildy walked out of the room.

Anne looked at Ellen, who stared back.

After coming to the nightclub with Kendall, Jillian had left him to entertain Hildy while she spent most of the evening dancing with Bart.

"You dance extremely well," Bart told her after a while.

"Thank you, kind sir," Jillian said. "You don't do such a bad job yourself."

"Is that why you chose to honor me by being my partner?"

"Of course. George only knows how to do a two-step, Douglass has no sense of rhythm, and Kendall prefers to jerk around to fast music. You were the obvious choice."

"Oh? How would you describe me?"

"Smooth, charming, demanding, and dangerous."

"In short, a good match for yourself."

"Perhaps. But I think you're also a romantic. So you will always come out on the losing end."

"You're not a romantic, I take it?"

"Not in the slightest."

"Tough for Peter."

"Peter has everything he wants."

"In that case, you must be a pretty good actress."

Eyebrows arched, she replied dryly, "Of course."

"Isn't there anyone you've ever cared for?"

"You mean besides myself?" Her eyes laughed at him.

"Naturally."

"Once, when I was much younger, I almost did something foolish. But I stopped just in time. It wouldn't have worked."

"Speaking of doing something foolish, how did you like Shauna's new look?"

"About as much as you expected me to."

"You mean you didn't like it?"

"That's the only reason you did it, isn't it? To annoy me."

"Shauna enjoyed herself."

"Did she indeed?"

"What's the matter? Are you so insecure you're afraid she'll attract more men than you?"

She swore at him, but he only laughed.

She would have turned and walked away, but his left arm tightened around her waist and his right arm gripped her wrist.

"Face it," he whispered into her ear. "I'm exactly what you've been looking for. A man you can't wrap around your little finger. Somebody who knows exactly what you are like and doesn't care. Think what we could do together."

"You have a high opinion of yourself."

"Tell me you don't like meeting the one man who could master you!"

"What makes you think I'd ever want a man who could, as you say, 'master me'?"

"All women like to know there exists a man stronger than them. Particularly if that man can give them everything they need."

"And what do I need?"

"My intellect, my charm, and my passion for you."

"You're wrong. I don't need anything from you." But her eyes met his and he could see the smoldering fire in them.

"There's only one problem," he said.

"Perhaps the fact that I'm married?"

"Not in the slightest."

"What then?"

The music ended, as if on cue, and he released her. "The fact that your sister is worth ten of you."

She slapped him with all the strength she possessed. The sound reverberated through the momentary vacuum of the dance floor, and people looked over to see what had happened. Jillian walked away, leaving Bart alone on the floor with one hand to his reddening cheek.

Douglass was dancing with Ellen, and George with Anne. Kendall and Hildy were talking at the table. She was telling him a story about an elderly recluse who had left an estate worth millions to her parakeet. Jillian came striding up. The music was beginning again.

"Kendall, I want to dance." She stamped one delicately shod foot. "Now."

Kendall's eyes met Hildy's; he shrugged philosophically and got up.

Once on the dance floor, Kendall asked quietly, "So what did my cousin the creep say to annoy you?"

"I intend to dance. If you prefer to talk, I can always get another partner!"

When Bart joined Hildy at the table, she was surprised to see that he was laughing to himself, though there was little laughter in his eyes. The red mark on his face was quite pronounced, but he ignored it, ordered a drink, and began talking with Hildy about her job and her young son. He was surprised to learn that Peter had seen his son only once since his marriage to Jillian, and that Jillian had never even met him.

"Not that I'd want to see her with any child, whether someone else's or her own," said Hildy with a good deal of venom.

Looking out at the dance floor, Bart nodded. "You're lucky the kid hasn't spent any time with her."

"Yes, that's why I—"

"Why what?"

"Nothing important. Perhaps being married to Peter will help her grow up."

"Maybe. But somebody sure needs to teach her a few things."

Hildy glanced into his face, but there was no expression.

His eyes met hers and he smiled. "But why waste time talking about her when I'm sitting beside someone as attractive as you?"

3

Sunday morning came in hot and humid. There was little movement, except for Lorry, who had mentioned to Ellen the day before that she would like to go to church if it wasn't inconvenient. Ellen had readily found her a map and offered her a car, and by 9:30, she was gone.

It was almost 11:00 before there was widespread movement.

One by one, the Brodies and their guests ventured downstairs and gathered on the patio. Except for Lorry, who had not yet returned, Jillian and Shauna were the last. Today Jillian wore an apricot and cream sundress. As usual, every hair was in place and her skin glowed with health. Shauna was in a Spanish-style bright orange blouse and full skirt, but she looked deathly pale beneath large sunglasses. All that remained of the stranger from the night before was the short hair.

Bart saw her and swore audibly.

Nick asked Ellen about Lorry.

"Oh, she's been up for hours. She went off early to church. Said she'd be back by one at the latest."

Thoughtfully, he went back to his table.

Jillian pecked at a fruit salad for a while and then sat looking at Shauna, who was across the table, eyes down, moving her scrambled eggs around the plate.

Between them, Peter dug ravenously into the mountain of pancakes with butter and syrup and bacon on his plate.

Jillian's face took on a look of disgust as she watched him.

He caught her gaze and smiled.

She pushed away her dish of fruit and walked into the house. In a few minutes, she returned with a magazine and sat reading on a lounge chair a short distance from the tables.

The others ignored Jillian and finished eating, except for Shauna, who went over to sit beside her. They spoke, with low voices. Bart, who was sitting at the closest table with Nick, Hildy, and Kendall, caught parts of the conversation. Several times he heard Shauna say, "I'm sorry."

"Well, you should be." Jillian's voice raised slightly. "He's no more than a two-bit con-man. His pockets are as empty as his brain. But of course," she added scornfully, "if you prefer his advice to mine…"

Shauna hadn't moved. Her head was down, eyes fastened on the empty glass she still held. "No, of course not. I'm sorry, Jillian. I won't listen to him again. It's just that he said I was dowdy."

Jillian's eyes narrowed. "I suppose he would prefer you to look the way you did last night. Like a stripper."

"I'm sorry," Shauna whispered, her eyes downcast.

"Stay away from him." Jillian gracefully stood up, and sauntered over to where Anne and Ellen were sitting together at one of the tables.

The conversation abruptly came to a halt and Anne, pleading a headache, hurried into the house. Jillian raised her eyebrows, but didn't comment. She calmly asked Ellen about getting season tickets to a theater she had mentioned.

Shauna hadn't moved. Her head was bent, eyes fastened on the empty glass she still held in her trembling hand. A man's hand reached down and pulled her chin up. She recoiled as Bart said harshly, "You moron. You wimp. Do you enjoy being the mat she wipes her feet on? Or do you let everyone walk all over you? You know, they outlawed slavery a long time ago, Rip van Winkle!"

Without replying, Shauna pushed his hand away and scrambled to her feet. The forgotten glass slipped from her fingers and splintered against the cement patio.

Bart watched her disappear inside the patio doors. He turned and saw Jillian laughing, presumably at something Ellen had said. But her eyes were on Bart. He strode away angrily in the direction of the garage.

He had to sidestep quickly as Lorry came around the corner of the house. She was dressed in a bright lime and turquoise floral dress and walking as if she hadn't a care in the world.

"Have a nice time at church?" Bart asked, his voice sarcastic. Before she could answer, he continued, "Did the preacher tell you who you should be nice to and who you should avoid? There are certainly a few people around here that a good little Christian ought to avoid."

"Well," replied Lorry carefully, watching Bart's face. "Actually the sermon was about some verses that talk about life in this world being only a vague shadow of reality."

"Sounds like a philosophy course," Nick said. He had hurried over the moment Lorry came around the corner.

"Perhaps," replied Lorry. "But the verses simply mean that we only see things through a haze now. So often, we don't understand why people act the way they do or why God allows certain things to happen. Often, we don't even understand why we ourselves act the way we do. One day, God will allow us to see more clearly than we do now."

"Meanwhile, we're supposed to trust and obey?" Bart's voice held sarcasm. "Do good to our enemies and all that stuff? Yeah, right. Too bad most preachers don't know much about reality. I guess they're all in this obscurity you're talking about." Leaving Lorry to stare at his back, he turned and walked across the terrace into the games room, where he went straight to the bar.

"Come and sit with Kendall and me," suggested Nick. "You can tell us all about the church you went to."

4

Forty minutes later, having finished a leisurely lunch while being entertained by Nick's and Kendall's stories of law school, Lorry went to her room to change. She found Shauna lying face down across her bed. It took a few minutes to coax her to sit up. Her face was red and puffy, the area around her eye purple and blue.

"Did your sister upset you again?"

"It's that stupid Bart! I don't know why I ever listened to him. I thought I could be somebody else, but I can't." She threw herself back onto her pillow, and her body shook with deep sobs.

Lorry knelt by the bed, but Shauna told her to go away. Lorry decided to change. She was putting on her sandals when there was a firm knock at the door.

Opening it, she found Jillian.

"I want to talk to Shauna," Jillian said as she walked in. "Alone. You'll have to go somewhere else."

Lorry took her time doing up the strap on her sandal.

"Who is this?" Jillian was holding the picture Lorry had placed on her night table.

"A friend," said Lorry.

"Looks your type." Jillian set the picture down carelessly. "Hurry up, I don't have all day!"

"Shauna," said Lorry, "I'll be outside on the couch. If you need me, just call." She looked into Jillian's eyes. "And if I were you, I'd watch your step. You're going to go too far one of these days. Sometimes the worm has been known to turn."

"You scare me half to death," Jillian said out of the side of her mouth. "Now would you please get lost? Go chase after Nick some more since that appears to be what you came to do."

Unspoken words fought to escape her lips, but Lorry made herself pick up a book and walk out.

Overlooking the staircase and front hallway was a small sitting area marked by a beautiful Persian carpet. On it were two love seats and a couple of tables covered with magazines. Lorry sat on one of the love seats and began to pray silently.

In the bedroom, Jillian was looking at herself in the mirror while she addressed Shauna. "I just finished talking to you after lunch, and I turn around and see you with Bart again. What do you think you're doing, encouraging someone like that? I didn't realize you were that desperate for a man."

Shauna sat on the edge of her bed with her hands in her skirt pockets and her eyes glued to the floor.

"I suppose you could use ignorance as an excuse," Jillian continued. "I don't expect you've run across anyone like Bart before." She adjusted the bodice of her dress. "But I thought you'd learned your lesson." She turned to look at Shauna. "Just see that you stay clear of him the rest of the weekend if you don't want him to make an even bigger fool of you, because that's all he's doing."

Inside the right pocket of her skirt, the comb Shauna was holding suddenly snapped.

Jillian ended her lecture. "If he tries to talk to you again, tell him to butt out. Or I will." She walked out.

Shauna stared at the closed door for a full minute. She used a word she'd never used before. Then, with a firm jut to her jaw, she ran to the closet and pulled out the suitcase containing her own clothes. Pulling off her skirt and blouse in such haste that she tore off a button, she changed into faded denim shorts, a white T-shirt, and a worn pair of running shoes before racing downstairs past a startled Lorry, who had been coming back into the room to make sure Shauna was okay.

5

The afternoon slipped forward. The hot sun poured down, proving once again its mastery over man as by ones and twos most of the guests sought the coolness of their air-conditioned rooms.

But not all were inside. Several of them had chosen the solitude of the outdoors. One lone figure was furtively hurrying toward the Japanese garden.

Inside the garden, where Jillian was sitting in the shade on a rustic bench at the edge of a clearing of soft grass, the only sound was the soft gurgling of water. Jillian's eyes were focused on a unique waterfall, but her eyes were unseeing, her mind indifferent to her surroundings.

Despite the beauty of the setting, she was annoyed. He should have been here before her. If he thought she would wait at his beck and call, he could think again.

She would give him five minutes, and then she had other fish to fry. Stupid expression, she thought. Her mother's, no doubt. Her mother's words were a parade of trite expressions, one after the other, and no matter how she tried to keep down that part of her life, it kept popping up, usually in the form of some stupid saying.

She held up the floral chain she had made in the first few minutes while she was waiting. She didn't know what the flowers were. They looked like daisies, but daisies were white. Roses and orchids and gardenias were the only flowers she was interested in. Hot house flowers arranged in expensive bouquets. Not flowers that grew like weeds in the outdoors. But they were a pretty yellow. And she had done a good job of making the chain.

When she had seen the flowers at the entrance to the garden, she had suddenly remembered being taught how to make a daisy chain. Seemed like ages ago. It was fortunate she'd had a nail file in her pocket. It had slit the stems very well. She pictured her former teacher coming up the path. She would surprise him with the chain—throw it over his head. And let him try to get away! She laughed.

Then she felt anger. Why was he so late? Even if he'd had trouble getting away unnoticed, he should have been here by now. Why was there no sign of him coming up the path?

While there may have been no sign of anyone on the path, Jillian was not alone in the garden. The other person, the one who was watching so as not to step on any fallen leaves or twigs that would crackle, ignoring the well-manicured grass where a footprint might remain, sticking to the hard cobblestone walk that meandered through the delightful Japanese garden, was moving closer, now leaving the walk, but very carefully. Stepping only where no footprint would remain.

The scattering of birds in nearby trees saw, and they flew away. Instinct, perhaps. A primitive sensing of danger.

Jillian had no such sense. Would have laughed at the very idea. So she sat unmoving, thinking how wonderful it was to be free of her family, to be a woman who could do whatever she wanted. With no one to stop her.

Laughter bubbled up in her throat. But even as she began to laugh, a gloved hand passed a cord around her neck, and she tensed with sudden panic. The laughter died unborn as the cord tightened. The floral chain dropped from her fingers.

Her lips were open, but no sound escaped. Eyes wide in disbelief, she arched her back and shoulders and flailed her arms in an attempt to pull away. The cord continued to tighten. She twisted and fought to escape. Her hands clutched at the cord, but it had dug into her skin and there was nothing she could do to loosen it. Her lungs screamed for air. None came. A short gasp, the rattle of death, escaped her open mouth and she slumped forward, her face an expression of sudden horror.

The murderer twisted the rope tighter and held it long enough to make certain she was dead, then casually loosened it. The limp body slid forward and collapsed in a heap on the grass. The sunlight could reach her now, touching her bare arms and legs. And she hadn't put on sunscreen. But the danger of the ultraviolet rays was no longer something she needed to worry about.

In a few moments the scene had reverted to nature.

The fountain, a deerscarer which consisted of a remarkable piece of bamboo and string architecture, was a conversation piece designed by an American from Sweden who had been brought in to do the gardens three years before. The fountain calmly continued its endless work, filling a large bamboo spout with water, dumping it out, filling it, and dumping the water over and over and over again.

The gurgle of the water every few minutes and the rustle of the leaves were the only noises discernible in the tiny copse. The birds had not yet returned.

Part II

A very great part of the mischiefs
that vex this world arise from words.

Burke

Chapter Seven

In his small private office on the third floor of the Yonge Street police station, Detective-Inspector Paul Manziuk signed his daily report. His hand was firm, letters neat and round and easy to read—the letters of a man who hated to write and felt uncomfortable doing it, as if his fifth grade teacher were standing at his shoulder shaking her head over the way he made each stroke.

But when the signature was complete, the anger he had been holding inside could no longer be contained. It found its way into his clenched fist, and Manziuk brought that fist crashing onto his desk, scattering papers to the floor and sending a large blue-and-gold marble rolling along the edge of the report.

Instinctively, Manziuk caught the marble, dwarfing it in his big hand. He opened his palm and rolled the marble over it, feeling the cool smooth surface.

Two months ago, the marble had been in the possession of an attractive twenty-two-year-old woman. A college student, she'd been using the marbles in an experiment with autistic children—on her way to becoming a very special kind of teacher.

There were twenty-four marbles altogether—specially made, larger than normal, very bright, almost neon—six of each color—red, green, blue, and yellow—all with sparkling gold mixed in. At least, there should have been six of each color. One of the marbles, a blue and gold one, was missing. For some reason, the marbles had been strewn all over the ground where the body lay, and they had only been able to find twenty-three.

Remembrance of the girl's lifeless body and the feeling of impotent rage that had overcome him when he first saw it broke in waves over Manziuk.

It could just as easily have been Lisa, his daughter, twenty-one and a student at the same college.

How could you protect your daughters against people who didn't need a motive? How could you defend them against men who seemed to think it was their God-given right to do what they wanted to any woman they happened to see? Being a police officer didn't help. In fact, it made things worse—he had to see the bodies, had to witness the pain and anger of relatives and friends, had to feel twice as helpless because he knew how little there was to go on in a case like this. And there had been three similar cases in Toronto since last October.

He grunted, remembering how his friend and fellow police officer, Joe Hanover from Detroit, had teased him about having a soft cushy job in "Toronto the Good." Though the nickname was still used now and then, the truth was the city was fast approaching the crime rate of others that were not so good.

And wishing it wasn't so didn't change anything. You had to deal with things as they came, keep going no matter how much you wanted to give up, try to make some kind of a difference.

Manziuk flexed his legs and thrust his powerful back against the chair as he pushed away from the cluttered desk. He picked up the reports, then paused to stretch his large bulk before walking to the office door and opening it.

"James." He didn't raise his voice, but the single word penetrated every corner of the outer office.

A young man dressed in police blue hurried over.

"Take these to Seldon for me, will you?"

The young man reached for the reports and, without a word, strode off down a hallway.

Manziuk stood gazing around the busy room. No one paid him any attention. He grunted once and then went back into his office, shutting the door with a snap.

He moved restlessly around the small room, glancing at his special commendations, pausing for a moment to stare at the picture his wife had given him the day after he'd complained that he never got out into the country anymore. It was a print of a young eagle spreading its wings above a peaceful valley, with a small mouse racing below. The hunter and the hunted.

He looked at the picture often. For some reason, it calmed him. Perhaps because it served as a reminder that throughout the natural world, life and death go hand in hand. No one being is more important than any other. Even the predator has its place.

It was good to remember that, since he had to deal with a lot of predators. And worse. Animals normally kill only for food. But in Manziuk's world there were those who killed, not for need, but for pleasure. Animals seemed to have it down better.

Manziuk walked around the room, pausing for a moment to look out of his narrow window at the street three stories below. Hot out there. Steam was rising. Or maybe it was smog. Young women wearing too little—not too little for the weather—too little because of how it gave some men an excuse.

He shut the venetian blind and walked past his desk and chair, past the filing cabinet in the corner, around to the leather chair in front of his desk. Leather was hot in this weather. Bare flesh stuck to it.

Flesh. The smell of flesh. He'd been called in at 2:00 AM because they thought a body they'd found might be related to his homicide case. The body had been there no more than a day, but intense heat had hastened decomposition.

On the chance it was a homicide, he'd pushed to get the autopsy done right away, but the cause of death had turned out to be accidental. She'd been drinking and doing drugs, and had fallen, smashing her head on a jagged piece of broken sink somebody had thrown in the alleyway.

Accidental. Nobody's fault. Or everybody's. The girl was a few months short of sixteen, from a good middle-class home. She'd run away, and her parents couldn't persuade her to come back. And the authorities had shrugged their shoulders and said she was old enough to look after herself. Nothing they could do.

So she'd been living with a guy in his twenties and taking drugs like they were candy and slurping beers like they were pop, and now she was dead.

Leaving Manziuk to tell her parents. To watch their eyes grow blank, and see their bodies shrink back from the pain, to feel their anger as they massed him in a lump with all the others who didn't care.

Only he did care.

Why'd he want to keep this lousy job, anyway? Twenty-nine years a cop, ever since he graduated from grade twelve as a fresh-faced idealist of eighteen. Going to set the world straight.

He looked at his watch. 12:20 PM. He'd spent the dawn hours on the teenager's body, and the rest of the morning following the last possible lead on the homicide he'd been dealing with for eight, no, nearly nine, weeks. But the lead had gone the way of every other lead they'd had.

There was nothing more he could do here. And he was tired. So tired.

He turned abruptly and went to his desk. For a long moment, he stared at it. Papers littered the top, spilling onto the garbage can and carpet. The picture of his wife and him on their twenty-fifth anniversary was on its back, partially hidden by the accumulation of files. The triple-frame pictures of his daughter and two sons had fared better. It stood there in its U with a cloth handkerchief draped unevenly over the faces.

Manziuk remembered using the handkerchief to mop his sweating face and neck half an hour before. He leaned his bulk forward to set his wife and himself up, in the process letting more papers tumble onto the floor. He swore under his breath and picked up the handkerchief. Before he put it back into his pocket, he mopped his face and neck again. This stupid weather! Air-conditioning was fine until the day it malfunctioned; then you were helpless; not used to the heat anymore. Soft. You drove to your air-conditioned office in your air-conditioned car and you went home to your air-conditioned house and the only time you were out in the weather was when you took a day off to see the Blue Jays or to relax with a drink in your backyard.

Unless, of course, you had to do leg work on a case. Like the one he'd just been on.

He went back to his door and opened it. Instantaneous quiet dropped like a shroud onto the outer office. One treaded softly when Manziuk was in a bad mood, and he'd been in one for the past three weeks.

"Craig," he barked.

A lined face peered over a terminal.

"I need you," he said brusquely, leaving the door open as he went back inside his office.

Detective-Sergeant Woodward Craig, age fifty-nine, hot, tired, and overworked, hoisted his sweaty body out of the chair he'd been dozing in and followed Manziuk. Manziuk, at six-five, 230 pounds, was not easily ignored. But more than that, the two men had worked together often over the years, and they had developed mutual respect. They each knew that when they were together, the other's back would be adequately covered. No words had ever been spoken on the subject. They were no more and no less than good cops who played by the rules and who would retire with a small pension and the knowledge that in a troubled world they had done a little bit of good.

"Your reports done?" Manziuk asked as Craig entered the office and shut the door.

"Took them down an hour ago."

"So what are you hanging around here for?" Manziuk barked.

"Didn't know if you'd want anything else." Woody stared at the chair in front of the desk.

Manziuk noticed. "You need my permission to sit down?"

Woody tried a grin, but his face was too tired to hold it for long. "It is your office."

"So it is. All right." With exaggerated politeness, Manziuk pointed to a chair. "Sit down, won't you?"

Detective-Sergeant Craig ignored the chair and leaned, half-sitting, half standing, against the edge of the desk, as if ready to move at a second's notice.

Manziuk turned and walked to the window. "This Matheson case is dead-ended. We thought we had a lead and we've busted our behinds following it up, but you know what happened. Not a blasted thing! We've searched every inch of the grounds where she was found, talked to everybody who lived in the area, suspected everyone who knew her. And we've got absolutely nothing! Not one more lousy lead to work on! So now we put it on a back burner and hope some guy confesses when we catch him for something else. And we hope to God he doesn't do it again. Fat chance! If he gets away this time, he'll do it again all right. Anyway, we're off it for now."

He turned to face Craig. "I know it's hard to leave it as a red mark, but we don't have enough men to keep the good ones running in circles chasing their tails. We can't do any more than we've already done. Maybe we'll think of something later. So we'll take a little break. Here it is, July long weekend. We've got nothing to do from now until Tuesday morning, so go home and get a tan or something. All right?"

Craig smiled. "All right." There was a moment's pause. "And you? Are you going home to get a tan?"

Manziuk glared at his sergeant for a moment, gray eyes meeting brown in understanding. "Yes. Soon as I get these blasted files out of here, I'm gone."

Craig slipped off the desk and began picking up the personal effects that were strewn among the papers. "I'll take these downstairs on my way out." He found the bag they belonged in and replaced the items, comb, keys, wallet, Kleenex, pen, notebook. He picked up the small chamois drawstring bag that held the marbles and put them back inside. As he was about to close the bag, Manziuk reached over and dropped in the marble he had been holding.

Manziuk's voice was tinged with the frustration he still felt. "I wish there was something else these things could tell us."

Craig walked to the door, then paused. "See you Tuesday, then."

"And not a minute before. No matter who gets it."

"Yes, sir." He went out.

Manziuk spent twenty minutes sorting and filing papers. At last, he took his battered hat from its hook (straw for summer—hated to wear it, but the small bald spot on the top of his head had been burned by the sun once, and once was one time too many) and barged out of his office through the adjoining room. As before, the atmosphere became quiet and efficient.

When he reached the elevator on the wall opposite his office, he pressed the down button, waited until the doors slid apart, and then turned to the people in the office. "It's all right," he spoke gruffly. "You're allowed to breathe again."

At 4:30 that afternoon, a different Manziuk was in the back yard of his house lounging on a white molded plastic chair set on the eight-foot slab of concrete which passed for a patio. In one hand, he held a half-full glass; in the other, a Dick Francis novel he had been wanting to read for at least four months.

In the background, the phone began to ring steadily.

On the sixth ring, he heaved his bulk out of the chair and lumbered to the patio door. His large bare feet made flapping noises.

On the eighth ring, he answered it.

He listened for a moment, then grunted. "Oh, sure. Tell that to somebody who'll believe you." More listening. "She's young, is she?" The answer coming in the affirmative, he swore. "Oh, you know I'll come. But I really didn't—Oh, forget it! Who's available for second?… Where's Woody? No, don't bother him. He needs some rest. Not as young as he used to be. Who else is available?… No way. Not on your life!… Do I have a choice?… No, don't bother him.… Oh, all right, give me Ryan and blast you all!" He slammed the receiver down and stared at it for a minute. "I knew I should have left town!" he muttered. But his wife Loretta was out shopping and there was no one to hear.

Loretta. The supper they were having tonight! It was the first time in months they'd been able to plan an evening with friends.

And now this! Not only did he have a murderer to catch, but his second was a green cop, brand new on the job, and a woman to boot! Maybe he was an old-fashioned chauvinist like his daughter said. Okay, he knew he was. But having women on homicide just didn't seem right.

Not his business, though. The directive from city hall said the force had to be half female in twenty years. Same as the population.

As if the criminals would follow the same directives.

But it wasn't his problem. Except for the fact that he had to go out there with an inexperienced partner. No, not just inexperienced. He could handle that. What bothered him most was the very real fear Ryan had been promoted solely because of her race and gender, and not her skill. To meet the numbers, play the political game. That scared him. He sure hoped the boys—and girls— in their ivory towers knew what they were doing.

But he didn't have time to worry about politics. He had a murder to attend.

He lumbered back to the patio and picked up his glass and the book. Shutting the patio door with a thump, he dumped the remains of his drink down the sink and found a marker for the book. He sighed as he put it back on a shelf. Little chance he'd get to it again before he had forgotten what he'd already read.

Then he headed for the bedroom. Couldn't go to see a lady wearing plaid shorts and nothing else. Not even a murdered lady.

2

On the second floor of the recently refurbished but still old police headquarters, newly promoted Jacqueline Ryan sat in the center of a desk swinging both shapely brown legs and laughing with her friend, Constable Beverly Champion, Vice Squad, a ten-year veteran and mother of two young sons.

"So, what do you think? Should I celebrate by a night on the town or a new outfit?"

Bev laughed. "How about a new outfit to wear for a night on the town?"

"Mmm. Not a bad idea."

"Have you told your family yet?"

"Yep. Told them at supper last night."

"They must have been so pleased!"

"They think I'm nuts!" Jacquie's normally musical alto changed to a shrill soprano, "What girl in her right mind would want to go around investigating murders?" A low growl, "Why don't you just find a good man and settle down?" A firm alto, "What do you think you'll do if you have to go after a murderer?" A threatening bass, "And what will you do if the murderer goes after you?"

"It must be fun having your aunts and grandmother and cousins all living close by."

"Fun? You think it's fun? Girl, you need to see more of life!" In one swift, graceful motion, Jacquie jumped off the desk and began to pace the small cubicle. "But, seriously, I do have one very real concern. Manziuk."

"Detective-Inspector Manziuk?"

"I hear he's a terror to work with." Jacquie's mobile face twisted into a scowl.

Bev's reply was cautious. "I've heard he doesn't miss anything. He hates laziness."

Jacquie continued to pace the tiny area, using her hands to punctuate each sentence. "What I've heard is he comes down like a ton of bricks on anybody who makes a mistake. And you know what else? He reminds me of a teacher I had in grade six. Big man, stomach the size of an oven, never so much as a hint of a smile. Hey, we thought if he ever did smile, he might literally crack his face. Well, that's who Manziuk reminds me of." Jacquie paused to arrange her features into a deadpan, chin thrust out, lips in a thin line, eyes cold and hard.

Bev laughed, then became serious. "But Manziuk's good, Jacquie. Everybody says so."

Jacquie's face relaxed, but she resumed pacing. "He's one of the best. But I'm still nervous when I think about having to work with him. Who knows what he'll think of me?"

"What's to think? You're a good cop. You graduated near the top of your class in criminology. You paid your dues in narcotics and juvenile. You just spent a year in vice."

"But he's old school. Worked his way up step by step. And the word is he doesn't have any time for cops who learn the business at university. And then there's my age. I'm only twenty-eight. How many homicide detectives are that young? Not to mention the fact I'm a woman. And black. And we both know that's why I got the promotion."

"Jacquie, that's not true!"

"Grow up, Bev! I'm not complaining. But I know perfectly well the police force has a mandate to promote more blacks and more women. So here I am—two for the price of one!"

"But you're a good cop!"

"Sure I am, honey. I just have to keep proving it to everybody."

"Well, don't get in a knot over it. He works with Detective-Sergeant Craig all the time. Maybe you'll never even have to go near Manziuk."

"I sure hope not. At least not till I know my way around."

The phone on Beverly's desk rang. After answering it, she held the receiver out to Jacquie. "You may have to put that celebration on hold. Homicide is looking for you."

3

Thirty minutes later, Manziuk was driving on a paved country side road past some rather enormous and obviously expensive houses. He turned in at an impressive gate that was the only apparent opening in an eight-foot stone wall that extended for about two hundred feet on either side. The gate was opened by an unsmiling police officer who carefully checked his ID. Once inside the gate, he found himself entering a circular drive which extended the full length of an immense brick house. In the center of the drive was a grassy oval highlighted by a large fountain with water cascading down. Beds of massed red and yellow flowers teamed with small green evergreens circled the fountain and softened the front of the house.

White police cars dotted the driveway, looking grossly out of place. Manziuk parked his Chevy wagon near the entrance to the house. It looked every bit as out of place as the squad cars.

An officer in uniform was talking on his car radio. When he saw Manziuk, he finished his conversation and hurried over. "Afternoon, sir. I'm Constable Waite. The body is in the garden. Forensics is here. They've done a preliminary search and taken pictures of the scene. They're ready for you."

"Is Dr. Weaver here?"

"No, sir, he's on a fishing trip. Dr. Munsen is here."

Lucky Weaver. A fishing trip. That's what he should have done. Only he didn't like fishing. Seemed too much like his job. Besides, the fish hadn't broken the law, so why should he catch them? Munsen was an adequate pathologist. Not as experienced as Weaver. More emotional, too. Likely you got less emotional with more experience. Besides, bad enough to have to look at a body without having to examine it minutely.

Aloud, he asked, "Witnesses?"

"No, sir. Constable Carnaby has the people from the house all in one room, sir. There's a weekend house party, so there are a number of guests."

"I understand the victim is the wife of a prominent lawyer."

"Yes, sir, that's what we were told."

"You took the call?"

"Yes, sir. Carnaby was right behind me. The body was found just after four by a group of three who were walking in the garden."

"Garden?"

"A rather spectacular garden, sir. Not your vegetable kind."

"All right. Area sealed off?"

"Yes, sir."

"Fine. Is Detective-Constable Ryan here yet?"

"No, sir, I don't think so. But there's a car coming now."

Manziuk turned to watch as a small red Toyota daintily threaded its way through the cars in the driveway and found a small spot to ease itself into. A young black woman got out of the driver's side. She was wearing a short-sleeved navy pantsuit with a light pink blouse. She stopped for a second to arrange the strap of her navy purse over her shoulder. The purse, which was plain and square and medium in size, matched her navy low-heeled shoes.

Business-like, Manziuk thought. For some reason, that annoyed him. He watched her striding purposefully toward them, and the resentment he felt against her presence threatened to surface. Stupid of him not to call Woody. Only—the truth was he was worried about the older man. Looked a bit gray around the mouth a few times this past week. No, Woody needed time off even if it did mean having to work with a green female.

The woman stopped a few feet in front of him, planting her feet about eighteen inches apart, knees flexed, like an outfielder ready to go either way the ball was hit. She was taller than average for a woman—maybe five foot nine. Sturdy—no, muscular. Manziuk suspected there wasn't an ounce of fat on her. Her hair was black and cut very short—maybe an inch long—with tight curls all around. Like she'd had a buzz cut a month before.

Aside from the hair, her features were unremarkable—neither especially ugly or pretty. A face you wouldn't notice in a crowd. No makeup. One very small silver stud in each ear. But you might notice her eyes. She had very intense dark brown eyes.

"Inspector Manziuk?" she asked coolly.

"That's right," he said. "You're Ryan and you're secondary."

"Have you seen the body yet?" Her voice was businesslike, well modulated.

"Just got here."

"Let's go," she said.

Manziuk raised his eyebrows, but he picked up his briefcase and acquiesced without a word.

Constable Waite led the way along the right front of the house and through an archway into a garden. They walked through beautifully pruned trees and shrubs, over several tiny bridges topping rippling streams, down a cobblestone path to a curved bench. There, in the midst of all this beauty, spotlighted by a beam of sunlight, lay the body.

Manziuk stared for a moment at the neat foot in the tiny beige sandal. Why did women wear such flimsy shoes? He followed the foot up the beautifully formed legs to the peach sundress. Good figure, he thought. He looked at the cascades of tumbled blonde hair—golden blonde, he thought they called it. Natural? Perhaps. Looked real. Nice tan. But it had a bluish tinge to it now.

He had a good look, then nodded to one of the men from the Forensics Identification Team, and the body was rolled over.

Manziuk looked at the flushed face for an instant, and then stepped back. Beside him, Ryan made a small choking sound and turned away.

A short man in a creased brown suit stepped toward them. "Not very nice, is it? I'll just finish my examination now."

Manziuk said, "Go ahead," but his voice was unsteady. God, how terrible it was. Even after twenty-nine years on the force, the sight of death still made him queasy, especially death such as this. He could understand mercy killing—understand, not condone; and he could also understand, but not condone, killing in anger. But this! No, he would never understand this kind of killing.

At his elbow, Ryan coughed.

He looked down at her and a smile twisted his lips. "First?"

She nodded her head. "This kind."

"Get used to it," he said, knowing he never would. "I've seen lots worse."

Ryan grimaced, then took a firm grip on the strap of her purse. "What do we do now?"

"We talk to the pathologist here and see if he can determine the cause of death. Shouldn't be too hard."

"You know?"

"I think so. What do you think?"

Ryan bit her lip and moved closer to see past the kneeling doctor. "Her face looks flushed, but that could be just lividity from the blood pooling there since she was lying on her stomach. However, I'd say the other facial features and the bruising on her neck indicate strangulation."

"That's right," agreed the small man, who stood up and began dusting the knees of his pants. "A lot of bruising on the back of the neck and a line on the neck. Straight line. No noticeable abrasions or scratching."

Manziuk was writing in a small coil notebook. "Something smooth?"

"That's right. Smooth and thin."

"Scarf?"

"Maybe, but I'd prefer something firmer. A smooth rope, if there is such a thing."

"Anything else you can tell me?"

"Rigor mortis is just starting. 'Course, it's awfully hot. Speed things up. Some lividity. Still on the warm side. I'd guess not earlier than 2:00 PM."

"The body was found shortly after 4:00 PM," Constable Waite said.

"No question it was murder?" Manziuk asked Munsen flatly, knowing the answer.

"None whatsoever."

"Okay."

"Terrible thing," said the pathologist. "I hope you catch him soon."

"Him?"

"What? Oh, I see. No, not necessarily. A strong woman could have done it. If it were done quickly, so the victim didn't struggle too much, it could have been over in a couple of minutes. No, you can't rule out the women." The slightly stooped, slightly shabby doctor leaned over to study the neck again. "See the marks on her neck there?" he asked. "She clawed at the rope. Not for long, though. Whoever did it had no hesitation. A very fast, clean job."

"When can you do the autopsy?" Manziuk asked.

"Got to stand in line. Not before three tomorrow afternoon. Do my best to work it in. Should be straightforward enough, poor thing."

"Was she killed here?"

"From her position, I'd suggest she was sitting on the bench and someone got behind her. Afterward, she toppled off the bench face first."

Manziuk looked around. About eight feet in front of the bench, a unique Japanese waterfall gave forth a tiny stream of water that likely fascinated many visitors to the house. He'd seen something similar in a Vancouver garden he'd visited with his wife years ago. Someday he'd like to put something like that in his own backyard. A curiosity. But for now that was beside the point. Not to mention impossible due to lack of time.

But he had more time than the girl who maybe a few hours ago had been watching that fountain but was now lying dead.

He continued to stare at the fountain and bench for a moment. Then, as if remembering where he was, he turned and saw the small group from Ident waiting. "I'm sorry," he said. "Thinking. You've done a preliminary search?"

"Yes, sir." Special Constable Ford stepped out from the others. "Not much. Considering it's outdoors, this place is clean as a whistle. We found a couple of cigarette butts, a wrapper from a chocolate bar, and this," he held out a paper bag and Manziuk took it. Inside was something that looked like a loose wreath made from some kind of daisies. "Could mean something, I guess," Ford said.

"Let me jot down a few things and then I'll release the body." Manziuk made more notes. Ryan watched quietly. Then he pulled out a sketch pad.

"What now?" Ryan asked.

"Now we do a sketch of the scene. Got a pad?"

"I have a tape recorder." She opened her purse and pulled out a tiny black unit.

"Nice. But what's that got to do with the scene?"

"I can describe it on tape. Same result. Besides, there's a team to take photos and a video."

"Sure there is. But what if the batteries fail or the film won't develop properly or the tape gets wrecked? What then?"

"All those things won't happen."

"Maybe. But I still do my own sketches. It helps me think."

There was silence as he began a quick drawing of the body, the bench, and the fountain. Then he pulled a measuring tape out of his pocket. He walked to the bushes behind the bench. He turned to look at Ryan, who was standing still. "Before we do anything else, we go over the crime scene with a fine-tooth comb. We talk to the witnesses later. After we have some kind of idea what we're talking about."

"What do you want me to do?"

"Watch."

She bit her bottom lip.

He went over every inch of ground in the clearing and the area surrounding the body, measuring and recording the measurements on the sketch he had drawn.

"I could be helping," she said at last.

"How many cases have you been on in homicide so far?"

"This is my first, but—"

"So watch and learn."

When he had finished the sketch, he pulled out his own tape recorder and went over the scene and the measurements on it.

"Okay, the body's all yours," he said to the Forensics Team as he put his notebook and tape recorder away.

4

A few minutes later, with Ryan hurrying to match his long strides, Manziuk followed Constable Waite's directions through the garden to the back of the house. In a way, he wished his wife were here. She would have enjoyed the garden.

Well, he couldn't say his job didn't take him to interesting places. Not all as ritzy as this, though. Not by a long shot.

When they passed through the wooden archway that marked the end or beginning of the garden, depending on which way a person was going, Manziuk took a few more long strides and then turned to look behind. Little chance that anyone not at the scene of the murder could have witnessed what had taken place. The shrubs and hedges and manicured trees were too dense.

He turned and gazed up at the side of the imposing house. There were five windows, three on ground level and two above. He'd have to have a look out them.

He continued down the pathway. In front of them was a large swimming pool surrounded by tiled patio. The patio in turn was sprinkled with pots of yellow, red, and white flowers, half a dozen red, yellow, and white striped lounge chairs, and three yellow tables with vivid red umbrellas and matching red chairs. Despite the intense heat, the patio was empty and rather forlorn-looking.

Beyond the pool area, he saw what looked to be another garden. This one was much less dense, though it did abound with trellises. The archway opening was lavishly surrounded with climbing roses.

At the end of the pool near the house was a low building which Manziuk took to be a change house. This sort of place would have something like that. All the frills.

Four sets of patio doors came out onto the patio, along with a regular door near the other end of the house.

At this door stood Special Constable Benson, a man Manziuk knew well. He was talking earnestly with another officer who looked to be standing guard.

Manziuk strode toward the two men, wondering as he went what awaited him inside the house. Thus far, the place was like a movie set, with the police running around like so many ants. But inside that house were real people, and one of them could be a murderer who might not take so kindly to the police running about.

"Well, Benson, what brings you here?" The question was given in a rather amused tone.

The young constable Benson had been talking with looked slightly offended at the interruption, but Benson ignored him. "Perhaps we should find a place to sit down, sir."

"Excellent idea. Lead the way."

Benson opened the door and went into a back hallway. The kitchen was to the right, a large pantry to the left. "This way, please. Mr. Brodie said we are welcome to use his study."

"That should do nicely," Manziuk replied.

It was a comfortable room with two walls of books, mainly legal ones, with a few mysteries, some popular novels, and old yearbooks, presumably from Brodie's university days, scattered throughout. There was a fireplace on the third wall, with two orange overstuffed chairs drawn up in front, a table with a typewriter tucked into one corner, a desk in the center of the room, and a few straight-backed business chairs. There was a laptop computer open on the desk.

"This will do quite nicely," Manziuk remarked.

"You take the desk," he said to Benson as he pulled one of the chairs around so it faced the desk. Then he noticed Ryan standing just inside the door. "Close the door and find a chair. Sam, this is Detective-Constable Ryan on her first homicide. Ryan, Special Constable Benson, public affairs officer."

Manziuk settled into his chair. "Okay, what have we got that brings you here?"

Benson leaned comfortably into the executive chair and stretched his hands behind his head.

"Want a cushy desk job?" Manziuk asked.

Benson laughed. "Not for a while yet." He sat forward again. "Okay, let's look at this one. You've heard of Brodie, Fischer, and Martin?"

"The name rings a bell."

"Law firm with a lot of important clients. Clients that don't want notoriety, if you know what I mean."

"So they have a lot of squeamish clients. What's that to me?"

"Jillian Martin, the victim, is the wife of the youngest partner, Peter Martin. It would be unfortunate if there was a lot of destructive publicity surrounding the case."

"So you want to do the talking to the press, is that it?"

"In a nutshell."

"And am I supposed to investigate thoroughly everyone who might be involved?"

"Absolutely. We don't want whitewash. But we don't want unnecessary speculation, either. And as little dirt as possible. So, have I got your cooperation?"

"You can tell the press anything you like. But you don't touch my investigation."

"You've got it."

"I mean it, Sam. I don't want any problems from sensitive toes calling headquarters because I accidentally trod on them."

"I'll let you have as much line as you need. But you know the score. So try not to churn up too much water unless you've got the fish hooked good and solid. Especially if it's a big fish. Okay?" Obviously Manziuk wasn't the only one who thought his job had a lot of similarities to angling.

"Fine. We'll need a search warrant for the house."

"It's on the way."

"Good. Now get out of here and let me do my job."

"One question. We've got a young woman here. What are the chances this is connected to the four unsolved cases you're working on?"

"Doubtful. The other four all had red hair. This woman is blond. The method used is similar, but the location is very different. And if it turns out it was somebody in this house, the chances are virtually nil."

"So you don't feel there's any connection?"

"It isn't totally impossible, of course, but it's doubtful."

"Okay. You know they'll ask."

Benson winked at Ryan as he left. He was whistling.

When he was gone, Manziuk turned and looked at Ryan, who was sitting stiffly on the edge of a chair several feet away. Her knees were together and her purse was on her knees.

"Well, what are you waiting for?" Manziuk asked. "This isn't sit-around time. We've got work to do."

"No weapon so far," Special Constable Ford, the head of the Forensics Identification team, stated ten minutes later, after Manziuk had settled Ryan at the desk and given her a notebook so she could take notes. "We've searched the garden and beyond. No rope in the water. We wondered if it could be a cord from a curtain or something like that."

Manziuk nodded, his eyes half shut.

"There's no reason to think she was sexually assaulted," Ford continued. "Apparently, whoever did it simply wanted to kill her. Unless he was disturbed before he had a chance to do anything else."

"Robbery?"

"She had on three rings. A watch. A diamond pendant."

"So we can presumably rule out a tramp."

"The grounds are bordered by other estates. There's an eight-foot stone wall all around the place. There are only two entrances—the front, where we came in, and a small gate at the back that is kept locked. The front has an electronic gate that is locked at night. During the day there is a buzzer that goes off whenever anyone crosses the entrance."

"Who hears it?"

"It rings in the kitchen and the garage. Apparently it was installed by the previous owner. The Brodies bought the place just before Easter and haven't changed anything.

"The gate at the back can only be opened by a key and it locks automatically. Behind, there are paths into ravines and such beyond it. Someone could conceivably come from back there, but getting in would be pretty difficult."

"Uh-huh," Manziuk said. His eyes were completely shut now. There was silence for about half a minute. Then he opened his eyes and said, "Go on."

"The only concrete thing we found might not have anything to do with it. It's a daisy chain."

"Yeah, I saw it. Learned anything?" he asked.

"It's made from flowers with their stems slit and the next flower inserted in the slit, and the last one making it a circle. Ingenious."

"She could have made it while she sat there."

"Yes. Or somebody else could have. All we do know is that these particular flowers only grow near the entrance to that particular garden."

"So whoever made it picked them on the way in and—what would you say—braided it later?"

"I suppose it could have been done while walking."

"Yes. Examine it thoroughly. Find an expert if you can."

"Yes, sir. That's about it for now. We'll start searching the house in a few minutes. The people here have been confined in one room since Carnaby arrived."

"All of them accounted for?"

"Yes, sir."

"Send someone to take his place and tell him to come here"

"On my way."

Ford left.

"Doing all right taking notes?" Manziuk asked Ryan.

Her dark eyes flashed, but she nodded meekly.

Constable Carnaby came in slowly and looked around, not sure where to sit. Manziuk pointed to the chair and he sat awkwardly in it, twisting his cap between his knees. He looked young—twenty-two or three, and out of place in this lavish setting. But he was obviously determined to do a good job.

"Now then," Manziuk said. "How long have you been here?"

Carnaby's voice was all business. "I arrived at four-sixteen. The call came on my radio at four-eleven and I was only a short distance away. Waite arrived about two minutes earlier. He sealed the scene and I did a quick search of the grounds and then isolated the witnesses. The Emergency Response Unit also arrived about the time I did. Waite allowed a paramedic in to see if there was a chance of resuscitation. When Worrell arrived ten minutes later, he did another search of the grounds. Ident and Dr. Munsen and the others arrived soon after."

"You talked to the husband?"

"Yes, sir." Carnaby flipped open a notebook. "Name of Peter Martin. Guests here for the weekend. The victim is his wife,

Jillian. She was found by a group of three who were walking in the garden."

"Did they move her at all?"

"Turned her slightly to be sure she was dead."

"I see. Did her husband have anything else to say?"

"He appeared completely devastated, sir. Answered yes or no to my questions and didn't volunteer anything." Carnaby looked up and said by way of explanation, "He'd seen the body."

"All right. Did you talk to anyone else?"

"Just Mr. Brodie, sir. The owner of the house. He and Mr. Martin are partners. Lawyers. There's a Mr.—" He consulted his notebook. "A Mr. Fischer as well. Mrs. Brodie had invited both partners and their wives here for the weekend."

"Who else is on the grounds?"

Constable Carnaby consulted his notebook again. "Well, sir. There are quite a few." The constable nervously cleared his throat. He read the names of the Brodies, Nick Donovan, and the Fischers.

When he identified Peter Martin as the corpse's husband, Detective-Constable Ryan couldn't keep the laughter from gurgling up at the inept description. She stopped abruptly. "Sorry," she said as Manziuk glanced at her, his face unsmiling.

"Who else?" Manziuk said, looking back at Constable Carnaby.

He read off the names of the rest of the guests.

"Is that it?" Manziuk tone was sardonic.

"Well, all but the servants, sir."

"How many?" he asked with a resigned sigh.

"The cook, Mrs. Winston. Her daughter, Crystal. And then there are two gardeners, but neither lives on the estate. And there's another man who comes to help with heavy jobs. And a woman who cleans weekly, but she hasn't been here since Wednesday.

"That's it?"

"Yes, sir. There's no chauffeur."

"No chauffeur?"

"Yes, sir. The people who lived here before had a chauffeur, but Mr. Brodie prefers to drive himself, as does Mrs. Brodie. So there's an empty apartment above the garage. Mr. Bart Brodie is staying there right now."

"Well, that makes one less person we have to talk to," Manziuk said. "I for one am glad they don't have a chauffeur."

"There doesn't appear to be a butler, either," Ryan added.

Carnaby looked from one to the other. "Is there anything else, sir?" he asked.

"Not now. Leave your list of names, though. I'll need it to keep this cast of characters straight."

Carnaby went out.

"You know," Manziuk said as he stretched out his legs and got comfortable, "if I wasn't involved in this I'd think I was reading it. This place is like a setting for one of those whodunits. Right out of a book."

"A setting for murder," Ryan echoed hesitantly. "Except this is no stage."

"And our corpse is on the way to the morgue for an autopsy. And we've got a whole list of people who could have murdered her. Or it might have been none of them. It's like a Rubik's cube, all jumbled up. Ah, well, talking about it won't do us much good. It's time we started listening. You check to make sure Ford has the house search going, and I'll go spy on the house party."

Chapter Eight

Manziuk walked along the plush hall carpeting until he found
Carnaby back at his post in the open doorway of the day room.

After a brief conversation, Manziuk entered the room. He
took in the floral curtains and matching loveseats and chairs. His
wife would like this room.

Talk died as one by one they became aware of his presence.
Without a word, he took control.

His eyes went quickly past the decor to the people. Seven
women and five men. One of the men was missing then. By the
look of it, several of them hadn't recovered from the shock. One
woman wasn't unhappy, though. She would bear examining.

A movement behind made him step further into the room and
turn.

"Sorry, officer, or whatever. Your title escapes me. I know we
were asked to stay in here, but, unfortunately, I needed to leave
the room." The man, who was much younger than his bald head
made him seem at first glance, spread his hands in a helpless gesture. "The bathroom is across the hall, so I didn't go far. Childish
of me, I know, but there it is." The man dropped his hands and
went past Manziuk. Then he stopped to observe the others before
turning back to the Inspector. "Charming group we have here,
isn't it? Has anyone confessed yet, or are you going to have to
give us all the third degree?"

"Bart, be quiet." The man with graying hair came forward.
"My nephew, Inspector. Please ignore him. He seems to think this
is funny. I can assure you the rest of us don't."

"Mr. George Brodie?"

"Yes, that's right. Officer, I don't know what to say. This sort of thing isn't in my line at all. I stick to corporate law, never touch criminal."

"All I need from you and everyone else is your complete cooperation so we can work as efficiently as possible."

George nodded. "Of course. We certainly don't want to hinder you in any way. Though frankly, I think whoever did this has already made good his escape."

"We aren't overlooking that possibility."

"Well, then. As long as you realize that." He looked around the room as if buying time. "I suppose you would like me to introduce the others?"

"If you would."

"My wife, Ellen." He moved toward the center of the room and the woman beside whom he had been sitting got up and came toward them. She looked about fifty-five, a few pounds overweight, with salt and pepper hair put up in a chignon, and a worried expression. Somehow she didn't fit the house. Not sure why he thought that. Just a feeling. Perhaps Ryan would figure it out. Could be a female thing. It hadn't occurred to him before, but it might be useful to have a woman's opinion.

"My partner, Douglass Fischer," George said of a big man who looked to be in his mid-forties. His wife, introduced as Anne, was the woman who had looked almost relieved. Anything but upset.

Peter Martin looked upset. Unless he was a very good actor, his wife's death had come as a complete shock. He sat off by himself, head sunk in his hands. When he glanced up during George's introduction, his eyes seemed to have trouble focusing—as if all this were some terrible nightmare he couldn't quite wake from.

A woman with coal black hair and a blue dress was hovering over him, getting him a drink, asking if he wanted anything. Hildy Reimer. Oh, yes, that was the neighbor whose apartment was being painted. She didn't look much like a neighbor right now. There was pain in her eyes. And the look she gave Peter Martin! No mistaking that look..

"And this is Jillian's sister, Shauna," George said of a nondescript girl in a brown print shirt and a pair of worn denim shorts. Colorless. Hard to believe she was the sister. You never knew, of course. One took after the father, the other the mother.

Not ugly; just plain and insipid. And why was she wearing sunglasses inside the house?

There were three others in a group near the bar. The two men both looked white and drawn. They had empty glasses in front of them. The girl in the middle had striking red hair. No, not red. There was a better word. Ryan might know it.

"This is my son, Kendall." The nearest young man stood up. He had brown hair and brown eyes and he looked upset, like someone with a stomach virus.

"My wife's cousin, Lorry Preston," said George. The redhaired girl looked up, her eyes serious. Manziuk nodded.

"This is a friend of my son's, Nick Donovan." The dark young man stood up somewhat unsteadily and held out his hand almost as a mechanical gesture. Manziuk shook it. The hand was cold and strangely lifeless considering the athletic build of the owner. He too looked as though he were ill.

"This is our housekeeper, Mrs. Winston, and her daughter, Crystal."

Mrs. Winston was a plump woman with bleached blond hair. She looked about forty. Her daughter Crystal was thin with very short blond hair that had a narrow green streak through one side, and about five earrings, all different, in each ear.

Mrs. Winston stood up. "I was wondering what to do about supper, sir. I can't finish making it while I'm in here, and I don't know what I should do about it."

George Brodie would have hushed her, but Manziuk's lips curved for the first time. "Well, what say I talk to you first and while we're talking, I'll have an officer look around your kitchen. Then you can go back to work."

"That's very kind of you, sir. I don't want to be in the way. Only it'll all be spoiling."

"No problem. Just give me one second." He raised his voice and announced, "I'll be wanting to talk to each person here individually. There's not much doubt we're dealing with a homicide, and the best way to find out what happened is to talk to all the people who were at the scene, so to speak. No one is under suspicion at this time. We merely have to get the facts straight so we know what we're looking for. I'm going to start with Mrs. Winston. I'd like everyone to remain here until you're called. Any questions?"

"Do you really think this is necessary, Officer?" the big man asked. George Brodie nodded as if in agreement with the question.

"I'm afraid so."

"But you surely don't suspect one of us?" The brittle voice belonged to the woman sitting beside the big man—Fischer, was that the name?—who had not looked upset.

"Just procedure," Manziuk said before turning to Mrs. Winston. "Now, if you'll come along with me?"

When Manziuk led Mrs. Winston into the study, he found Ryan standing in the center of the room as if wondering what to do next.

"Take the desk," he instructed, waving his arm to underline the words. "This is Mrs. Winston, the housekeeper." He seated her in one of the two easy chairs in front of the desk and took the other chair for himself.

"This all must be very upsetting," he said gently.

The woman nodded. "I've never been this close to such a thing before. Nor ever wanted to. There's some I know would be glad to be in my shoes, but I'm not. I'd as soon be off right now. But that wouldn't do. Mrs. Brodie needs me."

"That's right. I'm sure she does. And the sooner this is cleared up, the better for everyone."

She nodded vigorously, but added, "I don't know anything, though. I've no idea how it could have happened."

"Well, there might be something you know that you don't think counts. Or maybe you can help us just by telling about the people in the house. We don't know the people and you do. Now, let's see if you can give us any clues as to what's happened this afternoon. I understand there's a buzzer in your kitchen that goes off when someone enters by the front gate. Has it gone off this afternoon?"

"Only once, sir. That is, until the police started coming."

"And who was that?"

"Miss Lorry, sir. Mrs. Brodie's cousin."

"What time was that?"

"Shortly after one. We'd been serving brunch and she got back just before we started clearing up.

"Do you know where she had been?"

"Mrs. Brodie said she was going to church. She was the only one up for breakfast at eight, except Mr. Brodie. And she drove off some time after nine. Mr. Brodie opened the gate so she could get out."

"Did the buzzer go off at any other times today?"

"Not that I heard."

"Could it have gone off without your hearing?"

"I was in the kitchen all but maybe half an hour this morning, and this afternoon from one-thirty to two-thirty. But Crystal was in the kitchen this afternoon, so she'd have heard. The only time neither of us was near the kitchen was this morning from about twelve to twelve-thirty after we'd served brunch and I went up to see that she was doing a good job tidying up the rest of the bedrooms. Some of the people had just come out of their rooms then, so we had to try to tidy their rooms while they were eating."

"Would someone on foot make the buzzer go off?"

"Oh, yes, sir. Even an animal will, a cat, for instance. It's very sensitive, you see."

"Good. Now then, Mrs. Winston, you are by way of being a good objective witness. I'd like your opinion on a few things."

"I'll try, sir," she said anxiously.

"What, for instance, did you think of Mrs. Martin?"

"Well, that's hard to say." Her words came out slowly, reluctantly.

"Just tell me what you think," he urged.

"Well, I don't like to speak ill of the dead." Her eyes slowly raised to meet his. "I guess I didn't like her too much. She was never polite, like Mrs. Brodie, or that nice girl, Lorry Preston. Why, when I was getting breakfast for Miss Lorry this morning, she was so sweet about it! Didn't want to trouble me. Thanked me with a big smile. Now Mrs. Martin, never a thank you from her. Just orders and complaints. And I didn't for one minute believe her story about the broken vase!"

"Broken vase?"

"Water and petals and broken vase everywhere—splashed all over the walls and the door as well as the carpet. She said she was moving it because it was in the way. But you tell me how dropping a vase you're moving is going to smash it all over the place. I wasn't born yesterday."

"I see."

"Not that I want to say unkind things, but you asked what I thought."

"Yes, I did. What about some of the others? Mrs. Fischer, for instance."

"Keeps to herself. Probably has the migraine. My sister is like that. Goes out for a while and then has to hurry home to lie down. I heard her crying once, too."

"Your sister?"

Mrs. Winston looked at Manziuk reprovingly. "Mrs. Fischer. Maybe it's her time of life."

"Maybe," Manziuk agreed. But he was thinking that of all the people in the room she had looked the least unhappy, except for George Brodie's nephew Bart, of course.

"What about the nephew?" Manziuk asked.

"Oh, him," Mrs. Winston's face broke into a smile which she quickly wiped away. "He's the black sheep of the family. Comes around when he needs money. Mrs. Brodie's told me all about him. But you can't help liking him, anyway. He has what Mrs. Brodie calls 'charm.' Like today at brunch. What does he do but come right out into the kitchen, put on a frilly apron, and insist on helping Crystal and me take the food out to the patio."

"They all ate outside?"

"Yes, sir. A cold buffet beside the pool. Mrs. Brodie likes that on hot days."

"And everyone was there?"

"Yes, sir. Miss Lorry was a bit late on account of being at church, but the others were all there."

"Did you notice anything unusual today, or this weekend, for that matter?"

"No, sir. I don't think so…" Her voice trailed off.

"What is it?"

"Well, just a feeling, I guess. Likely silly."

"What sort of feeling?"

"I guess just that it wasn't a very successful party." She made a sweeping gesture. "I know it isn't now. After a murder. But I mean before. There seemed to be a lot of tension in the air. Crystal thinks I'm being silly. But I did feel that way."

"Do you still feel it?"

She looked at him in surprise. Her eyes grew round. "No, I don't," she said in a bewildered tone. "There's people upset, for it's a terrible thing to have happen, but it's like the storm broke. Like when there's electricity in the air and then the storm breaks and it's over. Isn't that strange?" she said, more to herself than as a question.

"Perhaps not," Manziuk said. "Well, if you think of anything else, just tell one of the officers. I'll want to talk to you again, likely, after we know more."

Mrs. Winston hesitated. "Did it happen quickly?"

He nodded, "Very quickly, I believe."

"That's good. You don't like to see people suffer. At least I don't." She turned to leave, then paused. "It was somebody strange, wasn't it? Some madman who didn't know what he was doing?"

"Maybe. We don't know yet."

She shivered, and then went through the door Ryan was holding open.

"Who's next?" Ryan asked when she was gone.

Manziuk didn't hear her. Eyes half shut, he considered Mrs. Winston. Tension in the air, indeed! He opened his eyes to find Ryan staring at him.

"Who will you see next?" she asked.

"I guess her daughter. Then they can make supper. Who knows? They might offer us some."

Ryan's face showed a fleeting glance of derision, but she quickly left the room, returning several moments later with Crystal Winston.

2

Manziuk thought Crystal looked composed. He guessed her age at eighteen.

She nodded.

"In high school?" he asked conversationally.

"I graduated this spring. In the fall, I'll be going to college. Ryerson."

His eyebrows lifted.

She shrugged. "I'm helping my mother for this weekend and the odd day. Normally, I work as a hostess and cashier at a restaurant a few miles from here. I'm part time during the school year and full time in the summer."

"Well, Crystal, can you tell us anything about this weekend? Did you hear the buzzer going off today, for instance?"

She answered quickly, as if she had already gone over the events in her mind. "Both times for Miss Preston. Then again after lunch. Twice in about twenty minutes."

"This was after Lorry Preston was back for lunch?"

"Yes."

"Do you know who it was?"

"Not for sure," she hesitated. "I think it was Bart Brodie. He looked terribly angry a little while after lunch, and I saw him going toward the garage. Of course, he's staying in the apartment above it, so he may have been just going there. But it was only a minute or so later that the buzzer went off."

"And it went again in about twenty minutes?"

She nodded.

"About what time would that have been?"

"Before my mom finished her nap."

"When did she finish her nap?"

"Always at two-thirty."

"And after that, were you out of the kitchen?"

"Only to take the lemonade."

"When was that?"

"I'd just put the strawberry shortcake in the oven. Mom and I had a cup of coffee after her nap, and then I made the shortcake. So it would have been around three o'clock."

"Did you see Bart Brodie again?"

"I saw him walking off with Ms. Jensen a little before we made the lemonade."

"Anything else you noticed this afternoon? Anyone going into the Japanese garden? Or anything that seemed unusual?"

"The Japanese garden?" she repeated slowly. "No, sir."

"So you were around the kitchen most of the afternoon, were you, Crystal?"

"Mostly. I cleared up things on the patio, of course, and I collected glasses from the bar, and I put some water in the flowers in the dining room and the day room. That's about it."

"Have you ever been troubled by strangers coming into the yard?"

"No, sir. They say the house two doors down was robbed during the winter when the owners were in Florida, but it turned out to be the chauffeur's brother-in-law who did it. They caught him pretty quickly."

"So this is a relatively peaceful area?"

"Yes, sir. There aren't many hitchhikers or hikers or such around here."

Manziuk sat up a bit and leaned forward. "What do you make of it, Crystal? Ever been involved in a murder before?"

"No, sir."

"Frightened?"

She leaned forward, her eyes earnest. "A little, I suppose. But more interested. Not everyone gets to be part of a police investigation."

"I guess that's true."

"Do you think it will happen again?"

"I doubt it. We rarely have two murders one after the other." She looked vaguely disappointed. "But on the other hand, you never know. It pays to be careful."

Crystal shivered.

Manziuk's tone was fatherly, "Any ideas as to who might have done it? Perhaps you noticed someone who didn't like Mrs. Martin."

Crystal tossed her head. "That's easy. Mrs. Fischer. She looked at her a few times like if she'd had a knife in her hand she'd have thrown it. Like when you read about someone looking daggers at another person? That was her."

"I see." He paused. "Anyone else?"

"I don't really think so," she said slowly. She looked down at her hands and then back at Manziuk. "Do you need to know everything?"

"I have to. We don't want someone running loose who might do this again, do we? No matter who it is."

Her right hand went up and touched one of her earrings. "Well, I know Mrs. Martin had an argument with her husband. They were in their room with the door shut, but I could hear them from the hallway as I went by. I don't know what they were saying, exactly, but they were talking loud, and then they quieted down like they were afraid they might be heard."

"Did you catch any words?"

"I didn't really. Not much, anyway." She looked embarrassed. "To tell the truth, I was trying to hear them."

Manziuk allowed a bit of a smile. Ryan, seated at the desk making notes, looked up and said, "Why shouldn't you? I know I would have."

Crystal turned slightly to face Ryan. "Well, you're supposed to try to ignore what people say. Eavesdropping and all."

"Honey, everybody listens," Ryan remarked dryly. "It's just that no one wants to admit to it."

"So what did you hear?" Manziuk asked.

Crystal shifted back to face him. "Well, from what I could make out, it was something to do with Friday night. Mrs. Martin had gone outside to talk to someone. I'm not sure who. But Mr. Martin was annoyed."

Manziuk nodded. There was a pause. "How did Mrs. Martin get along with the other guests?"

Crystal cocked her head to one side. "She flirted with all the men and ignored the women."

Manziuk laughed. "Not a feminist, I guess."

Crystal didn't deign to reply to this.

Manziuk stood up. "Okay, Crystal, we'll likely talk again. By the way, if you had to pick the murderer, who would it be?"

She looked up at him. "Mrs. Fischer, I guess. Or maybe Ms. Reimer."

"Who?" Manziuk couldn't disguise his surprise.

"Ms. Reimer. I think her name is Hildy."

"The neighbor," Ryan offered as Manziuk began to search the list of names Carnaby had given him.

"Why on earth would she do it?" Manziuk asked.

"Because she's Mr. Martin's ex-wife. And she crashed the party."

When Crystal had gone, Manziuk turned to Ryan.

"Who do you want to see next?" she asked. "Hildy Reimer?"

"Before I see anybody, I want to get two things straight. One is that I do the talking. Two is that you take the notes. Got it?"

"I thought I was helping."

"You haven't had enough experience yet to help."

"I've interviewed suspects and witnesses plenty of times."

"Not in a murder case, you haven't."

"Asking questions and trying to decide if people are telling the truth doesn't change whether it's murder, robbery or—"

"Maybe not. But I'll let you know when you can start asking questions. Okay?"

"Yes, sir." Her voice was stiff. "Who would you like to see now, sir?"

"Who found the body?" Manziuk asked.

Ryan consulted the list. "Kendall Brodie, Nick Donovan, and Lorry Preston."

"Let's have one of them in. Kendall. That's Brodie's son, isn't it? We'll talk to him."

3

Kendall quietly followed Ryan in and sat on the chair indicated. His face continued to look pale and sickly. His left hand twisted the school ring on his right hand.

Manziuk was in front of him, knees crossed, relaxed, slightly reminiscent of an actor in a cop movie from the 40's. But he was missing the fedora. "Now, Kendall," he said, his voice low and encouraging, "what we're interested in is fixing the time of death. You found the body, I believe?"

Kendall nodded.

"You were taking a walk?"

"Well, sort of."

"How do you 'sort of' take a walk?"

Kendall stared at Manziuk's waistline. "Oh, I'm sorry. The thing is I've been feeling pretty sick since it all happened. Did you see her? I did. It was horrible. She was so beautiful. And now—" He looked up apologetically. "I've never seen anyone before who was killed. My grandmother, but she died in her sleep and I only saw her for a second at the funeral home. Nothing like this."

"That's all right," Manziuk comforted, his eyelids half shut. "It takes a while to get used to. Strangulation isn't very nice. Take your time."

Ryan looked up. Avoiding Manziuk's eyes, she said, "Maybe you could tell us what you did right after lunch, Mr. Brodie?"

He cleared his throat. "I sat and listened while Nick and Hildy talked about skiing. Then Lorry came back and we talked about law school mostly. Afterwards, Nick and I went for a swim. Mr. Martin was in the pool already."

"Did you go to your room to change?" Manziuk asked, his eyes on Ryan.

"We used the change house."

"And after your swim?"

"Dad asked me to make a fourth for a game of snooker, so I dried off and went in."

"What time was that?"

"Two o'clock."

"On the nose?"

"Maybe five after. I looked at my watch while I was getting dressed."

"What time did the snooker game break up?"

"Around three. My mother called to say there was lemonade on the patio, so Hildy and I quit after two games. Douglass and my dad kept playing."

"Who else was on the patio?"

"Let me think. Lorry, Nick. Peter came out for a while, and then went back in to join my dad and Douglass. My mother was there, too, I think. Then Jillian came down."

"What about Mrs. Fischer?"

"She went upstairs right after lunch. I didn't see her again until the police herded us all into the day room."

"What about your cousin, Bart?"

"I think he went back to his room above the garage."

"After the lemonade, where did you go?"

"Everyone kind of wandered off to do their own thing. It was too hot for tennis. I decided to find a book I'd been meaning to read and settle down inside. Air conditioning, you know."

Manziuk smiled. "Yes, I know."

"I couldn't find the book in my room, so I decided I must have left it down here. I went into Dad's office to find it, but I started talking to him. I never did find the book. We talked about the firm and Nick's not wanting to join, and what I'll be doing in the first while. Then I realized Lorry had been playing the piano for quite a while. I'd promised at lunch that I'd take her to see the Japanese garden when it got cooler, so I went to see if she was ready to go for a walk. We met Nick outside, coming from the rose garden, and asked him to go with us. Some walk, huh?"

"What time was it when you went to your dad's office?"

"Around three-thirty."

"Which of you actually found the body?"

He thought for a minute. "Lorry, I guess. She was a little ahead of me, and Nick was behind me. She saw around the corner first and said something in a really odd voice about how someone was lying up ahead. I thought she was nuts, and so did Nick, but she wasn't. She went closer and screamed, and then Nick ran past us and lifted Jillian up and saw she was dead. She was—she was—" Kendall put his hand up to his eyes.

"What happened next?"

With an effort, Kendall continued. "Lorry clutched my arm. Nick said for us to call the police, so Lorry and I ran back to the house. She must have phoned, because I was feeling so sick I just headed for the nearest bathroom."

"Did anyone else see the body?"

"After she phoned the police, Lorry told Dad and they went up to Peter's room to tell him. I know he didn't believe it. I heard him arguing with her and telling her this wasn't a very funny joke. Then he insisted she take him to where the body was so he could see for himself. I waited for the police. I didn't want to see Jillian again. Once was enough, believe me. When I heard the sirens, I ran out to the front of the house and showed the police where to go."

"You have a very good memory for details, Mr. Brodie," Manziuk said.

A trace of a smile touched Kendall's wan features. "I ought to. I'm a lawyer."

Manziuk looked surprised.

"I just passed my bar exam. I'm joining my father's firm."

"Not bad," Manziuk said appreciatively.

Kendall smiled a little more easily. "I know I'm lucky to have the father I do. I only hope I won't disappoint him. So many people will assume I got the job because of Dad, and I guess it's true, but I want to show them I can handle it on my own merit."

"Did you know Jillian Martin?"

The muscles at the corners of Kendall's mouth tightened as if the question brought him back to reality with a thud. He looked down. "I'd seen her picture but never met her before."

"She must have been about your age."

Kendall looked up and smiled briefly. "Yes and no. I've just been a college boy up until now."

"This Shauna. That's Mrs. Martin's older sister?" asked Manziuk.

"That's right."

"Had you met her before?"

"I didn't even know she had a sister."

"Can you think of any reason for someone to want to kill Mrs. Martin?"

Kendall bit his lower lip. "You mean someone here, don't you? In this house?"

"Someone who knew her, yes."

"To tell you the truth, I think it'll turn out to be someone we don't know. I really can't see any of the people here murdering someone."

"You could hear Lorry playing the piano the whole time?"

"I couldn't swear that she played constantly, but it was pretty steady. The music room is next door to Dad's study, you know, so you hear the piano in the background, even with both doors shut. Of course, Dad and I were talking. I can't say I recognized anything she was playing."

"Is she that bad?"

"Oh, no, she's very good. But I didn't recognize the songs. When I asked her later, she said they were hymns, you know, from church."

"Just one more question. You said Nick was coming from the rose garden. Do you have any idea what he was doing there?"

Kendall shifted uncomfortably. "No, I don't. You'll have to ask him."

"Nick Donovan is your friend, isn't he?"

"We've roomed together for three years of law school."

"He's a lawyer, too?"

"On paper." Kendall's voice held a touch of bitterness. "Actually, he says he prefers skiing."

"But he graduated from law school. Is he a hard worker?"

"Him? He never works hard at anything. Just breezes through everything. And the girls all go for him, too."

"Do you think Jillian Martin went for him?" Ryan's voice interrupted and Manziuk frowned.

"Maybe." Kendall laughed, but not with amusement. "Why should she be any different?" He paused, then said earnestly. "Look, don't get me wrong. Nick is my best friend and a great guy. I'm just a little angry because I thought I was doing him a big favor by getting him a really good offer, and he casually turned it down. That's all."

"What was the offer?"

"To join my father's law firm."

"Okay, Kendall," Manziuk said. "If we need you again, we'll let you know."

Kendall left.

Manziuk got up and lumbered over to sit on the desk. "You don't appear to take directions very well," he said. "Next time, would you at least wait until I seem to have run out of questions before you jump in?"

"Sorry. It was an accident."

He snorted. "The trouble with women is they think they should do all the talking."

Sparks flew from her eyes and she opened her mouth to protest, but he cut her off as neatly as a surgeon. "Get me the girl who found the body. The cousin from out west."

Ryan got up and went out. Her footsteps were determined. Her closing of the door was quite firm both as she went out and when she returned.

4

Manziuk stood long enough to shake Lorry's hand and see that she was seated in the other armchair. "You're not from around these parts, are you?"

"No. I'm from a small town near Edmonton."

"The farthest west I've been is the Windsor-Detroit area. Though I have been east and south. I hear it's all pretty flat out there on the prairies."

"Parts are. But I live not too far from the Rocky Mountains."

"Hmm. Not flat there."

"No, sir."

Ryan, her voice impatient, asked sharply, "You were one of the ones that found the body, weren't you?"

Lorry turned slightly to look at Ryan. "Yes, I was."

"What did you see?"

Lorry's description of the events in the garden matched Kendall's.

"Had you become acquainted with Jillian Martin over the weekend?"

"We spoke a few times. That's all."

"What impression did you have of her?"

"She seemed very unkind to her sister."

"How so?"

She told them about the events of Saturday night.

"You believe Shauna murdered her sister?"

"Oh, no!" Lorry's face took on a horrified expression. "You asked me about Jillian and I told you what little I had observed. I never meant to imply that Shauna could have killed her sister. She didn't even seem to be angry with her."

"Shauna wasn't angry with her sister?" Manziuk's voice was heavy with disbelief.

"I know it's hard to believe, but she wasn't. She blamed herself for making Jillian upset."

"Could she have been putting on an act?"

"I really don't think so, Inspector. As a matter of fact, she reminded me of a couple of women I know. For the last eight months, I've been volunteering one evening a week in a shelter for abused women. The kinds of things Shauna said about Jillian were very similar to what some of those women would say about their husbands. How it was their own fault for making their husbands angry. One of the first steps that abused women need to take is to realize that they are not the ones who are to blame."

"So you feel Jillian was abusing Shauna?"

"It sounds really unusual, I know, but yes, I guess I do. Jillian was so angry, it was irrational. There was nothing wrong with the way Shauna looked. Jillian herself was wearing heavier makeup and a more revealing dress. It was ridiculous for her to attack Shauna."

"If Shauna didn't kill her sister, who do you think might have?"

Lorry's eyes widened. "Do you actually believe it was one of the people in this house?"

"There's a very good chance."

She shook her head in disbelief.

"You played the piano for quite a while this afternoon?"

"Yes. I have some music books along, and Ellen said no one would mind."

"What time was it when you began playing?"

"I didn't look at my watch, but we had lemonade on the patio about three, and I drank mine pretty quickly and then went upstairs to get my music. It was so hot outside. I guess I'm not used to this heat. So it was probably about a quarter after three at the latest."

"While you were playing, did you see or hear anyone?"

"Nick came in for a few seconds just after I had started to play. And Ellen looked in once. She was going upstairs to lie down for a few minutes. And then Kendall came to see if I wanted to go for a walk."

"When did Ellen come in?"

"I'm not sure. Maybe ten minutes after I started. I know Kendall came in at a quarter to four because we both looked at our watches."

"So you didn't see or hear anything that could help us?"

"I'm sorry."

"Okay. Don't hesitate to call on us if something comes to you." He showed Lorry to the door and then turned back to look at Ryan.

"Can you not understand that I know what I'm doing?"

"You were babbling on about the countryside."

"I was trying to make her comfortable. She just found a murdered woman about her own age. Whether she realizes it or not, she's likely in shock."

Ryan looked down at her notebook.

"If you can't keep your mouth shut, at least try to understand the track I'm on and follow it. Do you think you could handle that much?"

She looked up. Brown eyes met steel gray ones. "I know what you think," she said.

"And what do I think?"

"That I've been promoted because I'm a black woman."

"What if I do?"

"I would have been promoted anyway. Sooner or later. Because I'm good."

"Then stop trying to prove you can do my job and do your own!"

"I am trying to do my job." Her voice was even as she spit out each word.

"Right now, your job is to do what I tell you! Until you prove to me you can handle that, you don't do anything else. Now, I have a murder to solve. I don't have time to waste on you. Either do what you're here for or get out and let me send for someone else who isn't overly challenged by taking notes and watching for inconsistencies in the answers we get! Now, can you do it?"

She broke eye contact as she looked down at the page in front of her that she had filled with shorthand. "Yes, I can do it," she said quietly. She looked up again. "But I'm not a secretary. I'm a police officer."

"Then stop wasting my time and go get me the third person who found the body. Maybe he noticed something the others missed."

5

Nicholas James Donovan, known to his friends and acquaintances as Nick, sat stiff and straight in the old leather arm chair, eyes attentive as he waited for the Inspector's first question.

Keen, direct eyes, thought Manziuk. And, perhaps, just a trifle wary? Manziuk leaned back in his chair and asked lazily, "I understand you were involved in finding Mrs. Martin's body?"

"Yes." Nick's eyes moved away from Manziuk's.

"Ever found a body before?" Manziuk asked.

Nick looked back at him. "No," he snapped.

"An unnerving experience."

"Yes."

"Tell me about it."

"I thought it was a joke at first. I teased Lorry about imagining things. Then I saw her…"

"Not a very nice sight."

"She was so beautiful, so alive, and to see her like that…" He bit his lower lip and took a deep breath. "What exactly do you want to know, Inspector? I don't think you really want to chat about finding dead bodies, do you?"

Manziuk studied the handsome young man before him. A good-looking, bright young man. And a wary one. Was he afraid of being arrested for murder?

"We have to talk to all the people who were here at the time of Mrs. Martin's death."

"So you want my alibi?"

"If you don't mind. Say from about two o'clock until the discovery of the body."

"Very well. I ate lunch on the terrace with the others. Then I went for a swim and more or less lazed around. We had some drinks at approximately three o'clock, after which I wandered over to the rose garden. It was twenty past three, by the way. At about a quarter to four, I went back toward the house and saw Kendall coming out with Lorry. We went to the Japanese garden and found the body."

"So, from about three-twenty until three-forty-five you were alone in the rose garden?"

"Yes." Nick was looking directly at him. "I realize that isn't a particularly good alibi, but it happens to be the truth."

"Lorry Preston says you stopped in at the music room."

"Just for a couple of minutes, if that. It was right before I went to the rose garden."

"Why did you go to the rose garden?"

"To meet Mrs. Martin."

Chapter Nine

"You went there to meet Mrs. Martin?" Manziuk asked.

"Jillian," Nick replied. "Is that better?"

"And how long have you known Jillian Martin?"

Nick shifted uncomfortably in the chair. "I knew Jill Jensen. I met her just over four years ago. I was twenty-one; she was nineteen. We dated for about six months, and I haven't seen her since."

"Did you know she would be at the Brodies' this weekend?"

"Of course not. I'd heard the name Jillian Martin, but I never dreamed there was a connection."

"When did you first see her this weekend?"

"Friday when she arrived. I came downstairs and saw a bunch of people outside. I knew Mr. Brodie's partners were coming for the weekend and I'd never met them, so I glanced out just to see how they looked. Jill—Jillian—was in the car with the door open. At first, I couldn't believe it was her."

"Why not?"

"Because when I knew her, she was a waitress at a bar near where I was working for the summer. It wasn't a bad place or anything, but you don't really expect a cocktail waitress to show up with a high-class lawyer—not as his wife, anyway!"

"Who put an end to your dating Jillian?" Manziuk continued.

Nick stared at him for a moment. "She did."

"And why," asked Manziuk casually, "were you meeting her this afternoon?"

Nick had been sitting forward in his chair. Now he leaned back and gave a low laugh. "Look, I'd better go back and start over. This has all been so crazy. I mean, you don't expect your old girlfriend to show up married to a top lawyer and then get herself killed all in one weekend. I realize I'm a logical suspect. Motive jealousy or revenge or some such thing. And I also realize that if I don't tell you the 'whole truth and nothing but the truth,' you'll find out and that'll make it look worse."

"Okay, start from the top."

"The last summer of my college days, I worked for a small law firm in the sticks. Mostly, I sat in the law library and researched a lot of boring stuff. There was a reasonably classy tavern nearby, and I used to go there after five to wake up. Jill was a waitress. She was… the word 'beautiful' is inadequate—and I got interested—along with a lot of other people. She went out with me and we—or I should say *I*—fell in love." Nick's voice was slow and hesitant. "I asked her to marry me. I thought she would. I thought she felt the same as I did. She didn't. She said she had higher expectations. I told her I'd be a lawyer in a few years, and I'd also been asked to do some professional skiing, and that if I was any good at either I'd have no trouble supporting a family. But she said she wasn't taking any chances. She basically said that if I'd had money right then, she'd have married me, but since I didn't—" Nick paused for a moment and studied the floor. "I kept on trying to get her to change her mind. Finally, she got her point across. A couple of months later, I went back to the tavern once just to see if she had changed her mind, I guess. But the bartender said she'd taken a better job somewhere else and he didn't know her address."

"Do you have a girlfriend now?" Manziuk asked.

Nick flashed a grin. "Lots of them."

"No one in particular?"

"I believe in playing the field. When I met Jill, I was young and inexperienced. She did me a favor—showed a lot more sense than I did." He sat forward again, hands on knees. "Look, if she'd married me, it would have lasted about a year, if that. If you've got any idea that I'm still in love with her, assuming I ever really was, get it out of your head. After I got over the shock of seeing her, I was happy she'd done well. Martin is successful and seems like a nice guy. I was glad for her."

"She wanted to meet you in the rose garden?" Manziuk asked.

"Yes. She came over while I was in the pool and said she had a surprise for me and I should be in the rose garden at three-thirty sharp. She didn't wait for a reply—just smiled rather mysteriously and left."

"What time was that?"

"About one-thirty. We all had drinks later on, but I didn't want to question her with other people around. No one here knew that we had ever known each other and, frankly, I preferred to keep it that way."

"The rose garden? Not the Japanese garden?"

Nick shrugged. "That's what I heard her say."

"Had Mrs. Martin talked to you on Friday or Saturday?"

"Not really. She tried to talk once on Saturday, but I found an excuse to get away. I was afraid she might want to go over old times or something. So I guess I more or less avoided her. Nothing personal, but I'd pretty well forgotten about her and I wasn't sure how she'd take that."

"Did you think she was happy?" Manziuk asked with a little more sharpness.

Nick looked puzzled. "Happy? I guess so. She seemed to be having a good time."

"What were the attitudes of the other wives toward her? Mrs. Brodie and Mrs. Fischer."

"Ellen and Anne?" Nick shrugged. "Okay, I guess." He glanced from Manziuk to Ryan and back to Manziuk again.

"How about Mr. Martin? Did he and his wife get along?"

"I guess so."

"And Mrs. Martin's sister, Shauna? I understand there was a bit of a disturbance Saturday evening?"

"Saturday evening?"

"Miss Jensen and Mr. Bart Brodie were late for supper."

"Oh. Oh, yeah, I guess they were."

"I understand she looked quite different from before."

He shrugged. "She had a new dress or something. I really wasn't paying much attention."

"According to Lorry Preston, you stopped in at the music room around three-fifteen today."

"Yeah, I did. I asked her if she wanted to do something later. She said she was going to play the piano for a while. I told her I'd come back."

"And you went straight to the rose garden?"

"I knew I was early, but I wanted to think."

"What did you do when she didn't show up?"

"To tell you the truth, I was thinking about some other stuff and I had no idea how much time had passed until I looked at my watch and it was nearly a quarter to four. Then I decided she'd stood me up. I really wasn't worried about it. In fact, I was relieved."

"What would you say if I told you someone in this house had strangled Mrs. Martin?"

Nick continued to look perplexed. "I can't believe it was Mr. Martin or any of the Brodies or Lorry. I guess I don't know the others as well, but I can't see why any of them would want to do it." He looked at Manziuk and then relaxed a little. A disarming smile appeared. "I sure wish I could tell what you're thinking. You know, you remind me a lot of one of my law professors. Absolutely inscrutable."

Manziuk allowed the slightest of smiles to touch the corner of his mouth. "If you do think of something that might help us, don't forget it's your duty as a law-abiding citizen to pass the information along."

Nick laughed and walked out.

"I'll bet the part about having lots of girlfriends is accurate," Ryan commented dryly.

Manziuk stretched back and touched the fingertips of his hands together. "He doesn't seem to have noticed much this weekend."

"Perhaps he had other things on his mind," Ryan suggested.

"Perhaps."

"Who do you want to talk to next?"

"See if the husband is able to talk with us."

2

Peter Martin slowly followed Ryan in and sank without a word into Manziuk's chair.

Manziuk, who had been considering the titles of the books on the shelves of the study, squeezed himself into the other chair and studied Jillian Martin's husband. The man certainly gave the appearance of someone who had suffered a sudden shock. His eyes were puffy and red. An air of despondency seemed to have bent his shoulders.

"Mr. Martin, I'm very sorry to disturb you at this time."

Peter's hand came up as if to brush away a curtain. "That's all right," he said flatly. "You have a job to do. I just hope you get whoever did this. You know," he said with a small ironic laugh, "I'm one of those people who strenuously supported legislation against capital punishment. But right now I could beat the guy's brains out all by myself. I guess your viewpoint depends a lot on how close it comes to you, eh?"

Manziuk nodded. "Mr. Martin, do you have any idea who could have done this?"

Peter slowly shook his head. "I wish I did."

"She had no enemies you're aware of?"

"No. Oh, don't get me wrong. I'm not going to sit here and tell you there weren't people who disliked her. Everybody has enemies of some sort. But it takes something a lot stronger than dislike to murder someone that way. It takes pure hatred. I don't know of anyone who felt that way. Nobody who hated her."

"But someone murdered her."

"Then you'd better get busy looking for some lunatic."

"We have police checking this entire area. If there was a stranger on these grounds, we'll find out."

"Do that then. And find him."

"Mr. Martin, I understand your wife and her sister had an argument after supper last night. Can you give us any further information?"

Peter sat up straight. "You surely don't suspect Shauna, do you? That's absolutely ridiculous!"

"We're checking everyone."

"Well, don't get carried away. Yes, they had a difference of opinion. Jillian isn't—wasn't—very tactful. But by this morning, Shauna realized that Jillian was right and she apologized. Shauna adored Jillian."

"Jillian was the older of the two?"

"Well, no. Shauna was older. But Jillian was the one with the ideas, the vitality. Shauna's quite plain and not very outgoing. Most people would take Jillian to be older. She was out in the world more—knew what was what. Jillian used to say Shauna was an innocent babe. No sophistication."

"What about Bart Brodie? What part did he play in this quarrel between Shaua and Jillian?"

He shifted in the chair. "Who knows why he did it? Likely for his own amusement. Anyway, Jillian was good and mad at him. I wouldn't be surprised if she told him off. She had a temper, you know. Nobody'd walk over her." His voice showed his pride. "Ask Bart if you want to know what he was up to."

"You didn't go with them to the nightclub?"

"No. I'm not much on dancing and all the noise, especially right after a big meal. There's a good bar here, so I just took it easy."

"Nick and Lorry also stayed?"

"Shauna did, too. We had a game of pool and then sat around and talked. Mostly about religion."

"Religion?" Manziuk asked, surprised.

Peter Martin smiled for the first time. "Lorry's an unusual girl. Could have a lot of men on her string. But she seems more interested in God than in men. Don't remember how we got on the topic. Oh, yes. I asked her what she did. Goes to a Bible college. We got into a pretty good discussion about life."

"Did Nick say much?"

"Nope. Mostly Lorry and me. She can hold her own, too. Surprised me. I thought I'd have her rattled in a few minutes, but she held out all the way. Knows what she believes in and what she wants out of life, too. A lot like Jillian that way." His voice lost its animation on the last sentence and he stopped talking.

"Jillian was your second wife, I believe."

"Fourth. And I know where you're headed. You figure she married me for my money. Well, why else does a twenty-two-year-old marry a forty-three-year-old who's getting a pot and starting to go gray? Of course she did."

Manziuk again looked surprised. "You didn't mind?"

"Not at all. If having a bit of money can't get you a gorgeous young dame, then why have it? She married me for my money and I married her because I happened to want a young attractive blonde. We respected each other and I think we had as good a marriage as most people I know."

"What about your other marriages?"

"As I was telling Nick yesterday, you make a few mistakes. I got married early. College sweetheart and all that. It lasted twelve years. We got a divorce. I'd already met Hildy. She contracted to do some personnel stuff for the firm I was with before I joined this one, and we got married a while after my divorce was final. We lasted five years. I felt a little, shall we say, tied down, and she got mad and divorced me. I played the field for a while and then married Genevieve. She took me for a good deal of alimony and went off with some guy from a rock band. She could have done a lot better.

"I decided since my first wife had brown hair, Hildy black, and Genevieve red, it was time for a blonde. I met Jillian at a party. She was with a doctor. I took her away from him and we ended up married."

"Would you have gotten a divorce?"

Peter laughed. "What a question!" He leaned his face against the back of his hand for a moment, then looked Manziuk in the eye. "Yes," he said thoughtfully. "Sooner or later. One of us would have gotten itchy feet. As I was saying to Lorry last night, life is to live. I don't believe there's anything after. What difference does it make if you get married once or a dozen times, just so long as you enjoy yourself? But," he said more seriously, "a friendly divorce is one thing. No one has the right to cut off life, especially from someone who was so beautiful. Whoever did this deserves a very slow and very painful death." His voice quivered. "You get him. And when you get him—"

"Mr. Martin, were you aware that your wife knew Nick Donovan?"

Surprise, then bewilderment registered. "What exactly do you mean?"

"About four years ago, he asked her to marry him and she turned him down. That's what he says, anyway. Did she mention this to you?"

"That's what he says?" Peter repeated.

"Yes. However, he also says he has had no contact with her since, and was completely unaware of her marriage or that she would be here this weekend."

"I certainly don't know anything about it. Nick and Jillian, eh? That's a bit humorous. He reminds me a little of myself twenty years ago, except I was married with a couple of kids. Maybe he reminds me of what I should have been, unencumbered. So he tried to marry her? I wonder if she cared about him at all?"

"He says she would have married him if he'd had money."

Peter laughed. "Smart girl. She was no fool, inspector, no matter what anyone might tell you. She knew what she wanted and she worked hard to get it. I don't mind telling you I wasn't particularly in a marrying mood when I met her. But she said it was marriage or nothing. So I married her. She was one smart cookie."

"What's your opinion of Nick Donovan?"

"I've got a kid somewhere that must be nearly his age. Maybe a few years younger. Same age as Lorry, come to think of it." He paused momentarily. "But you asked about Nick. You know we offered him a chance to join us?"

Manziuk nodded.

"He turned it down. I told him he's making a big mistake because it may be his one big chance. If Nick goes into this skiing—say he's good for five years. He's what? Twenty-five. He can't last long. Most skiers are young. So a few years from now he wants to get a good place in law, who's going to want him?"

Manziuk consulted the list Carnaby had given him. "What about Hildy Reimer? Someone mentioned that she's your ex-wife. Did you know she was going to be here this weekend?"

"No, I did not."

"Do you know why she came?"

"I was told it was because she was having her apartment redecorated and she had no more idea of my presence here than I did of hers."

"Is there a chance Ms. Reimer is still in love with you?"

He raised his eyebrows. "Hardly," he said with a twist of his lips. "She divorced me."

"Why?"

"She didn't like my spending time with other women. As a matter of fact, she was surprisingly sticky. I thought she was more—well, modern, I guess. But she certainly didn't murder Jillian. I'm sure she was merely curious, no more. She's deceptive. Much softer than you'd guess."

"What exactly do you mean?"

Peter coughed and adjusted his position. "Well, she looks like a real hard-boiled female executive—and she is. She does a good job and she works like a man. But she's got a feminine side, too. She's a good mother and, I guess for the right man, she'd be a good wife. Like Ellen. Home and family first. But I wasn't the man she should have married, and we both realized it."

"There is a child?"

"Yes. A boy. She has custody."

"Have you seen him recently?"

"Look, no bones about it. I'm not the family type. My first wife and I had three kids. If they turn out okay, it will be entirely her doing. It's the same in Hildy's case."

"Has she tried to talk to you this weekend?"

"No."

"Did she try to talk with your wife?"

"Not to my knowledge."

"Mr. Martin, what would you say if I told you your wife asked Nick Donovan to meet her in the rose garden at three-thirty?"

"But she wasn't in the rose garden, was she? Or was she killed after that?"

"He says she never came. That one of them must have gotten mixed up as to which garden it was."

"Does he say why she wanted to see him?"

"He says he doesn't know. That it was her idea."

Peter smiled. "Likely miffed."

"What?"

"Well, if he really used to be her boyfriend, as you implied, she probably expected him to be still carrying a torch. Since he wasn't, she likely wanted to find out why. Make him sweat."

"He wasn't?"

"Not unless he's a very good actor. Of course, he probably is. But my guess is that our Nicky's been hit hard, and not by Jillian. Lorry Preston's the one who's got him in a tailspin."

"He could be using her."

"What? To make Jillian jealous? No, I won't say he might not have started paying attention to Lorry because of Jillian, but I'd put money on it that it's more than that now." Peter's face sagged, the animation gone. "Look, Inspector, I can't believe we're doing anything but wasting time talking about the people in this house. But if one of them did it, I want you to get him. Only a beast could do something like this! Whoever did this, I want him punished to the full extent of the law!"

"Don't worry. We'll find the guilty party. Now, can you tell me what you did after lunch today?"

"Me?" His face went blank for a second. Then he produced a wry smile. "I suppose I'm the prime suspect, am I? Well, don't waste any more of your time. I didn't do it. But if you want to know my whereabouts, all right. I ate on the terrace. Jillian and Shauna were at the same table. Jillian didn't appear to be very hungry. Neither did Shauna, for that matter. After lunch, I stopped for a drink at the bar. Bart was there. He appeared to be a bit out of humor. He finished his drink and went out. I finished mine and went upstairs. Jillian and I talked for a while."

"Talked?"

Peter flushed. "I suppose someone heard us. Yes, we disagreed. I didn't think she needed to be so upset with Shauna. She wasn't pleased with my suggestion. To be truthful, I liked arguing with her. She stood her ground so well. A worthy opponent. None of my other wives were nearly as capable. Jillian never gave way to tears or recriminations. Clear and cool, that was her.

"Anyway, after a while, I decided to go downstairs. George was getting up a game of billiards, and Douglass, Hildy, and Kendall joined him. I sat back with a cold one and watched. And we talked, of course. I think Jillian came down a short while later. She was out on the terrace."

"Actually, you were overheard talking about Friday night. Something about going outside."

He looked at the floor. "Oh, that."

"Yes?"

"Friday night, Shauna went out on the terrace with Bart. Jillian said she was going to see what they were doing. Frankly, I didn't buy it. So I pretended to go upstairs, but I slipped out front and went around so I could watch. I saw Jillian come out, and sure enough she went and found Bart and Shauna, and a few minutes later, they went in. Then Jillian stopped to say something to Douglass, who was sitting alone by the pool. I knew she'd be coming in a second, so I hurried back around the front and upstairs. Jillian came up a few minutes later, but I didn't say anything then. I did this afternoon, though. I told her that I didn't think it was up to her to protect Shauna. She's twenty-seven years old; surely she knows how to deal with men by now. That's what we were arguing about."

"Okay, go on with what else you did. You were in the games room, I believe."

"I watched for a while, and then I played some billiards with George and Douglass after Kendall and Hildy left. Practicing some shots, you know. Seeing who could make the hardest ones. Then about three-thirty, I went up to our room. Jillian wasn't there. I lay down with part of the newspaper, and after a few minutes, I fell asleep. When I woke up it was after four. I was on my way down to join the others when I was met by George and Lorry coming to tell me they'd found Jillian's body. I thought it was some kind of very unfunny joke. But of course I was wrong." Tears came to his eyes and he raised his hand to wipe them away.

Manziuk jerked his head at Ryan. She looked at him. He jerked his head again. This time she got up and walked around to Peter's chair.

"Constable Ryan will take you back to the others, Mr. Martin. If you think of anything we've over-looked, please talk to me later."

"Yes. All right." He stood up quickly, then swayed. Ryan started to help him. "No," he said, shaking his head. "I'm fine." He looked toward Manziuk. "Get him, Inspector."

Back in the day room, Peter sank down in a large easy chair and covered his face with his hands. Hildy Reimer immediately brought him a cup of coffee.

Peter looked at it. "Get me something stronger."

Ryan turned to look for Shauna. She was huddled in a corner of the room. When Ryan came toward her, she stood up.

"You're Shauna Jensen?"

"That's right," she said tonelessly.

"Inspector Manziuk and I would like to have a word with you, please."

"All right."

Ryan led the way and the woman followed. Her shoulders were hunched forward, and she looked like a rag doll, with no life in her.

As the two women walked out, Bart Brodie swore, then picked up the whiskey bottle he'd managed to sneak in from the bar. The cork was stuck. He finally got it out. He held the bottle up for a moment and looked at it. As if in a trance, he turned the bottle upside down and watched as the golden liquid spilled out into a large Rorschach blot on the soft rose carpet.

The others in the room, startled at first, said nothing, except for George, who told his nephew in unprintable terms exactly what he thought of him.

At this, Bart merely started, then laughed, his mood apparently evaporated. He stooped to help Ellen and Lorry clean up.

Chapter Ten

In the study, Shauna sank into the chair Ryan indicated and looked up at Inspector Manziuk. Remembering what Lorry Preston had said, he wanted to ask her to remove the sunglasses, but he chose not to comment for now. He hoped Ryan would keep her mouth shut.

"Well, Miss Jensen," he said in a fatherly tone. "This must have come as a great shock to you."

"Yes," she said softly.

"You realize that someone killed your sister. We have to find out who, so we'll appreciate any help you can give us."

She nodded.

"Can you tell me something about your sister? How old was she, for instance?"

"She just had her twenty-third birthday last month. There was quite a party."

"And your own age?"

"Twenty-seven."

"So Mrs. Martin was your younger sister. How long had she been married?"

"A year. She got married on her birthday."

"So her birthday this year was also her first anniversary?"

"Yes."

"This was her first marriage?"

"Yes."

"What did she do previously? Did she have a job?"

She shrugged.

Ryan coughed.

Manziuk ignored her. "She finished high school?"

"Yes. She worked as a waitress for a while, but then she left home to go to Toronto and, eventually, she got a good job in a women's store. A boutique. But she really wanted to be a model, or maybe an actress."

"And did she succeed?"

"She seemed to be doing pretty well. Then she met Peter, and he wanted to marry her."

"So she gave up her career?"

"I guess."

"You aren't sure?"

She shifted in the chair. "Well, I think she still wanted to get into films or something. Being Peter's wife wouldn't stop her from that, would it?"

"No, I expect not," Manziuk replied dryly. "Was she happy in her marriage?"

He was looking at her, but the dark glasses were like a brick wall hiding her eyes, hiding her thoughts. She took her time answering the new question, as if she had to consider it.

"Happy?" she said at last. "Well, she had what she wanted."

Ryan apparently couldn't keep herself from butting in. "She wanted to marry a well-off lawyer?"

Manziuk frowned.

"She'd have preferred a banker or someone in films. But a lawyer was too good to pass up." Shauna's voice was unconcerned.

"I see," Manziuk said. His glance at Ryan might have been perceived as apologetic. "Was Mr. Martin aware she had married him for his money?"

Shauna mouth dropped open. "Did she?"

"I thought you just said that."

"Oh." She moved in the chair. "Well, she wouldn't have married him if he didn't have any. But I think she liked him a lot. He's really very nice."

"Had your sister or Mr. Martin ever thought of getting a divorce?"

"I don't think so. She never said."

"When did you last see her alive?"

"We were at the same table at lunch. I went up first. She came to my room for a minute or so later on. Then I went out."

"Where did you go?"

"Walking. With Bart Brodie. There's a ravine behind the house. We went there."

"And you got back at what time?"

"I don't know. I was going to my room to change when I met Mrs. Brodie. She said she had to talk to me, and then she said Jillian was dead."

"Okay. Just a few more questions, Miss Jensen. Saturday afternoon you went and got your hair done and bought a new dress. I understand your sister didn't approve of it. Is that true?"

She stiffened. Her words were evenly spaced and without any emotion. "She pointed out to me that it didn't suit me. She was quite right."

"What did you do with the dress?"

"I'm not sure."

"Did Bart Brodie encourage you to get the dress and a new hairdo?"

"Yes."

"Was your sister angry with him?"

"She didn't think I should listen to him. She was right."

"I see. Well, thank you for your cooperation." He stood and opened the door for her. She was about to go out when he said, "Miss Jensen, if you had to pick the murderer, who do you think it might be?"

Her mouth twisted and for the first time she looked as though she might have some emotions after all. But it quickly passed, and she said evenly, "I can't imagine anyone killing Jillian. There's no reason. It was probably someone who escaped from a mental hospital. You know. For the insane. You'd do better combing the countryside than wasting your time here."

She started out the door.

"Do you always wear sunglasses in the house?" Manziuk flung at her.

"I—I—My eyes are very sore. Too much sunlight." She rushed out.

Ryan moved to the door and raised her eyebrows. But all she said was, "Who now?"

"Bart Brodie," Manziuk replied, a lazy smile on his face. "He seems to enjoy causing controversy. Let's see what he has to say about all this."

2

Before Ryan could respond, there was a sharp rap on the door.

George Brodie walked in. "I'm sorry to interrupt, but some of us have been talking and we have a few questions."

"For instance?" Manziuk asked lazily.

"Well, we..." For a corporate lawyer, Brodie appeared rather nervous. "We were wondering how long we have to remain together. Some of the ladies and Mr. Martin would prefer to go to their rooms. Are you planning to interrogate each of us one by one?"

"When we finish checking through the house, we'll certainly let you all go and be more comfortable. As to talking with each one—not interrogating, surely!—why, yes, I do like to have a little chat with everyone. So often some irrelevant little detail remembered by someone not even remotely connected with the murder can give us the clue we need."

"Do you seriously suspect one of these people?"

"Why not?"

George looked around his study, his eyes flitting from bookcases to desk and back to Manziuk. "Well, it's just—absurd! I know them. They're ordinary people. Not murderers!"

"You know Hildy Reimer? Did you know she'd been married to Peter Martin?"

George coughed. "No, I didn't know her. He's been in the firm five years. I knew the wife before Jillian. But my wife knows Ms. Reimer."

"She knows her well?"

He looked down. "No, I guess not."

"You know Shauna Jensen?"

"I've met her once or twice before." His eyes returned to gaze at Manziuk's face. "But surely you can see at a glance that neither of these women would have done a thing so horrible."

"No, I'm afraid I can't, Mr. Brodie. By the way, since you're here, what did you do after lunch today?"

"Surely you don't suspect me?"

"Just a routine question."

George's cheeks had reddened. "Inspector, this is outrageous! You should be looking for the criminal somewhere other than in my house. You are wasting taxpayers' money questioning my family and my guests. I've a good mind to call the police commissioner and see what she thinks of this line of inquiry."

"The commissioner would just tell you to cooperate with the police instead of wasting our precious time."

George didn't speak for a minute. He glanced away and breathed deeply, giving Manziuk the impression of someone gathering his anger back into a box. Then he said quietly, "After lunch, I came to my study to take care of some minor business items. My nephew found me here and we talked for a few minutes. I then played billiards with some others. Mr. Fischer, my son, and Ms. Reimer. Mr. Martin was also present. The others left after a while. When they were all gone, I stayed behind to tidy up. Then I came back to my office to answer some e-mail. Kendall came in a few moments later. I think he said he was looking for a book. He and I started talking, and I think it was about a quarter to four when he said he should see if Lorry wanted to go out for a while. I stayed here until Lorry Preston knocked on my door and told me what had happened. I was on my computer during that time, finishing up my e-mail."

"Can I have someone check your computer? It lists times, doesn't it?"

"That's right. I wrote a few messages before Kendall came in, and a few while he was here, and several more after he left. The computer is right there." He indicated the desk, where Ryan had pushed the small laptop to one corner.

"Any private ideas as to who, if it had to be one of your guests, might be the murderer?"

George's voice was dry. "The only one around here with the guts to commit murder is my nephew, but murdering a woman he didn't even know would be, I fear, beyond even him."

"Your nephew exasperates you?"

"My nephew is a leech I could do without." Brodie managed a tight smile. "If you ever find him murdered, you'd do well to question me first."

"Anything else you can tell us?"

"Nothing relevant to Mrs. Martin's murder."

"Thank you, Mr. Brodie. You can tell the others we'll move along with all possible speed."

"My guests were planning to leave after lunch tomorrow. Some of them would now like to go tonight."

"No, I'd like them to stay until tomorrow. And they'll need to leave their addresses with Detective Ryan here."

"Very well," George Brodie said as he went out and carefully closed the door.

The moment he was gone, Ryan leaned her chin on her hand and said matter-of-factly, "He's worried."

"Can you blame him?" Manziuk asked. "Not very good publicity to have a murder in your Japanese garden. Especially if the murderer turns out to be your law partner."

"You think Martin did it?

"It is most often the husband. But as he himself pointed out, he's already been divorced three times. Why not one more?"

Ryan was willing to speculate. "Perhaps she wasn't as compliant as the first three. Or maybe he's tired of paying alimony. Could be a dozen reasons." There was a pause. "I wonder," she said, sitting up and tapping the desk with her pen, "what she was doing in the garden? Was she alone or with someone else? I mean, if she'd been with someone she trusted, and he just casually walked around behind her, still talking, and then suddenly slipped the rope around—could that have happened?"

"Don't see why not," Manziuk said, but he stood and stretched as if bored. "How about getting Bart Brodie in here before someone else barges in?"

3

As Detective-Constable Ryan reached the games room, she saw that Shauna was sitting beside Bart on a loveseat, his shiny head bent close to her mousy brown one. As Ryan went forward, Bart glanced up and said something. Shauna quickly rose. She walked to another chair and sank limply into it.

Bart's eyes were hard to read, but Ryan's initial impression was that she had detected merriment in them. After tossing down the last of the drink he was holding, he followed her. "Lovely weather we've been having, don't you think?"

Ryan ignored him and walked quickly along the hallway to the study door, where she stopped and waited for him to enter.

He halted beside her, a smile on his face. "Now, do I go in first? Are you sure? Even though you are a cop, you're also a lady. One never knows what is proper etiquette. And I suppose I ought to have said policewoman, or perhaps police person. I must say you're the most attractive police person I've had the pleasure of meeting. Involved in too few murders, I guess."

"This way, please, Mr. Brodie," she said briskly, motioning for him to go ahead.

He sighed and raised his hands. "As you wish."

He entered and sat in the chair Manziuk indicated. He seemed relaxed, but his eyes on Manziuk's face were measuring. He laughed suddenly. "You must get confessions by just looking at people. Very intimidating. Shall I admit right now that I did it, or do you enjoy the thrill of the chase?"

"Just tell the truth, Mr. Brodie, and we'll get along fine," said Manziuk, continuing to lean back comfortably in his wing chair.

Bart also settled back, crossing his ankles and reaching into his pocket. "Mind if I smoke?" he asked casually.

Before Manziuk could reply, Ryan said brusquely, "I do."

"Then I certainly won't." He took his hand out of his pocket and laid it on the chair. "Although I may decide not letting me smoke is a form of torture."

"Smoking is a form of lunacy," Ryan said.

"That will do." Manziuk's voice was whip-like.

Bart looked from one to the other, waited for a moment, then said, "Fire away, officers. I'll manage."

"Why were you invited this weekend?" Manziuk asked.

"I wasn't. I literally dropped in out of the blue. Well, through the patio doors, actually. My dear Aunt Ellen was just sitting thinking about her party, and I fear I came close to causing a stroke. She definitely was not expecting me."

"Did she invite you to stay?"

"Not at first. She was all set to throw me out on my ear. In fact, when I said I couldn't so much as afford a sleazy motel room, she said a few days in the open air would do me good. Very un-aunt-like, I thought."

"You're broke."

"That's one way to put it. But I always bounce back again."

"You came here to get money?"

Bart smiled. "You're certainly direct. How about we say I came here to see if my uncle was interested in making a small investment?"

"And was he?"

"Not yet. But give him time."

"I see," Manziuk said dryly. "Why did your aunt decide to let you stay?"

"Well, she's got a soft side, you know. Love of family and all. And I am family. But primarily, she wanted me to keep Jillian and Anne from each other's throats."

"Why was that?"

He shrugged. "Apparently they weren't the best of friends. I rather got the impression Anne hated Jillian with all the anger of a jealous woman."

"Jealous?"

"You've seen them, haven't you? Jillian was early twenties, blond, gorgeous, et cetera, et cetera. Anne is early forties, ten or fifteen pounds overweight, getting a few wrinkles, with two teenagers and all the housewifely attributes. Why wouldn't she be jealous?"

"You implied more than a simple case of envy."

"Yes, well." Bart laughed easily. "Perhaps you'd better ask Anne or Douglass about that."

"What are you implying?"

"Just that there may have been more to it. I got that impression, anyway. I could be wrong, of course."

"You think there was something between Mr. Fischer and Mrs. Martin?"

"Merely an impression, officer. Nothing more."

"I see." Manziuk paused for a moment.

Bart watched him, eyes twinkling, gaze steady. "Anything else I can do for you?"

"You seem to have been involved in an argument between Jillian Martin and Shauna Jensen. Something about supper Saturday?"

"Oh, that. Nothing much to tell. Shauna needed to learn a few tricks to enhance her appearance, and I helped her."

"Her sister seems to have disapproved?"

"Since I have no reserves about speaking ill of the dead, I'll tell you right now that Jillian Martin was a self-centered witch. Despite appearances."

"Did she confront you?"

"Heard about the dance yet?"

"I know a number of you went to a nightclub."

Bart proceeded to enlighten them about his talk with Jillian and her resulting anger.

"So she slapped you right on the dance floor?"

"She had a temper."

"So we've heard. Can you tell me what you did after lunch today?"

"After lunch? Well, let's see. I think I went in and had a drink at the bar. Yes, that's right. Peter had one, too. Then he went upstairs and I went to my apartment above the garage. Used to be a chauffeur's place. Quite nice, really, if you don't mind a mouse or two. The little beasties have had their way with it for the past few months. Then what did I do?"

"Did you take a car out, perhaps?"

Bart laughed. "I wondered if anyone knew that. I wasn't going to mention it unless someone else did. My uncle prefers me to ask him, and then he's liable to say no. Yes, I did take one out for a short while. Then I got to thinking, why be cooped up in a car when there was a scenic backdrop behind the house?"

"Were you alone in the car?"

"Come, officer. I am of age. But, as a matter of fact, I was alone."

"And walking later?"

"No. I met Shauna at the back of the house and talked her into coming for a walk with me. Actually, I called her an idiot, and then she said she'd come. Amazing how her mind works. We were gone for quite a while."

"What time was it that you left?"

"I'm not generally known to go by a clock. No, wait—when I was changing, I remember it was about three. So it was maybe five minutes later we went out the gate."

"How did you get out?"

"I got the key from Mrs. Winston."

"And did you lock the gate again after you left?"

"I didn't have to. It locks automatically. And I know it was locked because Shauna tried it. She was annoyed with something I'd said and tried to go back inside. She couldn't get in, and I had the only key, so she stayed with me and cooled down."

"And you got back at—?"

"After four, I know. They'd just found the body."

"Did anyone see you walking?"

"Witnesses, eh? Well, as a matter of fact, I doubt it. It seems to me someone was on the terrace, but I can't say for a fact that anyone saw us leave, and I don't recall seeing anyone on the other side of the wall, either. Afraid you'll just have to take my word for it, officer. Of course, I realize I could have slipped back for five minutes and killed her, but really I can't think why I'd have done it. Or how I'd have known she was there. Can you?"

4

Ellen Brodie nervously fingered the chain around her neck as she waited for Inspector Manziuk to speak.

"Mrs. Brodie, I just have a few questions for you," Manziuk said in his calm voice. There's a chance you may be able to tell us something that will help."

"I'm sure I don't know what," she said disjointedly.

"Well, I'd like to know a little about how this weekend was planned, and your viewpoint on how it went."

"How it was planned?"

"Yes. Who did you invite first? That sort of thing."

"Gracious, I don't see that as being much to do with it. But of course, I'll try." She paused to think. "I invited Lorry first. You see, she's my cousin's daughter. Her mother, Patricia, was my very best cousin, you see. But of course, since she married and moved west to Alberta I haven't seen much of her. I think I've only seen Lorry twice. Lorry, from Lorraine, really, is the youngest of six. Patricia mentioned in her Christmas letter that Lorry would be in Toronto for part of the summer, so of course I wanted to have her here for at least one weekend. So I got her to come straight here. George or Kendall will drive her down to where she's staying on Monday."

"Who did you invite next?"

"Well, Kendall, of course." She blushed. "Oh, don't tell him, please. I thought—well, Kendall is twenty-five and settling down in the law firm. Lorry is a couple of years younger and a very nice girl. I know they're cousins of some sort, but it can't be too close. Second or third." She laughed self-consciously. "I can never figure out things like that." Then she became serious. "But, of course, it hasn't worked out as I planned."

"It hasn't?"

"Kendall would bring Nick with him!" She leaned forward. "Not that I mind Nick. He's always welcome. But I wanted Kendall and Lorry to get to know one another. And then Nick is so handsome. Not that Kendall is bad-looking. But he doesn't have that something. I don't know what it is. Nick's got it. Like a magnet, you see. Always gets the girls."

"And Lorry is attracted to him?"

"Well, I can't say for sure. She doesn't wear her heart on her sleeve. And it's just been since Friday. All I know is they've spent a lot of time together. So hard to tell."

"After you'd invited Lorry and Kendall, and Kendall invited Nick, what did you do?"

"Well, I wasn't satisfied, of course. And then George said he wouldn't mind having his partners and their wives out. We've had them over for an evening, oh, maybe two or three times a year. But never for a whole weekend. George thought it would be good. I wasn't keen on the idea, but he'd already asked them if they were free, so of course then I had to phone their wives. And I had no idea Jillian was going to bring her sister. Not until they were here."

"And Ms. Reimer?"

"She phoned in the afternoon. Friday. She had decorators at her place and she wanted out."

"Were you surprised?"

"I was rather. I wouldn't have thought she'd ask herself anywhere. We get along fine and all, but—well, I was surprised. And then when she got here and Jillian started laughing the way she did, so nasty, and Peter said quite unexpectedly that Hildy was his ex-wife. Well, you could have knocked me over with a feather!"

"And your nephew, Bart?"

"He's George's nephew, not mine." She smiled a little.

"Do you know if your husband has given him money recently?"

She shook her head. "I don't think so. George gave him quite a bit some months ago. He was very angry that Bart was back already—I don't think he's going to give him anything more than bus fare into the city."

"It was you who decided to let him stay for the weekend?"

"I had been thinking about how to entertain Jillian and Anne—I've nothing much in common with either of them and they'd none with each other. A woman likes to talk to an attractive man, and for all his faults, Bart is attractive. He knows a lot, too. Really. I hate to see him going to waste."

"You'd like to see him join the rat race and get a wife and three kids?" Manziuk said with a smile.

Ellen relaxed and smiled back. "Oh, yes, I would."

"I understand he's spent a lot of time with Shauna Jensen."

Ellen frowned again. "Really, he hasn't done what I wanted him to at all. I mean, what I wanted at first. But then I didn't know Shauna was coming. As it's turned out, it was very good he was here to look after her. Though what they did Saturday! So unexpected! Took us all several minutes to realize it was Shauna. Like a transformation."

Ryan chose this moment to get in a question that was on her mind. "Mrs. Brodie, how did you think Shauna looked Saturday night?" Ryan ignored the glare Manziuk was giving her. "Did she look terrible, or gaudy, or—?"

Ellen turned to look at Ryan. "You'd never have known it was the same person. The dress may have been a bit more than she needed for supper, but no more than Jillian's was. She looked absolutely stunning."

"I understand Jillian didn't like it," Ryan said.

A frown creased Ellen's face. "Really? I wonder why."

"You can't account for tastes," Manziuk said philosophically. "Now, the only question I have left is about what you did after lunch today. Just routine."

Ellen turned back toward him. "Yes, I see. At least, I don't, really, but of course I've nothing to hide, have I? Let me see. After lunch, I believe I helped Mrs. Winston a bit with the clearing up. Then I checked about supper. You see," she said confidingly, "I'm not used to all this. I've been an ordinary housewife all my life. George wanted me to have everything, so I let him buy this house and get a housekeeper, but really, I miss doing the work. Not that having time for helping with charities and such is bad, and of course George has always insisted I hire someone to help when we entertained, which was quite often, but, really, I especially miss doing the cooking. Some afternoons I have absolutely nothing to do, so I watch those foolish soap operas. Not really living, you know? So I guess I sneak off to the kitchen every chance I get."

"And after you were in the kitchen?"

"After that, I went back to the patio. I talked to Hildy for a while. Then Jillian came and joined us. Rather difficult to know what to say to the two of them, you know. Fortunately, Jillian went up to her room and then George asked Hildy to go and play billiards with Douglass and him. Then I guess I puttered around a little bit. Just doing some tidying up, you know. And Lorry came down and I sat and talked with her. It was the first chance I'd had to ask her about her family. After a while, we got thirsty, so I went to get lemonade. The others came to the patio in the next few minutes. Bart and Shauna were off somewhere. Jillian took drinks to George and Douglass and Peter. Oh, yes, Anne wasn't there." She made a face. "I tell you, I haven't known what to do about that. She's so obvious! I know she couldn't stand Jillian. Isn't that terrible, to be able to use the past tense about somebody so easily? What was I saying?"

"About Anne."

"Oh, yes. Well, she's spent most of the weekend up in her room, if you can believe it! She's blamed it on a headache, of course, and I suppose it could be migraine. Some people have a terrible time with them, I know. But it makes it rather awkward just the same. Anyway, what I started to say was that while we were all out on the patio, I happened to look up and there she was staring out the window—their bedroom faces the back of the house. I waved, naturally, but she ducked inside. Just as if she was watching us without wanting anyone to know. Silly, don't you think? It reminded me of an old woman who lived near us when I was growing up. You'd be walking past her big old house and you'd get an eerie feeling. Nine times out of ten if you looked back, there she'd be at one of the windows, peering out at you. And she'd duck away quickly when she knew you'd seen her. I remember lots of times I'd go the long way round so I didn't have to go past her house."

"There were hard feelings between Mrs. Fischer and Mrs. Martin?"

"Well," she said thoughtfully, "it certainly seemed so, though really I never heard either of them actually say anything. I suppose when you think about it, Jillian always treated Anne all right. Maybe a touch too lightly, I think. It's hard to explain. As if Anne weren't to be taken too seriously."

"Made fun of her?" Ryan put in.

Ellen puzzled over this. "But politely. The way one does in society, where you don't want to be uncivil."

"And how did Mrs. Fischer feel about this?" Manziuk asked.

"Well, I think—no, I'm sure, she disliked it. She's not that sort, witty and all. She's more like me, caught up in her family and friends. But it does seem that there was a problem, and I don't expect it had anything to do with Jillian. She has two teenagers, you know. I've raised one and I know it's not an easy job nowadays. It wouldn't surprise me one bit if it isn't those kids giving her the migraines."

"Yes, you could be right." Manziuk laughed. "You were on the patio having drinks when you saw Mrs. Fischer at her window. What did you do next?"

"I remembered something I wanted to make sure Mrs. Winston had ready for supper, so I went to tell her. Lorry had already gone in. She found it too hot. Hildy went in with me. She was going to her room."

"Where was Jillian?"

"She'd gone to the billiards room. She must have gone upstairs after that."

"How do you know?"

"Well, I came out of the kitchen after telling Mrs. Winston about the blueberry salad. You must try some. Not too sweet, but just delightful. And I popped in to see Lorry. She was playing the piano and it sounded so nice. I stopped in to tell her. Then I went upstairs. I passed Jillian coming down. She had changed to a very pretty peach sundress. I expect she was murdered in it, wasn't she?" Manziuk nodded and Ellen shuddered. "Horrid!"

"And what did you do after you saw Jillian?"

"Well, she said she was going outside and that she didn't need a thing—sounded quite happy. So I went upstairs to my room. No. I talked to Kendall for a few minutes. He was upset over Nick's turning down the job with the firm. But he said he was fine. He was looking for a law book, and I told him it was likely in his dad's study. Then I went into my room. I thought since everyone was occupied, I could have a quick nap."

"You say everyone was occupied. Two more questions. To the best of your knowledge, where were all the people? And what time was it when you saw Jillian?"

"The time I can tell you easily, I think. When I looked at the clock in my room, it was exactly three-thirty-five. So I must have seen Jillian about two or three minutes before. What else did you want? Oh, yes, the people. Where they were. Let me see. George and Peter and Douglas were in the billiards room. Of course, Mrs. Winston and Crystal were in the kitchen. I believe Bart and Shauna were out walking. Lorry was in the music room. Anne was in her room. Kendall had gone down to his dad's office to look for the book he wanted. I'm not sure about Hildy."

"And Nick Donovan?"

"Let me think. I left Nick and Kendall on the patio. But I know Kendall came upstairs. Nick may have come up, too, and gone to his room, but I really don't know." She shut her eyes. "So hard to believe this isn't a dream." She shook her head. "I wish I could wake up and discover none of it is true."

Manziuk eased her out of the room.

"Sorry," said Ryan.

"Yeah?"

"I butted in again."

"Hmm. You obviously aren't able to keep your mouth shut for half an hour."

She bit her lip to keep back the sharp retort that had sprung to her mind.

"Get Anne Fischer, will you? Let's find out what she really thought of Jillian Martin."

5

Anne Fischer entered the room and smiled brightly at Manziuk. "I'm glad you finally let me come in, officer." She took the chair indicated and arranged the skirt of her medium length pale blue sundress demurely around her.

"Sorry to keep you so long," Manziuk said. "We'll soon have it done. Nothing terrible, you know. We have to talk to everyone. Routine stuff."

"Yes, of course." She folded her hands in her lap. "I really am afraid I can't give you any help." She sounded pleased.

He observed her through heavy-lidded eyes. A trace of a smile touched his lips. "You have teenagers, I believe," he commented.

"Why, yes." She looked surprised.

"They keep you busy, I guess?"

"Well, I can't complain. They are both doing well in school. Trina's just graduated and Jordan has two more years. They're both active in sports and all sorts of things. Trina had the lead in the school play this spring. Really, she's very talented. And Jordan was an all-star in hockey and now he's into soccer. They're forever on the go. I told Douglass we need to get Jordan his own car. He's quite responsible. Trina hasn't needed a car because of her boyfriend Luc's having his own, but I think Jordan needs one so he can be independent. Don't you think so?"

"Certainly," Manziuk agreed, ignoring the fact that his own almost eighteen-year-old son was restricted to borrowing the family station wagon one night per week. "Now, I wonder, Mrs. Fischer. You look like an observant person. Do you think you can help us out by giving us some of your observations about the weekend?"

"Well, I'll try," she said, but her tone hinted at vagueness.

"For instance, did you notice anything unusual today? At lunch or after?"

She settled back in the chair, obviously going over the day in her mind. "No," she said at last, regretfully, "I don't think so. I had a dreadful headache after lunch. Migraine. I went up to my room and slept a good deal of the time. So difficult to come for a weekend and then feel just terrible. I'd have stayed home, but Douglass thought we should make an appearance. Now I'm sure he wishes we'd stayed home. This publicity!" She shrugged.

"Now, I have to get this straight for the records. You ate lunch on the terrace with the others?"

She nodded.

"And you went upstairs at about what time?"

"Right after lunch. About one, I'd think."

"Were you alone?"

"I suppose the maid has told you. No. Douglass was there, too. We actually had a bit of an argument. You see, he never gets sick himself. When I said I had a migraine headache, he thought I should make an effort to forget about it." She spat out the words. "I was, needless to say, upset by that. It's not as if I want to feel that way." She paused for a moment, as if experiencing the anger again. "Anyway, we argued for a while, twenty minutes, maybe.

Which of course only made my headache worse. Then he left and I went to sleep. I didn't wake up until much later. After four. Douglass was in the room sitting in a chair reading some papers. When I woke up, he said he was sorry for what he'd said before, and we talked for a while. Then George knocked on the door and told us about Jillian."

"I see. Did you notice anything during lunch or the rest of the weekend that might help us?"

She shrugged. "I don't think so. Perhaps someone followed her here. Someone from her past. Or perhaps she was involved with someone other than Peter. I should think there must be lots of men you could question."

"You don't feel she was faithful to her husband?"

Anne snorted in a very unladylike manner and crossed her ankles. "Her? She didn't know the meaning of the word. She was out for any man she could get."

"Had she shown interest in Mr. Fischer?"

"Douglass?" Anne sat back further into her chair and crossed her arms. "He's a happily married man," she said with an air of finality.

"So she's never said anything to him, maybe flirted a bit?"

"Likely she did," Anne said bitterly, "but it takes two to tango."

"So you didn't have any cause to feel, shall we say, a little jealous of Mrs. Martin?"

"Jealous?" Her voice became shrill. "Of that—that—! Never!" She lowered her voice and spoke appealingly to Manziuk. "Look, I didn't like her because she didn't belong where she was. Peter Martin may be a good lawyer, but he's not much for his choice in women. Give him a pretty face and a good figure and he doesn't seem to care about anything else. I think it's a shame. I don't know much about Hildy, but at least she had the brains to divorce him. He's a disgrace to the law firm. Bringing in twenty-year-olds to flaunt themselves in our faces! He's as big a fool as she was!" She finished her speech and sat staring at Manziuk, daring him to argue.

Mildly, he said, "I see. Yes, it would be frustrating to accept her as an equal. Well, thank you for your time, Mrs. Fischer. Would you ask your husband to step in now for a minute?"

Without another word, she rose and made her exit.

6

Douglass Fischer entered the room and, after taking his time looking around, sat in the chair indicated. He made himself comfortable, crossed his legs, and waited expectantly for the first question.

Manziuk eyed him. A big man, heavy-set, though neither as tall nor as heavy as Manziuk himself. Brown hair, beginning to recede at the sides. Strong, square hands. Square face. Keen eyes. The type to inspire confidence in clients. Not a man to be rattled easily, yet there was something. A slight tic on the left side of his mouth. He was nervous then. Just a little.

"Well, Mr. Fischer, I'm sure you know it's routine to question all people present when a murder is committed. Just a few things we need to know."

"Yes, certainly." The voice was brusque, matter-of-fact.

"Now, the first thing we need is your whereabouts from about lunch on. Can you do your best to remember for us?"

"I've already gone over it in my mind. Anne and I ate lunch together and went up to our room immediately after. I thought she should try to be more sociable. She convinced me she needed to lie down for a while, so I went downstairs and joined a few others in a game of billiards. It must have been close to two.

"We were there quite a while, maybe an hour and a half, and then I decided to go upstairs and see if Anne wanted to come down. When I got to the room, I found her asleep. I decided not to waken her. I had brought a file of things from work, so I sat down to read through that. I planned to get Anne to go down with me when she woke up. But she had barely awakened when George came and told us about Jillian. We both went downstairs after that."

"Did you notice anything that might be useful to us?"

"I didn't notice anything suspicious, if that's what you mean. Just a group of normal people enjoying a weekend together. Surely you don't think that one of us murdered Jillian. If it really was murder."

"Oh, it was murder all right. And there's a good chance it was one of your normal people."

"Well, I find that hard to accept."

"Murder is never easy to accept."

"Yes, I suppose that's true," Fischer conceded in his calm, soothing voice.

"Mr. Fischer, I have a rather awkward question to ask you. I hope you'll think about it before you give an answer. Remember we can always check to verify things we are told." Manziuk paused.

Fischer sat unmoving, waiting.

Manziuk went on. "We would like to know exactly what was the nature of your relationship with Mrs. Martin."

Without hesitation or any apparent discomfort, Fischer replied, "There was no relationship. Mrs. Martin was no more or less to me than my partner's wife. And I certainly hope you won't suggest any such thing to Peter. He has enough to bear without false rumors." He spoke earnestly. "I expect my wife suggested that to you. She seems to feel it's natural for a man my age to fall for a young, attractive woman. She's been going through a stage of insecurity lately and she hasn't yet redefined her role. Once she has accepted her age and found new interests, I think she will find it easier to accept the fact that I am more interested in her than I would be in a younger woman."

"Did you meet Jillian Martin by arrangement late Friday night?"

"What?" Douglass's mouth dropped open for a brief second and he sat forward.

"Outside. You were seen talking to her."

He shook his head. "No. You've got that wrong."

"I don't think so."

"Jillian and Bart had both been smoking a lot, and the air was musty. I went out to get some fresh air. Then I was going to come in and go up to bed. Jillian came out and we happened to meet. We talked about the house and the gardens. That's all. It was perfectly innocent."

"You hadn't arranged to meet?"

Douglass crossed his knees. "Of course not. We were talking about the house, just like I said."

"Do you feel your wife hated Jillian Martin?"

Fischer's hand went to his hair, ruffling it. He uncrossed and recrossed his knees. Then he regained his calm. "Hated is a rather strong word, don't you think? I believe she envied her for her youth and poise, and, of course, her beauty. But I don't think she 'hated' her. Certainly not, as you may be hinting, enough to murder her. My wife's struggle is against what Jillian represented—youth—and is solely within herself. I'm sure there was no personal animosity toward Jillian."

"If you had to choose someone in the house as the most likely suspect, who would it be?"

"I'll leave the speculation to you people. Criminal law was never my forte."

"You have no suspicions?"

"None. I find it extremely difficult to believe that anyone in this house could be a murderer and I expect you will come to the same conclusion."

"Who knows?" Manziuk said airily. "In mystery novels it's usually the person you least suspect."

"Then you'd better lock up young Lorry. I'm sure she would have the least reason." Douglass sat forward again. "Look here, Inspector, you can't seriously think anyone here has a motive for murder. I know what the normal reasons are: money, revenge, love. Well, she didn't have money of her own, so that's out. And the others are ridiculous. You'll have Kendall murdering her because he didn't want to join the law firm while she was Peter's wife or Lorry killing her because she didn't go to church. Look, she was just an ordinary young woman lucky enough to grab a rich and prominent husband. There's no logical reason for one of us to murder her."

"Then how do we explain the fact that she was murdered?"

"Maybe it was a tramp. What exactly do you have to go on?"

"At this point, not much. After Forensics is finished, hopefully, more."

Fischer nodded and went out. His shoulders drooped.

Manziuk said to Constable Ryan. "Good lawyer, I bet."

"Yes, but you threw him a few times. Do you think he's lying about his relationship to Mrs. Martin?"

"Could be. He looked like I caught him off guard once or twice. I also thought some of his other answers were a bit too pat, like he'd rehearsed beforehand."

"We've talked to everyone except Hildy Reimer."

"Yes, I thought I'd save the ex-wife till last. Give her time to figure out a good reason for being here."

7

Hildy Reimer, relaxed in a navy velour shorts outfit that showed off her more-than-adequate figure, placed both elbows on the armrests of her chair and waited for Inspector Manziuk's first question.

"Now, Ms. Reimer—it is Ms., isn't it?"

"Yes."

"Very well," he said easily. "You are a neighbor of the Brodies?"

"I live a couple of miles from here," she said stiffly.

"But you know Mrs. Brodie fairly well?"

"We both belong to a horticulture club."

"And you are friends?" he persisted.

She looked away. "Not close friends."

"But you felt free to ask if you could come here for the weekend when your apartment was being painted?"

Watching her closely, he saw a tinge of pink touch her cheeks. Her "yes" was quiet.

"Was your apartment being painted?" he asked casually. "We can easily check, you know."

Hildy shifted in the chair. Finally she said, "No."

Inspector Manziuk followed up. "Was it because your ex-husband was going to be here?"

She looked straight at him. The signs of discomfort were gone. "Yes."

"And why is that?"

"I wanted to see how he was doing with his new wife." Her voice was calm and direct.

"And did he appreciate that? Or did you perhaps want to make him uncomfortable, get back at him for divorcing you?"

Her reply was scornful. "He didn't divorce me; I divorced him."

"I take it that was because of the next young lady, Genevieve, whom he then married?"

"No. It was because he was a very poor husband and a lousy father. It wasn't until six months after our divorce was final that he married Genevieve. She was an exotic dancer and aspiring actress. That lasted a little over a year. It was some time later that he married Jillian."

Manziuk thought for a moment. "So you were simply curious as to how this marriage was going?"

"That's right."

"And how was it going?"

For a second, she looked off-balance. Then she visibly regained her poise. "Reasonably well. They both seemed satisfied."

"No more divorces for him?"

"I wouldn't go that far. But it would be amicable. Perhaps in a few years."

"Mr. Martin has a short attention span, has he?"

She gave him the hint of a smile. "You know that old saying about the grass always being greener!"

"Did he mind your being here?"

"Apparently not. I hadn't intended to say anything about the past, but after Jillian made sure everyone knew, he acknowledged me with good humor."

"Did you and Mrs. Martin know each other?"

"We'd never met. She said she recognized me from seeing my picture."

"Was she angry about your coming here?"

"She didn't seem upset," she said dryly.

"What was your opinion of Jillian Martin?"

She considered for a minute. "I haven't really thought about it. She was pretty, of course. Young. And a golddigger." She shrugged. "I really didn't know her."

"Do you know of any reason why someone would want to kill her?"

"No, of course not. There have been a number of murders of young women in the city during the last year. I assumed this was done by the same person."

"Perhaps," said Manziuk in an off-handed tone. "But it may have been someone she knew. Mr. Martin, for instance."

Up to this point, Hildy had been very self-controlled. But now her hands clenched the sides of the chair and her eyes blazed with anger. "That's ridiculous! Surely you're not such idiots as that! Or are you out to make headlines by sensational speculations? If you are, you'll soon find a libel suit on your doorstep."

Manziuk retained his relaxed manner. "So you don't think Mr. Martin could have killed his wife?"

She glared at him. "What possible reason could he have? If he wanted to get rid of her, he could just divorce her."

"Quite right," said Manziuk. "Just one more question. What did you do after lunch today?"

"After lunch? Oh. You want my alibi."

"If you don't mind."

Her face lost its flush and she visibly relaxed. "I'll do my best. I came down for brunch about a quarter after twelve. I sat at a patio table with Kendall and Bart and Nick. I was mostly talking to Nick about skiing. Then Lorry arrived. She'd been at church. Since I'd finished eating, I moved over to talk with Ellen."

"Who else was around then?"

"I think Jillian was reading a magazine in a lounge chair. And Peter was swimming. I remember because he was yelling at Kendall and Nick about something. I don't remember seeing anyone else."

"About how long were you talking to Ellen?"

"Maybe half an hour. Maybe longer. Then George came out and persuaded Kendall and me to join him and Douglass in a snooker game. We played for perhaps an hour, maybe longer." She shrugged. "I'm not that good at judging time."

"That's all right." Manziuk sat there looking sleepy "We just want an idea. Where did you go next?"

"I had some lemonade on the patio with Ellen. Most of the people were there."

"Including Jillian?"

"Yes."

"Do you have any idea what time it was?"

"Not really."

"Okay. After the drinks, what did you do?"

"I decided to go for a walk out front where it was quiet. You know, just to be able to think. I sat and watched the fountain for a while, and walked around the drive. I know it was four o'clock when I came back into the house, because the clock in the front hall was striking. I went up to my room to comb my hair, and as I came downstairs I heard people shouting. They had just found Jillian's body."

"So you were out front for about half an hour, say?"

"I think so."

"Did you see anyone else while you were there?"

Hildy shook her head. "For a while I heard someone playing the piano in the music room. Just in the background, you know. Very good. The person playing, I mean. I didn't recognize the music, though, and I didn't actually see anyone." She paused. "When did the murder take place?"

"We don't know exactly. Jillian seems to have been seen at about three-thirty. So some time between then and four, I would guess."

"So I have no alibi. But you people always say to tell the truth, don't you?"

Manziuk shifted his weight to get up. "Always," he said with a hint of a smile. He went to the door and opened it.

As she stood up, he thought of another question. "You have just the one child?"

She stiffened noticeably. Her voice lost its animation and became flat and mechanical. "Yes. A boy. His name is Stephen."

"He's in your custody?"

"Yes."

"Does his father see him often?"

"No." Her voice was like steel.

"You've been married just the once?"

"Yes."

"And the name Reimer?"

"My maiden name." Dark eyes flashed.

"You work?"

"I'm a personnel consultant with a national company."

"Good pay?"

"Very."

"Does Mr. Martin pay support?"

"Not a cent. I don't want his money."

"All right. Thanks for your time. I'll let you know if there's anything else." He shut the door behind her and turned to look at Ryan. His mouth was stern, but there was a twinkle in his eyes. "Well? What do you think of the ex-wife?"

"I didn't think I was supposed to have an opinion."

He stared at her.

She shrugged. "This is my first case, remember?"

"What's the matter, did I hurt your feelings?"

"No." Cheeks burning, she looked at the notes she had made.

"I asked what you thought of Hildy Reimer. Or don't you have an opinion?"

"I think she's one smart lady. The type you'd expect to see in an important job. Career woman."

"Got pretty nervy when I asked about her kid."

"Could have scratched your eyes out, as they say."

"Think she'd hesitate to lie to the police?" he asked with a raised brow.

"About as long as she'd hesitate to step on a cockroach."

"That's what I thought, too." He took several strides around the room, and she was reminded of a prisoner pacing his cell. Manziuk dwarfed the study, making it seem too small, too stuffy, and too confining. "Well," he said at last. "We've seen them all. Now the hard part begins."

There was a knock on the door. Constable Carnaby entered. "Mrs. Brodie wondered if they may go ahead with supper now that you've talked to everyone."

"Certainly."

"She also wondered if you would like a tray in here. Nothing fancy, she said. Just a cold supper."

"As befitting the circumstances," Manziuk said. "Yes, that would be fine. I'd like to talk with Ford now, too. See if he's finished inside. If he is, you can tell the people they are free to go around the house. But I'd like them to stay inside."

"Yes, sir. I'll tell them. I'll tell Special Constable Ford you're ready for him."

When they were alone, Ryan said, "Who do you think did it?"

"I rather think we don't know the half of what's been going on here. Why don't you start by going over their stories and figuring out where each of them say they were between when Mrs. Martin was last seen and when the body was found? That should prove interesting."

Ryan bent to her task.

There was a light tap at the door before it opened to let Ford in. He was only 5' 10" but was as sturdy as a redwood and could have played the heavy in any movie. To go with his stature, his voice was brusque and low, and a long scar ran across his left cheek. The kind of man a person would think twice before talking back to.

He sank into the empty armchair and looked at Manziuk. "Well, we don't have much. We've fingerprinted the girl's room. Not much hope. Masses of prints. But we'll check them out. Only thing of interest was this." He handed Manziuk a scrap of paper. "Two sets of prints, one of them likely hers. We're working on identifying the others."

Manziuk opened it. There were a few typewritten lines.

```
Jillian Darling,
     You may think it's all over and fin-
ished between us, but you're wrong. You
can't play games with me. I don't know
what you think you're doing, but you
said you loved me and wanted to marry me
once, and I know you meant it. I still
want you and I will have you. I won't
let anything or anyone come between us.
Nothing will stop me. I'm not afraid of
what will happen. And you should
```

The paper was torn and there was no signature.

Chapter Eleven

"Interesting," Manziuk said as he passed it to Ryan, who read it and then began hunting through her notes.

"Where did you find it?" Manziuk asked.

"That's the strange thing. It was in the Fischers' room," Ford said.

"Fischers'?"

"Yes, sir. Taped to the bottom of a drawer in the bureau."

"Well, that's certainly going to take some explaining," Manziuk muttered. "Anything else?"

"Not too much of interest." Ford opened a small worn notebook. "I'll give you a general idea. Peter and Jillian Martin. A lot of women's clothing. Expensive and very feminine. Lots of lace and ruffles. Much more than you'd need for one weekend. Expensive jewelry. Just a few men's things. Lots of cosmetics and such. Blood pressure tablets in the night stand. His. Prescribed four months ago."

Manziuk nodded.

"Hildy Reimer has a picture of a young boy on her dresser. Nice, expensive tailored clothes, some jewelry, cosmetics, not much else. Except for a gun hidden in a pocket of her suitcase."

"A what?" Manziuk asked in astonishment.

"A Browning .22 target pistol to be exact."

"Now what on earth is she doing with that?"

Ford and Ryan both looked at him.

"Okay," Manziuk said, "we'll have to ask her later. Go on."

"Kendall Brodie, room barer than you'd expect. Apparently he doesn't actually live here. A lot of car magazines. Also a number of trophies for debating and public speaking. Some law books. Clothes. Toiletries. Things from earlier years. Nothing that looked unusual.

"Nick Donovan is sharing the room. Just clothes and toilet items. Nothing personal except a couple of Dean Koontz paperbacks.

"George and Ellen Brodie. Large room. Decorated very nicely. Flowers everywhere. Clothes, personal items, a lot of pictures of people. Knickknacks. Not much of interest. Some medicine. Nothing prescribed except some mild sleeping pills. Hers. She got them about three months ago. Bottle is half-empty. And some pills for an ulcer. His. A month old.

"Douglass and Anne Fischer. Clothes and toilet items. Not a lot. Normal things. Tylenol 3 with codeine, a bottle of Seconal tablets, and an ice pack. The note I showed you. And one other item of interest—an empty brandy bottle in the back of the closet, behind a suitcase. We took prints.

"Shauna Jensen. Clothes of the same style as her sister's. One torn dress lying on the floor of her side of the closet. Looks like it was a sharp dress. A sketch pad with some pretty good drawings under her pillow. Also a brochure from an art school. And a suitcase with some clothes in it lying open on the floor. Nothing fancy. A few toiletries and makeup items. Lot of Kleenex in her wastebasket. Offhand, I'd say she or her roommate shed quite a few tears.

"Lorry Preston is in the same room. One empty suitcase. One full, unopened. Mostly clothes. Some hanging, too. Not expensive. Not too fancy. Jeans and such. Dresses and skirts without labels. Looked hand sewn but well-made. Toiletries and makeup, but not much. A Bible and other religious books, some music books, and a diary. Apparently she feels an interest in someone she met this weekend, and it bothers her. There seems to be someone back home she's not sure whether to marry or not.

"That leaves Bart Brodie. He's in an apartment above the garage. Interesting. Some very expensive items. Also some very cheap ones. Several books of poetry. Browning seems to be a favorite. Some copies of somewhat, ah, explicit magazines." He looked at Ryan when he said this. "Two hundred dollars in a wallet with his clothes. A couple of bottles of Scotch and two glasses. Same label as the Scotch in the house. Also same glasses. A packet of business letters about some kind of scheme for selling condos in Florida. Looks like it went bust.

"We also checked the bathrooms and the servants' rooms, and the kitchen. Nothing unusual. You can see the complete list after we've finished off the main floor. Thought we'd do it while they're eating."

"The grounds?" Manziuk asked.

"No indication anyone came in from outside. Neighbors saw nothing. Looks like an inside job to me. Not much help in the garden. You got that daisy chain thing?"

Manziuk nodded.

"Nothing shows on that path. No deep scuff marks or anything. Victim doesn't appear to have put up much of a struggle."

"That's it?"

"Well, we were looking for the murder weapon. We found two possibilities." He held up a plastic bag containing what looked like a black braided cord.

"What is it?" asked Manziuk, taking the bag to have a closer look at its contents.

"It's the cord off a housecoat. Frankly, it was the only thing I saw that looked like a possibility. There were a lot of belts and scarves and such. But Dr. Munsen said something about a smooth rope. Well, there it is."

Ryan was leaning forward, across the desk. "I've got a cord like that on some lounging pajamas. It's made of polyester or something, but it's braided like a rope. It would leave marks like a rope, but it wouldn't be abrasive."

"Where did you find this?" Manziuk demanded.

Ford consulted his notebook. "It was with the clothes belonging to George Brodie. A sort of kimono-style silk robe."

"And the other possibility?"

"Well, it's not any one thing in particular. There's a type of cord used in the garden. It's beige, but it's not twine. It's more like a smooth twisted cord. Maybe even cotton. It's used a lot. In some places, it's holding up plants tied to stakes. In a number of places, it's used to hold together little water fountain things. Like the one where the body was found. And in a few places, it's used to hold weights." Ford shook his head. "We couldn't make it out. Looks like whoever tied them there is trying to pull the branches down by weighting them. Never saw the likes of it."

"Did you find a loose piece of the cord?"

"Not yet, but we're looking for it."

"See if Mrs. Winston knows where the gardener would keep extra cord. Get a sample from somewhere and get both cords to Munsen right away."

"Yes, sir."

"Any other surprises you've been holding back?"

"That's it. I'll have the itemized lists for you by morning. This looks like a real dilly. Of course, that cord and the note may be all you need."

Manziuk nodded. "Could be."

"Need me for anything more?"

"No. Finish up here and then go home and get eight hours. We'll see how things pan out in the morning. Oh, there is one other thing. Get Moffatt looking through our files to see if we have anything on any of these people. Check them all. Noon tomorrow will be good."

"Will do."

When he was gone, Ryan asked, "Do you think Nick Donovan wrote that note? The bit about 'this time' sounds like him. She got away once."

"It certainly sounds like something he could have written. It was done on a typewriter, not a computer." He walked over to the corner table, where a Selectric typewriter sat under wraps. "This one, I expect."

"He was still in love with her and she wouldn't have anything to do with him. Maybe laughed at him. So he killed her. You saw what he was like. Distracted. Didn't seem to be all here. And his alibi is pathetic." Her voice became animated. "'One of us must have been mistaken about which garden.' Give me a break!"

"Maybe."

"You're not satisfied?"

"I don't like things to fall into place too easily. Takes the challenge out of it."

She rolled her eyes.

Fortunately, there was a knock on the door and Mrs. Winston appeared with a tray, followed by Crystal with a second. Manziuk and Ryan set themselves to eating. She finished first and busied herself with her notes. At last she looked up. "Okay, here it is."

"Alibis?"

"Uh huh. Want to hear them?"

He moved his chair closer so he could see the paper she had been writing on. He laughed. "Alphabetical?"

She didn't reply. "She was last seen at about three-thirty, so I've just looked for where people were starting then."

Bart Brodie – walking with Shauna from about 3:00 to 4:00

Ellen Brodie – napping in her room from 3:35 till 4:00

George Brodie – in the billiard room for a few minutes after 3:30, and then in his study talking to Kendall until about 3:45 and sending e-mail on his computer until Lorry arrived after four

Kendall Brodie – came out of his room about 3:30, went to his dad's study to talk. About 3:45, he went to find Lorry Preston in the music room and they went to the garden.

Nick Donovan – in rose garden 3:20 to 3:45, walked to the Japanese garden with Kendall & Lorry 3:45 to 4:00

Anne Fischer – asleep in room the whole time

Douglass Fischer – reading in room from just before 3:30 until 4:00

Peter Martin – asleep in bedroom from just after 3:30 until 4:05

Lorry Preston – playing piano (heard by several others) until Kendall came in at 3:45, went for walk

Hildy Reimer – out front alone until 4:00, heard clock ring hour as she came in

Shauna Jensen–walking with Bart from 3:00 until after 4:00

Mrs. Winston – in kitchen

Crystal Winston – in kitchen except maybe for a couple of brief trips to pick up dirty dishes

"Well, isn't that terrific?" Manziuk said. "Other than Bart and Shauna, the only ones who weren't alone for at least a few minutes are George and Kendall Brodie and the Fischers, and being father and son and a married couple, none of them would likely hesitate to lie for each other. So there's not one out of the lot of them that couldn't have done it! Well, Lorry appears to have been heard playing the piano by several people, but that's not to say even she couldn't have whipped out, killed Jillian, and got back to the room without anyone noticing. You don't pay that much attention to music you hear in the background. Or she could have even set up a tape to fill in. So none of them are out of this."

He circled the desk, then stopped. "Here, let's time this. You set your watch. I'm going to sneak out of the house into the garden, strangle someone, and sneak back here. Let's see how long it would take me."

So saying, he went out.

When he came back into the room, Ryan looked up. "Eight minutes," she said. "And a lot of luck. It's amazing somebody didn't see him, with all the people in this house."

"A lot of people, yes, but things seem to have been pretty quiet for those particular moments."

"But how could the murderer have known that?"

"Luck," Manziuk replied. "Or maybe he was seen."

"You mean someone might know more than he told us? Other than the murderer, of course."

A smile touched Manziuk's lips. "I'd guess at least half the people kept something back on purpose. And the other half kept something back without realizing it was of importance."

"That many?"

"That's normal. Well, we'll just have to see what we can do. I wish there was at least one with an iron-clad alibi. Then all we'd have to do is break it. But this mess!" Manziuk threw up his hands. "I don't think we can rule anyone out in terms of opportunity. So now we look at possible motives. Lorry also has no motive whatsoever, so, given she's neither an impostor or a maniac, I think we'll skip her for the time being. George, again, has no real motive. You don't strangle your partner's wife merely because she annoys you. Ellen—nothing I can see. Kendall had never met her before this weekend. Bart hadn't met her, although he seems to have enjoyed getting her upset. But I can't see why he'd murder her. Unless, of course, he knew her from somewhere else. But that would seem like an awful coincidence given Nick's story. Anne dislikes her, even hates her, but enough for murder?

Ditto Hildy. Her sister? I don't know. Could be something there. Douglass Fischer—is he telling the truth or not? Then there's Peter Martin, the husband. Or Nick Donovan. He looks the most obvious. He was in love with her once and she refused to marry him. The letter refers back to the past. He could have known about the cord from the bathrobe, if that is the murder weapon, because he's likely visited with the Brodies before."

"But the note was found in the Fischers' room," Ryan protested. That doesn't make sense. And despite Douglass Fischer's denial, I think something was going on between him and Jillian Martin. And his wife thought so, too."

"So you think one of the Fischers could have done it?"

"Why not?"

"Who else?"

Ryan thought for a moment. "Peter Martin, I guess, but there doesn't seem to be a strong enough motive for him."

"Anybody else?"

"Well, there's Shauna Jensen. She had good cause to hate her sister, if you believe Lorry Preston. But she was with Bart Brodie. Unless, maybe they knew each other from before. Maybe it was all part of a planned-out scheme."

"Now you're starting to think like a cop," Manziuk said.

She stared at him. "You really think Bart and Shauna could have been working together?"

"No, but you have to look at all kinds of options. Never take anything or anybody at face value. Who else?"

"Well, Hildy Reimer. Why was she really here? And why did she have a gun?"

"Okay. So now we have a starting list of suspects with Nick Donovan at the top of the list. So we go back to the station and get these notes typed up. Then we go over them with a fine tooth comb and come up with a list of questions we need to ask to clarify things. For instance, why did Hildy have a gun? How drunk was Anne Fischer when her husband went upstairs?"

"What?" She stared at him.

"The brandy bottle at the back of the closet was empty. He was drinking down at the bar. So who was drinking in the room? Or was it left over from some other guest?"

Ryan motioned toward the door. "Why don't we ask some more questions right now?"

"Because I want a few more answers first. Like have we found the murder weapon? Whose fingerprints were on that note? Was it typed in this house? Who stood to gain by her death?"

"Who stood to gain?"

Manziuk nodded. "For all we know, Peter Martin has financial problems and he took out a half-million insurance policy on her. The next time I talk to these people, I want it to be from a position of strength."

Ryan nodded slowly.

"If you jump in too fast, you can hurt your case. Now, you have your own car. I'll meet you in my office in half an hour."

She stared at him. "It's ten-thirty."

"Is that a problem?"

She made a face. "No, I love working all night."

"Get used to it."

2

In the dining room, most of the members of the house party slowly finished their late evening meal. Peter had been given a tray in his room. Shauna had gone to her room but refused food. Only Anne and Bart showed any signs of genuine hunger. The others merely toyed with the food. A mood of deep gloom, present since the discovery of the body, had sunk upon the house and most of the people.

"I wonder if they'll just pack someone off without any farewells." Bart mused as he set down his glass. "I guess they have a kind of protocol. Or it could depend on the whim of the arresting officer. What is his name again? Awful to have policemen with names you can't pronounce. Man-something. Tuck?"

"Shut up, Bart," his uncle said.

"M-A-N-Z-I-U-K," Anne said. "I asked that nice young officer. He said you pronounce it Man's hook."

"I've got him tabbed," Bart said. "He's the kind that likes to put you at ease till you're hardly aware of where you are and then, bang, he delivers his bomb. I wonder if he'll get a confession out of one of us that way."

"Dad said to shut up!" Kendall said, furious. "None of us killed her and you know it! You probably know a lot more about it than any of us!"

"Touché," Bart said with a smile. "I wonder if I should go and confess. Would that make it easier for the good Inspector Manziuk," he nodded toward Anne, "or would it muddy the waters? I—"

"Bart, be quiet!" his uncle thundered. "You seem to find all this a great source of amusement. Well, the rest of us don't. A young woman has been murdered here. One more word out of you and I will physically remove you from this house!"

Bart's eyes glinted, but any comment he might have made was forestalled by Manziuk's entrance into the room.

"Excuse me for barging in," he said. "Just thought I'd let you know that I'm leaving. I'll be back tomorrow, probably just after noon. I'd like everyone to remain in the house or on the terrace until I've had a chance to talk with some of you again. Perhaps all of you. And I'd like to repeat that if you remember something you haven't told me, even if you can't see its importance, I'd like you to tell me now or talk to the officers who'll stay here tonight. It is important that we catch whoever did this quickly."

"Why?" Bart asked insolently. "Is he likely to murder someone else?"

"That is always a possibility," Manziuk answered, refusing to be baited.

"Well, we'll all be very careful."

"This is no joke," Manziuk replied. "You'd do well to realize that."

Bart bowed.

"A few things have been removed from the house. When we are certain they have nothing to do with the crime, they will be returned. Ms. Reimer, could I see you for one moment in the hall?"

As the others all looked at her, she nodded. Without a word, she followed Manziuk out.

"Do you have a license for your gun?" he asked quietly.

She lowered her eyes to the beige ceramic tile of the hallway. "No."

"Then it will not be returned. Why did you have it?"

"I do a lot of driving at night. There have been a number of women assaulted lately. I was afraid. So I got it to keep in my purse at night."

"And the rest of the time?"

"In my glove compartment."

"Do you keep it loaded?"

"It wouldn't do me much good if I didn't, would it?"

"Have you ever used it?"

"No."

"All right. You can go back inside."

"I didn't kill her."

"Good. See you tomorrow."

After Manziuk was gone, the others wandered slowly back to the day room or toward the bar. Somehow it seemed wrong to play billiards or swim in the pool. Yet no one seemed to want to leave the others. Except for Bart, who headed for the bar and picked up a bottle. He took his drink and the bottle onto the patio where he lit a cigarette and nursed a double Scotch.

Shauna's voice startled him. "You seem to be enjoying yourself. You act like this was all a joke. But she was my sister. I guess you don't know how to care about anybody, maybe not even yourself."

Before he could come up with a reply, she had fled back into the house and up the stairs to her room.

Bart stared after her for a moment before finishing his drink and pouring another.

3

Hildy sat in the games room on a straight-backed Victorian chair with a tapestry hunting-scene cushion and ignored the desultory conversation being carried on by the Brodies and Fischers. Her eyes were fixed on a small painting of a fox hunt. Right now she felt rather like that fox.

She got up and walked out. She went to the study, where she found Peter hanging up the phone after talking to Mrs. Jensen.

"How are they taking it?"

"They're driving up tomorrow. They seem pretty upset."

"It's a shock."

"Yeah."

"How are you doing?"

"Oh, I'm okay, I guess. I heard the police talked to you again. What did they want?"

"They wanted to know why I had a gun in my suitcase."

He stared at her. "And what did you tell them?"

She shrugged. "That I'm out a lot at night and I get nervous."

"Lucky for you she wasn't shot."

"Yes."

She wandered around the room and Peter watched her. "It's nothing to do with you," he said at last. "You two didn't even know each other."

"No."

"It's crazy. Your being here this weekend. Meeting like this. And now the murder. Talk about a quirk of fate."

She stopped moving and crossed her arms as if she were cold. "I guess you'll find out sooner or later. The police already know. My being here was no quirk of fate. I came on purpose. I lied about my apartment being redecorated."

"But—but why? How did you know I'd be here?"

She didn't answer immediately. At last she said, "Because Jillian mentioned that you were going to be here."

"Jillian? When were you talking to her? You didn't even know her!"

"Didn't I?"

4

Shauna was packing her suitcase. She looked up guiltily when Lorry opened the door a crack. "Oh, it's you. I'm just—I—"

"I wondered how you are. Is there anything I can do?"

Shauna walked over and opened the door wide. "It's okay. You can come in. I have a lot of her clothes. I don't want them anymore. I'll wear my own." She had removed the dark glasses and was wearing her normal, black-rimmed ones. Her eye was still quite bruised, and there was a yellow mark on her cheekbone. Both eyes were also rimmed with red, and her nose was red and shiny.

"Can I help?"

"I only have a few things left. I want to take them to her room. I don't want them here."

"It looks heavy. I'll help you carry it."

Shauna put in the last items and Lorry helped her close the suitcase. Together, they carried it to the room Jillian and Peter had shared.

"I hope Peter isn't here," Shauna whispered as Lorry knocked on the door.

There was no response.

Lorry opened the door and they put the suitcase inside. Shauna was quick to step out into the hall again. "I don't want to see her things. I don't want to touch them again."

"I'm sure you won't have to," Lorry said calmly.

"I don't know. We wore the same size. Exactly. Except she filled them out better. On me, things just hang." She shivered. "I don't want to think about her."

They returned to their own room and Lorry shut the door. Shauna's bed had clothes strewn over it.

"Can I help you hang these up?" asked Lorry.

"They're mine," Shauna said defensively.

"I guess you don't have anything to put them in now?"

Shauna shook her head.

"Shall I see if Mrs. Winston has a shopping bag or something you could use?"

Shauna nodded.

"Would you like me to get you anything else?" Lorry asked. "A cup of tea or maybe hot chocolate? You seem cold."

Shaking her head impatiently, Shauna said, "You saw her, didn't you? You found her body."

"Yes. Nick and Kendall and I had gone for a walk in the garden, and we found her."

"She was strangled, wasn't she?"

"I believe so."

"When you're strangled, what does it look like? I mean, you can't breathe, right? It's like choking. Does—what does it look like? I mean, she didn't look like she was sleeping, did she?"

"No." It was Lorry's turn to shiver. "She didn't look like she was sleeping."

"Was it awful? Ugly?"

Lorry swallowed as the memory of Jillian's face returned vividly to her mind. "It's not very nice."

"I'm glad," Shauna said.

Lorry turned white. "You're glad?" she repeated.

Raising both hands to the back of her neck, Shauna took a deep breath. Then she intertwined her fingers in front of her face. "She was always so proud of her looks. She thought she was something special because she was so pretty. I'm glad she isn't pretty anymore."

"But Shauna, I…"

Lowering her hands, Shauna looked straight at Lorry. "You thought I loved her, didn't you? You thought I worshipped her. She told Peter that, you know. That I worshipped her. When we were younger, she used to make me her slave. I had to do things for her all the time. Because she was beautiful and I was ugly. And now she's not beautiful anymore. She's ugly! And she's dead." Her voice began to rise to a shrill pitch. "She's dead, she's dead, she's dead, she's—"

Lorry grabbed Shauna's shoulders and held her firmly until Shauna pulled away and crumpled onto the bed in a sobbing heap.

5

Back in the games room, George Brodie gave up trying to make small talk with his wife and the Fischers. They had exhausted the weather, the traffic, the difficulty in getting servants, and the interior of the house, being careful not to mention the gardens.

"Well," he said now, stretching his legs forward and crossing his ankles. "I guess we're going to be spread across the papers."

"Yes," Douglass agreed. "We'll have reporters all over the place soon."

"I'm surprised we haven't had some already."

"They're waiting outside," Ellen remarked. "They can't get at us because the gate is shut. And if anyone should manage to get in, there's a policeman on guard outside. But tomorrow, when the police leave, the reporters will still be there waiting."

There was a collective sigh.

"I think I should check on my kids," Anne said.

"Peter was phoning," George told her. "Better wait till he comes out of the study."

"Oh." Anne relaxed back into her chair. "Yes, I guess he'll have a lot of arrangements to make."

"Yes," George agreed. "There's always a lot to do when someone dies."

"Well," Douglass said, "I guess we'll have to meet with Peter and decide how we can cover for him this week. Do you know what he's working on?"

"Yes." George stood up. "If you ladies will excuse us, we'll get some drinks and talk about the firm for a few minutes."

When the men were gone, Anne turned to Ellen. "So dreadful this had to happen in your home, dear, but she sure got what she deserved, didn't she?"

Ellen took her time answering. "You and she, er, didn't get along, did you?"

"Huh!" Anne's snort was very unladylike. "There are some people you just can't like no matter how hard you try, and then there are those you wouldn't even bother trying to like. I don't see how anyone could. Little golddigger. I wondered when Peter would wake up and realize she only wanted his money."

"You don't think Peter—?"

"Of course I do. Who else could have done it?"

"Well," Ellen said without malice, "I rather thought it might have been you."

6

With some difficulty, Lorry cleared the bed and then got Shauna into it and stayed with her until she fell asleep. Then she turned her bedside light on and sat reading for a while. Her mind was whirling, but one thought was uppermost. Shauna couldn't simply be sent back to her family and her job without first getting some help. But how could Lorry do anything? Perhaps she should talk to Peter in the morning. It seemed unfair to burden him with Shauna when he'd just lost his wife, but who else was there?

Lorry looked down at the page she had been reading in her Bible. She had begun reading the book of Philippians the night before. Now, several verses stood out.

For I know that this shall turn out for my deliverance through your prayers and the provision of the Spirit of Jesus Christ, according to my earnest expectation and hope, that I shall not be put to shame in anything, but that with all boldness, Christ shall even now, as always, be exalted in my body, whether by life or by death. For to me to live is Christ and to die is gain.

"This shall turn out for my deliverance," she repeated, looking over at Shauna. Could Jillian's death result in Shauna's deliverance from the state of fear and oppression in which she had lived her life?

Deep in thought, Lorry was startled by a soft rap on the door. She got up and opened it.

Nick was there. "I was hoping you were still up," he whispered. "How is she?"

"Sleeping."

"Do you want to come down for a while? It's beautiful out on the patio. Kendall and Hildy and Bart and Ellen and I are just sitting out there."

She looked back at Shauna, who was breathing evenly. "Maybe for a few minutes."

As they went downstairs, Nick said, "I wanted to come up earlier and see how it was going, but I didn't think I'd be much help. Is she taking it hard?"

"Well," Lorry answered, wondering how much she should say, "she's pretty upset."

"I guess they were close, eh?"

"I guess. So, what have you been doing?"

He grinned. "Not much. No pun intended, but it's like a morgue here."

She didn't reply.

"I guess that wasn't funny."

"Not especially."

"I wasn't trying to be smart. The truth is I don't want to think about it. Only I can't stop."

"It was pretty awful."

"It was—words are inadequate."

She nodded.

They had reached the patio. Nick went to get Lorry a Coke while she sat down next to Bart.

"Nothing potent, I hope," Bart said when he saw Nick hand Lorry the glass. He slurred the words.

"No," Lorry replied.

"Too bad. I was hoping maybe this had unsettled you enough to get rid of your religious pretense."

"Bart, you are very offensive," Ellen said. "I would assume it's because you're drunk, except I've never known you to get that drunk. Or rather, I've seen you drink a great deal, but never seen it affect you."

"Maybe I'm losing my grip as I get older," he answered, "because I feel drunk."

"I'm sorry, Lorry," Ellen apologized. "This has certainly not been the weekend I had intended when I invited you here."

"It's not your fault."

"You'll just have to come again, Lorry," Kendall said, "when things are back to normal."

"Will they ever be normal again?" Bart asked of no one in particular. "Speaking of which, I need another drink."

"I think you've had enough, Bart," Kendall said.

"You do, do you?" Bart began to get up, but Nick was before him and pushed him back into the chair.

"Lorry, when I asked you to come downstairs, I didn't intend you to have to listen to a drunk."

"I'm okay," she said. "Everyone's upset. I think maybe we should all just go to bed."

"Yes," Ellen stood up. "Let's end this terrible day and hope tomorrow this will all be solved and we can put it behind us."

Hildy followed Ellen inside and Kendall took Bart's arm. "I'll take him over to his room. Be back in a minute."

"Better tell *him* where you're going." Nick nodded toward the police officer who was trying to make himself inconspicuous at the far end of the patio.

At Kendall's insistence, Bart got up and allowed himself to be directed to his apartment above the garage.

Lorry began to stand.

"Don't go," Nick said quickly. "Who knows when I'll have a chance to talk to you alone again."

"I—"

"This is kind of strange," Nick said. "I don't quite know what to say. But I don't want you to disappear on me. We're just starting to get to know each other."

She looked at him. His unruly black hair and bright blue eyes made her think of a mischievous little boy. But his handsome face and the white shirt with several buttons undone, revealing the tanned, muscular line of his neck and shoulders, quickly reminded her that he was a man. She caught her breath. "Nick, I don't—"

His fingers touched her lips. "Don't say it. I already know we have virtually nothing in common. Isn't that why they say opposites attract?"

"I have an engagement ring in my purse."

Part III

A man always makes his troubles less
by going to meet them
instead of waiting for them
to catch up with him,
or trying to run away from them.

Ralph Moody

Chapter Twelve

Try as he might, George Brodie could never sleep past six-thirty. And he couldn't lie in bed once he was awake. Consequently, on Monday morning he'd been in his study for over an hour before he came to the breakfast nook to see if Mrs. Winston had his breakfast ready.

A few minutes past eight, he was putting the finishing touches on bacon and eggs with toast with jam and two cups of coffee. He wasn't looking forward to the rest of the day, but for a few moments at least, he felt at peace with the world.

Mrs. Winston came in to clear up. "I expect Mr. Martin would like a tray in his room, do you think?"

"You're likely right. Perhaps you should have Crystal take a cup of coffee up and see if he's awake."

"Yes, I will, sir. At least…"

"Anything wrong?"

"No, sir. It's just that she hasn't come up yet." She continued hastily, as though suddenly worried that her employer might be unhappy. "Not that it's a problem. I haven't needed her yet this morning. I will a little later, when there are more up for breakfast. Perhaps I'll just go down and make sure she's up. She's one for watching a movie on TV late at night when she should be asleep."

George said nothing, so Mrs. Winston went back to the kitchen and then descended the back stairs to her daughter's room. From there, she checked the bathroom and the small lounge reserved for use by the servants. Returning upstairs, she stood in the middle of the kitchen floor for a few minutes before returning to the breakfast nook. But George had already gone to his study.

She thought for a moment, her forehead wrinkled, eyes narrowed. Finally, she walked along the hall to the door of George's study and knocked.

"Come in."

She peeked around the door. "Mr. Brodie, I expect I'm being foolish, but with what happened yesterday and all, well—"

"What is it, Mrs. Winston?"

"Crystal's not in her room. Her nightgown is on the end of the bed, and her bed's not made. She's not in the kitchen and she's not in the basement."

"Perhaps she's upstairs."

"No, sir, I don't think so. I've been in the kitchen since seven o'clock and she's not come up the stairs. I know her. She'd never be up earlier than that." She was getting more afraid by the minute. "She never gets up earlier than she has to."

"Have you looked outside?"

"I suppose she could be out there." Her doubtful tone belied the words.

"There's a police officer outside. Ask him if he's seen her. Likely, she's had an early swim and she's in the change room."

"Yes, sir." She left the study.

George shook his head. Women! Let one little thing go wrong and they started imagining all sorts of horrors. Well, perhaps he was being unfair. Jillian's murder wasn't exactly a little thing. But still. There was no reason to assume the worst!

When Mrs. Winston opened the back door, she saw the policeman sitting in a patio chair at one of the tables, his back to her.

"Excuse me, officer," she said.

He remained still.

"Excuse me," she called louder.

No response.

She stepped outside, moving toward the prone figure.

His arms were hanging at his sides, chin on his chest. She opened her mouth to scream, then saw his chest rise and fall. She shut her eyes in relief. He was asleep, then. Not dead.

"Officer!" Still no response. "Officer!" She shook him and was rewarded as he raised an arm slightly. She shook him again, calling "Wake up!" in his ear.

His eyes came half open and he shook his head. "Wha—?"

"You're not supposed to sleep, you know."

"Who are you?" He looked around. "Where am I?"

"You're guarding our house, and doing a lousy job if you ask me! Have you seen my daughter?"

"Who?"

"My daughter, Crystal. Have you seen her?"

"I don't—my head. Is there anyone else here? Can you call someone?"

"I'll call someone all right. And I'll report you." She turned to go back to the study to tell George, but a new thought made her walk instead toward the four-car garage. As she walked, she glared up at the window of the apartment Bart was using. "If he's involved—!" She mounted the stairs and knocked on the door.

After a couple of minutes, the door opened. Bart stood there, shirtless and barefoot. The black pants he wore were rumpled, as though he'd slept in them. His chin was unshaven. And his eyes were bloodshot.

"I'm looking for Crystal," the housekeeper said, folding her hands across her chest.

"Crystal?"

"My daughter, and don't bother pretending you don't know. I want her."

"My good lady, your daughter is not here. As a matter of fact, no one's daughter is here. Unfortunately, I am completely alone. Except for you, of course. But somehow, I don't think—"

"Mr. Brodie, this isn't funny. I can't find Crystal. I just want to know she's safe. If she's here, you tell me right now!"

For answer, he stepped back. "You can search the place. She's not here."

"Was she here? Mr. Brodie, I know what you're like. You can't fool me. Was she here?"

"Why does the woman persist in thinking I'm lying?" he asked the door.

She strode past him and looked through the three rooms. She checked under the bed and in the closet and shower. No one was hidden. No one was there. Bart's only companion appeared to have been the empty bottle of Scotch on top of the bedcovers.

She was holding back tears as she returned to the entrance.

Through his hangover, Bart finally sensed her panic. "You're sure she isn't around?"

"She's not in her room or in the kitchen or anywhere I can think of."

"When did you see her last?"

"She went downstairs about eleven last night. I haven't seen her since."

He sighed. "Let me get some shoes and I'll help you look."

By the time she had reached the bottom of the stairs, he had thrust his feet into loafers and thrown on a shirt. He buttoned the shirt as he went down the stairs and listened to Mrs. Winston's story about the sleeping policeman as they walked across the lawn.

The policeman was still sitting in the patio chair, head down, eyes shut.

"Problem, officer?" Bart asked as they came close.

With obvious effort, the young man looked up and said, "I—just call somebody, will you? My backup. And Manziuk. He needs to know about this."

Bart put two hands on the table and leaned against it. "What does Manziuk need to know?"

"I think—" the officer pressed one hand against his forehead. "I think I've been drugged. The last thing I remember is sitting down here just after midnight. I was drinking this." He pointed to a glass about a third filled with dark liquid. "A Coke. I didn't even finish it." He rubbed the back of his neck. "I feel lousy. Headache. Dizzy. And I could go back to sleep in a minute."

"So no one's been watching the house all night?" asked Bart.

Mrs. Winston swayed.

Bart caught her and helped her into a chair.

"She can't find her daughter," Bart explained. "I think I'd better phone Manziuk right now."

As Bart was moving toward the house, the back door opened and Ellen Brodie came out. "Is everything all right? George said something about Crystal's being missing. What should I do?"

"You stay here with Mrs. Winston while I get her a glass of water." He shook his head. "No, I'll get something stronger than that. Look, I'm sure Crystal is okay, but we need to find her. Her mother is pretty worried." He went into the house, and Ellen took a chair beside her housekeeper.

"They'll be wanting their breakfast." Mrs. Winston started to get up, but Ellen firmly pushed her back down.

"I'll look after breakfast. You stay right here until Crystal is found."

Mrs. Winston sat, hands tightly clenched around a handkerchief she had taken from her pocket.

Bart returned with a small glass of brandy, which he handed to Ellen. "Give her this." He looked at the policeman, whose only movement had been to lean forward to cross his arms on the table and rest his head on his arms. "I told Kendall to call 911. I'm going to look for Crystal."

He went back into the house.

Kendall came though the patio doors that led to the games room. He was carrying a cell phone. "Mom? Bart said the policeman was drugged. Was he? I called 911 and they said they'd tell Manziuk. Is anything wrong? I mean, anything else?"

"We can't find Crystal."

"She's not in her room?"

"Bart just went to look for her."

Kendall hurried back into the house.

The two men returned in a few minutes. At Ellen's anxious glance, Bart shook his head. They continued toward the change rooms. Mrs. Winston dissolved into hysterical tears.

Nick appeared at the door to the day room. "What's going on? Kendall just asked me if I'd seen Crystal? Why?"

"We don't know where she is." Ellen's own voice began to shake. "Oh, Nick, if something's happened to her—" Nick hurried forward and she clung to him.

Mrs. Winston began to weep inconsolably.

The police constable made an attempt to get up. But he immediately sank back down into the chair.

Lorry appeared at the back door, and Nick quickly told her about Crystal.

"People will be wanting breakfast. Peter and Shauna," Ellen said helplessly. "Lorry, could you manage, do you think?"

"Certainly. Would you like a cup of tea?"

Ellen glanced at her housekeeper. "Yes, that might help. And maybe coffee for the policeman. That might help him. There should be some left from George's breakfast."

Kendall came running from the change rooms. "We can't find her. Bart's gone to check the garage. I'll take the rose garden. Nick, do you want to look out front?" He stopped. "She wouldn't have gone to the other garden, would she?"

"I'll look there after I check out front. Sound the dinner bell if you find her." Nick hurried off.

Kendall was about to go, too, when Ellen said, "Kendall, do you think you could get your father? He's in his study. Tell him we may need his help."

2

Thirteen-year-old Win Fong was delighted that his best friend, Trent Cooper, had been able to stay for the weekend. This morning, they were going hunting. Win had been given a zoom lens for his birthday a week before and he wanted to test it out. The local fall fair had a photography contest for children up to fourteen, and Win felt the new lens gave him a good chance to win.

The subject he was interested in was birds' nests. With Trent's help, he thought he'd get some terrific shots.

The place they had chosen to hunt in was the ravine at the back of Win's house. And as soon as the two boys had finished breakfast, they were off.

They had climbed two promising trees, and Win had taken five pictures. The day was looking great.

"Let's try that tree over there." Trent pointed to a large ornamental crab fifty feet from where they were standing. "It looks big enough to have three nests in it."

"Yeah, it looks like a good one," Win agreed. "Race you there." He took off, and Trent willed his legs to move faster so he could keep up with his friend.

Win got to the tree first and started up. He was laughing and urging Trent to try to catch him.

Trent waited at the bottom for a minute, watching his friend until he had reached the first solid limb.

"Okay," Win said. "Come on up and I'll make room for you."

"On my way." Trent began to grasp the trunk with both arms.

"Put the lunch down, dummy."

"Oh, yeah. I forgot." Trent looked around for a safe place to leave the canvas lunch sack he had offered to carry. He took a few steps toward a small tree stump and then he stopped. His face blanched. "Win," he said quietly.

"What are you doing? Hurry up!" Win yelled from his perch on the tree limb.

"Win." Trent's voice was somewhat louder than before. But his friend either wasn't listening or didn't hear. "Win!" he yelled with all his might.

"What are you doing over there?"

"I think I'm looking at a dead person."

"You're what?" The voice was only slightly amused. "Aw, come on."

"I'm not joking, Win. I think she's dead."

Annoyed, but curious to see what joke Trent was playing on him, Win Fong climbed down the tree. He walked over to stand next to Trent. "Now what?" He looked to where Trent was pointing. He took a few steps forward and Trent followed. Both boys stood still for ten long seconds. Then Win grabbed Trent's arm. "Let's get out of here!"

"Should—shouldn't we tell somebody?"

"We can tell my mom. Come on! Let's get out of here. Maybe whoever did it is still here. Maybe watching us from behind a tree!" Wasting no further time, Win turned and ran full out with Trent close on his heels.

Kendall knocked on the door to George Brodie's study.

"It's open," George said impatiently. "Oh, it's you. Have they found that dratted girl yet? What a day for her to decide to take a holiday!"

"I think it could be a little more serious than that, Dad. The policeman who was watching the house seems to think he was drugged last night."

"What?" George stood up. "You mean no one was on guard?"

"That's right."

"So much for our wonderful police force. Get slipped a Mickey just like any rookie!" He thrust both hands into the pockets of his gray trousers.

"Mom's out back with Mrs. Winston. They're both pretty upset. She asked if you'd come."

"What does she think I can do?"

Kendall shrugged. "Just be there, I guess. Sympathize or something."

"Does she really think something's happened to the girl?" George frowned as he looked down at the papers on his desk.

"After yesterday, it's easy to believe something bad could happen."

"I guess the truth is I was doing my best to forget about yesterday."

The phone on George's desk rang. George listened for a moment, one hand reaching up to smooth his hair, his body sagging into the chair. At last he said, "Thank you, Mrs. Fong. We will check immediately. And thank you for calling the police. I'm sure they'll be in touch with you." He sat still a moment, staring at the picture on the wall next to the door. It was one of his favorites. A small study by Cezanne. He'd picked it up eight years ago at an auction. It had been a bargain.

"Dad?"

George looked up. Kendall's face was white, his eyes frightened. "Dad?"

George slowly shook his head. "It's her," he said softly. "I'm sure it's her." He leaned over to rest his forehead on his hands. "How are we ever going to tell her mother?"

3

Manziuk and Ryan drove up just after ten. Winding their way through a cordon of newspaper and television reporters, they were let in through the front gate, and Manziuk parked the car.

"I never thought I'd be glad of a house with walls like a prison, but I sure am right now. By the way, if any of the media people get through and try to talk to you, all you say is 'No comment.' Understood?"

"Yes."

"I'll bet," Manziuk muttered as he opened his door.

"Did you say something?" Ryan looked over at him.

"Still mad because I wouldn't let you drive?" He got out of the car and shut his door.

"The senior officer normally lets the junior officer drive," she said as she got out. "Except when he's prejudiced against women."

"I told you I'd get here faster."

"How would you know?" She walked toward the house.

Manziuk slammed the door shut and followed.

George Brodie met them inside the front door. "She's out back," he said in greeting. "Not on our property."

"How do we get there?"

"I'll take you."

Manziuk followed George Brodie through the house to the patio and across the yard to the gate. Ryan followed three steps behind.

The gate was open. Someone had brought a patio chair to keep it from shutting.

The two officers followed George another hundred feet. Now they could see Ford bending over something in the grass beneath a tree. Several others from Ident were gathered at a distance, just outside of a taped circle.

"Thanks, Mr. Brodie," Manziuk said as they came to about fifty feet from the body. "We'll take it from here."

George nodded and turned back.

Manziuk went over to Ford. "How and when?"

"I'd say several hours ago. And she was stabbed."

"Not recent?"

"She's cool," Ford said in response, "the corneas are cloudy, the blood's fairly dry, and there's rigor mortis in the jaws, neck, and shoulders, and starting in the arms. I'd guess six or seven hours minimum. Where's Munsen?"

"Should be here any minute," Manziuk replied.

"Who found her?" Ryan asked.

"Those two kids. They were just walking by." Ford pointed to a trio standing apart from the police officers. Two boys and a woman.

The woman stepped forward. "Excuse me, please. I'm Mrs. Fong, Win's mother." She motioned to the taller of the two boys. "I told them they had no business here, but they said they had to come and give their evidence."

"We were hunting birds' nests," Win explained. "Nothing bad. We wanted to get some pictures for a project."

"Yeah, we weren't going to hurt them."

"Okay, that's fine." Manziuk went over to them, stepping carefully. "You both saw the body?"

Win appeared to be the spokesman. "Yes, sir. Trent saw her while I was up in the tree. He said there was a dead person. I figured he was trying to get back at me—you know, make me waste energy coming down—because I beat him to the tree. But this was sure no joke, huh, officer?"

"No, this is no joke."

Trent spoke up. "At first I thought she was asleep, and I was just going to leave her alone."

"Did you touch her?" Manziuk said.

"Not a chance," Win said derisively. "We know you aren't supposed to touch anything."

"I knew she had to be dead when I saw the knife sticking up," Trent explained. "And that dark stuff. That was blood. It turns dark like that after a while, doesn't it?"

"We saw the knife stuck right in her," Win said reverently. He clutched his chest. "Right here."

"So what did you do?"

"We ran home to tell Mom, and we made her call the cops."

"Yeah," Win agreed. "We were scared the killer was still around."

"Good thinking," Manziuk said. "It pays to be safe."

Win's mother spoke again. "I'm afraid I didn't want to call. I couldn't believe it was true. But then I saw the headline in today's papers. And I remembered hearing police sirens yesterday. There was someone murdered here, wasn't there?"

"Yes, ma'am."

"So then I called. And it turned out they weren't joking. I only hope this doesn't damage them. Seeing a dead body like that. It's horrible!"

"I'll have to send an officer over to take a statement from each of the boys. But you can go now. Sorry, guys," he said as two faces fell. "But this is no place for you right now. We have to do a complete search of the area and as soon as the coroner gets here, the body will be moved." He reached a large hand toward them. "Thanks, guys. We sure appreciate your help. Mrs. Fong, was it? May I see you for a moment?"

The two walked a few steps apart.

"Mrs. Fong, right now these two think this is a swell adventure. They're going to get to tell all their friends they found a real body, and they're going to remember every drop of blood they saw, and they'll likely remember quite a few things they didn't see. But later, tonight or in a few days or a week or even a month, they could start having nightmares or being scared to go to school, or anything. It's normal. A reaction to shock. And we have people they can talk with to work it out. Okay?"

"Yes, officer. Thank you very much. I'll remember, and I'll tell Trent's mother."

They returned to the boys, and Mrs. Fong firmly took charge of them. One on either side of her, her arms around their shoulders, they moved away.

As they went, Manziuk heard the boy whose name was Win say to his friend, "We could have solved it if he'd just let us stay and help!"

"Yeah. Too bad."

"Manziuk!" a voice called from the gate. "Might have known you'd have me out twice on a holiday weekend.

"Hello, Dr. Munsen. Not my idea of a holiday, either."

"This is what we get instead of fireworks," Ford said. "Too bad they didn't use a gun. More fitting."

Manziuk led Munsen and Ryan toward the body. He knew he had to look at it. Examine it. Talk about it as though it was an inanimate object that had no significance except as the main piece of a puzzle to be solved. But, oh, how he hated his job right now. Most of the bodies he had to look at were of people he had never met before. This was a young girl he had spoken with, even joked with a little, the day before. Eighteen. With eyes that sparkled. Getting ready to spread her wings.

He looked down. It was Crystal all right. With her strange-looking hair that had somehow looked good on her. And her earrings. But she had changed her clothing. She had on stretchy black pants and a black long-sleeved T-shirt. To blend into the blackness of the night?

"What have we got?" Munsen asked from behind Manziuk. Ryan was a few feet further back.

"A knife sticking out of her chest," Ford answered. "Like in the movies."

"Yeah? Did they use ketchup?"

"Nope. Nice dried blood, not quite red and not quite black."

"Burgundy," Munsen said. "Used to be a color I liked, too."

"Nice and neat," Ford said as he stood up.

"Not strangled this time, eh?" Munsen said as moved into the spot Ford had vacated.

"Different MO or different perp?" Ford asked.

Manziuk shrugged. "That's what you're supposed to tell me." He had been kneeling beside the body. Now he stood up and walked a short distance away. He felt sick.

He glanced toward Ryan, who was standing about five feet back, hands clutching her notebook, eyes averted. Apparently she was more interested in the ornamental crabapple tree to one side than in the body.

"This isn't a sight-seeing trip," he barked. "You should be making notes."

She glared at him, but opened her notebook and got out an ergonomic ballpoint pen.

Munsen began looking at the body without touching it. After five minutes, he spoke to Ford. "Got your pictures?"

"Yep."

"Okay, let's look a little closer." Munsen's gloved hands began examining different parts of the body, starting with the head and neck. He carefully pulled the knife from the wound and Ford placed it into a plastic bag and labeled it.

"Ordinary paring knife," Ford said to Manziuk. "Like you'd find in any kitchen."

"Small wound," Munsen said absently. "Two wounds. The first to the lower stomach. Looks like a slanted entry. Could have done internal damage. Lots of blood. From the location, there's a possible liver puncture. Tell you later. Second into the lung. Can't tell for sure, but looks like a puncture. Bit of a sucking wound, but with the knife still in it didn't bleed as much as it might have. Don't see anything else. Need to get it to the morgue." He stood up. "I suppose you want a time?"

"As close as possible."

"Well, let's turn her over. You want any more pictures?"

For answer, Ford held up his camera and took several shots of the wounds. Manziuk came closer, stepping in the path Munsen and Ford before him had taken. He looked at the body, making comments into his tape recorder. Then he took out his notebook and made a few sketches and some notes, as well as some measurements.

He looked up to see Ryan standing watching him. "Won't be long," he said. He nodded to Munsen when he was through.

Munsen and Ford lifted the body enough to see that there

were no exit wounds visible, nor anything else unusual. Munsen made a brief check. "Okay, she died right here. No reason to think otherwise. Lividity seems to be pretty well fixed. I'd say seven to twelve hours ago. Be a tad more definite after I've checked her thoroughly."

"When?" Manziuk's voice was urgent.

Munsen sat on his haunches thinking. "I've still got your other one to do this afternoon."

"I'd say two murders at one location moves the priority up," Manziuk said. "We need to catch this guy before there are three."

Munsen nodded. "All right. Got a drunk from an alley to do, and a lady who died after an operation that should have been routine, but I guess I'll bump them and do yours first. Try to do them both right now. Provided nothing else turns up in the next few hours."

"I'd appreciate it," Manziuk stated firmly.

"Yeah. Can't have all these young women getting it." He paused. "I don't suppose these have anything to do with your other ones."

"I don't see any reason to think so," Manziuk replied. He turned to Ford. "Have you done a preliminary search?"

"Done it all. There's a spray of blood close to the path over there." Ford pointed with one gloved hand. "You can see where she was dragged here. Heel marks, no resistance. She was either dead or unconscious when he set her down."

"Can we work out what happened?"

"We'll give it a good try."

"All right." Manziuk pulled out his sketch book. "I won't be long. Tell them no one's leaving until I've had a chance to talk with them." He searched in his other pocket for a measuring tape. "Ryan, you may as well make yourself useful." He held the tape out to her.

She moved forward and took it.

4

Half an hour later, Manziuk, followed by Ryan, walked back toward the house. Before he reached it, he could see a small group gathered on the patio. One person separated himself from the group and strode toward Manziuk.

"You're back, are you?" Manziuk barely smiled. "And you want me to solve this before evening, no doubt."

Special Constable Benson grimaced. "It's not me, Paul. You know it's not me. But we've got the public very upset already. With this girl—well, you know what it's like. Are you sure there's no connection between these murders and the other ones? They're all young women."

Shaking his head, Manziuk said, "The other victims all had red hair and they were all strangled. But there's no clear pattern. A variety of locations. No connection between any of the women. Nothing in common except their hair color. Here, we've got a blond and a brunette, one strangled, which is similar to the others, but one stabbed, which is not. The first one pretty well had to be someone on the grounds. And I think this one was likely done to cover up the first. If you can find a connection, go ahead. But I'd need more to go on before I decided to pursue that avenue."

"The public is outraged that a serial killer is out there and we aren't catching him."

Manziuk scowled. "The public is no more outraged than I am. Does the public know how many hours we've spent sifting the small amount of evidence we have? Or how many times we've gone over what happened? Does the public know how many people we've pulled in? How many hours we've spent asking questions and not getting the right answers? Does the public care that we're doing everything we can?"

Benson crossed his arms in front of his chest. "The public wants results. Mostly, the public wants to know its daughters and wives are safe out of their homes. And in their homes," he added as an afterthought.

"This case is solvable," Manziuk said. "Just keep everybody off my back so I can do my job. As for the other, he'll make a mistake eventually and we'll catch him. I hope it's soon, but I can't guarantee it."

"The papers are full of this case. It's going to be a shooting gallery out there."

"I need time, Benson. I'm a cop, not a miracle worker."

Benson nodded, apparently satisfied. "I'll tell them you're optimistic this will be solved quickly."

As Benson walked quickly toward the front of the house, Manziuk muttered, "I'm always optimistic."

"He looks like someone who really enjoys his job," commented Ryan.

"Huh." He headed toward the small cluster of men on the patio, and Ryan followed.

One of the men was a police officer he didn't recognize. Another was Waite, one of the two who had made the initial response yesterday. The others were Bart, George and Kendall Brodie, Douglass Fischer, and Nick Donovan. A gathering of the menfolk, he thought idly.

"Inspector Manziuk," Officer Waite said as Manziuk and Ryan joined the group. "Have you heard Pratt's report?"

"I don't think so. Who's Pratt?"

"The officer who came to replace Fellowes, sir. Fellowes was on duty here last night, sir," said Waite nervously.

"Let's sit down. It's too hot for wasting any energy." Manziuk placed a chair in what he deemed a good spot with the sun at his back and sat. Waite sat back down. Kendall pulled a chair over for Ryan. "Now, who are Pratt and Fellowes and what's this about?"

"We thought you might have already heard," Waite said. "Officer Fellowes was left here to guard the house last night. This morning, Mrs. Winston, the housekeeper, called to him and found he was asleep."

"And where exactly," Manziuk said, "is Officer Fellowes? Is he not able to talk to us himself?"

"Yes, sir," Waite replied. "I mean, no, sir. He isn't here."

"I sent him to hospital, sir," said the officer who was standing behind Waite.

"Are you Pratt?"

"Yes, sir. I was to replace Fellowes at eight-thirty this morning. When I got here, I found the place in an uproar. A neighbor had just phoned to say there was a body outside the gate. I checked and saw that the young woman was indeed dead. Then I was told that Fellowes thought he had been drugged. He was still very groggy. He said he thought he'd been out most of the night. I looked at his eyes and decided he very well could have been drugged. I called an ambulance."

"So no one was guarding the house all night?"

"No, sir."

"Any idea how he was drugged?"

"There were three possible means. His own thermos of coffee, which was still full. He said he never drank any of it. Also, there was an empty tea cup and a glass of what I think is Coke. It had about a third of the drink left. I've sent them all off to be analyzed."

"Good work." Manziuk stood up and addressed George Brodie. "I'm afraid I'll need to use your study again."

"Do you mean we have to go through the whole thing again?" Douglass Fischer asked. "All the questions, just like yesterday?"

A beeping sound interrupted him. Manziuk's hand dove into the pocket of his trench coat and brought out a small pager. He stopped the noise, then stared at the screen as if trying to decide what to do with it. After a moment, he spoke to George Brodie. "I have a call to make first. But then I will want to speak with each of you. I was coming to talk with you again, anyway. I have some questions based on what we have discovered so far."

"Never fear," Bart said, "we just love to answer questions. What could give us more pleasure than to assist the police in their investigation?" He waited a moment. "Oh, by the way, Inspector, we're very impressed by what we've seen of the police thus far. Do you realize if your cop had done his job this wouldn't have happened?"

Manziuk ignored him. "Where is Mrs. Winston?" he asked George.

Kendall answered. "Mom took her to her room. She was pretty upset."

"Yes, I would expect so," Manziuk said. "Nevertheless, I'd like to see her if I may. Could you ask your mother if that is possible?"

"I suppose so." Kendall turned and walked into the house.

"Rather callous, don't you think?" Bart said. "The woman just lost her only daughter and you want to ask her questions!"

"It's my job," Manziuk growled. He walked a short distance away and, pulling a cell phone from his pocket, dialed a number.

No one else spoke as they waited for Kendall's return.

Five minutes later, Ryan followed Manziuk through the kitchen toward the housekeeper's room. Mrs. Winston had agreed to see them, but only if she could remain lying down for the ordeal.

Indeed, the woman looked as though she couldn't have walked five feet. Her hair was disheveled, her face red and swollen, her hands clasped on her bosom as if in supplication.

Ellen Brodie was sitting on a small chair beside the bed. She, too, for the moment, was teary eyed and frail looking.

Manziuk stood above the bed and placed his big hand on the housekeeper's shoulder. "Mrs. Winston, I can't tell you how sorry I am this happened."

"She was a good girl, Inspector. She never hurt anybody."

Manziuk nodded. Ellen Brodie slipped away and Manziuk settled his bulk on the small chair.

"What happened, Inspector? They said she was stabbed. Was—was that—all?"

"She wasn't sexually assaulted, Mrs. Winston. She was stabbed with a kitchen knife."

"Did she suffer?" The words came out in gasps.

"No. She likely didn't feel anything. It would have happened very fast."

"I wouldn't want her to have suffered."

"No."

"She was going to go to Ryerson, you know. Wanted to be a journalist. You know, work for a newspaper. Her teachers all said she wrote so well. And now—"

Manziuk said nothing.

"She was all I had. Her father died seven years ago. It's been just her and me." Her face dissolved in tears. "Now I'm all alone. What am I going to do?"

"I know it's hard to talk about, Mrs. Winston. But do you have any idea who could have done this?"

"Who would want to hurt her? She never hurt anybody. Never!"

"My thought is that she may have been killed because she knew something about Mrs. Martin's death. Did she say anything to you that could give us a clue?"

She shook her head slowly back and forth.

"Did she tell you anything about what she heard or saw?"

"Well, just about the Fischers fighting a lot. And the Martins, too. And about finding Miss Shauna's dress all torn. But she had no idea who killed Mrs. Martin."

"When did you see Crystal last?"

"She went downstairs to her room about eleven last night. Maybe a little before. That's the last I saw of her." Her voice became a whisper. "The last I'll ever see of her."

"And this morning? Tell me what happened."

She told him about Crystal's failure to appear, her own search of the house, finding the policeman asleep and going to the garage.

"Did you have reason to think Crystal would be with Bart Brodie?"

She shook her head forcefully. "No. It was my last hope that she might be there. I was so scared. And I was right to be scared, wasn't I?" Her eyes stared at him accusingly.

"Yes, Mrs. Winston. You were right."

"How did she seem last night?" Ryan asked from where she was standing behind Manziuk's chair. "Was she happy, unhappy, thoughtful, sad?"

"She was closer to happy than not. In fact, I said something to her about it not being fitting that she should be smiling in a house where there'd been a murder. And she laughed at me and told me that pretense wasn't in these days. That's exactly what she said. I said it wasn't pretending to respect the dead. And she said something I didn't quite catch. Something about one man's tragedy being another man's comedy. I told her to be quiet and do her work." The woman's voice stopped on a mournful note. "Now I'd give anything to hear her say it again."

"Was she having financial trouble?" Manziuk asked. "I know she was going to go to Ryerson. Did she have enough money?"

"She had a scholarship and a student loan, plus what she was saving this summer and what I could manage. It was going to be tight. The problem was how she was going to get back and forth. She would have liked to have a car, but we couldn't afford one."

"Thank you for seeing us, Mrs. Winston. You rest now and don't worry about the house. Mrs. Brodie can manage, I'm sure."

To his surprise, Mrs. Winston agreed. "Oh, yes, she'll do fine. She's a better cook than I am, and I pride myself on my cooking."

A few minutes later, Manziuk and Ryan sat in the study and once more looked at the list of people in the house.

"Who do you want to talk with first?" Ryan asked.

Manziuk was about to answer when there was a knock on the door of the study and it immediately opened. Douglass Fischer stood there. "Do you have a minute?" Fischer asked as he walked in, followed by George Brodie and a haggard Peter Martin. "Have you seen the morning papers?"

"I try not to read them," Manziuk said.

"You try not to read them?" Douglass echoed in disbelief. "Well, you might have a look at these. Our names are splashed across the front page! Look at this. 'Wife of Prominent Lawyer Strangled at House Party.' And then it goes on to name the firm and give details. How did they find out all this? Why do they have to write it up the way they do? It's indecent!"

"You think murder should be decent and orderly?"

Chapter Thirteen

Douglass had the grace to blush. "They don't have to write it up like this. It names everyone in the house."

"These things have a way of happening," Manziuk said.

"Did you talk to the press?"

"No. And neither did any of the other police members on the case. That I can guarantee you."

"I'd like to know who it was."

"Does it really make any difference?" Peter asked wearily. "We knew the press would have a ball with this, so let's try to ignore it and get on with finding out who did it. Maybe if we can solve it, the press won't hound us."

Douglass snorted. "Solve it? Instead of solving Jillian's death, we've got another one on our hands. It's going to be like a circus around here today."

"Don't get us wrong, Inspector," George Brodie said. "We are concerned about what's happened here. But we do have our firm to think of. This kind of publicity is going to do a great deal of damage to our reputation. We want to know what we can do to help—to see that it gets solved as quickly as possible."

Manziuk took up the suggestion at once. "Sounds good to me. The thing that will help me the most is to talk to some people again, please."

George sighed. "Who would you like first?"

"It's only noon and it's already been a long day," Peter Martin remarked as soon as his partners had left the room.

"Yes, I'm sure it has."

"Jillian's family is going to meet me at my apartment at four. That's if it's okay with you."

"Shouldn't be a problem. But I do need to search your apartment and any safety deposit boxes of your wife's."

"And you want my signed permission."

"Unless you want us to have to go to the work of getting a search warrant. We have to check her things. You're a lawyer. You know that."

"And you're hoping you'll find she has a diary and she wrote down that I was threatening her. Isn't that what you mean?"

"Not only a diary. She may have received threatening letters. There are a dozen things we might find."

Peter made a quick movement with his hand as though pushing Manziuk away. "Oh, all right. I know I didn't do it, so I have nothing to hide. And I don't care who it is, I want him punished." He took the papers from Ryan, signed them, and gave them back to Ryan, who took them out to give to Waite, who in turn would hand them over to Ford.

"Mr. Martin, there are some things I need to clarify. Did you know Ms. Reimer lied in order to get here this weekend?"

Peter looked steadily at his questioner. "She told me last night."

"Does this concern you?"

"I suppose in light of Jillian's death, it looks highly suspicious. But I don't believe strangling someone would be quite in Hildy's line."

"You told me before that she is a very controlled person. And your wife's murder was not a momentary act of passion. It appears to have been planned. As does the death of Crystal Winston," he added.

"You must be mistaken."

"No, Mr. Martin, I don't believe I am mistaken."

"Do you have proof?"

"Not conclusive yet. The bodies are being autopsied this afternoon. But I certainly have some things which are quite suggestive."

"Even if it was a planned murder, I don't think you can suspect Hildy."

"Mr. Martin, I'd suspect my own mother if she'd been in this house this weekend."

Silenced, Peter Martin sagged back into his chair. "Go on," he said after a moment.

"Tell me about the relationship between your wife and her sister."

"It was good. Jillian gave her things—clothes, money a few times. She helped out her whole family."

"How?"

"Money, mostly."

"Were they in need?"

"Well, with five daughters… And her father isn't the most… Well, he drinks a little too much, and now and then he loses his job. He's a good worker when he's sober, though."

"Does the family benefit through Mrs. Martin's death?"

He shook his head. "Just the opposite. The money she gave them was mine. She had none in her own name. Not to my knowledge, anyway."

"So her death cuts off a source of more financial help rather than increasing the gains?"

"That's right."

"Did you have insurance on your wife?"

Peter's voice immediately took on more than a hint of anger, "No, I did not. I don't stand to gain by her death in any way, Inspector. In fact, as far as I am aware, no one does."

Manziuk was sitting with his elbows on the arms of his chair, the fingers of his hands interlocked. He looked down at his thumbs for a second, then looked at Peter. "On the contrary, Mr. Martin. I believe you do benefit."

"What?" Peter's voice rose to a high pitch. "What are you insinuating?"

"According to the bank books in your wife's purse, in the last six months, she has invested over one hundred thousand dollars in stocks. Unless she left a will to the contrary, you, as her husband, would be the beneficiary."

Peter frowned. "How much did you say?"

"One hundred and fifteen thousand to be exact."

"I don't believe it."

"You weren't aware of this?"

"No. I paid her bills. And I gave her about two thousand in cash each month. There's no way she could have saved that much money!"

"She also had a bank account with just under twenty thousand in it. The bank account goes back several years and shows some fairly large deposits and withdrawals."

Unless Peter was a very accomplished actor, Manziuk believed he was genuinely puzzled. "I really don't know what to say. Are you sure about this?"

"We're sorry to have to break it to you this way, Mr. Martin," Manziuk said.

"No, no, it's all right. There must be a logical explanation for this. We'll find it."

"I hope so. Now, getting back to Shauna Jensen. Did it not occur to you that your wife was violent with her sister?"

Peter sat straight up. "What are you talking about?"

"When Mrs. Martin struck her Saturday night and tore the new dress she was wearing, didn't you consider that excessive?"

"Jillian had a temper. She didn't mean anything."

"Did she ever strike you?" Ryan shot back at him.

"No, of course not."

Ryan wasn't finished. "I see. She preferred someone who was weaker."

"No, that's not what I meant."

Manziuk quelled Ryan with an annoyed glare. "What did you mean, Mr. Martin?"

"Well, she just—oh, when you put it like that, you're right!" Peter's hands clenched. "She had no business getting so upset with Shauna. But I didn't know she'd struck her." He looked at Ryan. "Did she really?"

"It looks that way," Manziuk said gently.

"I don't know what to say." He stood and walked over to stare into the fireplace. "What do you want me to say?" His voice rose. "That I married a shrew who only wanted my money? Or that I was rapidly growing to hate her? That it was only a matter of time till I got rid of her?" He spun around. "But not like this! Never like this." He placed both hands on the back of a chair and grasped it tightly. "How can I get this across to you? You never knew her. She was so beautiful. Golden. Delicate. So fragile. So—*perfect* is the only word I can find. She made me feel like the luckiest man in the world. It was only after we were married that I began to realize it was all an act. That underneath she was cold and vindictive. And scheming. Always scheming to get her own way. I don't think she ever had a single thought for anyone but herself. She used people. So I decided I'd be the same. I'd use her. I wanted her for what was on the outside, so I kept her happy and she kept up her act with me." He sighed. "But, of course, it couldn't last. You can only live a lie so long. I'd already started thinking that I'd have to do something."

"You said she was vindictive. How would she have taken it if you had divorced her?"

He shuddered. "I don't know. She might have fought me. But we did have a prenuptial agreement. I got burned last time: I took measures to make sure I wouldn't get burned again. But even so, she could have made it very messy."

"Are you having an affair with anyone?"

"No, I'm not." He looked directly into Manziuk's eyes. "But I won't deny I've been thinking about it this last month. You need a woman who cares about you."

"And Ms. Reimer's being here wasn't planned?"

"I swear I had no idea she was coming. I couldn't believe it when I saw her standing there."

"You've talked to her since yesterday?"

Peter hesitated. "A little."

"She told me that she wanted to see how your marriage was going. I'm inclined to think she must have had a better reason than that. What do you think?"

Peter looked at the floor.

"Would you like to tell me her reason?"

"No, Inspector. I think you'd better ask her yourself. Then perhaps you'll understand why I'm feeling very low today. And not nearly as upset as I was with Jillian's murderer. In fact, I'm beginning to think he may have done me a big favor."

"Two more questions, Mr. Martin. Have you anything to add about Nick Donovan? Did your wife say anything to you about him? Anything at all?"

"No. Nothing. Only that Kendall's friend was good-looking and seemed to be interested in Lorry Preston. I think that annoyed her. She liked good-looking men to be interested in her."

"So Bart's interest in Shauna would have annoyed her?"

Peter's voice was dry. "Any man's interest in any other woman would have hit her the same way, Inspector. She thrived on male attention."

"One last question. Where were you between midnight and five this morning?"

"I was in bed sleeping."

"Were you alone?"

"I was."

"Did you have any trouble sleeping?"

"No, I didn't. I fortified myself with several drinks, but I think I would have slept even without them. Yesterday was an exhausting day."

"What time did you go upstairs?"

"Shortly after eleven-thirty. I had some calls to make. It was a very strained evening. I could have gone straight to bed, but after I talked with Hildy I sat in the bar with Bart and we hoisted a few. Not much of a good time. We barely spoke."

"Thank you, Mr. Martin. That will be all for now."

"They're doing an autopsy?"

"Yes, it's necessary."

"I know. Hard to think about, though. No matter what she was like inside," he said simply, "outside, she was perfection."

When Martin had gone, Manziuk paced the floor.

"Do you want me to get Ms. Reimer?" Ryan asked.

"Just a minute." He kept pacing. "Man, I hate this."

"Hate what?"

"All this..." His hand swept the room. "This poison. All the things that come out in a case like this. You can never take people at face value. There's always something—deep, dark secrets that come to light—alcoholism, abuse, affairs, drugs, you name it. Most of it has nothing to do with the crime we're investigating, but after a while, you get sick of it. Here's a pretty young woman. On the surface she's got everything she could want: a husband who's a popular lawyer, enough money, looks, everything she needs, and what do we find out? She's abusing her sister, she's got money that can't be accounted for, and her husband calls her cold and selfish and scheming. What a job we have, eh? Spending our lives trying to dig up the worst about people!"

Ryan took her time responding. "I know a lot of people hide things. But some don't, surely. There are innocent people, too."

"Sure."

She waited.

"Go get Ms. Reimer," he said at last.

She hurried out and after a few minutes found Hildy in the day room. Peter was with her.

"I guess it's your turn to be grilled," he said as Ryan entered the room. "Scream if you need help, and I'll send Nick and Kendall in to rescue you. I'm too old for that."

Ryan looked at him closely. His face was white and his lips had a blue tinge. Remembering the blood pressure medicine Ident had noted, she asked quickly, "Mr. Martin, are you all right? You aren't having any chest pains, are you?"

"What's this?" Hildy demanded of Peter. "Have you had chest pains?"

"Nothing serious. And, no, I don't have any now. I just feel tired, that's all."

"Have you had heart trouble?" Hildy's voice was brisk.

"My blood pressure was a bit high, that's all. Now go talk to the police before you get me upset and I keel over right in front of you."

"That isn't funny, Peter."

Ryan's voice was impassive. "If you'll come with me, Ms. Reimer, it won't take long."

2

Hildy followed Ryan to the study and sat facing Manziuk, who had returned to his chair. "What more do you need to know, Inspector?"

"The truth about why you came here. And why you were carrying a gun."

"The gun was in my suitcase."

"Why was it here at all?"

"It's none of your business. And it has nothing to do with the murder."

"I prefer to decide that for myself."

She sighed. "If I tell you, you're going to think I killed her. And I didn't!"

"I'm not a judge and jury. Just a cop trying to do his job. Do you know how many people have lied to me in the past?"

She looked down and pursed her lips. "Quite a few, I guess."

"Hundreds. Maybe even thousands. And I didn't throw any

of them in jail unless I was completely convinced they were guilty."

She clasped her hands around one knee. "Okay. I give up. I came here to see Jillian because I was tired of dealing with her by phone and by innuendo. I brought the gun because I wanted to use it to threaten her."

"Why?"

"She was trying to blackmail me."

"What did she have on you?"

"Nothing."

"Then how—"

"Maybe it isn't blackmail. I don't know the terminology. But she was threatening my son."

"How?"

"She was Peter's wife. Stephen is Peter's son. She was going to persuade Peter that I was an unfit mother and that Peter should have custody. Then she was going to send Stephen to a boarding school, the worst one she could find!"

"And what did she want?"

Hildy stood up and walked to the fireplace, an exact repetition of what Peter had done earlier. She stared at the unlit logs for a moment. Then she turned. "She wanted fifty thousand dollars."

"And you couldn't get it?"

"I'd already given her twenty-five thousand."

"I see."

"It was never going to end. Stephen is young. What kind of things would she do in the future?" She sighed in exasperation. "Oh, I knew Peter would likely divorce her at some point, or at least try. But it could be years."

"Why not tell Mr. Martin what his wife was doing?"

"I thought of that, but I wasn't sure he'd believe me. From what little I knew, he seemed to be crazy about her. Either he wouldn't believe me or he would be terribly hurt."

"This is your ex-husband we're talking about? Why would it bother you if he found out what his new wife was like? I'd think you'd be pleased to tell him the truth."

She looked away. "I'm not vindictive."

"No?"

"No," she said.

"Did you talk to her?"

"On Sunday afternoon, I found her alone in her room and I told her that I would kill her if she didn't stop her threats. I showed her the gun. She was very angry, but she wasn't foolish. I think she knew I was serious."

"And were you?"

She turned away. "I was very angry. But, no, I wouldn't have killed her. I have a son to think about. I was planning to take Stephen and go away. Change our identities. If you don't believe me, I can show you what I've done. Sold my condo as of the end of the month. Transferred money to a bank account in another name and sent out resumes to get a job out west. They're all in the name Annette Williams."

"So why bother with threatening Mrs. Martin?"

"I needed more time. She wanted the money this week. No way was I going to give it to her. I was hoping to buy some time so we could get away."

"Okay. Is there anything else you haven't told us?"

She shook her head.

"Where were you from midnight until five this morning?"

"In my room."

"Alone?"

"Yes. No witnesses."

"Were you asleep the whole time?"

"No. I was upset, worried, whatever you like. I knew your men had found the gun and that you would suspect me. And I was worried about Peter. I wasn't sure how much she had meant to him. I was afraid he was going to be hurt if the truth came out."

"The truth?"

"From something she said, I gathered I might not be the only one she was trying to blackmail."

"What did she say that made you think that?"

"On the phone, the first time, when I said I wouldn't pay her a dime, she said something like, 'You're all alike, but you all come through in the end.'"

"When was that first contact?"

"Two months ago."

"And you paid twenty-five thousand?"

"In cash."

"Okay, you can go for now. I may want to talk again later."

As the door shut, Ryan said, "You weren't kidding!"

"What?"

"Dirty secrets. Jillian Martin was scum."

"Yeah."

"Who's next?"

"Are you enjoying this as much as it sounds?"

She looked at him. "I suppose I'm enjoying it. Being on homicide, I mean. Shouldn't I?"

He leaned an elbow on the arm of his chair and rubbed his forehead. "Young blood, that's all."

"Would you like me to get someone else?"

"Get one of the Fischers. Him. Cold-blooded iceberg. Let's see if we can make him sweat a little."

3

Douglass looked anything but sweaty as he followed Ryan into the study. He was wearing a golf shirt and navy pants, and he looked very much in control as he sat down, set both forearms on the arms of his chair, and crossed his ankles.

"Just a couple of questions, Mr. Fischer."

"Fire away, Inspector."

"Does your wife have a career, Mr. Fischer?"

Douglass frowned. "I don't see what that has to do with anything."

"Oh, probably nothing." Manziuk leaned back comfortably in his chair. "Curiosity."

"As I told you yesterday, Anne has trouble with her nerves. Migraines, trouble adjusting to her age, and the kids getting older. I don't believe she could handle anything else right now."

"So she has a lot of time on her hands?"

"On the contrary, she's always been very active. Parents' groups, charity work, and looking after the house and kids. She's usually got something going on."

"And you wouldn't say she has any trouble dealing with her lifestyle?"

"Just a few minor health problems." He leaned forward. "None of which, Inspector, have anything to do with Jillian's or the Winston girl's murders, and therefore none of which are really any of your business."

"How long has she had a drinking problem?"

"What?"

"I said—"

"Never mind, I heard you. She does not have what you call a drinking problem."

"Then the bottle is yours?"

"And just what bottle are we talking about?"

"The empty one in the back of your closet."

"It might have been there for weeks."

"No, it wasn't. Constable Ford talked with Mrs. Winston and her daughter yesterday. They were horrified when he suggested the closet hadn't been cleaned before your arrival. They said it was completely empty and had been vacuumed that morning. So, I repeat, Mr. Fischer. Are you aware your wife has a drinking problem?"

Douglass stared at the empty floor between their chairs for a moment. "She takes a few drinks," he said finally. "She doesn't have a 'problem.'"

"That may be. For now, I just want to know whether the bottle was hers."

"Well, it wasn't mine and I didn't even know it was there. I never saw her with a drink." Apparently to himself, he added, "I rarely do."

"It's none of my business, Mr. Fischer, but you might want to consider getting some help for your wife. Some kind of counseling, maybe."

Douglass spoke through clenched teeth. "And you might want to consider that you're here to find a murderer, not to interfere in the lives of innocent people."

Ryan's mouth opened and she began to protest, but Manziuk silenced her with a look. "Quite right, Mr. Fischer," he said easily, "so we need to talk about the note you taped under a drawer in the bureau."

Douglass swallowed twice before saying, "I don't know what you're talking about."

"Fine. Then I'll ask your wife."

"No!" the other man shouted. "No. She doesn't know anything about it."

"The note appeared to be directed to Jillian Martin. Did you write it?"

Head down, Douglass mumbled, "No."

"Were you going to deliver it?"

"No."

"She gave it to you?"

"No."

"Then why did you have it?"

Douglass sat straight now and wiped his forehead with one large hand. He swallowed again. He fingered the suddenly tight collar of his shirt.

"I'm waiting," Manziuk urged.

Douglass shifted himself in the chair. "You're going to think there's more to it than there is," he said.

"Mr. Fischer, as a lawyer, you ought to know that the worst thing you can do is lie to the police."

Douglass sighed. "All right. But I sure hope you don't go off half-cocked over this."

"I'll try not to."

"I decided to go to my room a little before three-thirty. As I was coming out of the games room, I heard Jillian's voice. She had stopped on the stairs to talk to Ellen. I didn't want to bump into her, so I waited. When I'd heard her come down and go through the other hall, I went upstairs. I had left Peter in the bar, so I knew their room would be empty. I knocked quietly, and when no one answered, I went in. I was looking for something. That note was in Jillian's jewel case. I took it and got out."

"Did you find what you were looking for?"

"No."

"What was it?"

"I'd rather not say."

"Mr. Fischer, I have some people on their way right now to search Mrs. Martin's apartment. Do you want to wait until we've finished?"

Douglass wiped his face with his hand. "Oh, never mind the threats. I know when I'm beaten."

"I'll ask you again. What were you looking for?"

"She had some things of mine. A note from the hotel clerk. A copy of the register. And a copy of the receipt. To make a long story short, she was blackmailing me."

Chapter Fourteen

"Had you and Jillian Martin been having an affair?" Manziuk asked.

Douglass Fischer laughed bitterly. "Not a chance. Not with that viper."

"So what did she have on you?"

His voice was strong and clear now. "I made one lousy mistake. One! It was a business trip. I was sick and tired of Anne and her so-called headaches and her whining—so I took my secretary along with me on the weekend. It was just that once, I swear. And I—well, I feel bad. Believe me, I'd never do anything like it again. If only Anne..." He bent his head.

"How did Jillian Martin get hold of the items?"

His head snapped back up. "If I knew! But I don't! Two weeks later, she phoned me and told me all about the weekend. She sent me a copy of the three items and she offered to destroy the originals. For a price."

"How much?"

"Twenty-five thousand."

"You paid it?"

"Of course I paid it. What else could I have done! She was my partner's wife!"

"Did you get the items back?"

His voice continued to be bitter. "Oh, yes, I got them. But two months later, I found out she had kept copies and she wanted another twenty-five thousand. I paid it, but I told her that was all. I said I'd tell Peter if she tried to get more money out of me."

"And?"

"And last week she asked for more. Another twenty-five."

"What did you say?"

"I told her I didn't have it and I wouldn't pay. She told me Anne would be delighted to see the items." One hand ruffled his formerly well-groomed hair. "You've seen Anne. You know how jealous she is and how unstable. It would—I don't know what it would do to her. Maybe it wouldn't matter. I mean, we don't have much of a marriage. But I would hate it if it was me who put her around the bend. And there are the kids to think of. God knows I've been a lousy husband and a lousy father, but I couldn't add this to the rest."

"So you were going to pay?"

"I was stalling. Trying to scare her. Telling her I'd go to Peter. Bluffing that Anne wouldn't care. But she knew better. I went to search the room on the faint hope she'd brought the things with her. And when I found that note, I thought maybe I could pay her back. Threaten to show it to Peter. Maybe then she'd leave me alone. But I never even once thought of murdering her. Though I guess the truth is I'd like to thank whoever did. And I half hope he gets away with it."

"What time did you leave the Martins' room?"

"I must have been there about ten minutes. I kept praying Peter wouldn't come up. I have no idea what I would have said to him. Maybe the truth. And maybe he would have believed me and stopped her. I don't know."

"You went to your room after that?"

"I swear I did. And Anne was there, sound asleep, as I said."

Manziuk stared at him for a few minutes. When Douglass added nothing else, Manziuk asked, "What time did you go to bed last night?"

"About eleven-fifteen. Anne stayed downstairs for a change instead of going straight to her room. I think she was afraid to be alone. But the evening was pretty difficult. We talked for a while up in our room, but we were asleep by midnight."

"And you slept soundly?"

"Yes," he said. Then he changed his mind. "Well, I woke up once—about three. I went back to sleep about ten minutes later."

"Did your wife wake up then, too?"

"No. She had taken a sleeping pill. She slept through."

"All right. I'll need to talk with your wife now."

An anguished cry came from Douglass's lips. "You won't tell her?"

"About the blackmail? Perhaps not. I just have to find out if there's anything she hasn't told me."

2

"I've told you everything," Anne Fischer said a few minutes later. She crossed her ankles and smoothed the skirt of her pink and green floral sleeveless dress. Her brown hair, which was not quite shoulder-length, was loose, held by two green barrettes, and she looked more relaxed than Manziuk had yet seen her.

"Tell me about the brandy bottle in your closet," he said.

She clasped her hands and her face took on a wary look. "I don't have any idea what you are talking about."

"Your room was spotless when you moved into it. I have a witness who would swear to that in court. So where did the bottle come from?"

"I have no idea. Ask Douglass."

"I did ask him. He denies touching it. And our fingerprint department bears him out."

"You checked it for fingerprints? Why?" She had lost her superior edge and sounded frightened.

"Do you want to tell me about it, or would you rather I told you what I think?"

One hand smoothed her hair as she looked away from Manziuk and then back to him. "I'm not interested in what you think. Anyway, why shouldn't I have a drink if I want to? I'm over twenty-one. Just because the rest of them drink at the bar and I prefer to do it in my room, what business is it of yours?"

"Was that what Jillian Martin had on you?"

"What?"

"Did she know about your drinking?"

"Of course not," Anne scoffed. "She was the wife of Douglass's partner. She wasn't a friend. Not," she said defiantly, "that I care who knows. I haven't done anything wrong."

"We are aware that Mrs. Martin wasn't opposed to a little blackmail."

There was no surprise at the direction the interrogation was taking. "I suppose she left a notebook or something?"

Manziuk waited for her to continue.

When she didn't volunteer anything, Ryan said, "Every victim's nightmare."

Anne smoothed her skirt. "What?" she asked absently.

"You feel intense relief knowing your persecutor is dead. But you spend hours agonizing about who will find the incriminating documents."

"There were no documents," Anne replied. Realizing what she had said, she quickly back-pedaled. "This has nothing to do with me. Jillian wasn't blackmailing me."

"Very well. What was she doing?" Manziuk asked.

"I don't know what you're talking about."

"You had to have some reason for disliking her as much as you obviously did. What had she done?"

"I don't have to answer any of your questions." She was twisting her wedding rings now, her hands moving rhythmically, automatically.

"No, you don't. But it would speed up the investigation if I could eliminate you as a suspect."

She stared at him. "What's that supposed to mean?"

"It means that if I know the truth, I can often put the puzzle together and get the right answer. If I don't know the truth, I'm apt to suspect the wrong person, the one who's holding out on me, for instance."

"If I told you the truth, you'd think I killed her, and I didn't."

"Why is it," Manziuk asked wearily, "that everyone in this house seems to think I arrest people for being honest?"

"Well, it looks bad. And I have no proof."

"Proof of what?"

"She was threatening to take Douglass away from me." Anne's eyes filled with tears.

"I see."

"I don't," Ryan said.

"She—this is all so demeaning. She and Douglass were having an affair. I begged her to stop, to let him go, but she refused. She—" Anne's face crumpled and Ryan quickly reached to give her a Kleenex. "She said I didn't deserve him. And she's right. I don't do the things I should. I'm not sexy or—" She regained her composure. "We got married because I was stupid enough to get pregnant. It was my fault. I was taking the pill and I forgot. And

I didn't know what to do. My family would have been devastated. It was before abortions became easy. So Douglass married me." She paused, her mind wandering back through the years. "I was never good enough for him. I have only one year of college. All his years of university and law school, he had to support us. He had to work part time and he could never enjoy himself like his friends. And then, after, when we didn't have financial worries—I don't know, we just don't seem to have anything in common except the kids, and even there... He works so hard. He never seems to have time for them. And I don't seem to be doing a very good job of raising them by myself." She was crying in earnest by the time she finished. Ryan pushed the box of Kleenex toward her.

"Jillian told you she and Douglass had been having an affair?" Manziuk said.

"Yes."

"You believed her?"

"Of course."

"Why?"

"Why?" She seemed puzzled. "Why not? She was young and beautiful—everything I'm not."

"Why didn't you tell Peter?"

"She said Peter would never believe me. She dared me to tell him. I couldn't. She was right. He'd never believe me. And Douglass would have hated me for causing trouble."

"How much did Jillian want?"

Anne's voice became a whisper. "Twenty-five thousand."

"Did you pay?"

"I don't have any money. I buy the groceries and clothes and things, but that's out of our account. We keep about a thousand or two in it. I know we have retirement savings and some stocks and bonds, but I wouldn't have any idea how to get the money out."

"What were you going to do?"

Her voice was still a whisper. "I don't know. I really don't know. I thought of killing myself. I thought if I took the whole bottle of sleeping pills and drank several big glasses of whiskey or something like that, that I would just die and I wouldn't feel anything. And I thought they might believe it was an accident. I wouldn't want the kids to grow up thinking their mother killed herself. But I didn't know what else to do. Except let her have him. I guess maybe the kids and I could have managed." Her voice trailed away. "Though I don't know how."

"Did you think of killing her?" Manziuk asked.

"Once. I was cutting up some steaks, and I thought how nice it would be to have her come in and I could let the knife go into her and I could say it was an accident. But I don't think I could have done that." Her voice became bitter. "I wouldn't have the guts to do anything like that."

"May I suggest that you look into getting some counseling, Mrs. Fischer? And I think you'd better tell your husband what you've told me."

Her eyes widened in fear. "I couldn't."

"You'd be very foolish not to."

She said nothing, but her lower lip began to tremble. She fled from the room.

"Let's hope he was telling the truth," Ryan said dryly.

"Let's," Manziuk agreed. He stared at his hands for a moment and then said, "I have a phone call to make. Get Nick Donovan, will you, but don't rush."

3

Nick was playing cards on the patio with Kendall. As Ryan came up, she saw Nick spread his hand on the table and say, "Gin." His voice was anything but excited.

"Inspector Manziuk would like to speak with you again, Mr. Donovan."

"Oh, Lord," Nick complained, "already?"

"Afraid so."

"Can I grab a drink first? Something to keep my knees from shaking?"

Remembering Manziuk's suggestion that she could take her time, Ryan nodded. "If you think it will help."

"You're wonderful," Nick declared as he crossed to the bar and poured a drink. "My favorite cop. Usually they just glare at me as they write out the speeding tickets. But I guess you're way beyond that, aren't you?"

"You've got it," Ryan replied.

"Aren't you a bit young to be a detective? You don't look more than my age."

"I've got a few years on you, but yes, I am young to be a detective, not to mention being a woman."

"I was careful not to mention that," Nick said. "I'm well aware of all the politically incorrect things we shouldn't say. That's why I haven't noticed that you're black, either."

"Very kind of you, I'm sure," she said dryly. "Inspector Manziuk is waiting. If you've fortified your nerves, Mr. Donovan?

"Mustn't keep the good inspector waiting."

Manziuk was still on the phone. "Okay, tell him I'll try to get over this evening. And tell him not to worry. Sure, I miss him, but he doesn't need to think I can't do the job without him to nag at me.... Okay.... Take care, Arlie."

Ryan wondered why Manziuk had been making what appeared to be a personal call, but decided it was none of her business.

"Here I am," Nick said cheerfully as he sat in the chair he had used yesterday. "Ready for the third degree."

Manziuk took his time getting up and walking around to his easy chair. Ryan took her place behind the desk and prepared to take notes.

"So, Nick," Manziuk said as he made himself comfortable in the chair, "how's it going?"

"I can't say this has been one of my favorite weekends."

"Nick, I need to know what clothes you were wearing yesterday."

"You need to know what clothes I was wearing?"

"Yes."

"You mean in the afternoon, don't you? When Jillian was murdered?"

"That's right."

"You saw me. I was wearing a pair of white shorts and a red T-shirt."

"Thank you. Would you mind giving me the clothes before I leave?"

"You can have them." Nick leaned forward. "Look, Inspector, it doesn't take a genius to know where your mind is going. But I had no reason to kill her. I hadn't even seen her for almost four years."

Manziuk opened his notebook and took out the copy he'd made of the note that had been found taped to the bottom of the drawer in the Fischer's bedroom. "This looks like a pretty good motive to me."

Nick read it, then handed it back. "Where did you get this?"

"The question is, did you write it?"

"No."

"You'll forgive me if I think it sounds pretty appropriate given the circumstances."

"Look, I don't know if somebody is trying to frame me or if this is all a coincidence, but I didn't write that note and I didn't kill her."

"The note was typed in this house on the typewriter right over there." He pointed to the Selectric typewriter sitting on the small table in the corner.

"Not by me. I told you everything there is to tell."

"How about last night? Where were you from midnight on?"

"Kendall and I went upstairs at about a quarter past twelve or so. I was awake for a while. Kendall went to sleep right away."

"How long would you say you were awake?"

"I don't know. 'Till two-thirty at least."

"Why?"

"Gee, I don't know. Could it be because I was in a house where there had been a murder? Or maybe it was because I have a lot of other things to think about. Like what I'm going to do with my life."

"What made you think about the future?" Manziuk asked.

Nick's voice suddenly became more serious. "Jillian's death, I guess. I realized you never know when it'll come. I suppose I started to seriously wonder for the first time if I was making a mistake turning down the job offer. You know the routine: is this how I want to be remembered? Is this my contribution to mankind?"

"Did you see or hear anything that would help us? Crystal Winston died somewhere between midnight and three AM.

"All I can tell you is that neither Kendall nor I did it."

"All right, Mr. Donovan. If you could give those clothes to Detective Ryan… and we'll need your fingerprints, too."

"Yeah, sure." He strode out of the room.

As if knowing the timing was perfect, the phone rang.

"Yes?" Ryan said into the receiver. Then, "He's right here."

Manziuk took the receiver and listened. Ryan paced back and forth around the room.

After five minutes and a couple of questions, he hung up.

"That was the preliminary autopsy report on Jillian Martin. Munsen must have raced back to do it. All the tests won't be done for a day or so, but there's no doubt she was strangled. Not with the rope from George Brodie's robe. Munsen thinks the garden cord looks about right. There were a few fibers on her neck, and some under her nails, too. Other than the bruises on her neck and a crushed hyoid bone, both caused by the cord, there's nothing of interest.

"There's not much of anything else. She looks to have showered not long before going out. No foreign hairs on her. And no fibers, either. It's as if whoever strangled her did it without actually touching her."

"Could that have happened?"

"Let's try it," Manziuk said.

"What?"

He pushed the chair from the typewriter desk toward her. "Sit down and pretend you're watching something."

She looked at him as if he'd lost his mind, but complied.

"I'm not going to actually strangle you," he said. "Just in case you wondered. Hold up your arms."

She did as he asked, now totally puzzled.

Manziuk slipped a piece of rope around her chest, just under the armpits. "Okay, put your arms down." He pulled the two ends of the cord together and twisted.

"Ouch!"

"See. I'm not touching you at all. The chair back holds you in place. I've got the ends twisted around each other, and that gives me all the leverage I need. I can just tighten the rope and there's nothing you can do about it."

"How nice."

"It could have been forethought," he said, "or it could have been luck. I guess we'll know which when we find out who did it." He released the rope and she rubbed the area under her arms.

"I think it was Nick Donovan," she said.

"Maybe."

"You're not convinced?"

"I don't like it when things fall into place. Nick Donovan isn't stupid. Why would he write a note that we could find?"

"Everyone makes a mistake."

"I know. But one unsigned note that sounds as though it might have come from a certain person isn't exactly admissible evidence. Not all alone, anyway."

"But if he is guilty…"

"Crystal Winston's death becomes my fault. Is that what you're thinking? Because I had the note yesterday and I choose not to act on it?"

"It's possible."

"You're right. It is possible. And that's one of the things that makes this job difficult. Second guessing. Never knowing if your decision might have saved or taken a life."

"Could you have arrested him yesterday?"

"I didn't have the autopsy results. He denies writing the note. We don't have the murder weapon. Nothing concrete."

"If he is the murderer, he might give you the wrong clothes."

"Then get the clothes from him. Put them in plastic bags. And get a couple of people to identify them. Douglass Fischer. George Brodie. Somebody objective. And tell Lorry Preston I want to talk to her. I want an impartial observer. She's about the only one who I'm reasonably sure didn't do it."

As Ryan moved toward the door, he said, "What really bothers me is that there was nothing on her dress. That's what our serial killer does. He strangles people without leaving anything of himself. No traceable fibers, no hairs, nothing. I don't like this. It muddies everything up."

"You think there might be a connection?"

"Frankly, I don't know what to think."

Ryan couldn't find Lorry downstairs. Finally, she went to the patio, where Kendall was sitting alone.

"Where's Nick?" he asked when he saw her.

"Do you know where Lorry Preston is?" she countered.

"Likely in her room. She and Shauna have been there most of the day."

"Could you show me?"

He stood and she followed him into the house and up the stairs. They met Nick on his way down with a bundle of clothes.

"Where are you going?" Nick asked.

"She wants Lorry," Kendall replied. "Don't ask me why. I suppose they think she did it."

His voice sounding annoyed, Nick said, "That isn't funny."

Kendall turned to look at the policewoman behind him. "What's with him?"

"Maybe he doesn't like jokes about murder."

Ryan accepted the clothes and put them into two bags she had picked up from one of Ford's men. "Shoes, too," she ordered.

"Sorry." Nick turned to go back upstairs. The others followed. After getting and bagging the shoes, Ryan had Kendall take her to Lorry's room.

"I wish I knew what's going on," he complained before rapping on the bedroom door.

4

"Thanks for coming back to talk, Miss Preston," Manziuk said in a fatherly voice. "I know this must be difficult for you."

"I'm okay. It's been hard on everyone, but especially Mr. Martin and Mrs. Winston."

"Yes. Just a couple of questions. What was Nick Donovan wearing yesterday afternoon when you went for the walk with him and Kendall?"

She looked at him as if she thought he had lost his mind. "What was he wearing?"

"Yes."

"I'm not sure. Does it matter?" When he nodded, she said, "We saw him coming from the rose garden. Oh, yes. He had on white shorts and a red knit shirt. And sandals, I think. And he had on sunglasses."

"Would these be the shorts and shirt?" He held them up.

"Yes, I think so." Her voice was clearly puzzled. "Does it matter?"

"Maybe not. So, you think these are the clothes?"

"Well, I can't be certain, but I believe so. There was a small logo on the shirt—a crest. Yes, that's it."

"Just as a matter of record, what were you wearing?"

"A teal sundress and beige sandals."

"Thank you. That's blue, isn't it?"

"Blue-green."

"And Kendall?"

"He had on gray shorts and a striped shirt. Pink and white and gray."

"Was he wearing sandals?"

"I don't think so. I think he had moccasins or loafers. Something like that."

"Okay. Enough about clothes. Miss Preston, would it surprise you to learn that Nick Donovan was once romantically involved with Jillian Martin?"

"Jillian and Nick?" She seemed to be working to fit the two names together. "Yes, I guess it would. Neither of them mentioned it."

Manziuk thought she had lost some color.

"Would you be surprised to know that Nick Donovan is our prime suspect?"

This time her face definitely lost some color. "You think Nick killed them?"

"There's some reason to think that."

"I don't believe it," she said after a moment. "You weren't there when we found Jillian. Nick was the one who discovered she was dead. He couldn't have faked it."

"He couldn't have faked what?"

"His astonishment. He was very upset. I thought so at the time. It sounds crazy, because anyone would have been upset at finding her like that. But if they'd been close once, that would explain it."

"So you think he was surprised by her death?"

"I'm sure he was."

"And I'm sure that given the need, Mr. Nick Donovan could do a very fine job of acting."

Her large green eyes stared at him. Slowly, she nodded.

"Miss Preston, do you want us to find the murderer?"

"Yes, certainly."

"No matter who it is?"

"Yes." Her reply was firm.

"Will you give me some help?"

She stared at him. "But I don't know anything!"

"You are the one person in this house who is reasonably objective. You've never met most of these people before this weekend. You don't even know your relatives well. But you've been here the whole time. I'm restricted to what I can learn from people who may be lying or trying to cover up. You were here. You've seen them as they ate supper or played a game of pool or tennis. Do you get what I mean?"

"I think so. But I really haven't noticed anything."

"Okay. We'll leave it for now. How is Shauna Jensen?"

"I think what happened Saturday did something to her. She'd never before questioned Jillian's wisdom. And when Bart talked her into getting the dress and changing her hair and makeup and everything, she realized Jillian had been, at best, wrong. And then Jillian's anger—Shauna didn't understand. It was as if Jillian was angry because Shauna had taken the attention from her. And Shauna wasn't sure how to deal with it. I think she's dealing with a lot of guilt and confusion and anger."

"She hasn't said anything to you that leads you to believe she could have been angry enough to kill her sister?"

"Nothing like that. She's very mixed up. As I said, it's almost as if a spell had been broken, as though she'd just wakened from an enchanted sleep, and now she isn't sure how to evaluate the past or what to do next."

"Has she told you about her drawing?" Manziuk asked.

"Drawing?"

"Yes. She has a book of sketches in the room. According to Forensics, they're quite good. And there's a brochure from an art school. Looks like she was thinking about taking lessons."

Lorry shook her head. "She didn't say anything to me."

"Could be she was getting ready to sprout her wings before this weekend."

"So you think she might have planned this? To kill Jillian so she would be free of her?"

"It's within the realm of possibility."

"I don't believe it."

"Perhaps you aren't looking at it the way I am."

"What do you mean?"

"It has to be one of the people in this house."

She stared at him for a long moment. "It has to be?"

"Yes," he said. "So if you notice anything, or if you remember anything, tell me or one of the officers who will be here."

She nodded.

"And don't forget."

Her eyes locked on his. "You think Crystal knew something."

"I do."

"Something she didn't tell you."

"And now she never will."

"If I know anything, it's something I don't know I know."

"Yes, I believe you."

"What about Bart Brodie?" Ryan interjected. "Has he been in contact with Shauna Jensen since supper last night?

Lorry shook her head. "She's been in her room all morning. I got her a tray about eleven o'clock. Crystal's death has really shaken her."

"What about last night?"

"I think they may have talked for a little while right after supper. I don't know what it was about, but Shauna said something to me later about how some people couldn't be trusted. I'm not sure, but my impression was that she was talking about Bart."

"Okay," said Manziuk. "One last question. Where were you last night between midnight and five this morning?"

She thought for a minute. "I came up about fifteen minutes after midnight. Shauna was sound asleep. I wasn't feeling tired for some reason." She hesitated. "To be honest, the whole thing sort of got to me. I had a hard time going to sleep. I finally decided the best thing to do was just pray for everyone here."

He nodded. "That put you to sleep?"

She smiled. "No, but I felt better afterwards."

"So what time did you go to sleep?"

"The last time I looked at my watch it was twenty-five after two."

"So you can swear that Shauna didn't leave the room up until then?"

"She was sound asleep."

"And you didn't hear anything? The sound of a door? Footsteps in the hall or on the stairs?"

She shivered. "No. I didn't."

"Okay. Thank you, Miss Preston. This has been a very hard time for you. The events may come back to you often. Especially finding the body. You may want to talk to a professional. We can make arrangements at the station."

"Thank you very much, Inspector, but I don't think that will be necessary."

He escorted her to the door.

He put his hand on the doorknob, but paused without turning it. "Miss Preston?"

"Yes?"

"I think this is probably very far fetched. But there is a slight chance Mrs. Martin's murder may be connected to a series of four murders we've had in this city. All of the young women, who were about your age, had red hair."

Lorry's hand moved upward. "You think...?"

"No, not really. Jillian Martin's hair was a golden blond, not red. But whether it's the same person or not, you still have red hair. So take good care of yourself. You may be at risk here in this house; you're definitely at risk when you leave here and go downtown. Don't go out on the streets by yourself at night. Even in the daytime, it's risky for you to be alone until we catch this person."

"Thank you. I'll remember your advice. But I also believe God will take care of me no matter who might try to harm me."

"Believe in God," he said, "but watch your back just the same."

She went out and Manziuk turned to go back to his chair.

"Cold-blooded piece," said Ryan.

"You think so?"

"She finds a murdered lady one day, and she's as cool as a cucumber the next."

"Maybe."

"So, she identified the clothes. Douglass Fischer didn't know. Hildy Reimer was also pretty sure these were the ones. Recognized the insignia on the shirt."

5

Ten minutes later, Ryan brought Shauna Jensen to the room. The girl was wearing normal glasses and Manziuk could clearly see the bruising under her left eye. Her hair was unkempt and her naked face pale. Her clothes were untidy, too, as though she'd thrown on the first blouse and skirt that came to hand. She slumped into the chair across from Manziuk and stared at the floor.

"Just a couple of questions, Ms. Jensen," Manziuk said. "I know this isn't easy for you, so I'll try to be as quick as I can."

She shrugged her right shoulder; he interpreted the shrug as an indication that she didn't care what he did.

"Last night, when did you go to bed?"

"Ask Lorry," she said so quietly he had to strain to hear the words. "She'd know. I was too out of it."

"You were distraught because of your sister's death?"

"I guess."

"So much that you didn't notice the time?"

"I wasn't in the least thinking about the time!" Her voice grew in volume. "Would you have been caring what time it was when your sister had been murdered like that?" Her eyes came up to meet his. "I said to ask Lorry. She was looking after me. She's the only one here who cares how I feel."

"I'm glad you had Ms. Preston's assistance. Are you feeling better today?"

She had become much more animated. "Another girl is murdered and you think I should be feeling better? How do you know I'm not next?"

"Well, I certainly hope no one is next. I hope—"

"Well, you didn't do anything to help Crystal, did you? I heard your policeman was asleep."

"Drugged, not asleep."

She made a face. "Same thing. He wasn't watching like he should have been. You shouldn't make us stay here. I want to go home."

"I believe Mr. Martin is taking you to his apartment later today, where your parents will meet you."

She sat up straight and her eyes grew large. "My parents? Coming today? Oh, no!"

"Naturally, they'd want to—"

"I won't go back there! I won't, I tell you! I'm never going back there! They can't make me!" She was breathing hard. Now she paused and looked appealingly into Manziuk's eyes. "Can they?" she breathed.

Chapter Fifteen

"No one can make you go anywhere," Ryan said matter-of-factly. "You're old enough to decide what you do with your life."

"They don't think so." Shauna turned to face Ryan. "They all think I'm stupid. That I couldn't manage by myself."

"You're over twenty-one," Ryan said. "That means you're an adult. No one else can tell you where you have to live or what you have to do."

"At the same time—" Manziuk's eyes were on Ryan "— you have been through a shock and you may well need your family to care for you until you recover."

Shauna swiveled back to stare at him. "You don't understand at all, do you? You've never had people tell you you weren't capable of doing what you wanted to do. You've never had them go on and on at you until you didn't know yourself what you wanted. Well, I've just escaped and I'm not going back."

"Good for you," Ryan said, her eyes meeting Manziuk's without apology.

"What is it that you want to do?" Manziuk asked, his voice far more gentle than might have been expected.

"I want to study art!" Her voice was defiant, her eyes darting from Ryan to Manziuk and back as if daring either of them to laugh at her. "I want to illustrate books for children."

"That's a tough field," Manziuk said.

"Don't worry. I know." Her tone was bitter. "And I'm not smart enough to cope, and I'm not forceful enough to get myself known, and I'm not good enough to do it anyway. I know. My family has told me. Every time I ever mentioned it."

"What makes you think you can do it now when you haven't felt confident enough before?" Ryan asked.

"Because I just realized Jillian's been lying to me all my life," Shauna said simply. "How do I know the others haven't been lying, too? You know what? I bet they didn't want me to leave because they wanted my money. Every month I hand over nearly all my money from working in the library. That's why they don't want me to go away!"

Manziuk had no answer for this, so he changed the subject. "Did you leave your room after midnight last night?"

"I slept very soundly from before that till late this morning."

"Is there anything you haven't told us that might help us discover the killer of your sister or Crystal Winston?"

Mutely, she shook her head.

"If you think of anything, let us know."

She nodded. "May I go now?"

"Yes."

She almost ran to the door.

"She's in fine fettle," Manziuk said.

"She's stretched tight."

"You didn't exactly help with your 'You're an adult, you can do what you want' bit."

Ryan frowned. "Why shouldn't she study art? Ford thought she was good."

"We're cops. We don't give personal advice to witnesses or suspects."

"Right. Like suggesting that Anne Fischer get counseling."

"I suggested she get counseling; I didn't try to counsel her myself!"

She merely looked at him.

2

In contrast to Shauna, Ellen Brodie sat up straight in the chair, her eyes on Manziuk, her body language expectant. She wanted to help. She wanted to rid this house of the blot staining it.

"Mrs. Brodie, I need to know where you were from midnight last night until five this morning."

"I was in my room, Inspector. Shortly after midnight, I went to sleep and I didn't awaken until after almost eight."

"And your husband?"

"He was with me, of course. Except he got up at six-thirty, as always."

"If you were asleep, how do you know he was there?"

"I'm a light sleeper. I hear George get up every morning. I keep a book by my bed to read when he wakes me up."

"So if your husband had left the room during the night, you would know?"

"Yes, I would."

"And he did not?"

"No, he did not."

"Thank you. These questions must be asked. Now, Mrs. Brodie, can you tell me anything about yesterday or this morning? Anything unusual? Something someone said or did?"

"No, I don't believe so. Except of course the policeman who had been drugged. That's very puzzling, don't you think? Someone must have wanted him out of the way very badly to do something like that."

"Yes, you're right. Whatever Crystal Winston knew was damaging to someone. She had to be silenced."

Ellen shivered.

"I'd bet anything her murderer arranged to talk with her, maybe even to pay her something, all the time planning to kill her. And the murderer could strike again. That's why, if there is anything you haven't told us, it's risky to keep silent."

She thought for a moment. "You're correct, Inspector. I will tell you, but I do hope it is meaningless." She leaned forward. "Bart and Shauna told you they didn't come back until after four yesterday. But that isn't true. I saw them from the kitchen window just before I went upstairs."

"That was at three-thirty?"

"About then. I'd just stopped in to talk to Mrs. Winston for a minute to check on supper, and as I was leaving, I happened to glance out of the window and see them coming toward the house. I noticed them particularly because they seemed to be arguing. But that's all I saw."

"Could Mrs. Winston have seen them, too?"

Ellen thought for a moment, then shook her head. "No," she said. "She was at the stove stirring a sauce. She wouldn't have left it for a second."

"Was anyone else in the kitchen?"

"Just Crystal."

"Could she have looked out the window?"

Again, Ellen had to stop and think, obviously picturing the scene she was describing. "She could have. Now, mind, I don't know if she did. But she was walking about preparing to peel potatoes, and she might have looked out the window." Ellen leaned towards him. "But that doesn't mean either Bart or Shauna murdered Jillian."

"If they didn't," he said, "they have nothing to fear."

3

Bart Brodie looked anything but afraid when he entered the room a few minutes later. In fact, he looked bored. "So, we play Ring Around the Rosy some more, do we, Inspector?"

"I prefer Truth or Consequences," Ryan retorted.

"What's that supposed to mean?"

Manziuk glared at his partner, and she bent her head to take notes. "It means, the time has come for you to tell the truth. As in, for example, what time you came back from your walk yesterday afternoon. You and Shauna Jensen seem to have been half an hour premature in returning."

Bart laughed. "Is that all? Inspector, I haven't the slightest idea why she did that. Lied, I mean. You talked to her first, and she whispered to me that she'd said we came back after four. It was only polite for me to give you the same story, but naturally I thought someone must have observed us. I was quite surprised when you didn't question the time yesterday."

"There were several things I didn't question yesterday," Manziuk replied dryly. "What caused the argument?"

Bart raised his eyebrows. "You must have your little spies everywhere. How nice for you."

"You haven't answered my question."

"As you might have guessed had you put your mind to it, we were discussing Shauna's life, or rather, her lack of one."

"You were arguing."

"We interpreted some things differently. I told her she was a stupid imbecile. She didn't like my choice of words. In fact, now that I think about it, I don't think she liked anything about me."

"Did she eventually see things your way?"

"She ran into the house."

"Where did you go?"

"My apartment above the garage."

"So the truth is neither of you had an alibi for the time Jillian Martin was killed?"

"Actually, Shauna came up to my apartment about twenty minutes later. She'd been crying. Came to apologize. Said I was right, that Jillian had no business treating her the way she did. She didn't act or sound like somebody who'd just murdered her sister."

"You know what she'd sound like if she had?"

Bart grinned. "I suppose not."

"Was Jillian Martin blackmailing you?" Manziuk asked.

Bart appeared to be genuinely taken aback. "Was she what?"

"Just wondering."

"We'd never even met before this weekend, and I was completely unaware of her very existence."

"So you had no motive for killing her?"

"None whatsoever. And no, I didn't kill her because she was nasty to her sister, either. Nor did Shauna request me to do it for her. No Lady Macbeth she. Besides, it wasn't Jillian's fault that Shauna was so gullible." His voice took on a more serious note. "Are you serious about blackmail?"

"Have you spoken to Shauna since yesterday at supper?"

"Last night. Briefly." He studied the floor. There was silence until he suddenly looked up. "Oh," he said in surprise, "you want to know what we said, don't you?"

"Were you still arguing?"

"You know, I really think our conversation has nothing to do with you. We were neither planning another murder nor discussing how to hide evidence." He looked innocently at Manziuk. "You really don't have much of a sense of humor, do you?" His eyes focused on Ryan. "Must be highly tedious working with this man." He sighed. "We were discussing her dependency on Jillian and the rest of her family. I feel sorry for the little beggar. I was trying to put a little backbone in her, and I was doing it in what you'd call reverse psychology. Telling her I thought she was right to play it safe, that sort of stuff. Boy, did she get mad."

"Thank you. Now, can you tell me where you were last night after midnight?"

"Last night? Not the clearest one to pick. But I'll try. I went to my apartment around midnight. At least, that's what time I heard someone say it was. Ask Kendall; I believe he was my escort. A very nice bottle of my uncle's Scotch kept me company after he left. I expect I fell asleep some time, but don't ask me when. Mrs. Winston woke me this morning by unceremoniously banging at my door."

"Did you see or hear anything that could help us?"

"Afraid not, Inspector."

"A young girl is dead, Mr. Brodie."

"Believe it or not, Inspector, if I knew anything that could help you, I would not hesitate to divulge it even if it involved my dearest Aunt Ellen. But I don't know anything."

"Mr. Brodie, we've been checking on you. There are a few rather unsavory items in your past."

"Did any of them involve murder?"

"No."

"Assault?"

"No."

"Anything of a violent nature?"

"Not physical. But embezzlement, forgery, and misrepresentation of oneself are not exactly devoid of violence. They are passive violent crimes. They harm people."

"You're making me weep. Is there anything outstanding?"

"No. But I can't help wondering if Jillian Martin mightn't have hired someone like you to help her. Or perhaps someone like you gave her the idea."

"Are you serious that she was blackmailing people?"

"Dead serious, Mr. Brodie. I'm dead serious." With that, Manziuk stood and walked to the door. "If you think of anything that could help us…"

Bart stood up. "If I do, I'll toddle right along to let you know." He sauntered out of the room.

"Well, he leaves a bad taste in the mouth," Manziuk said.

"Do you really think he could have been working with Jillian Martin?" Ryan asked.

"Why not? There's nothing to say one of them might not have found the other. Like to like."

"We've talked to everyone except Kendall and George Brodie."

"What time is it?"

"After four."

"I wonder if Martin's left yet."

As if on cue, there was a quick rap at the door. It was Peter Martin, together with George Brodie. "Sorry to interrupt, but I'm wondering if I can go home, Inspector. Jillian's family will be there now."

"Yes. No. Just give me one minute. Unless… Could I have your suitcases brought to you later?"

Peter shrugged. "I guess so. Nothing in them I desperately need. And your boys have already seen everything at least twice."

"I'll have them delivered later today. Oh, by the way. You said you went straight to your room yesterday at three-thirty. I have reason to wonder about that. Want to tell me the truth?"

"I suppose someone saw me."

"Never mind. Where were you?"

Peter Martin looked away for a moment as if gathering his thoughts. Finally, he turned back to face Manziuk. "All right, I went to Hildy's room. She didn't answer when I knocked. I wondered if she'd heard me, so I tried the door. It was open, so I went in. She wasn't there."

"How long did you stay?"

Peter licked his lips. "This is hard to explain. I stayed about ten or fifteen minutes. There was a picture of my son Stephen on her night stand. For some reason I can't explain even to myself, I picked it up and sat on the bed staring at it for a long time. That's all I did."

"We'll be in touch," Manziuk said.

"Get him, Inspector."

"We will, Mr. Martin. You can bank on it. By the way, is Shauna Jensen going back with you?"

"I certainly assumed so."

"Shauna seems to be opposed to going anywhere near her family right now."

Peter sighed. "That's all I need. Okay. Thanks for the warning, Inspector."

"Good luck."

Ryan continued to stare at the door after Peter had gone out.

After a moment, she said, "If that doesn't beat all! Do you realize Douglass was going through Peter's room while Peter was sitting in Hildy's room and Hildy was walking around out front? Talk about musical chairs!"

4

George Brodie was waiting in the hall. Manziuk went over to him. "Mr. Brodie, could you spare me a few minutes?"

"Yes, certainly. Are you nearly finished with this? Several others are also wishing to leave."

"Let me make a call." Manziuk returned to the study and, dialing the number of the morgue, asked for Munsen. "Anything on Crystal Winston yet?" he asked when the pathologist came on the line.

"Two wounds. The first to the abdomen under the rib cage. As I suspected, the liver was pierced. The second to the heart. Either could have killed her. The combination of the two left nothing to chance."

"Anything else?"

"A couple of curious things. Her right foot was quite bruised on the top of the instep and toes. Her left wrist was also bruised. And there was bruising around the neck. My best guess would be that someone stepped hard on her foot, grasped her around the throat with his left arm, and grasped her left wrist with his right hand. The knife was apparently held in her left hand, since hers are the only fingerprints on it. Whether she was originally holding the knife or it was forced into her hand I couldn't say. My guess would be she had held it previously."

"Knowing she was going out to face a murderer, she may have taken it for protection."

"Nothing to say she hadn't."

"Okay. Anything else?"

"Only that if my analysis is correct, you are looking for someone quite strong. Someone who could have held her and forced her arm to stab herself."

"Not a woman?"

"Could be a woman, but it would have to be a strong one. Tennis player, swimmer, someone who worked out a lot."

"Okay. Thanks."

"I'll let you know if anything else turns up."

Manziuk hung up and turned to George Brodie. "Sorry, there's one thing more I need to check. Do you know if Ford's still here?"

"I believe so. There are still a number of policemen out back.

"Let's go see how they're coming."

Ford was still at the body site. He smiled when he saw Manziuk. "Good timing. Just finished up here."

"Find anything?"

"Just one thing which might help. A footprint that isn't hers or one of the kids. Over here." He pointed to a spot in the ground. "Looks like a man's size ten."

Manziuk nodded, then told Ford about Munsen's suspicions.

"Interesting," Ford raised his eyebrows. "I'll keep it in mind."

"What about the clothes?"

"Kelly's going to have a look at them tonight. Lots of blood. Leaves, grass, some dirt. It'll take a while to go over them. If she was holding the knife, she could have pricked him."

"We don't know what her right arm was doing either. She could have scratched his face. Okay, I've two more interviews and then I'll see what we have."

"Lots of fun," Ford said in parting.

5

Back in the study, Manziuk sat across from George Brodie and waited until Ryan opened her notebook. He had noticed that she had taken it with her when she went to escort Peter Martin. That pleased him. It wasn't something to be left lying around.

George took charge of the conversation. "What do you want to know? Where I was when she was killed? I understand it happened in the middle of the night. Ellen will already have told you we went to bed before twelve. I was up before seven. The rest of the time I was asleep and I don't know anything that could help you." He shook his head. "I can't believe this is really happening. It's unbelievable." He sighed. "I'm not a young man, Inspector. At the beginning of this weekend, I was looking forward to seeing my son come into the firm and thinking that in a few years I'd be able to retire and let him take over. It was a good feeling. I can accept the idea of his taking over, my taking Ellen on a cruise, enjoying what time we have left. But right now I feel a hundred years old and completely helpless."

"Murder of an innocent young person makes us all feel helpless, Mr. Brodie."

"I suppose so. But in my own home!"

"It's been violated. You've been violated. And you have to sit back and let me do my job. And tell me anything you know that could help me."

George shook his head. "I wish I knew one thing that could help you. But I've seen and heard nothing that makes me think I know who did it."

"Do you suspect anyone?"

"No." He dragged the word out.

"That didn't sound definite."

"Oh, it's likely just because I don't like him, but it seems to me Bart has the temperament for it. I don't know that any of these other people could have."

"Mr. Brodie, has anyone been blackmailing you? Jillian Martin, for instance?" Manziuk threw it out as a cast. He didn't expect George Brodie's face to turn ashen. "Mr. Brodie?"

"Do you know what you're asking me?" he asked in a rasping voice.

"I do," Manziuk replied.

"But I don't understand."

"Mrs. Martin seems to have found weak spots in several people. She didn't find one in you?"

"Are you telling me that she was blackmailing people?"

"Yes."

"Then that was what she was trying to do!"

"She had approached you?"

George stood up and paced back and forth in front of the fireplace. "She called in at my office one day and said she had a problem and couldn't ask Peter for help. Apparently she'd overspent her allowance. She asked me for money. When I said no, she suggested that I wouldn't enjoy having my background written up in the gutter press. Sensationalized, she meant. I'm not ashamed of my past, but that doesn't mean I want it smeared with the kind of headlines they'd use. They twist things so much you can't recognize them."

"Did you give her the money?"

"Certainly not. I simply reminded her that her husband's job depended on my firm's having a good reputation. If she were to do what she had suggested, we would lose clients, and all of the members of the firm would suffer. That set her in her place."

"She left?"

"Yes. But not happily."

"Did you talk to Peter about it?"

"I would have if she'd tried anything else." George shifted in the chair. "Look, I brought Peter into the firm because I wanted him, and I haven't regretted my choice for even a minute. Peter's a first-class lawyer. His personal life is nothing to do with me. Having said that, I should add that I do regret his choice of wives. At least the two I've known."

"Hildy Reimer was also one of his wives."

"She seems much more suitable, although her decision to crash our house party was deplorable."

"So Jillian said nothing else to you?"

"Nothing."

"Had you heard of anything else, or anyone else she might have approached?"

"I had no idea that this wasn't an isolated incident. You mean she was actually blackmailing other people who are here this weekend?" His voice rose in astonishment. "Douglass?"

Manziuk stood up. "I don't think we'll get into that, Mr. Brodie. Thank you for your help. I just need to talk to your son and then I'll be out of your hair. Could you ask him to come here?"

"Certainly. And if I think of anything that can help, I'll give you a call. I want this solved as quickly as possible."

"Bad publicity," Ryan said as the door shut behind George Brodie.

"What?"

"Does he actually care or is he worried about the bad publicity for the law firm?"

"Frankly, I'm not sure. I think he's right in what he said. He feels very old right now. Very helpless and confused. It's shock."

"Do you think he lied about not giving Jillian any money?"

"Could be. All I know is we've got more people with a motive for killing Jillian Martin than I'd have dreamed possible."

6

There was a knock at the door and Manziuk opened it to Kendall Brodie. "Nick and I were hoping to leave soon," he said. "Do you need to see me?"

"Just a couple of questions, Mr. Brodie."

"Good. I promised Lorry we'd drop her off on our way home. That okay with you?"

"Fine. Can you tell me where you were after midnight last night?"

"Sound asleep. Well, it might have been twelve-thirty when I got to sleep. We came upstairs about midnight."

"You didn't leave the room?"

"No. I was tired. I clicked out like a lightbulb."

"Can you testify that Nick was also in the room?"

"Well, we came up together, and we both went to bed. I assume he went to sleep. But I suppose I can't swear that he was. I mean, I was really out. But I'm sure I'd have awakened if he opened the door. I'd have heard that."

"Thanks. If you think of anything else that might help us, here's my card." Manziuk held it out and Kendall absently put it into his shirt pocket.

As Kendall started towards the door, Manziuk casually asked, "Oh, by the way, Jillian Martin wasn't by any chance blackmailing you, was she?"

Kendall stopped and stared. "What?"

Manziuk repeated the question.

"Are you crazy? First of all, I didn't even know her before this weekend, and second, what do you mean, blackmail? Are you telling me Jillian was blackmailing somebody?" His voice went from puzzled to angry. "Or do you think I have something in my life I could be blackmailed over? Just what are you talking about?"

"Oh, just a little thought of mine. Nothing to worry about."

"I don't think you should go around slandering people, even if you are a cop! Does Peter know what you're saying?"

"Sorry. That's classified," Manziuk said with an enigmatic smile. "You're going back to your apartment?"

"That's right. But I still—"

"I may drop in some time."

"That would be an honor," Kendall said. His voice was only slightly ironic. After a quick wave to Ryan, he left the room.

"Well, that's the lot." Manziuk's voice was tired.

"Looks like Nick Donovan, doesn't it? Kendall let out that Nick could have left the room without his knowledge, and then he tried to cover his tracks, but it didn't work. Perhaps she was never interested in Nick romantically. Maybe she was trying to blackmail him, too. Since she knew him four years ago, she may well have had something on him."

Manziuk looked at her in surprise. "Good thinking," he said. "All right, I need the search list from yesterday. See what size shoes Nick takes and whether he had a black shirt and pants."

"Black?"

"Just a hunch."

"We don't have the completed list yet. Ford wasn't finished when he was called here this morning."

"Okay, we'll just have to wait until we get all the facts. Meanwhile, put a tail on Nick. He'll be driving back to the apartment with Kendall. Make sure there are enough bodies to cover him."

7

A few minutes earlier, Peter had found Shauna sitting in the upstairs alcove drawing on a small pad.

"I'm driving back to the apartment now. Are you packed?"

"I'm not going."

"What do you mean, you're not going?"

"I won't go back and no one can make me."

He took a few steps in a half circle, then stopped. "Work with me on this, Shauna."

"What?"

"You came here with me and you're going back with me. Your parents and sisters are at the apartment right now. We have to go meet them."

She continued making marks on the paper. "I don't want to."

Exasperated, he grabbed her sketch pad. "Look at me!"

"Don't!"

"I'm trying to talk to you!"

"I don't want to! You can't make me!" Tears were flowing down her cheeks.

"Shauna, I don't understand. I know you're upset because of what's happened, but what do you want me to do?"

She stood up and grabbed the sleeve of his jacket. "Don't make me go back there. Please, don't make me!"

"To the apartment?" His voice was clearly bewildered.

"No! Back home!"

"Home?" He shook his head, completely lost. "Why don't you want to go home?"

She was still crying, but quietly. "I want to go to art school this fall. It may be my only chance."

"Art school?"

She nodded mutely.

It dawned on Peter that the object he was holding was a sketch pad. He held it up and looked at the page on which she had been drawing. His eyebrows raised. "You drew this?"

She nodded, her eyes desperately watching him, teeth biting her bottom lip.

He gave her an intent look; then glanced back at the drawing. "This is good," he said. "Really good."

"I've wanted to go for as long as I can remember. They'll never let me. If I go back, I'll never escape."

Peter leafed through the sketch pad. Page after page was covered with exquisite pencil drawings of dwarves, elves, fairies, dryads, centaurs, trees that breathed life, sea people, and a myriad of other imaginary yet appealing creatures. All drawn by Shauna. The realization acted like a sudden punch to his solar plexus. What a fool he was! Seeing only a gawky woman in horn-rimmed glasses and completely missing the delightfully gifted individual inside.

"Don't worry, Shauna," he said to her, his voice husky with emotion. "You'll go to art school. I'll see to it myself. And you won't have to go back home. I won't let them take you. You'll stay at my apartment until we can make arrangements. We'll get you into the best art school there is. I promise."

It was her turn to look intently into his eyes. "Do you really mean it? You're not just saying that so I'll go back with you?"

"You have my word. But first, you'll have to help me. All of Jillian's things—someone has to pack them up. And the funeral. There'll have to be one as soon as the police release the body. Will you help me get through that? Then, I promise you, as soon as your family goes back home, we'll start work on that art school."

She nodded and ran to her room to throw her clothes into the shopping bag Lorry had found for her.

Lorry Preston was in the bedroom putting the last of her clothes into her suitcase.

"I guess I'm going," Shauna announced.

"With Peter?"

"Yes. He said he'll help me go to art school."

"Shauna, that's wonderful!"

"He says I never have to go back home again."

"That's great."

"But I will have to. I have drawings hidden there. I'll have to go and get them some time. But not alone. I was wondering if you'd go with me? In a few weeks, maybe?"

"Yes, of course I will."

"Good. I have your number. You're sure you don't mind if I call you?"

"I want you to call."

Impulsively, Shauna walked forward and gave Lorry a quick hug. "I sure wish I'd had a sister like you," she said. Then she threw the rest of her clothes and toiletries into the shopping bag and ran out.

Lorry finished packing and sat down on the edge of her bed for a moment. Every bone in her body felt as though it was made of iron. She realized that the shock of the murders topped by the strain of trying to support Shauna had exhausted her more than she had realized.

She felt guilty, but nevertheless she couldn't wait to get out of this house. It would be difficult to ever come back.

There was a soft tap on her door.

"Who is it?"

"Nick. Can I talk to you for a minute?"

She hesitated, but then got up and opened the door. "Is Kendall nearly ready?"

"He'll be a couple of minutes. Look, I just wanted a moment to talk to you alone. This has been a heck of a weekend."

She stepped aside and he walked into the room and stood looking at her. At last, she said, "You wanted to talk?"

"I'm sorry. My usually ready tongue is on holiday, I guess. Maybe being the chief suspect in a murder investigation has done something to me."

"Are you?"

"Looks like it. Not that I did it. But there's a threatening note that looks like it came from me. Now they want the clothes I was wearing. If they match fibers, I'm in big trouble."

There was a long silence.

"Could they match fibers?" Lorry asked.

Nick looked steadily into her eyes. "So you think I could have done it?"

Her look was just as steady. "I don't know."

"You really think I could have done it?"

"I've only known you since Friday. How could I know what you might do?"

He walked over to the window. His voice was low, tinged with bitterness. "I thought you… at least…"

"Oh, Nick, this isn't a movie. This is real."

He faced her. "What are you talking about?" he asked impatiently.

"In the movies, when everyone thinks some man did it, there's always a woman who says she knows he couldn't have done it. And she never has any reason for believing he's innocent other than that 'she saw it in his eyes' or 'she just knew' or something like that."

"Is that so impossible?"

"Yes."

Neither spoke for a long time. Nick turned to look out the window again.

"Nick, I wish I could say that I can't believe you could ever murder another person, but I would be lying."

He spun to face her. She could see the anger in his eyes and his clenched fists. "Well, you'd better get out of here then. Don't you think you're being a little too brave, being alone in a room with a murderer?"

"Oh. Nick, I didn't say I wanted you to be the one! Or even that I thought you were. Just that I don't know you well enough to know. Does anyone ever know another person that well?"

"Well, if it's not me, it could be a relative of yours, couldn't it? So I guess it better be me."

"Not necessarily. There's Hildy, or Shauna, or—Oh, don't you see, Nick, it could be anyone! Any person here, including myself, is capable of murdering another person. Anyone here."

"Oh, come on! Ellen? Anne? Shauna? They couldn't. You couldn't, either."

"How do you know?"

"I know, that's all. Instinct."

"Well, I think you're wrong. For different reasons, perhaps. But anyone could kill another person if the reason was right."

"Self-defense, maybe. But not cold-blooded murder."

"Every person could, Nick. Not just some people. Every one. I don't know what could drive each of us to murder, but something could."

"Thanks."

Lorry's exhaustion overwhelmed her. Not knowing what else to do, she picked up her suitcase and started for the door.

But Nick moved quickly and reached it first. He was a foot in front of her. She stopped and looked up into his face. With a sudden shock, she realized that he was under a great deal of strain. His eyes were dull and the muscles around his mouth sagged. Without realizing what she was doing, she put her free hand out.

Nick grasped her hand in both of his. "Lorry, do you have any idea what this weekend has been like for me? First, I feel really bad because I'm disappointing my best friend by turning down a job offer he went out of his way to get me—one anyone in his right mind would kill for. Then, as soon as I get here, who do I see but a girl I once asked to marry me and who turned me down so hard I decided I'd never allow myself to be vulnerable with any woman again. Right after that, I meet you and all the barriers I've put up against women go flying in all directions. It's as if all my life I've been stumbling around in the dark and now the sun has come out and I can see what's possible. And then I realize you are definitely not likely to be attracted to me, and what happens? I want you even more!

"And now I'm likely the prime suspect in two murders. And if it wasn't me, who was it? Somebody else who was here. Maybe even somebody I care about. And I don't know if I want them to find the real murderer or not. And now you're leaving and I don't even know if I'll see you again, and—I feel lost. Like I'm in the middle of a maze and I don't have the foggiest idea how to find my way out."

"Oh, Nick." Lorry set her suitcase down and reached up to touch his face with her free hand. "I don't know what to say, either. I hardly know you. This would have been difficult even if the weekend had been normal. With everything that's happened, I just don't know what to do."

"I thought—never mind." He let go of her hand and moved aside. "I'm being stupid. You're right. You barely know me. I'll carry your suitcase. Is this the only one?"

"The other one is already down. Bart took it."

"All right. Let's go. Don't forget your purse."

"Nick, I—"

"Come on!" He strode out of the room. There was nothing for her to do but go back to pick up her purse and follow him.

Peter and Shauna had gone. Hildy had gone. Douglass and Anne were getting into their car. Kendall was waiting in his car. His parents stood together, a short distance away. Bart stood alone.

Nick managed to fit Lorry's suitcase into the space left in the small trunk. He and his suitcase squeezed into the minuscule back seat. Lorry hugged Ellen and shook George's hand and then got into the front beside Kendall. As Manziuk had suggested, they made sure all the windows were rolled up and the doors locked.

George shut the door, Kendall turned the key, and a moment later the small car was through the main gate. A television crew and a number of reporters were waiting, but although they tried to get him to stop, and one cameraman ran in front of the car for a short distance, Kendall resolutely shook his head and kept moving until they were through. Soon they were on open highway. The house party was officially over.

Part IV

Never, never pin your whole faith
on any human being:
not if he is the best and wisest
in the whole world.
There are a lot of nice things
you can do with sand:
but do not try building houses on it.

C. S. Lewis

Chapter Sixteen

"I'm glad you had a nice time at Aunt Susan's," Hildy said as she and her son carried their suitcases into their apartment. "What did you and Diana do?"

"Played Nintendo a lot. And Lego. I know what I want for my birthday."

"You do, do you? And what would that be?"

"They have some really neat new Lego sets."

"Oh, I see. Well, perhaps. No promises, though. I might like to surprise you."

"Mom?"

"Yes, Stephen?"

"What you said before, about how we might be moving away from here. We aren't, are we?"

"Well, Stephen, the fact is we might not have to go now."

"How come?"

"It's hard to explain. Why don't you unpack and then when your room is tidy I'll make us some hot chocolate?"

"With marshmallows?"

"With marshmallows."

He started rolling his suitcase toward his room, then stopped and looked at her. "I'd miss Aunt Susan and Uncle Art and Diana. And the new baby when it's born. Aunt Susan let me feel her stomach. It's neat how the baby seems to be kicking. She says it isn't really kicking. Just moving around. It's getting to be a tight fit. I wouldn't want not to see the baby when it's born."

"I know, Stephen. I really hope it won't be necessary for us to go away."

"Me, too."

He went into his room and she went into hers.

She shut her door, but instead of beginning to unpack, she sank onto the bed. For the first time since her arrival at the Brodies', her control gave way and tears streaked down her cheeks. After a moment, she pulled back the duvet that covered her bed and buried her face in the pillow so Stephen wouldn't hear her. Between sobs, she whispered, "Peter, how can you be such a fool! Oh, Peter!"

2

Peter Martin was not having an enjoyable evening. Jillian's parents and her three younger sisters along with several aunts and uncles had been waiting on the doorstep when he and Shauna arrived.

He had to explain three times what had happened, how the body had been found, and what the police were doing. They wanted to know why it had happened, but he couldn't answer that. They seemed to think he should have prevented it, but how they thought he could have managed that was a mystery.

Shauna, too, was bombarded with questions and recriminations, and at one point Peter realized Mrs. Jensen had all but said she wished it had been Shauna instead of Jillian. Shauna took it without so much as batting an eyelash. For one brief moment, he wished he could have left Shauna with the Brodies. Then he imagined the barrage of questions he'd have faced if she hadn't been with him.

As the evening wore on, his head began to pound. When he could stand no more, he went to bed, leaving them to their own devices. If Anne Fischer could get away with it, why couldn't he?

Just before he went to sleep, he thought of Hildy. It had been nice to see her again. So sensible and competent. It was good that she, and not Genevieve or Jillian, had had his child.

He pulled open a drawer and found the picture Hildy had sent him last Christmas. It was a smaller version of the one she'd had in her room. He sat and looked at it, studying the resemblance to himself in the nose and coloring. But the determined chin was Hildy's. And so was the serious look in those eyes. Accusing eyes.

He was a cute little kid. Had a birthday coming up soon, Hildy had mentioned. He'd have to send something. Hildy had wondered if he could come for the party, but he didn't think so. Didn't want to get the kid's expectations up. Better not to have a father coming in once in a while messing everything up. That was what his father had done! Thrown everything into chaos, and then, just when Peter got used to his being around again, took off again. No, he wouldn't do that to Stephen. Better no father than one who only blew in to mess up his life. Come to think of it, he wouldn't even send him a birthday present. Better not get his hopes up. Hildy would take care of him. No fear. Maybe one of these days she'd meet a good man. He hoped she would. She deserved to be happy.

Happy. That's what he'd talked to Lorry about. How this life was all there was and a person had to grab his happiness. Well, he wasn't feeling too happy right now. He'd never had a wife die before. He wondered how long he should wait after the funeral before he asked his secretary out for dinner. Maybe if he chose a nice secluded restaurant? On the other hand, there was no reason they couldn't have a business lunch some time soon. A long private lunch.

3

Anne and Douglass returned home to find Jason and Trina in the middle of a loud argument. Something to do with the mess in the kitchen and living room.

"What's going on here?" Douglass strode between them.

"I'm not cleaning up for him!" Trina yelled.

Jason swore at her.

"Shut up!" Douglass shouted. "You don't use language like that in front of your mother. Now what happened here?"

Trina spoke when Jason didn't. "He had a party. I've no idea how many kids. And they got raided by the cops."

"We did not get raided!" Jason stamped at his sister. "How many times do I have to tell you? Some idiot on our street complained about the number of cars, and the cops came because of that!"

"Yeah, right. And the noise had nothing to do with it, I expect?"

"You make me sick! Why don't you tell Mom and Dad how you just got back? How you haven't been here since Saturday? Why don't you tell them you spent the whole time with Luc?"

"Trina!" Anne exploded.

"Oh, get off it. I'm old enough to know what I'm doing. And don't worry, we know how to be safe. You don't have to be afraid you'll be a grandmother for a while yet. Maybe ever!"

Douglass turned on her furiously. "Trina, don't you dare talk like that to your mother!"

Trina rolled her eyes. "Like I should care what she thinks."

"Trina!"

"I—can't—take—this." Anne walked out of the room and slowly went up the stairs.

"Jason, you get this place cleaned up. Now. I'll talk to both of you later." Douglass turned towards his study.

Jason sneered. "Mrs. Young can clean this up tomorrow. That's why we have her. She's our cleaning lady, remember?"

"Where is she? She should be here."

"I told her to leave on Saturday," Jason said. "All she did was complain about the noise."

"Why didn't she phone us?"

"Because neither you nor Mom thought to give her your phone number. And I certainly wouldn't."

"You two are impossible. I suppose you think we've had an easy time. With two murders!"

"Two?" Trina's eyes were wide. "I only heard about one."

"Naw, they said on the radio today there were two," Jason answered before Douglass could. "Wish I'd been there."

"I don't suppose you or Mom did it, huh?" Trina asked.

"No, we didn't do it!"

"I didn't think so."

"Yeah, they wouldn't have the guts," Jason remarked in a low voice.

"If I were going to murder anyone, it would be you kids." As he said the words, Douglass saw the contempt in their eyes and realized with a stabbing pain in his stomach that he didn't know these two people—his son and his daughter.

Nor did he know his wife any more. She had fled upstairs. Likely she had a bottle up there. Just as he had one in his study. He turned toward it. But fifteen minutes later he sat in his chair with his face buried in his hands. A few drinks from a bottle only brought a moment of forgetfulness. They wouldn't help these strangers become a family.

4

"That was some long weekend." Kendall sighed as he and Nick entered their apartment.

"So, what do you have on this week?" Nick asked.

"Not much. Marilyn said something about a party she wants us to go to on Friday. I thought I'd go into the office tomorrow. Start looking things over. I guess both funerals will be this week, won't they?"

"It all depends on when the police are through with the autopsies."

Kendall shivered. "I hate to think about all that stuff. Cutting them open and everything."

"Not for most people," Nick said.

"I'd be the one who fainted."

"Good thing you chose law over medicine, then."

"Actually, I felt stupid back there. It was so—embarrassing. I'm in the bathroom throwing up while Lorry handles everything. Not exactly something I'm proud of. It should have been the other way around."

"Lorry isn't your average woman."

"Got it bad, don't you?"

Nick threw a pillow and Kendall laughed as he caught it.

"Remember that conversation we had on the way up there?" Kendall asked. "You were so sure no woman was ever going to get under your skin."

"Drop it, will you?"

"So when are you going to see her again?"

"Probably never."

"Oh, come on—"

"I mean it, Kendall. Stop bugging me about it. You never know when to stop!" Nick slammed into his bedroom.

Kendall stood still for a moment, his face thoughtful. After a moment, he walked over to the phone and dialed. "Marilyn?... I'm okay.... Yeah, well, a lot happened.... I don't know. I haven't looked at the papers.... Of course Nick didn't do it! I don't care what the papers say. I ought to know if he'd commit a murder or not. Although I think he did want to murder me a minute ago… I'm joking. Marilyn, I missed you this weekend."

5

"My house party didn't exactly turn out the way I'd planned."

Ellen's understatement got a quick laugh from Bart. But as he saw her puzzled look, he coughed.

"I wasn't trying to be funny," she said.

"I know. But it was rather a peculiar way to put it."

"I suppose." They sat together in the day room, Bart with a drink in his hand, Ellen with a cup of tea beside her.

"How's Mrs. Winston?" Bart asked after a moment.

"The pills Dr. Felmer gave her seem to have done the job. She's fast asleep."

"Still have to face it when she wakes up."

"I know. But tomorrow I may be more equipped to help her."

"Yeah, there's that to be said." He took a cigarette from his case and lit it.

"When are you going to give up that disgusting and filthy habit?"

"No immediate plans."

"You don't care what it does to your insides?"

"Frankly, no. I figure you gotta go some time, so what's the difference?"

"The difference could be several years."

He raised an eyebrow. "So?"

"I do feel sorry for you."

"Thanks a whole lot, but I don't remember asking you for sympathy."

"No, you only ask for money."

"Touché."

"I can just see you thirty years from now, still coming around begging for money. Only then you'll be asking Kendall instead of George. Won't that be awfully demeaning for you?"

"Well, you've just told me if I keep smoking I won't have to worry about old age, so I guess I'll assume that the gods will look after me and I'll be history by then."

"Speaking of that…"

"Speaking of what?"

"Well, God, I guess."

"Were we?"

"You said something—it doesn't matter what. I was only going to say how curious it is that Lorry is so religious. I mean, going to church here even when it meant going to a strange place where she wouldn't know anyone. And then, what she's doing for the summer. I don't think she makes any money. Helping kids on the street. Likely most of them don't even want help."

"Strange girl, all right."

"So much like her mother. Not always, of course. We were great friends as girls. But Patricia met this young man who was going to seminary. At first, she was sorry for him. Such a waste, you know. She thought she could change him. But as she got to know him better, she was the one who began to change. She began to believe what he said—that you could know God. And the next thing we knew she was married and gone off out west with him. Happy, too. That's the surprising thing. Not just in her letters, but I've seen her a few times. She's never had a house with enough rooms, and he's never been paid enough to manage properly, but she's genuinely happy. Just like Lorry. Rather peaceful to be around."

"Almost like she knows something you don't," Bart mused.

"Yes, that's it exactly. That's what Patricia was like. So annoying, yet, sometimes, I've wondered if there was something I missed. Not that I'm unhappy," she said hastily.

"Of course not," Bart dismissed the topic. "Now, about the money situation. You implied that if I helped you out this weekend, you'd see that I went away with a little more in my pockets than I had when I arrived."

"You'll have to give me a chance to talk to George. He's in his study just now working on a case that's going to court this week, so I wouldn't want to interrupt him. Perhaps later tonight. You don't mind staying overnight, do you?"

"Not at all. Although I would prefer to move into the house. If the truth be told, mice aren't really my favorite companions."

"Oh, certainly. I'll change the bedding and give you the room Hildy was in, shall I?"

"That would suit me just fine."

Alone in his study, George sat nursing a Scotch and trying to concentrate on the file before him. It was a tricky civil case. One of two partners had exercised an option to call for the other partner to buy him out, only to discover that his partner had no intention of doing so, but was exercising a smaller clause which gave him the right to refuse and force the first partner to buy him out. In other words, the first partner's bluff had been called, and he couldn't come up with the necessary capital. It was a real mess. If only they could work together... but it appeared that by calling the option into effect, all chance of the two men's working together harmoniously had ended. The firm of Brodie, Fischer, and Martin was representing the second partner.

Normally, George would have enjoyed preparing for the case, but today he was unable to concentrate for more than a few minutes at a time.

He thought back to Friday afternoon and the feeling he'd had of impending doom. Well, he had certainly been right, hadn't he?

And as if to add insult to injury, Bart was still in the house, likely out there cajoling Ellen into giving him money. George supposed he'd find himself writing out another check. Likely, he'd be doing that for the rest of his life.

Well, Bart was family. Besides, George had the money to spare. Only it galled him to think that he was making money only to have Bart go and throw it away. He could tell Bart this was the last time. Make it sound convincing. But of course, Bart was Bart, and that was it.

George remembered telling Manziuk that Bart likely had the temperament for murder. He hadn't been serious, of course. Just annoyed. The truth was Bart was too lazy to do anything that would expend energy either to commit or to cover up. No, Bart hadn't done it. And George sincerely hoped no one close to him, including Bart, fell under suspicion. Let the police arrest Shauna, or perhaps Hildy. Even Nick, although he liked Nick. But not a member of his family or someone from the firm! Although they did say that more often than not it was the husband in these cases. That would be great publicity!

Oh, well, they'd live through it. He just hoped the police made their arrest soon. If they didn't arrest someone, all of them would remain under suspicion. And that would do the firm no good at all.

George sighed. His stomach still felt queasy. Maybe he should watch what he ate more, like the doctor had said. Or was it his ulcer acting up? Maybe it was his instinct again. Maybe there was more trouble to come.

He picked up the papers he had been trying to read. There would be a lot of trouble if he wasn't ready to go to court with this case. He would have to force himself to concentrate.

6

Across town, in a much less affluent neighborhood, Lorry Preston was concentrating on unpacking in the small, third-story room which would be hers for the summer. It was less than a quarter the size of the room at the Brodies', and she had to share a second-floor bathroom with the members of the family as well as another summer intern, but it would be comfortable. The walls were papered in a blue gingham check, and the spread and curtains were off-white and reminded her of old lace. There was a rocking chair, too, with matching blue pillows. The picture of Jesus with little children around him was one she'd often seen before. She felt much more comfortable in this home than she had in the Brodies'.

She looked at the framed photograph lying face down on the spread. She sat on the edge of the bed and picked it up. Dean's familiar smile stared at her.

She hadn't written to him yet. He'd be worried. Perhaps she should phone. With a start, she realized she hadn't telephoned her parents, either. What if they read about the murders in the papers?

She opened a drawer and set Dean's picture inside. Then she hurried downstairs to phone both Dean and her parents. She wouldn't have to do more than tell them about the murders and that she was fine. She would call Dean later in the week to talk about other things.

But while the short talk with her parents proved very simple, once they were certain that she was all right and that she was away from the site of the murders, the conversation with Dean was more difficult.

"I should never have let you go," he said in a troubled voice.

"Dean, it was never a question of your letting me go. Don't be so melodramatic."

"Lorry, do you know how hard it is for me when you're thousands of miles away and involved in a murder? Anything could happen."

"I'm fine."

"That's not the point. I want to look after you. How can I do it when you're so far away?"

"I thought I was relying on God to look after me." Her voice was teasing.

"I know that, but he can use me."

"Oh, Dean, God doesn't need you to look after me. He can do fine all by himself."

"You sound as if you don't care if I'm around or not."

"Why must you be so serious all the time?"

"You could have been killed!"

"Dean," she said, her voice perplexed, "I trust God. I thought you did, too. Remember? 'If I live I live for God, if I die I go to be with him.' I thought you believed that."

"I do, but not where you're concerned, Lorry. I'd go crazy if anything happened to you."

She hung on to the receiver, her fingers showing white around the knuckles. "Dean, that reminds me. I found your ring in my purse."

"Put it on, Lorry."

"I told you I wasn't ready to make a commitment."

"I slipped the ring in at the airport. I thought you might change your mind while you were away."

"Dean—"

"I love you, Lorry. That's why I get so concerned about you. What more do I have to do to make you understand? I'd marry you tomorrow if you'd agree."

"I have to go, Dean. I'll call you in a few days."

"I wrote you a letter. You should get it soon. Lorry?"

"Yes?"

"I really believe God wants us to be together. He wants me to take care of you."

Her hand tightened on the receiver. "I'll talk to you later, Dean."

She hung up and went back to her room where she sat in the rocking chair and gently rocked back and forth. She had attended the same church as Dean while she was going to college in

Edmonton. During the last couple of years, they had drifted together because they enjoyed doing a lot of the same things. But she had only thought of him as a friend. She wasn't ready to get serious. There were so many things she wanted to do before settling down and having a family.

Lately, however, being with Dean had become very difficult. He was so certain they were right for each other. So sincerely convinced. He had declared his love for her on several occasions. Once in front of several of her friends.

He seemed to be a perfect match. But was that enough? Wasn't there something more? Something she should feel? Like the way she'd felt several times when she was with Nick Donovan? Or was it simply because Nick was so experienced in making women feel at ease?

She shook her head as if to shake off her thoughts. Nick Donovan was nothing to her. They didn't have anything in common. Face it, she was feeling sexual attraction for the first time. She'd thought she was immune to such things.

She would fight it, though. She would have nothing to do with Nick Donovan. She laughed. As if she would ever see Nick again! He had only been flirting with her because there was nothing else to do all weekend. Likely he'd already forgotten they'd ever met.

Why did that thought make her feel even worse than she already did?

7

Shauna had been talking with her family all evening. When her parents finally went to bed, and her three sisters, all of whom reminded her of Jillian, were asleep, she fell exhausted onto the leather couch in Peter's study.

There had been talk only of Jillian and the funeral and the disposal of Jillian's possessions. It was all settled now. There would be a service in the city and the body would be taken back home and buried there. Mrs. Jensen wanted it that way and Peter didn't seem to care. As for her clothes and jewelry, Mrs. Jensen was to take everything home with her. So everyone was happy.

The difficult time would come when they got ready to head home and Shauna refused to go with them. Peter had said to leave everything to him, but she would need a backup plan just in case Peter didn't really mean what he'd said. No matter what happened, she wasn't going home with her family.

After a long time, Shauna fell into a troubled sleep, tossing and turning, seeing Jillian's face, stained with blood, coming toward her, threatening her, and Bart's eyes mocking, telling her she was a spineless idiot. She woke up more than once, determined that from now on she would live her own life no matter what anyone said.

8

Manziuk and Ryan also had a busy night. It was nine-thirty when they returned to the station, having grabbed a couple of hamburgers at a drive-through window.

Ryan led the way to Manziuk's office and kicked her shoes off before sitting on the edge of the desk.

"Don't do that!" he barked.

Startled, she jumped off the desk. "I'm sorry. I—"

"No." His voice was penitent. "I'm sorry. I just—it was a stupid reaction."

Manziuk hadn't shut the door, and now another man walked in without knocking.

"Long day, Manziuk?" the middle-aged man asked. He was fairly tall, with a solid build, fair hair, and a long, droopy mustache. His nose looked as though it had been broken at least once. The picture of an ex-hockey player, even though he'd never laced on a skate.

"Hello, Seldon. You've met, I trust." Manziuk indicated Ryan.

"Yes." Ryan said. "Superintendent."

He nodded to her, then turned to Manziuk. "Been over to see Woody yet?"

"No chance. I talked to Arlie this afternoon for a few minutes. That's it."

"I was over at four. He's looking pretty good. Quite a scare, though. He was asking about you. Worried that you're on a case without him. Good thing he was where he was when it happened." He shook his head in disbelief. "There's one good mother-in-law story, eh?" He hit his fist into the palm of his hand. "Well, on my way out. How's it going? Your report ready yet?"

Manziuk looked at him.

"I guess you've been busy. How close are we to making an arrest?"

"I haven't got the reports from Forensics yet. There are some things I need to know. Fiber checks, mainly. Details."

"Try to have something for me by noon tomorrow."

"Provided we don't have another murder before then."

"Cross your fingers." He stepped toward the door. "There's some fresh coffee out in the hall."

Seldon left and Manziuk looked at Ryan. "Well, you heard the man. Let's get to work. Ford should have something for us by morning."

"Was that Sergeant Craig you two were talking about? Did something happen?"

"He had a heart attack this morning while visiting his wife's mother in the hospital. He was gone, but they brought him back."

"You've worked together a lot, haven't you?"

"Yeah."

"Go and visit him. I'll start transcribing my notes. When you get back, we can go over them."

"No, I can't leave."

"You're going and that's an order," she said, holding out his hat. "After you get back, we can work all night if necessary. But Sergeant Craig needs you now."

He stared at her a long moment before taking his hat and walking out of the room.

Manziuk flashed his badge and was ushered into Woody's room without any argument. He was in a private room in coronary care, hooked onto a whole battery of machines, and at first glance Manziuk didn't even recognize him. His eyes were shut, and he looked like an old man. His chest rose faintly, and Manziuk knew he was alive. But that was all.

Manziuk quietly sat down in the chair that was drawn up beside the bed. Likely where Arlie had been sitting most of the day. He made little noise, but suddenly Woody turned his head slightly and opened his eyes.

"Paul?"

"Yeah, it's me," he said gruffly. "Thought I'd make sure they were treating you okay."

Woody gave a small chuckle. "Oh, pretty good. You hear what happened?"

"You came to visit Arlie's mother and you keeled over."

"Yeah. Pretty good, huh? Pays to look after your mother-in-law. They said if I hadn't been here, I never would have made it."

"Fate, I guess. They knew we needed you around."

Woody smiled. "Yeah."

"So, I guess you'll have to take it easy for a while."

"Yeah, I guess." Woody's voice was frail, almost a whisper. "You hear they stuck me with a woman?"

"Arlie told me. She thought it was funny. You think it's funny?"

Manziuk snorted. "She's bossy and she can't keep her mouth shut. And she fights imaginary dragons."

"Sounds like you twenty years ago. Come to think of it, sounds like you now."

"Thanks a lot."

Woody smiled again.

"Well, the nurse told me I couldn't stay long. Seems you need a lot of sleep right now." Manziuk stood up, his immense size making the figure on the bed look even less alive. "So you do what you're told and get out of here ASAP, you hear?"

"I'll be back before you know it."

"All right." Manziuk put his hand on Woody's shoulder and squeezed gently. Then he turned and quickly left the room. His eyes were misty, and he didn't want Woody to see. That would have worried him.

Manziuk drove back to police headquarters and worked with Ryan until midnight.

Loretta was in bed reading when he got home. "Did you see him?" she asked when he walked into the bedroom.

"Not for long. About two minutes."

"Didn't he look ghastly?"

"I don't know. A bit gray. But not too bad."

He was undressing as he spoke. Methodically. His shoes next to the door with fresh socks in them. Pants and shirt hung over the valet Loretta had bought for Christmas years ago—after he'd bumped his head on the dresser trying to find his pants in the dark when he'd been called to a murder scene in the middle of the night. His shoulder holster was on the night stand, ready to his reach. The phone at his hand. Alarm set.

He pulled back the covers and collapsed onto his back. His six-foot-five frame made a long mound in the bed, which had been made specially for his bulk. Beside him, Loretta's five-foot four-inch, one-hundred-twenty-pound form was barely notice-able. "Arlie taking it hard?" he asked after a moment.

"As expected. She's a good cop's wife. Just a bit off-putting that it was a heart attack and not a gunshot wound." Loretta reached over and slid her arm around his neck. "Rough day?"

"Rough year."

"You could always sell insurance." It had become a joke, but it was no less the truth. Loretta's brother was a successful life insurance salesman who had been trying for twenty years to get Paul to go in with him.

Paul grunted. He turned and put his right arm around his wife. "Kids okay?"

"Yes. They were here when Arlie called. Michael was upset. Lisa went to the hospital with me."

"Mike okay now?"

"Yes. But I think he's worried it could have been you."

"He always worries."

"It's tough being a cop's kid."

"Anybody could have a heart attack."

"But Woody isn't anybody. He's your best friend. And he's closer to the kids than their real uncles."

"I know. How do you think I felt? Out on a crazy case with a girl who's wet behind the ears as secondary! Knowing Woody almost died this morning, and still might, and all I could do was keep talking to this bunch of lunatics and try to keep the cop who's taken Woody's place from saying something stupid!"

"Did you know Woody wasn't well? Arlie said Seldon told her you made the call not to bother him when you got pulled in yesterday."

"I just thought he looked tired. He's not a youngster, you know. He'll be sixty before he knows it."

"He won't be back. At best, he'll get a desk job. More like-ly, they'll retire him."

He groaned and buried his face against her long black hair. "I've worked with him so long," he said after a minute.

"You'll survive," she said coolly. Changing the subject, she added, "I called Conrad."

"How is he?"

"Fine. London is terrific. Scotland was wonderful. He can't wait to get to Paris."

"Did he like Oxford?"

"Loved it. And he thought the people he talked to seemed impressed."

"So he thinks he'll get the fellowship?"

"He's very hopeful."

"Dr. Conrad Manziuk, Professor of Ancient History, of Oxford University. Sounds good, doesn't it?"

She snuggled against him. "Sounds very good."

"Lisa okay?"

"Yes. She was sorry she missed seeing you. She'll try to get back in two weeks. Hopefully, you'll be able to get some time off."

"Do you hate being a cop's wife?"

"Not as long as you're the cop."

He smiled. "You know, there's no way I could do this job if I didn't have you to come home to."

"Do you want to tell me about this case?"

"No. I just want you to be here."

9

Jacquie Ryan's mother was sitting in the living room talking to her aunt Vida, her cousin Precious, and her grandmother. As was their custom, they were all wearing dressing gowns and slippers and sipping green tea.

As soon as Jacquie opened the front door, she was showered with a barrage of questions.

"Where have you been so late? It's after midnight." Her mother's voice.

"What's happening with your case?" Her cousin Precious was the bloodthirsty one.

"Are you all right?" Her grandmother was always concerned with her health.

"Did anything exciting happen?" Precious again. "Did you arrest anybody?"

"Do you have your gun?" her mother chimed in. "Put it somewhere safe so it doesn't go off."

"Mom, you tell me that every single day!"

"Well, one of us has to remember."

"Okay," Jacquie said with a sigh. "I'll put it in a safe place."

"Then come back and tell us everything," Precious said.

"You know I can't tell you much!"

"Come and have some orange spice tea, child," her grandmother said. "Did you have enough to eat today?"

"I suppose you ate at some greasy joint," her mother said. "I'll get you a chicken sandwich."

"I can warm up some pea soup if you'd rather." Her grandmother was always warming up something or other.

Jacquie came back from her bedroom, where she'd kicked off her shoes and locked her gun in its drawer. "I'm not hungry. We stopped for food around eight-thirty. I'd like a glass of milk. And I need to get to sleep soon. I have to be back to work by eight in the morning."

"Child, it's none of my business, I know," her grandmother said, "but don't you think you'd rather have a job where you keep regular hours?"

Her mother took up the theme. "I just wish you'd find a good man and settle down and raise a family. I want to be alive to see my grandchildren."

"Are any of these policemen you work with single?" Her aunt finally got a word in.

"My goodness, Vida, where did you get your brains?" her grandmother asked, hands on hips. "Not from me, I hope. You don't want her marrying a policeman. He'd never be home!"

"Well, how she's ever going to meet any men except policemen while she's working these hours is beyond me!" her mother complained.

Her aunt was not going to be ignored. "Are there any nice men among the suspects in your case?"

Chapter Seventeen

By eight AM, Manziuk and Ryan were hard at work, piecing together the evidence. At 8:10, they had their first argument.

Manziuk was sitting at his desk studying the file, thinking to himself, saying nothing.

Ryan was pacing the floor. Suddenly she stopped and whirled to face him. "I am here, you know. Awake."

"I know," he said without looking up.

"So?"

"So?" he repeated, his mind still focused on the paper he was reading.

"So, aren't we going to talk about it?"

"Talk about what?"

"The case," she said. "Duh."

He had silver-rimmed reading glasses perched on his nose, and he looked over the top of them at her.

"You look like a university professor," she said. "An absent-minded one, at that."

"Could you possibly stop chattering and let me study these notes?"

"Could you possibly think out loud so we can both work on the case and not just you work on it and me stand here watching you? Or is that what you're used to? Does Sergeant Craig let you do all the thinking?"

"Sergeant Craig has learned that I like a chance to get my thoughts organized before I talk about them. Less time wasted that way." Okay, that was true. But it was also true that Woody didn't say much. Now and then he helped with the thinking, but rarely. Most of the time, he sat and waited while Manziuk looked for inconsistencies, threads of ideas to explore, new directions to check.

"Well, I'm not Sergeant Craig," Ryan said.

"I've noticed," he replied dryly.

She stood in front of the desk, placed her hands on it, and stared him in the eyes. "Nothing against him, but I don't want to watch you solve the case. I want to be part of it. All of it."

"Fine. Go get us some coffee and you can sit and think while I watch."

She glared at him.

"You want *me* to get the coffee?" he asked.

By 8:30, Ford had sent in his written report.

"Okay," said Manziuk, who was still seated at his desk with Ryan on a chair pulled up beside him. Papers covered every inch of the desk, with two empty coffee cups sitting in the midst of them. "You want to do this together, we'll do it together. So pay attention. I don't like repeating things." He put on his glasses and picked up Ford's report. "The Forensics people say there's very little to link anyone with Jillian Martin's body. No foreign hairs or anything else on her. No prints that could be determined as belonging to the murderer, no skin or blood under her nails, no scratches on any of the possible suspects. The weapon is likely the cord we found—or at least a piece of cord identical to that one, but there is nothing to link it to anyone."

"What about the flowers in the circle?"

"Let me read the report. There were a couple of tiny scratches on her hands. Also some traces of leaves. Feeling is she made the flower chain herself. By the way, the flowers were Gerbera. Some kind of daisy."

"What about Nick Donovan's clothes?"

"Hang on." He read more of the report. "Nothing much here. There were a couple of hairs on Nick's shirt as well as a trace of powder that belonged to Jillian Martin. So we do know that at some point he was in contact with her. But the fact that her face powder was on the front of his shirt implies that she was facing him. If, as we suspect, she was strangled from behind while seated on a bench, it doesn't seem likely that her face would touch his shirt. So…" He paused as if checking to see if his mind had all the facts straight. "Now we'll see about Crystal Winston." He scanned the second report. "Not much more. A footprint, size ten men's running shoe. The shoe—rather a pair of shoes—was found in the change room by the pool. Belong to Douglass Fischer. He says he left the shoes in the change room after playing tennis Saturday. Never thought to get them."

"That's just great!" Ryan's voice was tinged with annoyance. "Did Ford notice if they were there Saturday night?"

"Yes, they were."

Restlessly, Ryan stood and walked around the edge of the room. "Anything else?"

Manziuk watched her for a moment before answering. "There were no hairs or different-colored fibers on Crystal Winston; however, there might have been a few fibers that were black but of somewhat different content than the clothes she was wearing. The guess is the murderer was also wearing black."

She stopped. "That's what you thought. You asked them to look for black clothes."

"A hunch."

"Do you have hunches that good all the time?"

"Now and then."

"So what did they find?" She resumed walking slowly back and forth.

"There were several possibles. Turtleneck shirts owned by Nick Donovan and George Brodie, a T-shirt owned by Bart Brodie, and a sleeveless sweater belonging to Anne Fischer. And there was an old jogging suit belonging to Kendall Brodie in a closet near the back door. Jacket and pants. All were made of similar synthetic fabric and all could have been the item that left the traces. The jogging suit, however, had hairs belonging to Crystal Winston and blood stains. The problem is anybody could have borrowed it. They're going over it. Both Kendall and George Brodie have used it, and even Ellen sometimes has put on the jacket when it was cool outside and she just wanted to go out for a minute. She thought it possible Crystal or Mrs. Winston had worn it, too. And there are no fingerprints on the knife except Crystal's. No skin or blood under her nails.

"Oh, and Ford found the things Douglass Fischer had mentioned in the bottom of a drawer in Jillian Martin's bedroom. Nothing else incriminating."

"So we haven't budged far from square one."

"What about the list we made last night?"

"Okay, let's look at it." She came back to the desk and, after tossing some of the papers around, held up a single typed sheet with three columns. The first was titled *Not Very Likely*. The names under it were Ellen Brodie, Kendall Brodie, Shauna Jensen, Lorry Preston, and Mrs. Winston.

The second column was titled *Maybe, But...* and contained the names of George Brodie and both the Fischers.

The third column was called *Most Likely* and had four names: Bart Brodie, Nick Donovan, Peter Martin, and Hildy Reimer.

The third column was the important one. These four people had no alibi for either murder.

"Nick Donovan and Hildy Reimer had the best opportunity," said Ryan as she sat down. "They were both alone and outside."

"Except most people who plan murders like to have a rock-solid alibi."

"Maybe it wasn't planned."

"That's certainly possible. Particularly given the choice of weapon. We still haven't figured out where the murderer got the cord that was used. Was it a new piece, or did he just untie a piece that was being used in the garden?"

"We may never know that."

"Hmm."

"Nick Donovan looks the most likely to me," Ryan said.

"Except that the connections to him are purely circumstantial. Someone else could have written the note. And the hair and powder from Mrs. Martin could have gotten on his shirt any time that day."

"So who do you think?"

"Douglass Fischer would get my vote. He says he was searching the Martins' room, where he found the note, and then he was in his room, where his wife was asleep. But he could have found the note earlier, or even taken it off Jillian's body. Though why he would take it and not destroy it, I don't know. He may not have known about her connection to Nick. "

"You'd think we'd find some trace of the killer!" Ryan protested. "Fibers, hairs, prints, something! It's almost like he or she knew we'd look for them."

"Any one of these people could know a lot more about forensics than the average person. Especially if the murder of Jillian Martin was planned. We're dealing with top-notch lawyers, Hildy Reimer is a very capable woman, Bart Brodie is no dummy, Shauna Jensen works in a library. The killer might have made sure to read up on forensics just to avoid making a mistake."

"Surely not."

"Why not? These people are highly intelligent."

"But murder isn't often that cold-blooded, is it?"

"No. It's usually done in the heat of the moment. And most murderers leave clues. But every now and then you find one who doesn't. Or the clues left lead us in circles."

"But there's always something."

"Yeah? Have you been following the case of the four women murdered here since last October?"

"Certainly I'm aware of it."

It was Manziuk's turn to get up and pace the room. "Four women. All young. One university student, one college student, one nurse, and one hairdresser. None of them knew each other. Nothing in common except all of them had red hair: two natural, two from a bottle. All killed by being strangled from behind with some kind of black cord by someone who didn't touch them. Suspects include a couple of boyfriends, the neighbor of one, and a few guys we've had our eye on for a while. Leads? None. Evidence? Nothing. No hairs, no nothing. From the look of it this guy just walks up to a perfect stranger who has red hair and puts a cord around her neck without creating suspicion and then pulls it tight until she is dead." He stopped pacing and stood with his arms crossed. "This guy is either a complete psycho whose randomness in killing makes him very lucky, or he's a very smart guy. Because the bottom line is we don't have a clue."

"Have you tried decoys?"

"Where? When? This is a big city. The guy's chosen four different locations. No method. The first was October seventh. The second January eleventh, the third February eighth, and the last May second. We can't just put red-haired decoys out indefinitely. And we don't even know where to put them. It's like he just cruises the streets till he sees a redhead, trails her until she's alone, and then, bam! One less redhead in the city."

She said nothing.

He moved over to his chair and leaned on its back. "At least in this case we have some obvious suspects."

"So what do we do with our suspects?"

"Who's first?

"Bart Brodie."

"Okay." He began walking again, now and then stopping to straighten a book or adjust the blind. "Lied about being with Shauna. Says it was because she lied first. Could have told her to lie. Says he was in his apartment above the garage. Also there during Crystal's murder. Had been drinking heavily."

"The drinking makes it unlikely for him to have murdered Crystal."

"Not necessarily. He could have been acting drunk to give himself an alibi. We need to see if anyone noticed just how many drinks he had and exactly what he was drinking."

"But he has no motive."

"No motive we're aware of. No evidence he was being blackmailed, for instance. But what if he was? He could have arrived on the scene because Jillian had told him she would be there for the weekend."

"How could we find that out?"

He stopped. "I want a couple of people to visit restaurants in the vicinity of the Martin apartment. Take pictures of Jillian and Bart and Nick and see if she was seen meeting either of them. Also, check with the doorman of the apartment and find out if either of them have been seen going up."

"Okay." Ryan was taking notes again.

"Next, Nick Donovan. He's got a tail. Later today, we'll check and see what he's been up to."

"Hildy Reimer?"

"Check to see if she really has been preparing an alias. But I think she's going to be okay. If she had done it, she probably wouldn't have given us the alias she was going to use."

"Unless she has two just in case."

"Good point. Have it checked out."

"Peter Martin?"

"I believe I'll pay him a little visit today. Meanwhile, we need a check on his finances. Four divorces would be pretty expensive. Maybe he couldn't afford to pay any more alimony."

She nodded. "Is there anyone else we should check out?"

"Either the Fischers or the Brodies could be covering up for one another. We can check into their finances and particularly see how much was paid out to Jillian Martin. She had a good scam going. Used the Fischers' fears very nicely. George Brodie sounded less convincing. He said he didn't pay her a dime. That he threatened her back. Could be she tried another angle, one he didn't have a backup plan for. Surprising what some people find embarrassing. Especially once they're successful in the eyes of society. So we'll check into his past thoroughly. See if there's something he would pay to keep hidden."

"One thing that needs explaining," Ryan said thoughtfully, "is how Jillian got the information about Douglass Fischer and his weekend."

"The woman was his secretary. Peter could have known about it and perhaps let something out."

She nodded. "But I'd still like to know more about how she operated."

"You wondering if she might not have been doing it alone?"

"What if she married Peter Martin because of his money, but she was really in love with someone else. Someone like her."

"Someone like Bart Brodie?"

"Yes."

"Not a bad idea. We'll do our best to find out."

2

Bart might have been insulted by the suggestion that he was like Jillian Martin. Or he might have been pleased with it. But right now, he was merely impatient. He wanted to get some money from George, and he wanted to leave. George had proved to be difficult.

"Look, it isn't as if you don't have the money," Bart argued.

"That isn't the question. However, since you choose to put it that way, how about looking at this? Whatever money I have, I earned. Note the word I use. 'Earned.' I—"

"Don't tell me. You started out with nothing and worked twenty-hour days and made yourself what you are today. Wonderful. We applaud you. But is it really necessary for every-one to emulate you? Why can't you simply realize you enjoyed every minute of it and now you have more than you need and you have a responsibility to your family to see that none of us starves?"

"What my sister ever saw in your father!"

"Yes, you've mentioned that before, too. I'm just like him. So sorry, but I have no choice. My mother never once said to me, 'Child, we're planning to bring you into an imperfect world where you can't choose your relatives or circumstances, and we'd like to know if you want to come.' I had to come, willy-nilly."

"You may not have had a choice in being born, but you do have a choice in what you do with your life. So far, you've chosen poorly. Well, I have a choice also. And I choose to ignore you. If I'd done that years ago, you might be a lot better off."

"And if—"

"And if you follow through with your threat of a few days ago and try to give a story to one of the trash magazines, it will harm you more than me. You are not my son, merely a relative. I have no obligation to you, and I will make sure the papers are aware of everything I have already done for you. I have no doubt I will come out smelling like roses and you will look exactly like what you are—scum we could well do without."

There was a long moment of silence. Finally, Bart said, "You're bluffing."

"I am giving you five thousand dollars. That is because Ellen feels you were helpful this weekend and she wants me to be certain you have something to start with. But you had better use it wisely, because there will be no more. Absolutely no more. I know you think I'm bluffing, but I'm not. It's the last money you'll ever see from me. And that includes after my death. Your name is not in my will. And if you think Kendall will support you, you are very mistaken."

"I—"

"That will be all. I trust you will be gone before lunch." George held out the money in cash, and Bart took it. "Unless you do something to show me that you have reformed your lifestyle, you will not be allowed on this property or in my office again. As far as I am concerned, from this moment on I have no nephew."

"You're making a big mistake."

"Close the door when you leave."

Bart slammed out of the room.

George leaned back. Should have done that years ago. And who knew—it might even work. He felt good.

But now he needed to get to the office and do a day's work. Time to put the events of this nightmare weekend behind and get on with life. Stupid thing to say, when two people were dead. Yet not much he could do about it.

And, strangely enough, the feelings of impending doom that had been bothering him since Friday had lifted. Coincidence? Probably more like stomach acid. Which reminded him. He needed to take the pills his doctor had given him to coat his stomach.

Twenty minutes after George was gone, Ellen watched Bart get into a cab in front of the house. He had given her the gist of George's message, but she had offered no sympathy. She liked him too much, she said, to see him continue to waste his life the way he'd been doing. Maybe if he knew he didn't have George to bail him out he'd do something to improve himself. That or get his legs broken by a gambler he couldn't pay or wind up in jail for forgery or something like that. She didn't know what all he'd done and she didn't want to know.

She waved.

The cab drove away.

He was gone. They were all gone.

Only she and Mrs. Winston were left.

Of course, Mrs. Winston was unable to do anything. It was Ellen's turn to take care of her. She smiled. Unhappy though the time might be, it would be nice to get back into a kitchen again without feeling guilty.

A small car came into sight. It was old and battered. The gardeners. She'd forgotten they would be coming in. They had a key to the gate and had apparently come to work on the gardens, as usual. What was she going to say to them?

3

Peter was at the office by nine in the morning. Anything to get away from his in-laws. Shauna would just have to cope. He'd make it up to her later.

He accepted sympathy from his secretary and the others in the office. "I'll be fine," he said as soon as there was a quiet moment. "I just want to get back to work. It helps to have my mind on something." He smiled in his engaging way, and the secretaries and law clerks fell over themselves agreeing with him.

He went into his office and shut the door, leaning against it for a moment before sitting at his desk. Now what? He needed something to do. He leaned forward to buzz his secretary.

"Yes, Mr. Martin?"

"What have we got to work on today?"

"You have that litigation for Mr. Devlin."

"Ah, good, good. Bring the file in, please. And your notebook. I have a couple of letters to write."

"Yes, Mr. Martin."

She was there in three minutes, seated across from him, efficient, agreeable, eager to please, easy on the eyes, and, to the best of his knowledge, not in the process of blackmailing anyone. She should take his mind off things nicely.

Douglass would much rather have been in the office, too. But Anne had been in such a state the night before that he had finally phoned her doctor, who had recommended she take two of the sleeping pills he had prescribed several weeks before and come in the next day if she thought it necessary. A lot of good that was.

She had drunk half a bottle of vodka, and he hadn't wanted to give her a pill on top of that. But he had looked for them.

And found more than he'd bargained on.

Three bottles of sleeping pills. Along with a suicide note telling him he was free to go to Jillian and begging him to look after the kids.

He slept little during the night. His mind was grappling with too many things. His wife was so miserable she was ready to commit suicide. His two children were so out of hand he had no control over them. And it didn't take a genius to see they were both heading for trouble.

Douglass Fischer, age forty-four. And what did he have? A guilty conscience because of one foolish weekend. A good job that took most of his time and interest. A miserable home.

He got up at eight and made sure there was an ice pack for Anne. When she woke up, she would need it.

He shut himself up in his office and began to write out a list of everything that was wrong with his life.

4

Lorry was busy, too. Dave Spalding, the tall black man at whose home she was staying, had taken her over to the small store that had been remodeled to make an office for the mission. Now, he was showing Lorry the basic operation. Besides the office, where the staff tried to help by counseling, finding jobs and places for the kids to stay, or reconnecting them with their families, they had a small doughnut shop manned by kids who had been on the street, a house converted into bedrooms for kids who had nowhere to go, another house that served as a halfway stop for kids trying to get their lives back on track, and a community center where kids could hang out.

Lorry was going to work on the counseling and referral end, talking to kids who came in, helping them figure out what they were doing on the street, suggesting ideas for what they could do with the rest of their lives, trying to give them hope.

Dave was the director. There were three other full-time staff, a couple of part-timers, a number of volunteers, and two summer workers other than Lorry.

They had been horrified to learn about Lorry's long weekend. But she was already tired of discussing it. She wanted to get busy and put the taste of the last few days behind her. So she was glad to go with Dave, slowly walking around the streets, meeting a few of the kids who were regulars.

But in spite of a strong effort to keep her mind on the mission, every young man with dark hair reminded her of Nick Donovan. And every pair of blue eyes reminded her of him, too. It was very annoying.

5

Shauna was annoyed with herself. How had she put up with these people all her life?

The phone rang and Mrs. Jensen grabbed it. "Martin residence.... Shauna?... Who's calling?... She's quite busy. If it's anything to do with Jillian, I can—I didn't say she was out!" She set down the receiver and said, "It's for you. The nerve of some people! I don't know who this man is, but he's quite rude. I had a good mind to hang up on him. You tell him not to call again."

Shauna took the receiver. A rebellious thought made her want to run into Peter's bedroom to use the extension, but she knew that if she were to do that her mother would listen on this phone. Besides, who would be calling her? Likely Inspector Manziuk. He could be rude and get away with it.

"Hello," she said softly.

"Who's the harridan?"

"Pardon me? Who is this?"

"Don't you know me?"

"Bart?"

"See, you do know me."

"Why did you call?"

"Why not?"

"I—you—we—"

"You sound confused, woman. Because of the old battle-ax?"

"That old—er—that's my mother."

"Then you'll welcome a chance to escape. How about ten minutes out front? I rented a car for the occasion."

"Where did you get the—" Realizing that her mother was listening, she stopped short of questioning his finances. "I can't."

"Sure you can. Ten minutes. If you don't appear, I'll start honking the horn and keep at it till I get a ticket."

"I really can't."

"Imbecile. Who's telling you what to do now?"

He hung up, and she carefully replaced the receiver.

"Well, who was it?" her mother demanded.

"Just a friend."

"You don't have any men friends in the city, I hope. Or was it one of Jillian's friends?"

Shauna didn't answer. Instead, she walked toward the kitchen.

"I asked who it was!"

"It was nobody important."

"Shauna Jensen, you come right back here and tell me who was on the phone!"

Shauna turned and stared at her mother. She felt strangely aloof, as though she were watching a scene on a stage. Her thoughts surprised her. Her mother must have been pretty when she was young. Likely she had looked a lot like Jillian. Or would have if she'd had the money. It wasn't purely Jillian's fault she'd grown up the way she had. Grasping. Selfish. Just like Mom. Why had she never seen that before?

The funny thing was that Jillian had gotten away with it. She'd never have let their mother ask about her phone calls. Jillian would have said it was none of her business and their mother would have shut up. If not, Jillian would have told her to shut up. And who was the favorite daughter? The compliant Shauna or the defiant Jillian? Let that be a lesson to you, she thought.

"I'm going out," she said. "Not sure when I'll be back."

"You can't go out and leave us. Your father will want to have lunch soon. And I thought you could look after your sisters while he and I do some shopping."

"Sorry." No, that was wrong. Don't say you're sorry. Jillian never had.

But her mother had heard the word. "You're sorry? You will be sorry!"

Shauna ignored her and glanced into the mirror in the hall. Hopeless. Nevertheless, she picked up her purse and headed for the front door.

"Shauna, I said you're not to go out! What are you doing? Who was on the phone?"

"Bye," Shauna said sweetly.

She was standing at the curb when Bart drove up in a shiny new Mazda.

"So you do have some sense," he said in greeting.

She glared at him. "You shouldn't waste your money renting cars."

"You'd rather walk?"

"Walking might be good for you. You could stand to get in better shape."

"What's that supposed to mean? I'll have you know I'm in great shape. Not a pound overweight."

"No, but your muscle tone isn't very good. And you could do with more stamina."

"I suppose you're an expert on physical fitness."

"No, I'm not. But I do exercise to keep in shape."

"Can we talk about something else?"

"I need to buy some clothes, get some contact lenses, and have my hair done."

"You do, do you?"

She adjusted the seat belt and settled comfortably back against the plush cushions. "I decided I'd let you take me," she said confidently.

6

Manziuk and Ryan were meeting in the large squad room with the rest of the team on the case.

Benson was there, too. Just to give them all a friendly reminder that there was a lot of outrage felt by the public—whose taxes paid their salaries. The public wanted results. Benson wanted results. So did the police chief and the commissioner. And the mayor, for that matter.

So when was Benson going to be able to tell the public (in the form of the media) that they were once more safe, that the murderer had been apprehended? Did they know how difficult it was for Benson to have to keep answering questions with, "We're working on it," or "We won't give up until we've got him," and the like? All pat answers. All answers he'd grown to hate. He concluded, "So get to work and get this case solved!"

Manziuk waited until Benson was out of the room before going to the front. "Okay, let me tell you what we've got so far." He then outlined the case from the first finding of Jillian Martin's body to his and Ryan's list of probable suspects. When he was finished, he said, "Okay, what else have we got?"

"We found out who gave the story to the newspapers," said one young policeman. "Crystal Winston phoned it in Sunday evening. She negotiated a fee up front and then more or less dictated the story. The reporter who took it spiced it up a bit, but basically the story was as Crystal read it to them. The payment check will be sent to her mother."

"All right," Manziuk said. "What else?"

"I have the statement from Officer Fellowes, sir." An officer Manziuk recognized as one of the Forensics Team held out an envelope. "And the results of the tests on the three items that were found beside him."

"Good. Anything we can use?"

"I think so. Fellowes brought the thermos from home. It had coffee in it. He said he hadn't drunk from it. That appears to be true. It was full of coffee, nothing else. Secondly, we had a tea cup with traces of Earl Gray tea and sugar. According to Fellowes, Ellen Brodie gave him the tea around eleven-thirty. Finally, there was the glass. It was about one-third full of Coke—loaded with Seconal. It's lucky he was just groggy and not out of it for good."

"Even though he'd only drunk two-thirds of it?"

"Yes, sir. Someone had dissolved about ten tablets in the soft drink."

"How fast does Seconal act?"

"Anywhere from instantly to, say, half an hour."

"So it isn't surprising that Fellowes was asleep before he finished the Coke?"

"No, sir. Particularly since he says he was sipping it slowly rather than just drinking it down. He figured it was going to be a long night and he may as well make it last."

From her seat near the front, Ryan suddenly asked, "Wouldn't it have been easier to put in the tea?"

The officer from Ident looked uncertain.

"She asked if it wouldn't have been easier to put in the tea," Manziuk said.

"It wasn't, sir. There was no trace of it."

Ryan turned to face him. "I know it wasn't in the tea. But it seems to me it would dissolve more readily into a hot substance. Which one would be more likely? The cold Coke or hot tea?"

The officer looked at Manziuk.

"Well?" he asked impatiently.

"I guess—well, the tea. It would be a lot more work to dissolve tablets into the cold liquid. But that's what happened."

"Thank you," Manziuk said. "Since Detective-Constable Ryan is secondary on this case, I hope you will answer her directly from now on."

"Sir?" An officer in the back raised his hand.

"Yes?"

"How is Sergeant Craig?"

"He's had a heart attack. But the doctors are optimistic that he'll pull through. Whether or not we'll see him back here in the near future, I can't answer. Now, what else have we got?"

"Nick Donovan left latents on the typewriter keyboard," Ford said.

"He did?"

"Yes. So we know he could have typed the note we found."

"Any other prints? What about on the note itself?"

"It was a mess. One clear one that was Jillian Martin's. A couple of Douglass Fischer's. There are a lot of other smudges. I don't think we'll find anything else. It looks like it was handled quite a bit."

The meeting ended half an hour later. Nothing of great importance had been added. Neither Nick nor Bart had been seen at the Martins' apartment building. Several waiters and waitresses from nearby bars and restaurants recognized Jillian, but neither of the two men.

However, there were still a lot of places she could have gone. They needed to keep the circle spreading wider. And Ryan suggested they expand who they were looking for. Maybe she had been having an affair with Douglass after all.

In the early afternoon, Manziuk was working at his desk, piecing together what they had for the fourth or fifth time.

Ryan walked in suddenly. "Inspector? I've been going through my notes from the interviews again."

He looked at her and waited.

"Two things. The first is that Lorry Preston mentioned going into the study on Saturday and finding Nick Donovan there. She said he was not pleased that she had come in. Could he have been typing the letter then?"

"She didn't say what he was doing?"

She shook her head. "Only that she was surprised because he seemed annoyed that she'd come in."

"All right. What else?"

"Something Crystal Winston said. It might be meaningless, but when you asked her if she'd been in the kitchen the whole time Sunday afternoon, she said she was. But later she mentioned something about getting glasses from the bar and doing a few other housekeeping things in the day room."

"So?"

"So she was out of the kitchen. She could have noticed someone going through the games room or past the house toward the Japanese garden."

"Or coming back."

"And she could have kept quiet about it and later asked for money."

"Yes, you could be right. It doesn't narrow the list of suspects, but it does give us a good idea of what she might have been up to."

"If she'd told us right away…"

"She'd still be alive."

"Why would she try to deal with someone she knew was a murderer?"

"Maybe it was someone she thought she could trust. Maybe she didn't realize the implications." He stood up and shuffled some papers, presumably in an attempt to tidy the top of his desk. "Okay, we've been here long enough. Let's go talk to a couple of people."

Ryan had to run to keep up with his long strides.

Chapter Eighteen

They found Lorry in the mission office looking through a list of kids who were regulars, memorizing names.

"Sorry to bother you, Miss Preston," Manziuk said. "Just one or two questions."

She indicated a couple of mismatched chairs in front of her desk. "Won't you sit down?"

"We want to clarify a couple of things," Manziuk said as he perched uncertainly on an old brown wooden kitchen chair. It held. "You mentioned seeing Nick Donovan in George Brodie's study on Saturday. Was he by any chance typing?"

"Yes, he was." Her eyes questioned him.

"On the typewriter or on the computer?"

"On the typewriter. It's in the corner."

"When was this?"

"In the afternoon. Maybe around four. Nick and I had gone for a walk earlier and then had some lemonade. I went up to my room for a while. We had planned to play tennis around four, so I went down to look for him. Kendall told me he was in the study; I went in to ask him if he was ready."

"Did you happen to notice what he was typing? A form, a letter, something else?"

"I didn't look at it. I was just surprised at how fast he was typing."

"What was his reaction to your going into the room?"

She hesitated, looking down at the desk in front of her.

"Was he pleased to see you?"

Lorry continued to stare at the blank paper in front of her. "No," she said at last. The words were slow and very quiet. "He seemed annoyed that I had come in. I left right away."

"Did he say anything later?'

"He followed me out. He started to say something, but I stopped him. I said I was sorry for bothering him." She shrugged. "I don't like to be interrupted when I'm concentrating on something, either."

"And then you went and played tennis?"

"I talked to Hildy for a few minutes at the pool while Nick went to his room to change."

"How long was he?"

"Maybe ten minutes. He had said he was almost through with what he was working on, so I assume he finished it first."

"You haven't remembered anything else that might help us, have you?"

She looked up and shook her head. "No, I'm sorry. You don't really think Nick did it, do you?"

"Several things point to him."

"Are you going to arrest him?"

"Not for the moment. But if he comes around, I would make sure I wasn't alone with him."

Manziuk and Ryan left, but Lorry continued to sit at the desk. For a long time, she stared at the closed door.

Outside, Ryan said, "Well?"

Manziuk let out a long sigh. "Looks like it, all right. Let's talk to Mrs. Winston and then maybe we should pay a visit to Peter Martin."

"I can drive," she said, thrusting her chin forward in challenge as she headed for the driver's side.

"In your dreams," he replied. As he unlocked the driver's door, he said, "When I want to be driven around by a young woman as if I were a doddering old fool, I'll let you know."

"So it *is* your pride," she said. "I thought so. It's okay for a younger man to drive you around, but not a younger woman. How ridiculous. And sexist. I could report you."

"Do your worst. You still aren't driving."

2

The gate swung open once they buzzed and told Ellen who they were. She answered the front door. "Oh, my! I wasn't expecting you, was I?"

"No, Mrs. Brodie. We dropped by to clear up a few things. Is Mrs. Winston able to talk with us?"

"I don't know. I gave her the medication the doctor left. So she'd sleep, you know. She was very distraught yesterday. But of course you know that. Anyway, I can go and see if she might be awake."

"Do that, please. And if she is asleep, I'd like you to try to wake her."

"Oh, but—? Oh, yes, I see." She left them standing in the hallway for ten minutes. During that time, neither spoke.

"Oh, dear," she said as she returned to them, "my manners have gone right out the window. I'm so sorry. I never would have left you standing here if I'd been myself. I was thinking about Crystal, of course, and how sad this all is, and I—"

"You were seeing if Mrs. Winston could see us," Ryan said. "Is she awake?"

"Yes. I expect you're in a hurry, aren't you? And me rattling on. She's awake. I don't know how alert she'll be, though. The doctor said she could be a little groggy. And then she's apt to burst into tears, you know. At any time."

"We'll take a chance," Manziuk said.

"Come on, then." She started toward the kitchen. Over her shoulder, she said, "But I expect you know the way, don't you?"

They found Mrs. Winston in bed in her room adjoining the kitchen. The bedclothes were twisted and pulled out at the bottom. Several pillows lay in a heap on the floor. Mrs. Winston had apparently been having a rough time. Her hair was askew, face swollen and red; her hands, on top of the old quilt, were twisting each other in an odd, wringing motion.

"Mrs. Winston," Manziuk said as he sat on the chair beside her bed. "We're sorry to have to bother you again."

"Have you found him?" Her voice was rasping.

"You mean the one who did it. No, we haven't yet. There are a couple of things I need to know. They might help me discover who it was."

"He had no business hurting Crystal. She never did anybody any harm." Her agitation continued to manifest itself as she twisted her hands in quick, jerky motions. "She was young. She never hurt anybody."

"I know, Mrs. Winston. I wish I could bring her back. She

didn't deserve dying like that. But I can't bring her back. I can only make sure that whoever did it doesn't do it again."

"She didn't deserve it."

"No."

There was a long moment of silence.

Ryan opened her mouth to speak, but a sharp look from Manziuk made her shut it again.

Into the silence, Mrs. Winston at last spoke. Her voice was shaky, but determined. "What do you want?"

"I need to know," Manziuk spoke distinctly, "whether Crystal was ever out of the kitchen on Sunday afternoon?"

"She was in the kitchen. We were working on supper."

"I know. But it's easy to forget. Did she go out to get glasses from the bar?"

"Glasses?"

"Dirty glasses. From the bar in the games room. Did she go to get them?"

"Dirty glasses. Oh, yes. I remembered them because of Bart. He was on the patio and I saw his glass. I don't know why, but it made me remember that we hadn't collected the ones from the bar since early in the morning. There were quite a few there from the night before. In the morning, Crystal put out fresh ones and we took the dirties to the kitchen. A little while after I saw Bart, I sent her to get the dirty ones and take a tray of fresh ones. She was hardly gone any time at all."

"I see. So there were still people on the patio when you asked her to go?"

"Oh, yes. Quite a few. They were having lemonade."

"Did Crystal go anywhere later? Say to check the flowers?"

"Flowers? I don't remem—no, wait. She did go to the dining room to make sure the flowers were fresh for supper."

"The dining room?" Manziuk's voice betrayed disappointment. "But that's at the front of the house."

Ellen had come in and was listening, but now she interjected, "Yes, certainly. Is anything wrong with that, inspector?"

"No. I just—"

"What about the flowers in the other room?" Ryan asked. "Not the games room. The other one."

"Oh, you mean the day room?" Ellen asked with interest. "Did you want her to go there?"

"Not particularly," Manziuk said, his voice putting a damper on Ellen's enthusiasm.

"She did, you know," Mrs. Winston said, her voice weaker than before. "She told me she had just given them water because they still looked fine."

"So she was in the day room?"

Mrs. Winston nodded. "Right after she picked the flowers."

"What?" The word burst from Manziuk's lips and exploded into the small, crowded room.

"She picked flowers for the dining room arrangement. Just a few. Most of the flowers were fine, but a few had wilted. She picked some Shasta daisies and some roses."

"Which garden?" Manziuk asked, his voice under control again, but eagerness in every line of his body.

"Why, the rose garden, of course," Ellen answered. "The Shasta daisies are just this side of the entranceway, and there are lots of roses."

"Is the arrangement still in the dining room?" Ryan asked as she started toward the door.

"Goodness, yes," Ellen replied. "Who's had time to think about flowers in this house?"

It was fairly easy to tell which roses Crystal had added to the vase. A few were clearly fresher than the others. And a quick walk to the garden showed that the roses had been picked from two bushes that were near the entrance—a beautiful reddish orange tea rose called Tropicana, and a majestic pink bloom named Queen Elizabeth.

"Who knows what she saw?" Manziuk muttered half under his breath after he and Ryan had taken their leave of Mrs. Winston and Ellen and seated themselves in the front seat of their car, with Manziuk at the wheel.

"The question is, did he see her?" Ryan added.

"Or she."

"Yes, or she."

"In any case, we now have a good possibility as to what happened. She came out here and saw someone either coming from or going into the Japanese garden. She didn't think anything of it. Who knows if she'd even put it together when we interviewed her? It may have been later that it occurred to her to wonder what that person had been up to."

"Or perhaps he, or she, approached Crystal."

"Whatever, we now have to figure out who she saw."

"You know," Ryan said, "she might have gone to the garden herself and murdered Jillian Martin, though I can't imagine why."

"Unless it turns out Crystal was Peter's secret girlfriend, I don't think I'll buy that."

"Stranger things have happened."

"True. But I hope not in this case."

"How about money?"

"If you mean that Jillian was blackmailing Crystal, or if, as I suspect you may mean, you think someone paid Crystal to kill Jillian, I don't think so. I think she saw something and decided to make a profit from it."

"Then it would have to be someone she wasn't particularly afraid of."

"According to Kendall and even Nick himself, Nick Donovan has no trouble getting women to fall for him. I think if he had spun Crystal a good enough tale, she'd have believed Jillian's murder was justified."

Ryan nodded. "If a sensible girl like Lorry Preston is attracted to him, no doubt Crystal would have been."

"Hmm." Manziuk found a parking place. "Well, let's go check out a few more things with Peter Martin."

3

After a quick glance at Manziuk's ID, Peter's secretary buzzed her boss and watched with interest as Peter hurried out of his office to usher Manziuk and Ryan inside.

"Any news?" he asked as they seated themselves on the plush leather.

"No arrest, yet, but there may be one soon," Manziuk replied.

"Dare I ask who?"

"Not for the moment. Mr. Martin, this is a rather delicate matter, but one I need to clear up. Your partner, Douglass Fischer, was on a business trip a couple of months ago. He took his secretary."

Peter stared at him. "Even if he did, what's that got to do with Jillian's murder?"

"You are aware of the trip?"

"Yes. Douglass, er, asked me for advice when he got back. You are, I take it, referring to the fact that it turned out to be more pleasure than business?"

"What I would like to know, Mr. Martin, is if you said anything to your wife about that weekend? Anything at all?"

"To Jillian? No, of course not. I wouldn't..." His eyes looked away and a tinge of pink touched his cheeks.

"You remember something?"

"Yes. Not about the weekend. But—look, what's this got to do with Jillian's murder? You surely don't suspect Douglass or Anne, do you?"

"Mr. Martin, your wife was blackmailing Mr. Fischer. She knew all about the weekend and had obtained evidence."

"Oh, my God!"

"We need to know her source."

"All I said to her—and it was unintentional, a slip of the tongue—was that I didn't blame Douglass for slipping the leash. And I said something about his secretary—Miss Kayne—being attractive. Then I realized I shouldn't have said that much and I changed the subject. That's all."

"Would it be possible for us to talk to Miss Kayne?"

"Douglass isn't in yet. You could talk to her in his office where it's private."

Five minutes later, the young woman was threatening tears. "It's so terrible about Mrs. Martin. She was so nice. So friendly."

"Did you tell her about your relationship with Mr. Fischer?"

"Not what you'd call a relationship. Just that one time. My boyfriend Randy would kill me if he found out."

"You told Mrs. Martin about that one time?"

"She asked me about him. You know, about me working for him. Said she knew how hard it was to work with someone every day and not get—I think the word she used was 'involved.'"

"And you told her about the weekend?"

"Well, not right out." She looked at her hands. "I—well, I asked her what I should do. You know, if my boyfriend ever found out, he'd be really mad. Really mad."

"What did she say?"

"She asked me if there was any proof. You know, letters or such. I said no. And I said there wouldn't be any trouble because we had signed in with our own names. You know, we had separate rooms."

"Did you mention the name of the hotel?"

"I might have." She looked at him, suddenly curious. "Why? You aren't going to tell anyone, are you?"

"I don't think that will be necessary."

"Randy won't find out?"

"Not from us."

"Good. I sure wouldn't want him to find out. And you know," she said confidingly, "I thought it would be exciting, but it wasn't. We were both too worried somebody would find out." Her voice was wistful. "It wasn't any good at all."

4

Douglass Fischer sat alone at his desk. Before him was a paper full of writing; in his right had was an empty glass.

He had a decision to make.

Life couldn't go on this way. He couldn't take it. Neither, it appeared, could Anne.

Manziuk had recommended counseling. But he didn't know a good counselor. There were a lot of duds out there. How did a person find one worth taking the chance on?

And would Anne even go?

Well, it was that or what? Give up?

Who should he blame for the way his life had become? His kids? Anne? His job? Society? Himself? And why on earth had he not realized what was happening? Why had he never once sat down and thought about it? Anne had tried. He had to be honest. She had tried to get him to talk about the kids. About her needs. But he had been too busy to listen. No. That was a cop-out. He hadn't wanted to listen. Hadn't wanted to bother.

And now look at the mess they were in.

But it wasn't too late, was it?

They were still alive.

They were still young enough to change.

Well, there was no harm in trying.

Maybe Anne's doctor knew the name of a good psychiatrist.

He looked at his empty glass. A refill? No, he really should go into the office.

No. No more escaping. No more running away. He would go upstairs and talk to Anne if she was awake. And if she wasn't awake, he would sit in the chair across from the bed until she woke up. And then he would do something he hadn't done for a very long time. He would tell his wife he loved her.

5

Bart and Shauna ate a late lunch. She had ordered contact lenses, bought several new dresses and other items of clothing, and made a hair appointment which she would keep right after lunch.

Bart told her what George had said. He expected sympathy. He got scorn.

"You are ridiculous," she said simply. "I may not know anywhere near as much as you do, but at least I can support myself."

"Oh? What's this about Peter's sending you to art school?"

Her cheeks flamed. "I'll pay him back. Every penny. It's only that I've given most of my money to my family. Otherwise I'd have enough."

"You aren't giving them any more, I hope."

"Not my parents. But I'll have to see if I can help the girls. Otherwise, they're sure to end up like Jillian. They may, anyway, but I'll have to try."

"Well, Sleeping Beauty, you seem to have awakened with a vengeance."

"What's that supposed to mean?"

"Nothing. Where is this art school?"

"New York, I hope. Peter said something about Paris, but that's a bit much."

"Who knows? If you have talent, and I think you do, the world is yours."

"I don't want the world."

"What do you want?"

"Just to be left alone. To be able to be me. Lorry said something about everyone's needing to be loved and to have a sense of importance—something you do that is yours. I can't really expect someone to love me, but I can do what is inside me to do. Maybe—I don't know—maybe that will be enough."

"Why can't you expect someone to love you?"

"Why should I? Anyway, that's out of my control."

"Not entirely."

She looked puzzled.

"It partly depends on you."

"I don't understand."

"Imbecile. Do you think I called you up because I had nothing else to do?"

Her eyes widened in dismay as she whispered, "Oh, no!"

6

Hildy set down the phone. It was done. She had reserved two tickets to Vancouver. In one week they would be gone.

Was she being foolish? With Jillian dead, there was no apparent reason to do this.

She shook her head. They had to go. It would be difficult. Hard to be so far from her sister. Hard for Stephen to leave his school and friends. But they had to go. Had to start a life someplace else where every street corner didn't remind her of Peter.

For a brief moment back at the Brodies' she had thought maybe there was a chance. That Jillian's death might have changed him. When he told her that he'd been in her room looking at Stephen's picture, she held her breath, barely daring to hope. But it was no good. Peter didn't love her. And he didn't love Stephen. He liked them. But deep in her heart, she knew he didn't care.

Next Friday, she would start a brand new life with nothing to remind her of Peter. And in time, who knew? A boy needed a father. No, a dad. Somebody to play catch with him and build a train with him and teach him to drive a car. Someday, maybe, she would find a man like that.

Someday. But not right away. Just now the very thought gave her a choked feeling in her throat.

Blindly, she grabbed a pitcher from a side table and threw it across the room. It hit full-on against a mirror and the two crashed together onto the floor, showering the room with a thousand bright slivers. "Oh, Peter, I hate you! I hate you! I hate you!"

A tremulous young voice said, "Mother?"

She spun around.

Stephen was standing in the doorway of his bedroom. His face was white, his chin quivering. "Mother? You're scaring me."

7

George Brodie opened the door of his office and came face to face with his son. This was a moment he'd waited for. A proud moment.

"We have an office all ready for you," George said as he put his arm around Kendall's shoulders. "I think you'll be pleased."

They walked down the hall, and George opened a door. "We'll have your name put on it tomorrow."

Kendall looked inside. A mahogany executive desk. A large matching credenza. Wine leather chairs. Heavy wine and cream curtains. Cream carpets. His face broke into a wide grin.

"Like it?" asked George.

"Like it? I love it! It's perfect!"

"We're still looking for a secretary for you. Should have one by the end of the week."

"No problem. Although the secretary is a good idea. I never have been very good at typing. Nick has usually done it for me."

"He hasn't changed his mind?"

Kendall shrugged. "He told me this morning that he's moving out at the end of the month. Says we'll be living in different worlds now. I'm not sure where he's going, and neither is he. But that's his problem. If he's going to turn down all this—" His hand swept the office as he spoke. "He's got only himself to blame."

8

It was pouring rain when Lorry walked out of the mission office. Nick was walking toward her.

"Oh! Nick! I—I didn't expect to see you here."

"Have you any plans for dinner?"

"I'm staying with the man who runs the mission. At his house, I mean. I'll be eating there."

"How about going someplace with me tonight?'

"I—" She searched for an excuse that would sound reasonable. "I think that might be rude. I mean, considering I just arrived yesterday."

"I need to talk to you."

"Can't it wait?"

"I'm here now."

"I—I'm not sure."

"Lorry, can't you spare me a couple of hours? Or do you prefer giving your time to strangers?"

Her laugh sounded forced to her ears. "Nick, you're basically a stranger. I've only known you since Friday!"

His eyes begged mutely as he said, "But I don't want to be a stranger."

"Nick." Her voice implored him to leave.

"Lorry!"

"I don't know what to say."

"We don't have to go far. There must be someplace around here we can eat. Just for a little while. Please?"

"You're impossible. And you're getting soaked. Oh, all right, but I'll have to tell Dave and Marie."

Nick took the umbrella from Lorry and held it as they walked through the rain to the house where she was staying.

She invited him inside to meet the Spaldings. Marie's pale skin and straight blond hair contrasted with her husband's ebony skin and curly black hair. Both expressed delight in meeting Nick.

"Never mind going out to eat in this miserable weather," Marie said cheerfully. "I made stew and there's a ton of it. You're more than welcome to eat here."

"Are you sure you don't mind?" Lorry asked, ignoring the look in Nick's eyes.

"Of course not. You'll soon learn that we love company. Lorry, if you'll just set another place. Dave, fill a pitcher with water and finish the salad for me, please. Nick, I wonder if you would mind giving Darren the last of his cereal?"

"I don't know anything about feeding kids."

"Oh, he's easy. Just get half a spoonful and put it in front of his mouth. He loves his cereal."

After a last pleading look Lorry chose to ignore, Nick took off the light jacket he had worn because of the rain, and sat on the old chrome kitchen chair beside the baby's highchair. He dutifully began to spoon cereal into the wide-open mouth. "I thought babies spit this stuff out," Nick said after a few minutes.

"Not all babies," Marie replied cheerfully. "And not all the time. Only if they aren't hungry or they dislike the taste. But Darren seems to be always hungry, and so far he loves his cereal. Brenda was a lot fussier."

"Brenda?"

As if on cue, a three-year-old wandered into the room with her doll. Seeing Nick, she bounded over to him. "Hi!"

"Uh, hi."

She held out a dark-skinned doll. "Can you feed my dolly some, too? She's hungry."

"I don't think so. She can't eat this stuff."

"I know that." The tiny girl shook her black curls scornfully. "You just 'tend feed. Don't you know anything 'bout dollies?"

Two hours later, when the meal was over and the dishes washed and Marie and Dave had excused themselves to put their children to bed, Lorry and Nick sat in the small living room on well-worn unmatched chairs and looked at each other. Seeing clearly was rather difficult. Though it was only eight o'clock, the clouds and rain had made it dark outside. An old ivory floor lamp and a newer ceramic table lamp provided the only light.

"This wasn't exactly what I'd planned," Nick said.

"Oh?" Her voice was innocent.

"Can we go for a walk?"

"In the rain? Anyway, I've been told this isn't a good neighborhood to go for walks in at night."

"Don't you think I could look after you?"

Manziuk's words hung in Lorry's mind. "Why do you want to get me alone?" she asked bluntly.

"Why do I—?" His voice was puzzled. "I don't want to 'get you alone.' I just want to talk to you, and it's a little hard to say what I want to in front of other people. Especially people we don't even know."

"They aren't here right now."

"I know that, but..." He rubbed his forehead with both hands, and then threw his arms out, palms up, "Okay. I give up. I wanted to—" He made a fist of his right hand and pounded it into the palm of his left one as he spoke. "This isn't exactly easy. Mostly, I just want to say I'd like to get to know you better."

"This is me." She indicated the room.

"What?"

"This room, this house, these people, small children, thanking God for the food and asking his blessing on our lives, talking about other people we're trying to help—this is me."

"You mean what you're used to."

"That's right. My home is similar to this one. And I fit in here. It's what I want out of life."

Nick caught her mood. "Church on Sunday, a car that needs a check-up, toys everywhere, people dropping in for a meal. I get the picture."

"It's very different from your life."

"I know."

"I won't change."

"I know that, too." His eyes stared intently into hers. "I'm the one who has to do the changing."

She felt as though there was a lump the size of a golf ball in her throat. Her voice, when she finally found it, was husky and low. "Do you want to?"

"Last Friday afternoon, before I met you, I'd have said there wasn't a chance on this earth. Now—I'm not so sure. I've never met anyone like you. I don't understand how you think and I won't pretend I do. I don't honestly know if I could live like this and do all the things you do. But right now, I have to consider it." He stood and paced the small area that was free of chairs and toys. "Don't think I haven't tried to put you out of my mind, because I have. I've told myself I'm crazy. Only—no luck." He stopped pacing and sat down again, leaning forward to take one of her hands. "What I need, Lorry, is to know that if I do decide to change, you'd be there."

"You mean is it worth it?"

His mouth twisted into a curve. "Yeah. I guess. You said there was a guy back in Edmonton. What about him? And, bottom line, do you think you could care for me if I were to change?"

She didn't answer for a moment. When she did, her voice was so low he had to listen intently. "Nick, when you offer to change so you will be acceptable to me, it's very flattering, but it just doesn't work. You can't simply change the way you are on the outside. When people change, it has to be from the inside out.

"The bottom line, as you put it, is that we have very little in common. You like partying and drinking and going out with a lot of girls and having a good time. If you simply try to act as though you don't like those things, first of all it won't last, and second it won't be real. You'd grow to hate me for making you false to yourself."

"But, Lorry, I've never met anybody like you. I didn't even know people like you existed! It's not just that I'm attracted to you because you're beautiful or anything like that. I like being around you, talking to you, even arguing with you. I can't imagine not seeing you again."

He stood up and went to a window. With his back to her, his face hidden from her, he said, "Lorry, I don't understand myself. Maybe it's got something to do with seeing Jillian. It was like opening an old wound that I thought was healed. She hurt me, badly, and I guess I just covered it up.

"Four years ago, I thought Jillian was what I wanted, but seeing her on Friday, I didn't feel anything. In fact, it wasn't very long at all before I wondered what kind of total idiot I was to ever think I wanted to marry her. And I guess that got me wondering if I was still a total idiot."

He still had his back to her. "The truth is I started off spending time with you because Kendall had asked me to. He was afraid his mother was trying to matchmake, and he already has someone. He asked me to look after you so Ellen wouldn't get her hopes up. But by Saturday night, I was hooked. Then you and Peter talked, and I realized just how totally different we are. And how hopeless it is."

He spun to face her. He was next to the floor lamp and the light it cast made half of his face look overly bright and haggard while leaving the other half in shadows. "It isn't that I want to pretend to be the kind of person you could—you could care about. I want to *be* that kind of person. I want to be the person you need! But I don't know how."

There was a knock on the front door.

They both turned to look at it. The knock was repeated. Lorry got up to turn on the outside light and open the door.

Manziuk and Ryan stood there.

Manziuk said. "Is everything okay?"

"Yes."

"Nick here?"

"Yes."

"We hate to interrupt, but I'm afraid he's going to have to come in for questioning."

Nick came up behind Lorry. "Are you arresting me, Inspector?"

Chapter Nineteen

"I want to ask you some questions," Manziuk said. "Will you come with us now?"

"You could ask me your questions right here," Nick said.

"I'd prefer for you to come down to the station."

Manziuk's voice was light but Nick heard the iron behind it. "How did you know I was here?" he asked. "Were you having me followed?"

"Will you come, please?"

Nick's jaw dropped. "You were, weren't you? You had someone following me. You really think I did it!"

"Mr. Donovan, I'd rather discuss this at headquarters if you don't mind," said Manziuk.

Nick noticed that Ryan had put her hand inside her purse. "Okay, I'll come peacefully." He turned to Lorry. "Sorry to put a damper on your evening. Or were you hoping this would happen? It certainly came at a convenient time for you, didn't it?" As he put on his jacket, he looked into her eyes. "Still think I did it?"

"I never said I thought you did it."

"You came close enough." He went past her. "Okay, officers, I'll go peacefully. Hey, should I represent myself or should I get a real lawyer? What do you think?" His words were flippant, but Lorry had seen the whiteness around his lips.

He walked out between Manziuk and Ryan, and Lorry stood watching until the car had driven off, water splashing from the tires as it went.

Dave came down the stairs. "I thought I heard someone at the door. Has Nick gone already?" he asked.

2

At the station, Nick was taken to Manziuk's office and Ryan indicated where he should sit. She sat nearby: Manziuk took the chair behind the desk.

"Okay, what's this about?" Nick asked.

Manziuk took his time answering. "Mr. Donovan, you have no alibi for either murder. You were alone in the rose garden when Jillian Martin was killed. You could easily have gone to the Japanese garden and back to the rose garden. You could even have walked with Mrs. Martin to the Japanese garden and then killed her. You had time to go back to the rose garden and make it look as though you were just coming out. We are quite certain Crystal Winston was near the entrance to the rose garden at one point in the afternoon. There is every chance she saw you either going to or from the Japanese garden." He leaned forward to continue, but Ryan suddenly interrupted as an idea hit her.

"Or perhaps," she said, "it was what she didn't see. Perhaps she didn't see you in the rose garden."

"Possibly," Manziuk said. "Now, what else was I going to say?" He put his glasses on and picked up a notebook. "Oh, yes, we know that at some point on Sunday you were very close to Jillian Martin. Several of her hairs and traces of her face powder were found on your shirt. Also, your prints were on the typewriter and you were seen typing. Why not the note threatening Jillian?

"When Crystal realized what she'd seen—or hadn't seen—" he bowed toward Ryan, "she spoke to you, and you asked her to meet you at the back of the house. You knew she could easily get the key to unlock the back gate and if you went out to the ravine the body wouldn't be found right away. Also, if she cried out back there, no one would hear. You may have agreed to pay her. Or she may have thought she was in love with you. Either way, you used her trust to get her alone and then you killed her.

"You used Douglass Fischer's tennis shoes, which happened to fit you and happened to be placed conveniently in the change house. You knew about the black jogging suit in the hall closet, so you put it on over your clothes. And you told Crystal to wear black so she wouldn't be seen.

"But you made one mistake. You didn't put quite enough Seconal in the Coke you gave the policeman who was guarding the house. I got his report this afternoon. He says you were talking to Bart and Kendall on the patio late Sunday night. You left for a short time and came back with Lorry Preston. Kendall and Bart went off to Bart's apartment. He got the impression Bart was intoxicated and Kendall was taking him home as opposed to simply going with him. You and Lorry talked quietly until Kendall returned, at which point Lorry went into the house. You and Kendall talked for a few minutes. Then he went in and you came over to the officer, told him the show was over for the night and he may as well make himself comfortable. You offered him a beer and he declined. Then you said it was a long night and would he like anything else. He said a soft drink would be nice. You went into the games room through the patio doors and returned with a glass which you said was a Coke. After handing it to him, you went into the house. He drank the Coke and that's the last he remembers until Mrs. Winston woke him."

"Do you deny that?" Ryan asked.

Nick shook his head. "No. That's what happened. But I didn't put anything in the glass except the contents of a can of Coke."

"You should have given him the can," Manziuk said.

"I thought he'd want ice."

"So you put ice into the glass?"

"Yes."

"And nothing else?"

"Nothing."

"Do you have an alternative suggestion as to how Officer Fellowes was given the sleeping medicine?"

"Is that what it was?"

"It was Seconal, fairly high strength. The same thing Mrs. Fischer had in her room. She can't be sure, but she thinks some of her pills were gone. It wouldn't have been difficult for someone to see the bottle lying on her nightstand right out in the open and borrow a few tablets."

Nick's voice broke, betraying him. "I didn't do it. I didn't do any of it. I know it sounds damning the way you put it and I expect you'll get a conviction, but I still didn't do it." He shut his eyes and breathed deeply.

"That's all you're going to say?" Ryan asked.

"I'll say 'not guilty' when you take me before the judge, but I don't expect it will do me any good."

"All right. Ryan, take him downstairs and book him."

Nick pulled himself to his feet. His hand shook as he held it toward Manziuk. "Manziuk, look at me!"

The Inspector complied.

"Do I really look that stupid? If I had done it, would I have given him the drink so openly? Left my prints on the typewriter? Written the note in the first place? Look, I know I'm no angel, and I may have done some stupid things, but surely even you can see I wouldn't have done this! I might as well have left you a confession and signed my name to it!"

"What were you typing?" Manziuk asked, interested.

"A letter for Kendall. He'd been asked if he would consider working with a legal aid agency, and he had to let them know he wasn't interested."

"Why were you doing it?"

"I do all his typing. He's lousy. Like he's got ten thumbs."

"Why were you annoyed when Lorry Preston came in?"

"Not because I was typing a threatening note! I was—embarrassed. Oh, what the heck! I wanted her to think I was this macho guy, and here I am typing like some nerd. And I'd been thinking about her at the same time. And suddenly she was in the room. I felt stupid. That's all, I swear."

"Jillian Martin meant nothing to you?"

"Not anymore. And certainly not after I'd met Lorry."

Ryan interjected, "You would have traded Jillian Martin for Lorry Preston? I find that a little hard to believe."

"Believe it! Look, Inspector, if you'd asked me what I thought about love at first sight, I'd have laughed in your face. I didn't even believe in love. I mean, real love. Overnight love with consenting adults I believed in. But if anyone had told me I'd be thinking about chucking my skiing and going off to the slum area to try to help street kids who need legal aid I'd have—well, you get the idea."

"So you're thinking of applying for the position Kendall had been offered?"

"Considering it."

"Good story," Manziuk said. "Maybe it was typing the letter for Kendall that gave you the idea of writing Jillian."

"Manziuk!"

"Take him down and book him as a material witness."

"You can't!"

"If I were you, I'd go peacefully. The middle of a police station isn't a good place to pick a fight."

"Manziuk, you're making a huge mistake. I didn't do it!"

"Then how did the Seconal get into the glass of the Coke you gave Officer Fellowes? Was anyone else around?"

Nick shook his head. "No." He walked across the room and stood looking at the picture on the wall. An eagle soaring through the air. A mouse racing along the ground below.

Manziuk's voice interrupted his thoughts. "Mr. Donovan? I'm waiting."

"I know," Nick mumbled.

"You don't have an answer, do you?"

"I put ice cubes into a clean glass. I opened a can of Coke and poured it into the glass. I didn't add anything else."

"Or perhaps you can tell me about this?"

Nick turned. Manziuk was holding up a picture of a chain of flowers. Nick walked closer and took the picture from him. "I used to make those. My mother taught me how. I haven't made one for years."

"Did you ever make one for Jillian?"

"I think so. Yes, I know I did." He paused and stared at Manziuk. "Did you find one of these?"

"Beside her."

"I didn't make this one. But I do remember teaching Jillian how to make them. She could have made it while she was waiting for me."

"While she was waiting for you in the Japanese garden. But you were in the rose garden. Why?"

"I guess I went to the wrong garden."

"You seem to have made quite a few mistakes this weekend, Nick. Can you tell me why you were in the wrong garden? Or perhaps, where you really were?"

"I can't."

"Do you want to call a lawyer?"

Nick walked over to the window and stood looking out for a long time.

Ryan opened her mouth once, but Manziuk shook his head violently. Although she gave him an annoyed look, she didn't say anything.

At last, Nick turned to face them. There was moisture in his eyes, and his voice shook. "I guess maybe you'd better go ahead and book me. You don't have much choice."

"Who are you protecting?" Ryan asked bluntly.

That shook him a little. But he quickly answered, "Nobody."

"Then why won't you tell us the truth?"

Nick smiled ironically. "Is this where I plead the fifth?"

Thirty minutes later, Ryan returned with a list of the contents of Nick Donovan's pockets and a report that he was duly booked and had offered no resistance.

Manziuk was on the phone, but he quickly ended the conversation when he saw Ryan.

"So?" he said. "Not very happy?"

"Do you think he did it?"

"I'm inclined to doubt. But that may be because he's so likable. As a matter of fact, a lot of murderers are very likable."

"But if he isn't guilty, who is? Peter Martin?"

"I could make a case for him. Or for Hildy Reimer, although I can't see her framing Nick. Or for Bart Brodie, though we still have no proven motive. Or for the Fischers, but while they may be guilty of a lot of foolishness, I don't believe either of them is a murderer. Then we have Kendall and George Brodie. If Nick is protecting someone, it would be Kendall. Or Lorry, perhaps—but that could all be an act. Nick says he was awake and Kendall was asleep while Crystal was killed. If Nick isn't the murderer, he could be giving Kendall an alibi. But George and Kendall were together when Jillian was killed."

"Could there be two murderers?"

"I sincerely hope not." Manziuk sighed. "But we can't rule it out. Maybe Nick killed Jillian, and then Kendall killed Crystal to protect him."

"How would we ever prove that?" Ryan asked.

"A confession would be nice."

"Yeah, right." She thought for a moment. "What about Peter Martin? Have we ruled him out?"

"I don't see how he could have drugged Fellowes."

"So it has to be Nick Donovan?"

"It seems that way. And if by any chance it isn't, holding him might make the real murderer relax and make a mistake."

"So we wait?"

"We wait. And we continue to sift every bit of information we have."

She turned to leave. "Oh, did you want this?"

"What is it?"

"The list of the contents of Nick Donovan's possessions when he was booked."

"Anything interesting?"

"Not that I could see."

"Okay, put it on the desk. I'll look at it later. I want to have a talk with Ford. See if there's anything Forensics could have missed."

3

Ellen was busy in the kitchen. George would be home soon and she wanted to make sure everything was perfect. She had cooked all his favorite foods.

She added a hot cup of tea to a supper tray and carried it in to her housekeeper. It had been a long day for Mrs. Winston. She had been by turns hysterical, weeping, tired, querulous about making funeral arrangements, and worried about what was going to happen to her. She had taken it into her head that George would fire her because of what had happened, and Ellen had used a good deal of her remaining energy to persuade her housekeeper that George would do no such thing.

Right now, Mrs. Winston was relatively calm. She had been crying again, but she was not anguished as she had been earlier. More like shock, Ellen thought. Crying but not quite knowing why. Not really understanding what had taken place.

Ellen helped her sit up in bed and made sure the tray was in the right spot.

"I'm shivering. That air conditioning makes it so cold when you aren't working."

After three tries, Ellen found the right sweater. She had to move the tray to help Mrs. Winston get the sweater on. Then she arranged the tray again. "Just call when you've finished. Or if you need anything. I'm getting George's supper ready, so I'll be in the kitchen."

Her housekeeper nodded.

"Would you like the TV on?"

"Yes. It might take my mind off things."

Ellen found the remote, turned the TV on, and left the control at Mrs. Winston's right hand.

She went back to the kitchen, found one of the cups she'd kept from their old set of dishes, and poured some tea for herself. She was about to sit down when the phone rang.

"Ellen?"

"Yes, George."

"How is everything?"

"Not too bad. We're having the funeral Friday. Jillian's is Thursday, isn't it?"

"Yes."

"Are you on your way home?"

"Doesn't look like it. I've got a lot of work here. And since I'll be going to the two funerals, I thought maybe I should work late so I can keep on top of things. You don't mind, do you?"

"No, I suppose not."

"You aren't afraid of being alone there, are you?"

"No, of course not. I'll make sure the gates are locked. And the doors."

"The police could send someone over if you were worried. Goodness knows we pay enough taxes."

"That's silly. There's nothing for me to worry about."

"Speaking of that, Kendall just got a call from Nick. He's been arrested."

She jumped. "Nick?"

"From what he told Kendall, sounds like a pretty strong case. I'm sure glad Nick hadn't joined the firm. If he had, the press would be twice as bad. Anyway, with him arrested, I don't think you have anything to worry about. Don't wait up for me. I have my keys."

She hung up the receiver and sat for a long time staring through the patio doors. All thoughts of the food cooling on the counter were gone. She didn't hear Mrs. Winston calling for her to come get the tray. "Oh, Nick," she said at last, shaking her head. "Not you."

In his office, George pulled out a file and began reading through the notes his law clerk had made. He'd had his secretary order up a ham on rye and a bagel with cream cheese. As he read, he ate. But after a while, the words blurred. He went over to the water machine and poured a glass of water. Two pills went down. That would help his ulcer.

So they'd arrested Nick. When Kendall had called to let him know, George had at first felt relief that the case had been solved and then anguish at what the arrest would mean. George had already phoned Bradley and Pattison to make sure Nick had the best defense possible.

George considered the trial. He wondered what evidence the police had. Likely circumstantial. Bradley and Pattison were the best. They'd get Nick off, all right. But it would be messy. They'd all be called as witnesses. And the press would have a field day. George's feeling of impending doom sank onto him. He'd been so hopeful that when the police made the arrest, it would be over. But of course, this was only the beginning of the next act. And there was nothing he or anybody else could do about it.

Trying to shake the feeling off, he sat down and began reading, willing himself to concentrate.

4

Kendall Brodie was pacing in his apartment, wondering how Nick was enjoying his prison cell. Kendall picked up a pillow and slammed it against the wall. Nick wasn't guilty. Not of murder, at least. Of being an idiot, maybe. But if Nick wasn't guilty, who was? And why couldn't the police solve this without hurting innocent people?

He kicked the back of a chair.

He'd been so angry with Nick for not wanting to join the firm, and now he couldn't care less about that. Nick could ski until he was ninety, if he wanted! Funny how a person's perspective changed.

Of course, that was assuming Nick got out of jail.

Kendall grabbed the pillow and threw it against the sofa. It had about as much effect on the sofa as he was having on the police investigation. This helplessness was horrible. But when he'd asked his dad what he could do to get Nick off, his dad had said to stay out of the way and let Bradley and Pattison handle it. They were the experts.

Come to think of it, that was what Nick had ordered him to do, too. Sit tight. Only he didn't want to sit! He wanted to do something!

He threw a second pillow, but the storm in his eyes didn't abate.

Was this what it felt like to have a brother? Was this what it felt to love somebody? He would have laughed if anyone had said he loved Nick. But he did. And he wasn't going to let Nick be the hero this time. No matter what it cost.

5

Shauna was finished at the hairdresser by five-thirty. They had supper at a small Italian restaurant. Then she asked Bart to take her to a certain address. She wouldn't tell him why.

When they arrived at a plain, brick, three-story office building, she went inside alone. She came back a few minutes later and thrust a brochure at Bart. It was from Alcoholics Anonymous.

"I don't need this," he protested.

"From what I saw this weekend, you need it."

"Give some people an inch and they take a mile."

"That's a cliché."

"Maybe it is, Miss Librarian. But it's also true. I only said I liked you."

"No, you said you were intrigued by me."

"Did you know that half the time I have to keep myself from wringing your neck?"

"And the other half?"

"Never mind." He started the car. "And if I want to stop drinking, I'll stop. Notice, I said *if* I want to stop."

"You'd better stop smoking while you're at it. Or don't you read the newspapers?"

As he pulled out of the parking spot he said, "Did anyone ever tell you you're bossy?"

Her face lit up. "Am I?"

"Yes."

"I've never had a chance before."

He glared at her. "So? The first guy you meet who doesn't ignore you and you think you have to boss him around?"

"Watch where you're going," she said.

When his eyes were on the road again, she said, "It's for your own good. You don't want to end up like my father, do you?"

"How should I know? I've never met your father."

"He's back at Peter's apartment. He'll drink with you. Smoke with you, too. And you can tell each other about all the jobs you've lost."

"I've never lost a job."

"Don't you mean you've never had a job?"

"Do you have to assume that if I'd had a job, I would have lost it?"

She just looked at him.

"Battle-ax," he said.

She smiled, her eyes dancing, and he nearly lost control of the wheel.

6

Anne and Douglass Fischer forgot about supper until eight o'clock. They had been in such intense conversation that nothing else seemed to matter. When Jason came up to the bedroom to ask what he was supposed to eat, he found his parents sitting together on the love seat in the bay window. His father's right arm was around his mother's shoulders, her left hand holding his.

"Send out for pizza," Douglass said lazily.

"Suits me," Jason replied and went downstairs to comply.

"I should have made supper," Anne protested.

"Pizza will be fine."

"Yes. I guess it will. Douglass?"

"Hmm?"

"Do you think the counseling will be expensive?"

"I don't care. We're worth it. I can't believe what a fool I've become."

"You're not a fool."

"A man who's so caught up in his job that he has no time for his wife or family is a fool."

"Well, you aren't one anymore."

"I hope not. Don't ever let me forget again what's most important."

"And don't ever let me be the witch I've been."

7

At nine o'clock, Manziuk was in his office going over the report from Forensics for the third time. Maybe there was something they'd missed. Some little detail that would lead them to something else that would lead to the murderer. But nothing rang a bell. Maybe he should quit. Nick Donovan was the obvious choice. So why wasn't he satisfied?

There was a knock on his door and Ryan strode in. "Well, guess what."

"You found something?"

"I didn't. But one of the men checking restaurants did."

"What?"

"Are you ready for a shock?"

"I should tell you I don't care for high drama. Just give me the facts."

Ryan rolled her eyes and leaned toward him. "Okay." Her voice became Jack Webb's from Dragnet. "You want the facts, nothing but the facts?"

Manziuk stared at her in astonishment.

"Oops," she said, jumping back. Then, quickly, she added, "She was seen at a restaurant with someone other than Peter Martin. Apparently, she met him there several times, the last one being Friday morning."

"Who?"

"You remember this morning you said to widen the search? Include Douglass Fischer?"

"Yes. So it was—"

"Not him. One of the officers added pictures of all the men involved. At my suggestion." She paused for him to digest this. "She was meeting Kendall Brodie."

Manziuk was silent for several minutes. Finally, he said, "He claimed he had never met her."

"He lied."

"Maybe we'd better have a talk with him."

They were walking out of the station when Kendall came running up behind them. Unfortunately, he was forestalled by three reporters who had been hanging around looking for news.

"What can you tell us, Inspector?" a dark-haired woman with a black umbrella and tan trench coat asked.

"Who's this? You new to Homicide, miss?" This from a young man in a hooded jacket.

"How's Woody doing, Paul? Don't tell me they replaced him with a woman!" A white-haired man with a leather jacket and cigar spat in disgust.

"No comment," Manziuk said. "Talk to Benson."

Kendall ignored the reporters. "Inspector Manziuk, I was up at your office and they said you had just gone out. Do you have a few minutes to talk?"

"Aren't you Kendall Brodie?" the female reporter asked. "I understand that Nick Donovan has been arrested. He's your roommate, isn't he? Do you have any comments on his arrest?"

"Nick is completely innocent," Kendall said.

"Inspector?" The young man wanted agreement.

"No one has yet been arrested for murder," Manziuk said. "Now if you'll excuse us—Mr. Brodie, I'd keep my mouth shut if I were you."

Manziuk was pushing back toward the station, taking Ryan and Kendall with him, the reporters blocking every step.

"Get out of my way." Ryan pushed against the young man in the hooded jacket. "If you don't move, I'll arrest you for impeding justice."

"Who's the spitfire, Manziuk?" asked the older man with a grin.

They ducked into the building, leaving the reporters behind.

"We were going to look for you," Manziuk said to Kendall.

"Nick told you?" Kendall sounded surprised.

Ignoring the question, Manziuk said, "Why don't we go to my office where we can be comfortable?"

A few minutes later, seated in his office, Manziuk studied the younger man. Pale, definitely nervous. "You remembered something?"

"Not exactly."

"Well?"

"Didn't Nick tell you?"

"Nick hasn't said anything to us that concerns you," Manziuk replied.

Kendall relaxed. "I didn't think he would." He seemed to be putting his thoughts in order. "Okay. Nick called to tell me he'd been arrested. He says you claim the Coke he gave the police officer was drugged. I don't know anything about that, except I was with Nick all evening up to a few minutes before he gave the officer the Coke, and I think you're crazy to think he put drugs in it. When would he have gotten them? And how would they have dissolved so quickly? He came upstairs a couple of minutes after I did."

"So you don't think there was time?"

"No, I don't. And I don't believe Nick would have done anything like that, anyway. We've shared an apartment for three years. I think I'd know if he was capable of murder."

"Or perhaps you would feel bound to help out a friend."

Kendall stood up suddenly. "Never!"

"That's what you came to tell me?" Manziuk sounded bored.

Kendall sat down again. "No," he said quietly. "It's about the garden. Nick wasn't in the wrong garden." He took a deep breath. "Jillian was."

"And you know that because…?"

Kendall rose once more and walked to the window. "She had told Nick to meet her in the rose garden. I told her Nick wanted to meet in the Japanese garden instead, because it was more secluded."

"When did you tell her this?"

"I was watching for her. When she came out of her room about twenty-five after three, I went out and talked to her. I told her Nick had asked me to give her the message, and that he might be a few minutes late because he had to get away without Lorry."

"Mrs. Martin believed you?"

"Yes."

"Why did you lie to her?"

"Because I wanted to talk to her myself, and she wouldn't give me a chance. I knew that we would be all alone in the garden, and I thought I could make her listen." Kendall's voice had become a whisper, his head drooping.

"So you followed her into the garden and tried to make her listen, and she wouldn't. And you became angry and killed her."

"No. That isn't what happened." Kendall's voice was barely audible.

Ryan couldn't keep quiet any longer. "Kendall, we've found the restaurant where you and Jillian used to meet."

He looked up. "I wondered if you would think about that."

"How long have you known her?" Manziuk asked.

"About a month. She called me one day and asked if I would have lunch with her. She said she wanted to get to know everyone connected with the firm and since I was George's son, she wanted to meet me."

"So you met her."

"Yes." His voice had once more become a whisper.

"What happened?"

Kendall looked up, his cheeks red. "I fell for her."

"She encouraged you?"

"Oh, yes." His voice was bitter. "I think you could say she did everything she could to encourage me. She told me that she would leave Peter for me once my position with the firm was secure."

"Why?"

"Well, at the time, I thought it was because she was in love with me, but now—I really don't know." His voice rose. "When I met her for lunch last Friday, she basically told me it was over." His voice was slow and sounded honestly perplexed. "She acted like she was telling me I couldn't have another cup of coffee. Like she didn't care one bit."

"Is that why you killed her?"

"Let me finish! I didn't kill her. When I saw her at my parents' on Friday, I tried to talk to her, but she ignored me. I wrote her a note Friday night, but when I handed it to her in the hallway, she tore it in half without even reading it and threw the pieces on the floor."

"You typed it?"

"Yes. Mom asked me where I had been for so long, but I'm such a lousy typist I had to redo it about five times. I told Mom I'd had some calls to make."

"And you typed a personal note like that?" asked Ryan.

"I'm a lousy typist, but my handwriting is even worse. Everybody is always telling me they can't read what I write. The last thing I wanted was for Jillian not to be able to read the note. So I typed it to make it as clear as possible."

"What did you do with the first attempts?"

"I burned them in the fireplace. I wanted to make sure no one else saw them."

Ryan moved closer. "You said she tore it into two pieces. We only found one. What happened to the other half—the half with the signature?"

"That was weird. After she threw the pieces down, she got a funny look on her face." He bent his head and took a deep breath before looking up again. "I don't know if I can explain it. She was looking at me—almost like she was daring me to do something about it. Then when I just stood there staring at her, she looked down, just her eyes, without moving her head, as if she was reconsidering what she'd done. Not that she was sorry she hadn't read it—something else. Then suddenly she dove down and grabbed the piece closest to her. I reacted instinctively and grabbed the other piece before she could get it. She glared at me—like she would have fought me for it, but just then Hildy's door opened and she started to come into the hallway, so Jillian put the one piece in her pocket and took off."

"What did you do with the piece you had?"

"I tore it into tiny pieces and flushed it down the toilet. I felt like a fool."

"Did you feel Jillian was playing games—that she was playing with you?"

"I didn't know what was going on. I was completely at sea."

"So she wouldn't talk to you or read your note?"

"By Sunday, I was getting desperate. Then just after lunch I saw her come up to Nick and more or less throw herself at him and kiss him. I couldn't believe it! He just pushed her away, and she went into her room. She was laughing. I was furious with Nick. That's when he told me he'd known her before and that she was trying to get him to meet her, and I saw my chance."

"Did you tell Nick the truth?"

"Not then."

"So you followed her to the garden?"

"Not immediately. Mom was coming upstairs, so I talked to her for a few minutes. I didn't mind if Jillian had to wait. I wanted her to think Nick wasn't coming so she'd be fed up with him. And then I thought I'd better check to make sure she hadn't gone to the rose garden anyway. But I saw Nick, and he was alone. So then I went to meet her." His gaze fixed on Manziuk's face. "Here's the part you aren't going to believe. When I got there, she was dead. Lying on the grass, just like you saw."

"What did you do?"

"I ran up to her and—" His voice broke. "I saw she was dead. It must have happened just moments before I got there. In fact, I looked around, thinking I'd see whoever it was running away. But I didn't see anyone."

"Did you hear anything?"

"I don't think so, but I wasn't thinking very clearly." He paused and took a deep breath. "I didn't know what to do. I couldn't believe it had really happened. Then I realized I had to get the police, so I hurried back to the house. I knew Dad was in his study, so I went there."

"Did you tell him everything?"

"Pretty much."

"And you made up a story about being with him the whole time?"

"Before, just after Jillian had gone downstairs, Mom had come up. I was still in the hall, so I told her I was going to look for a book. She said it was likely in Dad's study. So Dad said to just expand on that. Say I'd gone down to the study and we'd talked while he finished sending his e-mail."

"Why?"

"Because you'd be sure to think I was guilty, and I wasn't."

"Was it your dad's idea for you to take Lorry to the garden and 'discover' the body?"

"Yes." He shuddered. "I didn't want to go back there, but he said I had to, because we needed to get the police on it right away. So I went and got Lorry, and then we saw Nick. You don't know how relieved I was when he said he'd come with us. I offered to let them go alone, but they wanted me to come, too, so I thought I'd better. I thought it might look funny if I didn't go."

"That's it?"

"Yes." He looked straight into Manziuk's eyes. "That's it. I know Nick didn't do it. He was in the rose garden, like he said."

"Could anyone have overheard you telling Jillian to go to the Japanese garden?"

"We were in the hallway outside several bedrooms. I suppose someone could have heard us."

"You're ready to swear that this story is true?"

"Yes, sir. I didn't like lying to you before. But I didn't kill her, and I knew you'd think I did."

"When did you tell Nick the truth?"

"Sunday night. After we went up to go to bed. I told you I was asleep, but we talked for a long time. At least an hour."

"And what did Nick say?"

"He told me I was a total idiot, but that I was right to let you think I hadn't known her. He said it would just complicate things and lead you on a wild goose chase. But I didn't know you'd think he did it. I thought it would just help you concentrate on finding the real killer."

"We still have no explanation for the Seconal's being in the Coke Nick gave Officer Fellowes," Ryan interjected.

"Nick didn't give anybody Seconal," Kendall said with conviction.

"Okay, why don't the two of you go get Nick and let him know what you've told me. Let's see if he has anything to add," Manziuk said.

When Ryan and Kendall Brodie had gone, Manziuk sat staring at the picture on his wall. The eagle had great eyes. It could see little mice scurrying on the ground far below.

Sometimes Manziuk felt like that eagle, trying to see the one key detail that was buried among all the masses of facts or observations they had. And that one detail was often like a key that opened the door to making all the facts fit together.

But this case wasn't coming together. Everything they discovered led to more confusion.

What was it that was nagging at him? Something at the back of his mind. And why did he keep thinking about the other murders? Because he had spent so much time on them and they were still unsolved? Because Lorry Preston had red hair?

But that was irrelevant, unless of course she happened to be the next redhead the murderer ran across. He hoped she would take heed of the warning he had given her. Many women with red hair were now wearing hats or dying their hair just in case.

But that wasn't it. There was something else. Something in the back of his mind.

He put aside the report from Ford and glanced through Officer Fellowes' statement. How else could the drug have been administered? How else except by Nick?

Idly he picked up the list of Nick's possessions when he was arrested:

346

package of matches with two gone
wallet with credit cards and $180.00
driver's license
small plastic package of Kleenex
$3.24 in loose change
keys on a chain with a skier
paper with a single phone number
cat's eye
half-empty roll of breath mints
pen with a local chiropractor's logo
appointment card from the same chiropractor

The phone number had turned out to be the one for the mission Lorry Preston was working with for the summer.

The chiropractor he visited occasionally to keep his back in line for skiing.

There was nothing else of interest. What on earth was a cat's eye? And why would Nick have one in his pocket? And why did that seem to trigger bells in his brain?

The door opened, and Ryan, Kendall, and Nick walked in. Nick was holding a plastic bag filled with odds and ends.

"Good, you've got your possessions," Manziuk said without preamble.

"What?" Nick stared.

"The bag. Put them on the desk. All the contents of your pockets."

Nick did as he was asked, looking at Manziuk as if he thought the other man had lost his mind.

There it was. Some people might call it a cat's eye. He called it a marble. It was quite large and swirled with gold and blue. That was the detail that had been buried in his mind, just beyond reach. He'd seen it before. Back in George Brodie's office when he'd first interviewed Nick. Nick had been rolling it in his fingers. But it hadn't registered on Manziuk at the time.

Manziuk's voice was stern and cold. "Okay, Nick, I have to ask you one more time if you want to be represented by counsel?"

Chapter Twenty

Even Ryan stared at Manziuk in surprise.

"You just had them release me," Nick said, obviously bewildered.

"Yeah, well, I seem to have changed my mind."

"We've already gone over this." Nick looked at Kendall. "I don't get it. I thought you said you told him."

"What's this?" Manziuk held up the marble.

"What?"

"It's a marble. It was in your pocket. Why?"

Nick shrugged. "I don't know. I don't remember seeing it before."

"Is that right? Well, let me tell you that's not good enough. These marbles are unique. They're extra large. Specially made for an experiment with autistic children. Easier to hang on to than regular marbles. There were twenty-four of them. And one was missing. So I know where it came from. And I think I know how you got it."

Nick stared at him. "Well, you know more than I do. I don't have a clue where it came from. I'll go further than that. I've never seen it before in my life."

"Nick, you're about to be booked on six counts of murder. The game—"

"I came here and told you the truth!" Kendall exploded. "He didn't kill Jillian or Crystal! Why are you badgering him? And what are you talking about? Six counts of murder?"

"Sit down! He knows what I'm talking about. All those women, Nick. Why did you do it?"

"You're crazy!"

It was Ryan's turn to protest, "Inspector, are you sure?"

"Did Jillian find out, Nick? Was she blackmailing you?"

Nick's face was slowly turning red. "You're nuts! I didn't murder anybody!"

Manziuk jumped up and stepped menacingly toward Nick. "You smile and almost persuade me you couldn't possibly be the killer, and all the time this is sitting in your pocket, laughing at me. I ought to—"

"Inspector!" Ryan's voice was sharp, in command. "Don't you think you need to make dead certain of this?"

Manziuk stood silently, looking at Nick. The younger man was staring straight at him, with not so much fear showing in his face as confusion. Maybe... Manziuk stepped back and took a deep breath. "All right. Why don't we all sit down?" They found chairs. "Okay, Nick, let's look at this rationally. Did your mother have red hair?"

"Did my—? What are you talking about?"

"Did your mother have red hair?"

"My mother has dark brown hair. You might even call it black. I expect she has some gray, too, but she visits the hair-dresser now and then."

"Do you have an alibi for any of these evenings?" Manziuk scrambled through his notebook and held out a page of it.

Nick shook his head. "I don't keep track of everything I do."

Kendall was staring at the dates. "Wait a minute. The last date. May second. Yes. Yes, he does have an alibi. One of our professors gave a dinner party, and Nick and I were both there. We had dates, too. I took Marilyn and Nick took Candace. We were there from seven until one and it was after two when Nick and I got back to our apartment. We didn't leave it again that night."

"Whose car did you take?"

"Nick's. I didn't have mine then. I mean, I'd sold my old one, and Dad gave me the Porsche the next day. It was my graduation present."

"I'll need the full names and addresses of the two women and your professor."

Ryan spoke up again, "Are you sure this marble is what you think it is? That there couldn't be others?"

"So sure, I—" Manziuk forced himself to speak slowly. "Look, I've got four young women dead with no apparent reason. Wouldn't you want to grab the guy who did it?"

"Of course," Ryan said.

Kendall and Nick both stared.

Ryan turned to Nick. "If you aren't the killer, where did you get this marble?"

Kendall answered. "He picks things up all the time. Even in class, he's likely to be making a paper airplane out of his notes. It's as if his hands can't be idle. Half the time he doesn't realize he's doing it."

Manziuk stood up. "Well, this time he's going to remember. The two of you can just sit here until you do!" Manziuk left them there and went out to find Ford.

2

An hour later, Manziuk was back in his office. Nick Donovan and Kendall Brodie both had indisputable alibis for the murder of Cerise Matheson on May 2nd. And all Nick could tell them about the marble was that he must have picked it up somewhere. Reluctantly, Manziuk sent them both home. Then he told Ryan she may as well get some sleep.

"And you?" she countered. "I'm not going until you do."

Reluctantly, he called it a day. Maybe he'd be able to think more clearly after a few hours of sleep.

But Manziuk didn't sleep much that night. Loretta had been to the hospital with Arlie to visit Woody. Seldon had been there, too. Seldon was just talking about ordinary stuff, but apparently Woody had asked point blank if this was the end of his career, and Seldon's face had given the answer. Woody had decided there was no point in the doctors' saving his life if he wasn't going to be allowed back on the force.

Arlie, Loretta, and Seldon had spent half an hour trying to convince him life still could be worth living, with him getting more upset all the time, and then Michael, the Manziuks' seventeen-year-old son, had come into the room and walked over to Woody's bed and said, "Uncle Woody, what would I ever do without you?" And Woody had begun to cry and everything was okay again.

After hearing all that, it was hard to sleep. Between thoughts of Woody and wondering what his family would do if he weren't around, his brain was busy trying to figure out a solution for all six murders. He figured he got about three hours' sleep all night.

Beside him, Loretta, as usual, slept like a log. "Clear conscience." That was what he always said.

3

Manziuk was at his desk by eight.

They were back to square one with no apparent next move. Well, maybe not that bad. He had the marble, and Ford said it was identical.

There was a note from Benson lying front and center on the desk, and another almost identical one from Seldon. What was all this about releasing Nick Donovan? Did he think they were running a circus? Was he about to make a real arrest? How soon? The public was anxious. The police chief was anxious. The commissioner was anxious. The mayor was anxious. What was he doing? And would he come to see them as soon as he got in?

Manziuk sat and stared at the notes, his mind far away. Had Nick picked up the marble? Or had it been planted on him? And if so, by whom? Bart Brodie was the obvious choice. He could have committed both murders at the Brodies'. And he was the right type for a serial killer. A drifter and a leech. But they had no evidence to connect Bart to Jillian. Unless he was simply insane and killed when he got the chance.

Who else? Peter Martin? Opportunity, yes. And he seemed to have a love/hate relationship with women. Douglass Fischer? He gave the impression of a man under control, but a man whose control was about to snap. He was capable of murder. George Brodie? He had lied for Kendall. But he had been in his office sending e-mail when Jillian was killed and with his wife when Crystal was killed. And somehow, he didn't seem the type to do anything irrational.

What about the women? Hildy Reimer? Not if he knew anything about character. She could have killed Jillian Martin as a lioness would kill to protect her cub. She might have killed Crystal out of fear. But not the four women who had died needlessly. That was the work of a man. Ditto for Anne Fischer and Ellen Brodie and Shauna Jensen. No, it had to be one of the men. Bart, Peter, or Douglass.

They'd had a psychiatrist do an analysis after the third mur-

der. He had told them to look for someone who had been reject-
ed by a woman with red hair—possibly a mother, a girlfriend, an
idol, another family member or close friend.

"About time you showed up," he snapped at Ryan as she
came in. "Get the background checks on everybody in this case.
I have to go make some public relations calls. And then go
through the reports. Maybe there's something we've missed."

4

When Manziuk came back three hours later, Ryan was bleary-
eyed but pleased.

"What have you got?" he asked.

"First of all, Nick Donovan had the marble in his pocket
Sunday. It's in Ford's list as one of his possessions. It was in his
pants pocket along with his loose change. Second, no one in
Douglass Fischer's background had red hair. At least, no one we
know about. But Peter Martin's third wife, the one who took him
for a lot of money, had red hair. And I think Bart Brodie's mother might have, too."

"What do you mean, you think?"

"Her name was Francine, but she was known as Carrots," she
said with a smug smile.

He turned toward the door. "Let's go."

"Where?" She scrambled to grab her notebook and purse.

"I put a tail on Bart before he left the Brodie house. Let's find
out where his travels have taken him."

As they waited for the elevator, Ryan turned to look more
closely at him. "You don't look so hot. Aren't you feeling okay?"
A sudden thought sobered her. "Detective Craig isn't…?"

"No. He's fine. I didn't get much sleep last night. And I just
spent three hours getting hauled over the coals."

Her indignation caused sparks in her eyes. "What for?"

"Because we're taking too long to solve these bloody murders!" The elevator door opened and he hurried forward. "Now
are you coming or do you want to stand around here wasting
more time? And don't even mention driving. I'm not in the
mood!"

5

They found both Peter and Bart at the Martin apartment. Peter answered the door. He looked completely done in. No wonder, Manziuk thought a few minutes later after Mrs. Jensen had given him the third degree about their search for the murderer.

"Is there a place we could talk?" he asked Peter finally.

Peter led Manziuk and Ryan into a small study. Mrs. Jensen seemed to think that if this had anything to do with her daughter, she should come, too, but Ryan stood in her way and said, "That'll be all for now, Mrs. Jensen. We'll call you if we have any questions."

As soon as the door was shut, Peter said to Ryan, "I'm impressed. She actually listened to you. She always used to act as though she was a little afraid of me, but that's gone now."

"You look terrible," Ryan said frankly. "Can't you get rid of them?"

"As soon as the funeral is over, they're out of here even if I have to hire bouncers."

"Mr. Martin," Manziuk said, "we have some questions we need to ask you. Your third wife, I believe her name was Genevieve, had red hair?"

"That's right. So what?" He looked from Manziuk to Ryan.

"Can you give me any idea what you were doing on these nights?" Manziuk held out a paper.

Peter took it. "Not off the top of my head. Is it important?"

"Very."

"I'll get my appointment book." He went out and came back a moment later with a small computerized datebook. "It should be here. At least the ones this year." He pushed buttons and stared at the small screen. "Well," he said at last, "I don't have anything specific. I worked a bit late on February eighth, but the other two nights I was home here with Jillian. But I guess she can't vouch for me. I don't know about the one in October, but I may have a record of it at my office." He looked up. "Can you tell me why these dates are important?"

"You've heard about a serial killer, haven't you?"

"You mean the four women." Peter's voice broke. "The four red-haired women who were murdered?"

"Yes."

"You think there's a connection?"

"It's a possibility. Have you seen this before?" Manziuk held out the marble.

Peter stared at it. "No. Never. Is it a clue?"

"It may well be."

"Well, I hope you catch him, but if you think, as I suspect you do, that I murdered four women with red hair because of Genevieve, you're crazy."

"Can you check on that date in October?"

"You're really serious, aren't you?"

"You'd better believe I am."

Peter picked up the phone and dialed his office.

Twenty minutes later, his secretary had confirmed that on October 7th he was at a conference in Los Angeles. Jillian had gone with him.

Bart was with Shauna in the kitchen washing up after lunch. Shauna's appearance was stylish and smart. The sight of Bart Brodie in the bit of lace Jillian Martin had considered an apron was nearly too much for Ryan. She bit her lower lip to keep from laughing.

"I have a few questions, Mr. Brodie," Manziuk announced after he had persuaded the rest of the Jensen family to return to the living room.

"Yeah?" Apron or not, Bart looked belligerent.

"Did your mother have red hair?" Manziuk asked sternly.

"Did my mother have red hair?" Bart repeated, his face suddenly a picture of bewilderment. "What on earth?"

"Answer the question."

"Why?"

"Answer the question."

He looked at Shauna, then back at Manziuk. "All right. Yes. It was kind of an orange-red. That's why they nicknamed her Carrots when she was little. And if I didn't shave my head, I would have red hair, too. Which is one reason I shave it! So are you going to arrest me because you don't like the color of my hair?"

"I may need you to come down to the station."

"Because my mother had red hair? Or because I do?"

"You've heard of the murders here in the past few months?"

Bart put his hands on his hips. "Oh, no, you don't, buddy. You aren't going to try to nail those on me."

Ryan covered her mouth with her hand to keep from laughing out loud. Bart Brodie in a dainty lace apron with his hands on his hips was more than she could take. All he needed was a wooden spoon in one hand.

Both Manziuk and Bart ignored her.

"We've made a connection," Manziuk said.

"Are you serious?"

"What is all this about?" Shauna's voice was perplexed. "Does he think you killed Jillian?"

Bart ignored her and ripped off the apron. He held out his hands. "Okay, Inspector. Get the cuffs. I confess. My mother had red hair and the fact that she gave it to me made me want to kill every redheaded woman I met. Don't ask me why I killed Jillian and Crystal and left Lorry alive. Maybe I decided it was time to switch hair colors."

"Give it a rest," Manziuk said, but his voice was abstracted. Somewhere inside another bell had rung. If only he could make the connection.

Ryan finally got control of herself and stood up. "Have you got any alibis for the evenings of these dates?" Ryan took the paper from Manziuk's hand and held it toward Bart.

"How should I know?... Wait a minute." He began to laugh. "Yes, as a matter of fact I do have an alibi for one of those dates. The best alibi money can buy. I spent the night of January eleventh in jail. I had been in a club that got raided. Gambling without the appropriate license, I believe. I went there at eight. With two friends. And from nine-thirty until the next day at eleven I was in a cell with plenty of witnesses."

"You know we'll check that," Manziuk said.

"Check to your heart's content," he said.

Manziuk turned on his heel and walked out.

Ryan had to run to keep up.

"Now what?" she asked when they were in the car.

"Check on their stories. Find out if Bart really was in jail and if Peter really was in L.A."

"And Douglass?"

"Yes, we're down to Douglass."

6

They reached the Fischers' house half an hour later. Anne opened the door. "What do you want?" she asked bluntly.

"We have a few questions for Mr. Fischer. Is he home?"

"No." Her voice was ungracious. "He'll be back soon. I suppose you want to come in."

"Yes, if it won't bother you too much," Ryan said sarcastically before Manziuk could respond.

Anne stepped back so they could enter.

"What is all this about?" she asked. "We've already told you everything we know."

"We have some new questions," Manziuk said.

"What about?"

"Is Mr. Fischer going to be long?"

"I guess you can sit down in the living room." She led the way into a spotless green and yellow living room.

They sat in silence until the front door opened about ten minutes after their arrival.

"Douglass!" Anne jumped to her feet. "The police are here. They want to see you!"

He walked in the room and both Manziuk and Ryan were conscious of a change. For one thing, Anne had rushed over and put her arm around him. He had responded by pulling her close. But, more subtly, Douglass Fischer looked relaxed, like someone who had gotten the monkey off his back.

Still with his left arm around Anne, he walked over to Manziuk and held out his hand. "Good to see you, Inspector." He nodded to Ryan. "Sergeant, isn't it?"

"Constable," Ryan corrected.

"I can never keep titles straight. You wanted to ask me something?" He propelled Anne onto the sofa and sat down beside her.

"Mr. Fischer, did anyone in your family have red hair?"

"What?" He laughed in apparent bewilderment. "Is this some kind of joke?"

"No, Mr. Fischer, it isn't. We have made a connection between the murders at the Brodie estate and four murders of young women in the Toronto area this past year."

"So you think I—?"

"We're checking everyone."

"I don't see what people with red hair have to do with it."

Anne broke in. "They had red hair! All those girls!"

"That's right, Mrs. Fischer," Manziuk said. "And the psychologists told us to look for someone with a connection to a red-haired woman."

"Then I'm not your man, Inspector, because I don't have any relatives with red hair. Nor have I ever been involved with anyone with red hair."

"You realize we can check?"

"Of course, I do." Douglass smiled. He seemed completely at ease. "I really have nothing to worry about, Inspector."

"Can you remember where you were on any of these dates?" Manziuk asked, holding out the paper.

It took a few minutes, but Anne had a habit of writing all appointments on a calendar in the kitchen. And on May 2nd, she and Douglass had been at a party hosted by one of Douglass's clients. They had dined and danced from seven to one while on a cruise boat touring the Toronto harbor.

7

"Now what?" Ryan asked as the door shut behind them. "Every single one of them has an alibi."

Manziuk didn't answer. He walked to the passenger side of the car and said, "You want to drive?"

"You trust me?" Ryan was clearly incredulous.

"Right now, I don't trust me." His voice was flat and tired. He got into the passenger seat.

"There has to be something we've missed," she said as she sat behind the wheel.

"We seemed so close."

"One of them could be lying."

"I wish. But I don't think so."

"So who did it?" she asked.

"Maybe Nick's remembered where he found that marble."

"Maybe." There was silence for several blocks. "He was with Lorry most of the time. Would she have noticed?"

"Let's find out." Manziuk picked up the phone.

After a moment's thought, Lorrie said, "Yes, I do remember Nick's having a marble. On Friday night after supper. We were all sitting in the day room talking. It was just before Hildy Reimer walked in and surprised everyone. Nick seemed rather abstracted. I noticed he had an unusually large blue and gold marble in his hand. He was rolling it around. I'm not sure he was aware he was doing it. He put it back into his pocket after Hildy came."

"Did you see him with it again?"

"He might have had it Sunday. He often seemed to have something in his hand. Is it important?"

"It might be."

"Do you still think he did it?"

"Do you?"

There was a long pause. "No," she said at last. "But perhaps that's because I don't want him to be guilty."

"Well," Manziuk said, "if it's any consolation, neither do I."

"So he had it early Friday evening," Ryan said as Manziuk hung up.

"Let's go and talk to him again."

"Where does he live?"

"Turn left at the next street. I'll phone and see if he's home."

8

Manziuk and Ryan arrived thirty minutes later. "Traffic was bad," Manziuk apologized to Nick when he opened the door.

"That's okay. I wasn't going anywhere."

Kendall was sitting on a comfortable-looking off-white chair. In an identical chair, feet tucked neatly under her, sat a short-haired blonde in blue jeans and a pink man-style shirt.

Kendall stood up. "Inspector, this is Marilyn Garrett, my alibi for the second of May."

Marilyn smiled. "I'm pleased to meet you, Inspector. And I hope you aren't here to arrest either of these two."

"I'll try not to," Manziuk said. "This is Detective-Constable Ryan."

"Detective-Constable, nice to meet you," Marilyn said. "Please have a seat."

"Yeah, sit down," Nick said. "I know what you want. The marble, right. I just don't remember. I've tried."

"Lorry says you had it Friday night before Hildy came into the room," Ryan said to prod his memory.

"I did?"

"Yes. So where were you before that?"

"We were at supper," Kendall said. "And before that we were in the rose garden with Lorry."

"And before that I was in my room. And your mother gave me a quick tour of the house. And before that we were in the car." Nick's face suddenly went white.

"You've remembered," Manziuk stated.

"No, I couldn't have."

"Nick, let's not have any more lies."

Nick looked at Kendall. "It's just…"

"Nick, whatever it is, tell him," Kendall urged.

"All right. But, I don't—" He stopped and thought for a moment. "No, it doesn't make any sense."

Manziuk glared at him.

"Okay." Nick ran his fingers through his hair. "After we left here, we drove up the Don Valley Parkway. The traffic was terrible. We were crawling along. Kendall was harping about the job with the firm. I took off my seat belt and started to open the door. I threatened to jump out if Kendall didn't stop talking about the job. When I was putting my seat belt on again, my hand went under the seat cushions and felt something round. I remember pulling it out and glancing at it. I was going to throw it in the garbage, but it looked interesting. I thought maybe it was Marilyn's, so I dropped it in my pocket. I meant to give it to Kendall later, but I guess I forgot."

"Marilyn, have you seen it before?" Ryan asked.

Manziuk held the marble out.

Marilyn looked at it closely. Then she shook her head. "No, never."

"That tears it," Manziuk said. The others looked at him. "I had hoped that there was a connection. But now—anyone could have put that marble there. Even a workman back at the garage. How long did you say you'd had the car?"

"I got it the day after the dinner party. So, since May third. Not many people have been in it. And it's locked all the time."

"Then we're looking at a very narrow list of possibilities," Ryan said.

"It could have been sitting for a while at the car dealer's," Manziuk said.

Kendall quickly shook his head "No, it wasn't. It was a special order."

"We'll have checks done with the factory and the dealership," Ryan said. "Kendall, you make a list of everyone who's been in the car."

Manziuk and Ryan were on their way out the door when a thought suddenly struck Manziuk. He spun around so quickly Ryan almost went flying. "Kendall, what color was your grandmother's hair?"

"My grandmother's hair?"

"What color was it?"

"I don't remember. No. Wait. I believe she may have had red hair. Like my aunt's. I'm not positive. But I think so."

"Speaking of red hair," Nick said quietly. "Lorry's got red hair."

Bart had said the same thing. Lorry has red hair.

"A lot of women have red hair," Manziuk said harshly. "Why shouldn't they?"

"Where to?" Ryan asked after they'd given the list to Ford.

"There's one person we haven't talked to for a while." He started out. "And I'm driving. We're in a hurry."

"What was wrong with my driving?" She hurried to keep up with his long strides. "And what makes you think I can't drive as fast as you?"

9

Ellen Brodie was awakened by the buzzer from the front gate. She sat up suddenly and then felt dizzy. She put her hands on the arms of the rocking chair she had dragged into the kitchen and stood up. She tottered over to the intercom. "Who is it?"

"Mrs. Brodie, it's Inspector Manziuk. May I come in?"

"Oh, Inspector. I'm sorry. I was asleep. I'll press the button. You have to open the gate and then shut it behind you."

The button pressed, she went to the bathroom to check her appearance. Not good. Hair a mess, makeup smeared. Foolish to go to sleep like that. She looked at her watch. Seven o'clock.

Ellen opened the door just as Manziuk was reaching for the doorbell.

"Mrs. Winston is sleeping. I didn't want to wake her up, poor thing."

"Is your husband here, Mrs. Brodie?"

"George? Why, no. He's at the office. Working late. He worked late last night, too. He was in court today, and he has the two funerals tomorrow and Friday. Thought he should get as much done as possible tonight. I expect he'll be here soon, though."

"Does he often work late?"

"Not a lot. But sometimes, certainly."

"Mrs. Brodie, did you hear that Nick Donovan had been arrested?"

She sighed. "Yes, and I was so worried. But then you let him go, so I thought it was all right."

"You didn't want it to be Nick?"

"I don't want it to be anyone except the guilty person," she said with dignity.

"You realize, don't you, that I am going to have to arrest someone."

She nodded.

"Neither of us want an innocent person to go to jail, do we?"

She mutely shook her head.

"Is there anything you need to tell me?"

She looked at the ground. Finally, she nodded.

"You lied, didn't you?"

"I was asleep. Nothing could have awakened me. He put sleeping powder in my tea. I knew when I woke up later than usual in the morning. My head felt fuzzy."

"Why did he do it?"

"You'd both better come in and sit down, Inspector."

Manziuk and Ryan followed her into the kitchen. They found chairs, and pulled them up to Ellen's rocking chair.

"I've been sitting here all day trying to decide what I should do. What's best." She clasped her hands. "I even considered turning myself in and saying I was guilty. But that wouldn't really solve anything, would it?"

"Mrs. Brodie, have you noticed a change in your husband over the last while?"

"I've been thinking about that today, too. I think I've noticed it without realizing, if you know what I mean. His insistence on buying this house, for instance. I never wanted it. All my friends are in the city. But he had to have it. And the firm. Seeing it continue and be successful. It's always been important to him, but lately he's become obsessive about it. Everything has to revolve around Brodie, Fischer, Martin, and Brodie. He was so pleased that Kendall was joining. I think it would have killed him if Kendall hadn't wanted to. And you know, deep in his heart, I don't think Kendall does want to. I think that's why he was so upset with Nick. Because he isn't comfortable with being there himself.

"You might think because of this house and his Porsche and all, that Kendall is used to having a lot of money and things, but he really isn't. George made sure he didn't think he was special because his dad had a successful law office. He delivered newspapers and had to earn his money just like any other kid. I think he could be perfectly happy anywhere—in his and Nick's apartment, which isn't fancy at all. Now—now—none of that matters now, does it?

"Did your husband tell you what happened? Was Jillian trying to blackmail him?"

She stared at him. "Jillian? No, not Jillian. Crystal."

"Crystal? All right. Tell me about Crystal," Manziuk said.

"She saw Kendall coming out of the garden," Ellen said simply. "She told George she wouldn't say anything. She liked Kendall and knew it must have been Jillian's fault. She didn't want Kendall to go to prison.

"So George asked her what it would take to get her to keep it to herself. She said she needed a car to get back and forth next year, and he said he'd get her one. And then she said she'd be awfully tight for money for gas and insurance, so he said he'd give her ten thousand dollars. She wanted some of it up front. So he told her to meet him that night." She shook her head. "He took the money, but something went wrong. She threatened him with a knife. When he tried to get it from her, it slipped." She looked at them. "You don't believe that, do you? But I'm sure it's true. George would never do anything like that on purpose. He has too much stake. The firm. His family. He was only doing it to protect Kendall, you see."

"So George told you that Kendall murdered Jillian?"

Tears trickled down her cheeks. "She told him she was going

to marry Kendall. George hired a private detective and found out Kendall had been meeting her. He seemed to be in love with her. So George paid her a lot of money to stay away from Kendall. And he got a tape of her telling Kendall it was over. It was last Friday morning.

"But Kendall was upset. He thought Jillian had been lying to him; that she had been toying with him." She leaned forward in the chair, eyes brimming with tears that splashed down her cheeks, her gaze imploring Manziuk to believe her. "She mesmerized him. Like those women in that story about Ulysses. Sirens. She made him think he was in love with her. And then when she told him it was all off, he didn't know what he was doing. He never would have done it if he was in his right mind."

"So Kendall killed Jillian and then told George?"

"No, George only realized Kendall was guilty when Crystal came to him."

"George told you all this?"

"Not then. But after I woke up Sunday morning, I felt so funny. And then they said the policeman had been drugged. So I knew George had put something in the tea."

"Could he have?"

"I made the tea," Ellen said. "But I left it in the kitchen. George brought me a cup. Then he gave me a second cup and suggested I take it to the policeman. I thought it funny that he would think of that, but it never occurred to me that—well, that it was wrong. And he seemed pleased. The policeman, I mean.

"I drank my tea and went to bed. I barely made it. In fact, I think George had to finish undressing me and put me into the bed. And in the morning, I felt so strange. I knew something was wrong, but I didn't know what. Then when Bart said the officer had been drugged, I realized what had happened.

"Of course, George made a second cup after he got back from—from the meeting with Crystal. He washed my cup and the officer's and put them away. And he crushed the Seconal in the Coke that was left."

"Why didn't you say something?"

Her eyes filled with tears once more. "I thought—I thought he must have an explanation—or a good reason—something…" Her voice broke and she took a few moments to compose herself. "Last night, after you had arrested Nick, I got up the courage to tell him I knew. I told him I wouldn't let anything happen to Nick. But he said I shouldn't worry, that Nick would be represented by the best counsel. But that wasn't enough. I didn't want Nick to go to trial at all.

"But George said there was no other way if we were going to protect Kendall. He just assumed, you know, that I would agree with him. That I wouldn't tell you. I've always supported him in the past, you see. Never questioned what he did. So I've been sitting here all day wondering what to do." She was sitting on her hands now, rocking back and forth, "How can I ever tell Mrs. Winston? She's all alone now, her beautiful daughter gone…"

Her voice trailed off and she looked down. "I wouldn't have let Nick take the blame, you know, or anyone, even Anne. But Kendall—" her eyes filled with tears, and her whole body trembled. "To think that I should have to lose him this way! And George, too. I've lost them both, haven't I? I've already lost them?" Her eyes appealed to Manziuk for support.

"Once you've killed, you aren't the same person you were before," he said.

She nodded.

"Do you have a friend we could get to stay with you tonight?"

"My friends are all down in the city where we used to live. George doesn't seem to understand that."

"What about Hildy Reimer?" Ryan asked.

"Good idea," Manziuk said. "See if she can come over. Try to get hold of Kendall and Bart Brodie, too. And have someone go by George Brodie's office and pick him up."

Twenty minutes later, Hildy was on her way, having dropped Stephen off at her sister's. There was no answer at Kendall and Nick's apartment. Bart had left Peter's apartment, and neither Peter nor Shauna had any idea where to find him. He was going to pick Shauna up for the funeral the next day.

George Brodie was not at his office.

Manziuk stopped to talk with Ellen for a moment before he left. "Mrs. Brodie, I hate to have to tell you this, but I think your husband was lying to you. I don't think Kendall killed Jillian Martin. I think your husband did."

Her eyes grew wide. "But—"

"Kendall says he found Jillian just moments after she had been killed, and I'm inclined to believe him. He said his dad told him to say they were together in order to provide Kendall with an alibi. But I think it was really to provide himself with an alibi."

She clasped her hands together and half-covered her mouth. "But he said he was in his office at the time she was killed. He said he was sending out e-mail. He said he could prove it from the times they were sent."

"Sent," Manziuk said. "Not written. With some e-mail programs you can write e-mail and then set the computer to send them whenever you want. Just like turning your oven on with a timer. George likely had been writing e-mail earlier in the weekend but hadn't bothered to send them because no one would be at work. He was likely going to send them all on Monday. I think he was about to come upstairs when he heard Jillian and Kendall talking at the top of the staircase. Kendall told Jillian that Nick would meet her in the Japanese garden but that he might be a few minutes late. So George whipped into his office and set the timer to send the e-mail and then hurried out to kill Jillian. He knew it would appear that he'd been working the entire time."

"When did you figure all this out?" Ryan interrupted.

"While we were talking to Nick. I realized that if Nick really hadn't drugged Fellowes, and frankly I never could see him doing that, then the only other way the Seconal could have been given was in the tea. You said yourself yesterday that it would be much easier to dissolve the Seconal in a hot substance. And I rather think Fellowes would have noticed that much powder in his Coke."

Ellen's tears were flowing freely again. "How could he do that?" she whispered. "Telling me it was Kendall when all along—his own son! I'll never forgive him for that. Never!"

"Mrs. Brodie, I don't think your husband is the same man you once knew. I think this past year he's been doing a lot of things you're going to find hard to believe."

But her mind was fixed on one point. "Are you sure about this? Are you sure Kendall didn't do it?"

Manziuk nodded.

She relaxed slightly. "It's bad enough to think one of them could be a murderer. But both! It was more than I could bear."

She wiped her eyes and took several deep breaths before reaching in to her pocket. "You'll need this. One of the gardeners brought it to me. He noticed it because it was tied wrong. I expect it was the—the one he used." Breathing hard, she slowly pulled out a piece of smooth beige cord.

Manziuk pulled a plastic bag from his pocket and had her drop the cord into it.

"So Kendall found her there." Tears were again overflowing. "I can't think what it was like for him to find her—if he was really in love with her."

"I think he's realized by now that it wasn't love," Manziuk said gently.

She gave him a tremulous smile. "There's a part of me that can't believe this is really happening. I keep thinking I'll wake up and it will all be back to normal. Crystal will be here. Anne and Jillian will be saying nasty things to each other. And George will pop out of his study to see what I'm doing." She wiped her eyes and rocked in the chair. "All I could think about before this weekend was that maybe Kendall and Lorry would hit it off. That's all I wanted." She buried her face in her hands as her tears overwhelmed her.

"Yes, I know. But I think there is someone else. Someone you'll like. But right now, I need you to answer some questions about your husband's mother. First, did she have red hair?"

Ten minutes later, Manziuk was on the phone to Seldon, who had been at a fancy dinner party with the mayor. "His mother had red hair?" Seldon questioned.

"Mother and sister."

"And he delivered the car to his son the day after the last murder."

"Right."

"Should we put out an APB?"

"Already done."

"Benson will be waiting in your office when you get there. He'll want all the details."

10

Lorry looked at her watch. After ten. Dave had told her not to stay this long. But she was finished. And she was finally feeling that she knew what was going on in all parts of the mission.

Now she could really start to be useful.

"I'm ready to head out, Lorry." Aaron, the other young intern who was staying with the Spaldings, stuck his blond head around the corner. "Everybody else is gone. You should come, too."

"I have to clean up," Lorry said. "I'll only be about ten more minutes."

"I'll wait for you."

"I'll be as quick as I can."

"I'll make sure everything's locked up and sweep the floor."

Ten minutes later, Lorry shut off the computer and put away her notebook and the pen she had been using. The sound of a tapping on the front door made her look up, but the desk Lorry was using sat in the far corner of the room, the view blocked by a couple of large orange cloth dividers.

"I'll see who it is," Aaron said.

"I'm nearly ready." Lorry tidied a few papers and made sure she had left everything clear for the computer's morning user. Then she reached for her purse.

She heard Aaron open the door, heard him say, "What are you—?" Then a thud and the sound of the door shutting. The lights went out.

"Aaron?" she called into the darkness. Although he didn't respond, she could hear movement in the outer office.

She reached for the phone.

A black figure came around the divider, and a hand in a black leather glove caught her hand before it reached the receiver.

She tried to pull away from the hand but failed. As she rose from the chair, trying to back away, the figure came around behind her and kicked the chair away. Another hand reached in front of her neck, passing a black electric cord across it.

Chapter Twenty-one

The phone on the desk began to ring. It startled them both. Lorry used the moment to twist sideways and then lean backwards toward the person behind her. She stamped hard on the place where she thought the person's foot should be, and hit something. A man yelled in pain. But the hands holding the cord grasped it like a steel vise.

The phone continued to ring, but neither of them paid attention to it.

In the darkness of the mission office, Lorry struggled against the cord that was cutting into her throat, holding her fast. She tried to scream, but barely any sound came. Tried to pull the cord away, but she couldn't get a grip on it.

The cord was being pulled tighter, cutting into the soft flesh, making each breath difficult.

With all the strength she had left, she brought her right heel up hard to where she guessed the man's crotch would be.

He gasped with pain and dropped his hands for an instant. The cord swung free. Lorry fell forward, stumbled, scrambled to get to her feet.

She could see him now, but he was wearing a black ski mask. All she could make out were his eyes, which glinted with hatred. He was coming after her, murderous cord held tightly between gloved hands.

She wanted to get to the open doorway, or at least knock the receiver off the still-ringing phone, but instead she had to backpedal, keeping her eyes on the man who wanted to kill her. Oh, God, help! she thought.

The phone had stopped ringing.

Her back hit a wall. The man lunged forward and grabbed a handful of her hair. As he yanked her toward him, Lorry screamed.

Neither of them heard the car screech to a stop outside or running feet on the sidewalk.

The masked man got the cord around her neck once more and began to pull it. But at that moment, two figures rushed into the room. Someone yelled, and Lorry recognized Nick's voice.

A moment later Nick grabbed the man from behind, and the cord went slack. Kendall pushed Lorry out of the way. The masked man threw Nick off as if he were a puppy clinging to the man's leg. Kendall stood between the madman and his prey.

The man stepped toward him.

"Get out of here, Lorry!" Kendall yelled. "Call the police!"

She fled. Kendall continued to back away. The man was hurrying now, only aware that someone was blocking him from getting to Lorry. He dropped the cord and pulled something else from his pocket. As Nick tackled the man from behind, a gun went off. The bullet grazed a desk and spun off harmlessly into the air. Then the three men went down in a tangled heap.

For a moment there was a wild melee. As the gun fired again, Nick yelled in pain.

Another figure shot through the doorway and joined the battle. Three to one at last prevailed. The masked man was pinned to the floor with Kendall holding his shoulders and Dave Spalding holding his feet. Nick kicked the gun beyond reach and then grabbed his upper right arm and doubled over.

"You okay?" Kendall panted.

"No." Nick's voice was strained.

"You creep!" Kendall grabbed the ski-mask and pulled. Immediately, he jerked back in horror. "Dad?"

Police sirens burst like firecrackers upon the stillness of the dark night.

George Brodie babbled nonstop as they led him away, telling them his mother never really loved his father, begging them to understand how hard he'd tried to take his father's place, complaining that nothing had ever satisfied her, sobbing that just the sight of her with her red hair, dyed an even brighter red as she grew older and tried to hide the grey, made him feel sick to his stomach.

He told them he'd finally found a way to stop her from demeaning his father and complaining about everything he did for her. He knew how to shut her up now. The only thing he couldn't understand was how, after a while, he'd see her coming back again and have to shut her up once more. But he'd keep doing it just as long as he had to, until he finally silenced her voice forever.

"He stole a Toyota," Ryan said. "It's parked down the street. The owner reported it about ten minutes ago."

Manziuk shrugged. "I expect George Brodie was hot-wiring cars before he was ten."

"You people were a little late, Inspector." Nick Donovan and Lorry Preston walked up. Nick was clutching his arm, which had a blood-stained towel wrapped around it. "If we hadn't got here, she'd have been dead."

"Did you figure it was him?"

"Are you kidding? We thought it was Peter."

"Good thing you came."

"Yeah."

"You look like you need a doctor. "

"I think I have a bullet in my arm. But it's Kendall who's in real pain."

"Where is he?"

"He and Marilyn followed his dad down to the police station in my car. He thought maybe he could help."

"Marilyn was here?"

"She wanted to come. We left her in the car to park it and call 911." He thought for a moment. "You two must have been on your way already."

"We were on our way here after talking to Ellen."

"Does she know?"

"Some of it. Not about the other four girls."

"Man," Nick shook his head. "That's going to be rough."

"She's a tough lady. As long as she has Kendall to see her through this, I think she'll make it."

"Nick needs to get to a doctor," Lorry said. She had been standing impatiently beside Nick while he talked to Manziuk.

"Put him in the ambulance, then. Anybody else injured? How about you?"

"I expect I have a few bruises, but no more." She rubbed her neck. "And Aaron is going to be okay. Fortunately, George only knocked him out with the gun. He's groggy, but it could have been a lot worse. God sent Nick and Kendall just in time."

Manziuk shrugged. "Let a doctor make sure you're okay."

Nick and Lorry were duly loaded into the ambulance and driven away. Dave Spalding was assured that the police themselves would see that Lorry got back safely.

Manziuk and Ryan got into their car and sat for a moment looking at each other. Manziuk was in the driver's seat.

"That was close," Ryan said.

"Too close. We should have had her guarded."

"She wasn't alone."

"The other kid didn't know he was there as her bodyguard."

"They shouldn't have stayed so late."

"You're right there. When Dave got home and discovered Lorry was still at the office, he phoned to tell her to stay put until he got here. When no one answered the phone, he ran out to meet them and was in time to help Kendall subdue George."

"She was lucky," Ryan said.

"I never in a million years thought he'd go after her so soon."

"Do you think killing Jillian and Crystal might have snapped something? They were the first ones he killed that he knew."

"Crystal for sure. I expect he may have felt pretty bad about that. Assuming he had any feeling left at all."

"Will he get off on insanity?"

"There's a chance."

"Poor Mrs. Brodie."

Manziuk nodded. "It's going to be hard. But I think she'll survive. Kendall is going to have a harder time, I think. I hope he has the sense to hang on to that other young woman. She looked like a winner to me."

One of the other officers came up. He was holding out a small plastic bag. "Is this evidence, sir? It was in the stolen car."

Manziuk took it. Inside the bag was a credit card belonging to Nick Donovan. "I expect George was going to leave it there to give us a nice, neat case. "

"Don't you love it when the good guys win?" Ryan asked.

Special Constable Benson was waiting for them when they got to the station. He beamed as he grabbed both their hands and congratulated them. "This is terrific," he said. "The public loves a solution like this. Everything wrapped up neatly and tied with a bow. Caught in the act. No ifs, ands, or buts. You two are going to be the toast of the town. The mayor's already phoned. He wants to give you a special commendation. And the commissioner's office called. She's out of town tonight, but she'll be back tomorrow and she'll definitely want to express her gratitude. You've made my day! Now give me all the dirt so I can address the media. I've got a press conference scheduled in half an hour."

2

The sun was creeping along the horizon, casting long shadows on the ground, when Lorry and Nick arrived back at the Spaldings' house, courtesy of a police car.

Nick had been fortunate. The bullet had gone through the fleshy part of the arm, missing the bone completely, and would heal with no ill effects.

The officer would have driven Nick home, but Lorry offered to take care of him.

"You'd better come in," she said to Nick. "You're too exhausted to worry about getting home."

He followed her inside the house and let her help him up the stairs to her room.

"You sleep here," she said. "I'll use the couch downstairs."

"No. I'll sleep on the couch."

"Nick, for once in your life, do what you're told."

He sank onto the bed. "Oh, man, this hurts."

She took off his shoes, then went for a glass of water to give him one of the pain pills the doctor had sent along after Nick refused to stay at the hospital any longer.

"I can't believe this," Nick said as Lorry gave him the water. "George Brodie killing not only Jillian and Crystal, but four other girls he didn't even know. Not to mention trying to kill you. I just can't believe it!"

He took the pill and then Lorry covered him with a quilt. She picked up a few things and started to leave.

"Lorry?"

"Yes."

"Remember what you said that time? How anyone is capable of murder because we're all human? I thought you were crazy. But you were right. I never would have believed George Brodie was capable of murder. If I hadn't seen it with my own eyes, I'm not sure I'd believe it yet."

She said nothing.

He raised his head. "Lorry, what makes you so different from other people?"

She sat on a chair near the bed. "My faith, I guess. I really believe God is in charge and he looks after me."

"But tonight, Kendall and I rescued you from George."

"Who do you think gave you the idea that I was in danger?"

He smiled and shook his head.

3

Peter Martin was at his desk by nine the next morning. He would have to leave in a couple of hours for the funeral at one, but he'd had to get out of the house. Fortunately, Jillian's family would be leaving the next morning. He would have to go, too, of course, since the body was being taken back to her childhood home for burial. But he would drive out by himself. Shauna was going with Bart, so she would be okay.

He nodded good morning to his secretary. She was even prettier than usual today. Another new dress helped. But it was the glow on her face that he really noticed. She looked—radiant was the only word for it. Did she already know what he was thinking?

The only question was whether he should wait until next week, after everything had settled down, or call her in right now and ask her to book a restaurant for a business lunch for just the two of them. For Friday, maybe. That would be appropriate.

He had his finger ready to buzz her when the intercom went.

"Mr. Fischer wishes to speak with you, Mr. Martin."

Blast it! Why did Douglass have to want to do business now? He hadn't even seen fit to come into work the day before, and now, on the day of Jillian's funeral, he wanted to talk!

Douglass walked in. "Have you heard?" he asked without preamble.

"Heard what?"

"Misty Pauling from the *Toronto News* just called me. They've arrested George Brodie!"

Peter half-jumped out of his chair. "What?"

"He's being arraigned right now!"

"George? That's impossible!"

"He killed Jillian and Crystal. But that's not all. George killed all those other girls who were strangled this year. They caught him last night trying to kill another one."

Peter felt as though the floor had suddenly exploded, leaving a gaping hole at his feet. He sank back into his chair. "What will we do?" he asked. "George is the senior partner. What will happen to the firm?"

"The firm?" Douglass curled his lip. "You're worried about the firm?"

"Aren't you? We're going to lose clients in droves. We have to do something fast. Who's the best criminal lawyer we can get? We have to hire him right away. Maybe we can leak a story about the cops' being mistaken. Maybe it should be stronger. What do you think? The cops have it in for us? Is that better?"

"Count me out, Peter," Douglass said dryly.

"You're kidding, right? If the two of us work together we can salvage something from this."

Douglass sighed. "Right now, I'm much more interested in salvaging my family. We're putting our house on the market and moving out of the city. I'll start a small practice. We feel it will be better for us to get out of the rat race. I'm afraid you're on your own, Peter. Good luck."

Douglass walked out.

Peter remained seated at his desk for several minutes. Okay, so it was left to him to call the shots. Well, he was up to it.

On the other hand, maybe it would be better to let George go. After all, it was his wife George had killed.

Did he need George? No way. He could take over the firm, squeeze flesh, do what was necessary. He relaxed.

Where had he been? Oh, yes, about to arrange a meeting with his secretary.

He buzzed. "Miss Parker, could you step in, please?"

As she walked in, Peter sighed. She really was a picture.

But before he could speak, she said, "Mr. Martin, I'm afraid there's something I have to tell you."

"You've heard about the arrests?"

"Yes, sir. Mr. Fischer told Miss Kayne."

"I see. Well, don't worry about that. I have another idea I wanted to discuss with you. One I think—"

"Mr. Martin, excuse me for interrupting. But with Mr. Brodie gone and Mr. Fischer leaving, both Mrs. Estmanoth and Miss Kayne will be free. Before you speak to them, I thought I should give my notice."

"Notice?" Peter echoed the word mechanically. What was the woman up to? Was she so sure of him—?

"Yes, Mr. Martin. I was going to tell you yesterday, but with everything happening I decided to wait." She blushed. "I'm getting married. To Dr. Anderson." Seeing Peter's blank stare, she added, "Fourth floor. He's a psychiatrist. We met in the elevator a few months ago. I knew at once that we were meant for each other. He took a little convincing." She giggled. "But not much."

4

Jillian's funeral took place that afternoon. It was a hot July day, with bright sunlight and not a cloud in sight.

Hildy was there, dressed in a navy blue suit with a matching hat and veil, looking as well-groomed and capable as ever. She sat where she could see Peter. She noticed the new lines on his face, the grim set to his mouth. And behind the veil, her eyes grew misty. But her determination increased. This was the last time she would see Peter. She would concentrate on making a home for Stephen. That's what was important now. If only the boy weren't such a picture of the man.

Douglass and Anne sat together, her hand in his. They had an appointment the following morning with a marriage counselor Manziuk had recommended. And she had stopped drinking.

Bart was there, with Shauna at his side. They were at a distance from her family, who were incensed by the thought that Shauna was with a relative of the man who had killed their beloved daughter.

Ellen had spent an hour closeted with Bart early that morning. He had agreed to move in with her until the house could be sold and another bought in Cabbagetown where Ellen's friends lived. He would be paid a monthly salary to act as her assistant and advisor throughout the move and protect her from the media during the trial.

Shauna had told Bart that she was going to New York in September for one year of art school, but that she would consider marrying him the following summer if he did a good job for Ellen, stopped smoking and drinking, and took an art appreciation course so he didn't keep calling her pen and ink drawings scribbles. He was holding out for one drink per day and no more nagging, but every time he looked at her dancing brown eyes or her trim figure in the bright new clothes, he lost a little more of his resolve.

Ellen and Kendall were there. Ellen looked her normal self, though somewhat older and very tired. Kendall looked as though he was sleepwalking. It would be some time before he would be able to grasp what had happened to his father or decide what he was going to do with his life. Fortunately, he would have plenty of support. Marilyn Garrett was in the middle of the two Brodies, an arm around each of them. Her slight frame seemed to support both of them, and to be quite capable of going on that way.

Nick and Lorry sat on Kendall's other side. Nick's right arm was wrapped in bandages and anchored with a sling. His left arm was around Lorry's waist. She had written to Dean to tell him not to wait for her. And Nick had an appointment in the morning to lease the vacant building near the mission office. Dave was overjoyed with the thought of an on-premise legal advisor.

The funeral went on. Jillian Martin's uncalled-for death was mourned, as was her short life. No mention was made of her true character. Peter was consoled as the grieving husband. Her family was mentioned. Then it was over, and Manziuk and Ryan were walking back to the car.

"Inspector?" Ellen Brodie was with a woman about her age, whom Manziuk had noticed come in toward the end of the service. An attractive older woman with reddish-gold hair and a gentle face.

Manziuk stepped forward. "Mrs. Brodie. Is this your cousin?"

"Yes, this is Patricia, Lorry's mom. She's going to stay for a few weeks while we settle what has to be done. All the arrangements about the law firm and the lawyers and so much. I've never had to deal with business matters. George always treated me like I was made of china. But I guess I'll have to do some things now.

"Glory-Ann—that's Mrs. Winston, you know—and I will find a place in our old neighborhood. After what George did to Crystal, I have to take care of her. And we will be all right. It may seem a strange arrangement, but we've both lost someone we love through this, you see."

"Yes."

"I wanted you to know that I don't hold any grudge. I know some people do. As if it were all the fault of the police. But I don't. You were only doing your job. I'm just glad Lorry wasn't hurt. If I'd ever thought he'd do anything like that—or those other girls—I still can't believe what he did. It's just—just awful. And so unlike anything he'd ever done before. He's always talked about being so proud of his mother, but the doctors say he really hated her—that he blamed her because his father was weak. It's so puzzling how the human mind works, isn't it, Inspector?"

EPILOGUE

For now we see through a glass, darkly;
But then face to face;
Now I know in part;
But then shall I know even
as I am known.
   Paul's 1st Letter to the Corinthians, 13:12

"Got your report done?" Manziuk asked Ryan two days later.

"You must be joking. I'll likely be at it till midnight."

"Well, let's hope no one decides to bump anyone off today."

"Do you have yours done?" she asked.

"You must be joking," he deadpanned.

A smile touching her lips, and she moved into the room. "You know, I used to be terrified of you."

"You should be," he said, still without expression.

She sat sideways on the corner of his desk, her eyes on him. He winced.

She jumped off. "Sorry," she said. "That's a bad habit of mine."

"I yelled at you for doing that before, didn't I?"

"Yes, you did. I'm sorry. I guess you don't like informality."

He shook his head. "No, it's not that. It's just that Woody sits—sat—there a lot."

"Oh," she said in a small voice. "How is Detective-Sergeant Craig coming along?"

"He seems to be doing fine. Except he'll have to take early retirement. But as soon as he's recovered from the bypass, he should be able to go fishing and take a world cruise and do a few other things he's talked about."

"You'll miss him."

"Yes."

Neither spoke for a moment.

"He was a good cop," Manziuk said.

She diffidently moved some papers. A marble rolled along the desk and dropped to the floor.

She stooped to pick it up. "Did we ever find out how this got into Kendall's car?"

"Oh, didn't I tell you? When they opened the safe in George Brodie's office, they found three objects that made no sense. Turned out one belonged to each of the women he'd killed. He must have picked up the marble to put with his collection and somehow lost it in the car. When Forensics went over the car, they found clear evidence George had used it at some time, and the only opportunity he had was the day he picked it up from the dealer. And, of course, it was that night the Matheson girl was murdered. And George just coolly gave the car to Kendall the next day."

"He was getting pretty sure of himself."

"He was beginning to think he was invincible, I guess. Otherwise, he'd never have murdered Jillian the way he did. But Crystal was the real problem; he couldn't strangle her the way he had the others because she had a knife. And really, he didn't want to kill her. I think that made him more vulnerable. The truth is, if not for this weekend, and Nick's habit of picking up small objects, who knows if we'd ever have caught him. Though I think we would have eventually. Murderers always get too cocky."

Ryan thought for a moment. "In my psych class, we were told most serial killers want to be found."

"Could be. I just wish we could find them before they start out murdering in the first place."

"So the case should be open and shut?"

"Oh, I'm sure he'll have a fancy lawyer that will find all kinds of ways to get around the evidence. But they're doing DNA tests on the cord he used to attack Lorry Preston, which by the way was a spare computer cord he kept at the office, and they think they'll be able to prove it was used on the other women. I think a jury will come up with the right verdict."

"Yes, but he's insane."

"That's tricky. Did he know what he was doing? Yes. He had a very sharp mind. Was he rational? No. But are murderers ever completely rational?"

"What bothers me most is the total waste. He killed women he didn't even know, apparently because he hated his mother. Maybe if at some point he'd talked to somebody—a psychiatrist, a priest, even a friend—about his early life, they would have uncovered his irrational hatred and recognized that his mind was becoming confused, and he could have been treated."

"But he would have had to agree to the treatment. If he had never broken a law, there's no way anyone could have forced him to get treatment."

"You're saying we have other people out there just like him, living more or less normal lives, but hiding all kinds of resentment and jealousy and hatred, and there's no way we can identify them and keep them from killing one day?"

"Most people don't go that far. But there is no way to identify people who need help unless they ask for it or their family or friends recognize the problem and encourage them to get help."

"Maybe we should have a yearly mental health check-up as well as a physical."

"But who decides what's normal and what isn't?" The phone rang. Manziuk picked up the receiver.… "Oh, that's just great! I don't have the report done for the last one. You know, I think I'm overdue for a few days R & R.… Yeah, well, I'm going on a cruise with Woody when the doctor says he's fit enough to travel, and you won't be able to call me in the middle of the ocean.… Secondary? Who've you got?"

Ryan took a couple of steps to where she could stare at the picture on Manziuk's wall. She gazed intently at the tiny mouse just visible in the grass, and the eagle searching for prey. Ryan bit her bottom lip. She was barely breathing.

"Yeah, I guess." There was a long pause. "Okay, I'll take care of it."

He hung up. "So, they've got another body."

Ryan continued to stare at the picture as though fascinated.

"Oh?" she asked, as if it were no concern of hers.

"I guess nobody bothered to tell the perp I'm tired and need a rest."

"I guess." She moved toward the door. "Well, good luck."

"I'll need a secondary."

She stopped and turned to look at him.

"You doing anything?"

He was looking directly at her, his eyes measuring.

She put one hand on the doorknob. "You want to take along a female who can't keep quiet?"

He shrugged. "It doesn't get boring with you around."

She put her free hand on her hip. "I'm not sure my blood pressure can stand working with you."

He kept his eyes on her. "If you'd do your own job instead of trying to do mine as well, I wouldn't have to yell at you more than once a day."

"Thanks a lot." She shifted her weight so it was on the balls of her feet. "You just need to pay more attention to what I say. You aren't the only one who can think, you know."

He stood up. "Are you planning to talk all day, or are you going to back me up here?"

Her jaw set, she faced him "Just tell me one thing. Do you want a partner or a secretary?"

"What makes you think I need a secretary?"

She released the door and took a step toward her. "You *don't* need a secretary."

He stepped out from behind his desk, grabbed his hat from the peg it hung on, and pushed past her to lead the way out of the office. "You a baseball fan?" he asked over his shoulder.

"No," she answered quickly. "What does that have to do with anything?"

"A body's been found at the stadium. In the bullpen."

She had to run to keep up. "Murdered?"

"Looks like it."

"How?"

"The officer who found him thinks he was clubbed to death with a baseball bat."

As they hurried through the silent outer office, she made a quick detour to grab her purse. Lunging into the elevator as the door was closing, she asked, "Did you say they found the body in a bullpen? Why on earth would they have cattle at a baseball game?"

N. J. Lindquist is an award-winning author and speaker. She grew up reading the works of Agatha Christie, Dorothy Sayers, and P. D. James, and has chosen to write contemporary mysteries in their classic style. N. J. is the executive director of The Word Guild and a member of Mystery Writers of America, Sisters in Crime, Crime Writers of Canada, and the Writers' Union of Canada. She and her family live in Toronto, Canada.

Books by N. J. Lindquist

Mystery
Manziuk and Ryan Series
Shaded Light

Teen Novels
Circle of Friends series
Best of Friends
Friends Like These
Friends In Need
More Than Friends

Growing Up and Taking Hold series
In Time of Trouble

Teen Non-Fiction
The New You
The Bridge: Volume 1
The Bridge: Volume 2

Play
Behind The News: Report From Bethlehem

www.njlindquist.com

info@njlindquist.com